★ PENTAGON COUNTRY ★

BOOKS BY CLAY BLAIR, JR.

NOVELS:

The Board Room
The Archbishop
Pentagon Country

NONFICTION:

The Atomic Submarine and Admiral Rickover
Beyond Courage
Diving for Pleasure and Treasure
The Strange Case of James Earl Ray

COLLABORATIONS:

The Hydrogen Bomb,
    with James R. Shepley
Nautilus 90 North,
    with Commander William R. Anderson,
    U.S.N.
Always Another Dawn,
    with A. Scott Crossfield

Pentagon Country

★ A NOVEL BY ★

CLAY BLAIR, Jr.

McGRAW-HILL BOOK COMPANY

New York   St. Louis   San Francisco

Düsseldorf   Mexico   Toronto

PENTAGON COUNTRY

Library of Congress Catalog Card Number:
79–167490

First Edition

07–005602–1

To my mother and father

★ Book I ★

Sunday
Evening

★ 1 ★

William Montgomery King, Jr., Captain, United States Navy, sat at his den desk in shirt sleeves and stocking feet writing with a pen on a white Navy-issue tablet. He was a compact man with crew-cut brown hair going gray at the temples, and wide-set hazel eyes. Halfway through the page, he stopped, reread what he had written, then tore the sheet from the tablet, balled it up, threw it in the trash can. Then he began again with a fresh sheet, writing quickly and easily, pumping his right leg unconsciously.

The den was a small room, with plywood paneling made to resemble real mahogany planks. Along a high shelf, Captain King had placed models of the naval vessels on which he had spent nineteen of his twenty-five years' naval service. They were all submarines. A World War II Fleet Boat, the *Runner*. A post-World War II Guppy, the *Irex*. A new-design submarine of the Korean War era, the *Trigger*, the first nuclear-powered submarine, *Nautilus*, a *Skate*-class nuclear-attack submarine, *Swordray*, and finally, a *Polaris* missile submarine, the *John Paul Jones*.

There were a half dozen pictures on the wall. One was a blowup of a 1930s snapshot of his father, standing on the tiny deck of an R-class boat at the Submarine Base in New London, Connecticut. Another was an official Navy photograph of Vice Admiral Sidney M. Zimmerman, "father" of the atomic submarine. It was autographed. There was a color photograph of the *Swordray* surrounded by ice at the North Pole. Another picture frame held the citation for Captain King's prize-winning essay in *Naval Institute Proceedings*, entitled: "Seaborne Strategy for a Nuclear

Age," composed when he was attending the Naval War College in Newport, Rhode Island. Directly over the desk, there was a framed excerpt from a poem by Rudyard Kipling:

> It's Tommy this, an' Tommy that, an'
> "Chuck 'im out, the brute!"
> But it's "Saviour of 'is country" when
> the guns begin to shoot.

One wall of the room was a bookcase. It contained three or four dozen books, all about submarines: official Navy histories, memoirs of U-boat captains, and the like. The bottom shelf was packed solid with back issues of *Naval Institute Proceedings* and *National Geographic Magazines*, all gathering dust.

The door to the living room opened. Captain King's wife, Nancy, came into the den, carrying a piece of paper, a letter. She was his age, forty-six, yet seemed ten years younger. She was pretty, with a firm figure. She had bright blue eyes and wore her hair pulled straight back and clasped into a single, short ponytail.

"I've got to talk to you, Monty," she said with urgency.

"I'll be done in a minute," he replied without looking up.

"*Now*," she said harshly. "I can't wait another minute."

He looked up from his work. His wife handed him the letter. It was from the Dean of Men, University of Wisconsin. He read:

"Dear Mrs. King,

This is to notify you that your son, Paul King, has officially withdrawn from his classes. . . ."

"When did this come?" he asked, returning the letter.

"Yesterday."

"Why didn't you tell me?"

"Because you were too busy."

"Do you have any idea why?"

"No. I called his landlady. He left last week without giving notice. Left all his books. She said he ran off with a blonde girl . . . a hippie-type girl."

Nancy burst into tears. She sat down on the green leatherette sofa.

"I'm worried sick," she said between sobs.

"You should have told me."

"I started to last night. But you were on the phone all evening. Working all day today."

They moved into the living room. There was a fire smoldering and popping in the fireplace. Outside, rain fell hard. Nancy sat in the Queen Anne wing chair by the fire. Monty stood in stocking feet, staring down into the ashes.

Monty did not understand his son Paul. Paul had different genes, coming down, most likely, from Monty's mother. He did not even look like Monty. He was hollow-chested and frail, moody, a book-worm. Something apart. So very much unlike Mike, the oldest, whom Monty *did* understand. It had not helped that Nancy had spoiled Paul, indulged him, when a firm disciplinary hand was needed, he thought. That was the root of the problem. Now he was angry.

"Do you know anything about the girl?" he said. "Was it Doris?"

"No. It wasn't Doris. This girl has blonde hair. And that's *all* I know."

"Did you call Doris?"

"No."

"Why not?"

"Because they broke up six months ago. At Thanksgiving. Don't you remember? I'm sure she doesn't know anything."

"Nancy, to tell the truth," Monty said, with resignation, "I'm not surprised. I don't understand that boy. I think he has a bad streak."

"You've said that before. In Charleston you said you thought it was brain damage."

"Yes. Well. . . ."

"His problem, Monty, is that he has never had a father."

"That couldn't be helped," Monty said.

"He clearly needs a father now."

"What he needs is to learn some values. Like Mike. For example, the meaning of a buck. He has no concept of money. He. . . ."

"Monty, he needs a *father*."

Monty stared down into the fire, thinking of Paul, his own father.

"And I need a husband," Nancy added.

"I know you're upset," he said. "I don't blame you. I'm sorry. Come on, pull yourself together. If we have a real problem, let's deal with it promptly, the way we've always done."

He went to her side, stroking her head.

"A child will be what you expect him to be," Nancy said, choking down sobs. "Mike was your boy. You didn't know Paul. You ignored Paul. You still don't know Paul. You didn't try to know Paul. And now Paul is turning out to be just what you expected."

"I've always thought Paul was fine," Monty said. "Different, but basically. . . ."

"That's not true, Monty. Don't you know he *heard* you say he had brain damage? My God!"

"How did he hear?" Monty said, feeling a chill.

"Maybe he didn't hear exactly. But he *sensed* it. Don't you know that children sense everything? You can't disguise your feelings. They *know*."

Monty sat in the wing chair opposite Nancy.

"All right," he conceded. "Maybe I did goof. I'm not a genius. I'm sorry. I didn't mean to. These children, they're so complicated. Especially these days. Everybody seems to be having trouble. It's not the end of the world. They snap out of it. So, let's get organized and do what we have to do."

"You really love Paul?" she said.

"Yes, Nance. I really do love him. He takes some getting

used to. But, yes. I really love him. He's my flesh and blood. How could I not love him?"

"Do you love me?"

"Certainly. Come on, now."

"I didn't sleep all last night," Nancy said.

"No wonder. You should have told me."

"I was hoping for some word, first. I hoped he would call. Asking for money. Anything."

"He's not very considerate of your feelings," Monty said. "Or mine. After all you've done, it's a bit high-handed to upset you like this. Very selfish."

"Monty. Paul might be *dead*."

Captain King weighed this possibility. Then he said calmly: "No. I'm sure he isn't. If so, we would have heard. He carries a draft card. ID. The girl would have called. Something would have turned up. No, I think he's probably all right."

"Do you think he's *living* with the girl?" Nancy asked weakly.

"I don't know," Monty frowned. "But we'll find out. To-morrow morning, I'll call the dean, the authorities out there. They must know something. There must be some way. Friends or something."

The telephone rang. Monty answered in the den.

"Captain King, here."

"Monty, this is Jim Caldwell. I'm down at the Pentagon—got the duty. I thought maybe you'd be interested to know that SecNav has drafted an ALNAV announcing our Selection Board and the precepts. It got on the circuit this after-noon. . . ."

"Shoot," Monty said, tearing off the top sheet of his tablet, pen poised. As Caldwell read the ALNAV, Monty made notes on the number of admirals to be picked, the spe-cialties, the Year Groups to be considered and other tech-nical details.

"That's it," Caldwell said. "I guess that time's come, old

buddy. They're gonna separate the men from the boys. Oh hell. I've got to go. The other phone's jumping."

"Thanks very much," Monty said, hanging up.

"Who was that?" Nancy asked, when Monty returned to the living room.

"Jim Caldwell."

"What did he want?"

"Oh, nothing much."

"He was calling about the Selection Board, wasn't he?" she said.

"Yes. It's been announced."

Nancy looked at the carpet. Then she looked at her husband and said: "Monty, I don't want you to stand for selection. I want you to retire."

"What?" he exclaimed. "Retire? Are you crazy?"

"No, I don't think so."

"Well for Christ's sake, you sure sound like it."

★ 2 ★

"You don't have a prayer of being selected," Nancy said. "How many men are in your Year Group?"

"Three hundred sixty-four."

"How many vacancies?"

"Five."

"About one chance in seventy-two," she said after a pause.

"But . . ."

"Be realistic."

"I'm being realistic. My chances are good."

"You're a submariner. The aviators run the Navy."

"Not so much any more."

"Come on, Monty."

"There are many more submarine flag billets now. I've had War College. Major command. Damned good fitness reports. Admiral Starr said he was putting me in for another Legion of Merit for this tour. He's on the Board. He swings a lot of weight. I stand well with Rollow, who will be President of the Board."

"Look in the mirror, Monty. You're exhausted. You're lucky you haven't had a heart attack like Admiral Zimmerman and Pete Kane and . . ."

"I'm in good shape."

"Monty, I'm sick of this life. You understand me? Sick. I've been waiting on the beach for twenty-five years. You said this job was shore duty, that you'd be home. I've scarcely laid eyes on you for the last twenty-one months. Look at you. Sunday. You've been working all day."

"I'm sorry. I didn't know it would be like this."

"Nobody else in government works like you."

"Oh yes they do. Everybody I know."

"Well, you're *all* crazy. Here you are, a senior captain, in the zone, knocking yourself out and you don't make as much as a carpenter or plumber. You don't even have a private office."

"I'm not doing this job for money."

"If you get selected to rear admiral, you'll just go to sea again."

"Not necessarily."

"That's what you always say. And you always go to sea. Why wouldn't you? They'll give you a *Polaris* Division. You'll go straight to Rota or Holy Loch or Guam. I'll be left right here, rattling around in this empty house another two years. For what? It's a wonder I haven't gone out of my mind. I'm afraid to be here alone."

"Honey . . . "

"Why are you knocking yourself out? Nobody gives a

damn about the military anymore. It's Tommy this and Tommy that, all right. Anytime the press can make you look stupid, they do. Nobody has any respect for the military. Christine told me Bill's *afraid* to wear his uniform when he travels."

"That's ridiculous. I'm sure he didn't say that."

"Read the papers."

"I read the papers," he said. "It's just the Eastern press establishment. In the Midwest . . . "

"They're rioting out there, too. They burned the ROTC building at the University of Nebraska."

"Since the cease-fire I haven't seen much rioting. They didn't like the war. But who did?"

Nancy jumped up, walked to the piano. The top was covered with family photographs. She picked up one with a silver frame and waved it toward Monty.

"This was your daughter. Joanie. Remember her? I gave birth to her and then I saw her die in that damned sick bay in Key West. Where were you? At sea. Her life had no reality for you. Where were you when Paul was born? And Mike? At sea. Always at sea."

"I couldn't help it," Monty said. "The Navy's been good to us. To your family. My family. We owe . . . "

"We don't owe it anything," Nancy said, returning to her chair. "Nothing. I told you, I want a husband, not another tombstone in Arlington. Or an address to write at some fleet Post Office. And I want a father for Paul. He's never had a father. That's his problem. Look what the Navy's done to your family."

"Honey, the Navy didn't kill Joanie."

"Yes it did. If they'd had a decent doctor on duty . . . "

"And what's wrong with Mike? He's Company Commander . . . "

"Monty, he's a robot, just like you. He's been brainwashed, never had a chance to think for himself. He's going to go blindly through life, just like you. Annapolis, then twenty-five years at sea."

"Nineteen years at sea," he corrected. "A good, honorable life."

"It hasn't helped your family."

"How long have you been thinking this?"

"About twenty years."

"Why didn't you say something before now?"

"Because I was stupid. Naive."

"Why did you marry Navy? You knew what it would be like."

"I don't know. Maybe I *am* crazy."

"You're just upset about Paul."

"I decided this long before Paul disappeared."

"But . . . "

"Monty, do you realize I sat for six years in Charleston by myself, waiting?"

"I got home fairly often. Every two months. That *Polaris* was the best duty I ever had."

"For you. But what about us? Do you know we're both going to die someday?"

"Of course. What's that got to do . . . ?"

"Do you want to die without even knowing why you were here?"

"I don't understand."

"We've got to take time out. Read. Talk. I want somebody to *talk* to. I want somebody to make love to me. You haven't slept with me for thirteen months!"

"I tried."

"No you didn't. You must *hate* me."

"I don't hate you. That's ridiculous."

"You don't love me. You can't . . . "

"Stop that."

"No. I'm not going to stop it. We're going to talk. Why won't you sleep with me?"

"I don't know."

"You're too tired."

"I guess so. Anyway, we can't afford to retire. How are we going to pay for Paul's college with me on retired pay?"

"You'll make three-quarters of what you make now. We have equity in this house. Besides that, I have a nest egg."

"What nest egg?"

"You remember the $10,000 I inherited when mother and daddy were killed?"

"Yes. Certainly."

"I invested that. Plus, I've been pulling out something every month from the household account."

"*What?*"

"Yes. I invested it all. The whole thing's worth more than $40,000 now."

Monty looked at Nancy with disbelief in his eyes.

"You mean . . . "

"Yes. $40,000."

"How?"

"I bought New England Shipbuilding stock."

"What? You mean . . . ?"

"Yes. We have exactly 1,000 shares."

"But, honey. Jesus. I can't believe it."

"How's that for a nice surprise?"

"You shouldn't have put it in New England Ship!"

"Why not?"

"Because I could be nailed for a conflict of interest. Don't you realize I do business with them?"

"*I* don't do business with them."

"But . . . "

"Plenty of Navy families own New England Ship. I never heard of a Navy family selling stock, have you?"

"No, but . . . "

"Stop being so sanctimonious. I didn't do anything dishonest. You ought to be thankful you have such a thrifty wife."

"I know . . . I'm sure . . . but . . . oh hell. My God. I can't believe this. You're not kidding me are you?"

"No. Call Scottie MacIntosh if you don't believe me."

"He's your broker? Oh God."

"He knows you don't know. So he can't ever accuse you."

"But he might think I really did know and put it in your name."

"No. He wouldn't think that. Anyway, as soon as you retire, we're going to put it in tax-free municipal bonds. They're yielding about 7 percent interest nowadays. That'll give us about $2,500 a year more. Paul can live at home— I want him to live at home—and go to a local college. The way they package foods, three can eat as cheaply as two. So . . ."

"Honey, never mind the stock. We'll figure what to do with it. But I can't retire. That's madness. Here I've put in twenty-five years, my Board's been announced. This would be absolutely nuts. Just crazy. Besides, I've spent twenty-one months of my life pushing ULMS . . . we've got it to the point they're almost ready to sign the contracts for the long lead-time hardware . . . I couldn't just up and quit. Hell, I want to see this thing through. Zimmerman and Starr are counting on me."

"To make *them* look good."

"I'll look good too. That's another point in my favor. I've done a damned good job on ULMS. Damned good. If I don't get selected, I've got a job waiting at New England Ship as project manager on ULMS."

"I don't want you to work for New England Ship either," she said. "That's more of the same. I'll never see you."

"That's not true. I won't be going to sea."

"You'd be traveling all the time. Like when you worked for Admiral Wright in Special Projects."

"This is a desk job."

"You always say that."

"Honestly, this time I mean it."

"I don't want any part of it. I want *you*, Monty. I've given twenty-five years, my youth. Now I want you to give me something in return. Is that too much to ask?"

"It's a lot."

"Then you must not think much of me."

"That's not fair, honey. One of the biggest problems we have in the Navy is that all the good people are retiring. The best people. You can't keep an organization together when all the talented people quit. We're in trouble now."

"What the hell do you care? The Navy will survive without you. It has for two hundred years. You're not indispensable. You're just one more Pentagon Indian. So what if there's one less? Anyway, they are going to cut your budget again. They'll want people to retire early."

"No, they're not going to cut the budget. They can't cut the budget. We're operating on a shoestring as it is."

"Of course they're going to cut your budget. They ran for election on an antimilitary platform."

"I haven't seen any signs of it. They all say that. Then they get in there and find out they can't."

"They'll cut it. You wait."

"There's no way."

"They'll find a way."

"They'll have a hell of a fight."

"That'll be somebody else's problem."

"I'm not going to retire. That's crazy!"

"Let me say one more thing. I've given this a lot of thought. Monty, how many really wonderful men have you seen destroyed by the Selection Board? They were just like you. Riding up against the Board like knights in a jousting tournament. Confident. Gallant. Reckless. Blind. Then unseated and crushed. Told, in the prime of life, they were no longer fit, no longer needed. Rudy Johnson. Louis Brooks. Sam Carpenter. Kent Peterson. All good men with good credentials—Annapolis, War College, blah, blah, blah. Where are they now? A lot of them just empty hulks at the

bars in the officers' clubs acoss the country. Alkies and
bores. Monty, they might as well have *died*."

"I'm not an alcoholic."

"But you're human, just like everybody else. What if you
get passed over? Won't that be a terrible psychic shock?
Have you considered they might pass you over?"

"Yes."

"Really considered? Be realistic."

"No. I've always felt my chances were good."

"Could you take it if they passed you over? I'm asking
you to be honest with yourself, Monty. Really honest."

"It wouldn't be easy."

"It would be like getting kicked in the head by a horse."

"Maybe . . . "

"So you can spare yourself, Monty. I've made it financially
possible for you to get out now. You can get out and come
home and be a father and husband, lead a normal life, and
we can travel, go to all those fabulous places you were always going to take me to and never did, and all the rest of
it. You've not had time to think about it. I have."

"But . . . "

"Will you think about it? Really seriously?"

"All right. I'll try to think about it.'

★ Book II ★

Monday

★ 1 ★

There was a blue and white sign on the wall in the corridor identifying Monty King's Pentagon office:

ROOM 4C600
SUBMARINE WARFARE DIVISION (OP-31)
RADM. CHARLES M. STARR (DIR.)
CAPT. W. M. KING, JR. (DEP. DIR.)

Monty arrived there at 0630. It was a small dingy area, jammed with gray metal desks and file cabinets, old oak swivel chairs. Monty's desk was in a corner by the inner door leading into Admiral Starr's office.

The chief yeoman, John Zempfke, was already on board. He had collected the mail and papers from the Naval Communications Center down the corridor, the pneumatic tube station and the Navy post office. Now he was making fresh coffee in the office percolator, which stood on a shelf behind the file cabinets.

"Good morning, Captain," Zempfke called out cheerfully.

He was a dark-haired, old-time Navy chief, remarkably well-preserved. Trim and tawny. Like the other enlisted men in the Pentagon, he wore a uniform. The hash marks on his sleeve added up to thirty years' service. Monty had first met him fifteen years ago, when they were both assigned to the *Nautilus*. Since that time, Zempfke had served almost continuously with Monty, first on the *Swordray*, then *Jones*. He was a man of many talents: amateur artist, photographer, journalist, heraldist. On *Nautilus, Swordray* and *Jones*, Zempfke had put out the ship's newspaper, composed rough drafts of the official voyage reports in addition to his normal duties as secretary-clerk in charge of getting out the ship's enormous load of paperwork. In the twenty-one months he had served Monty in OP-31, he had proved to be an excellent office manager and right-hand man.

Monty laid his heavy attaché case on the desktop, hung his Navy blue gabardine coat on the wobbly tree by the dingy window. He sat down with a heavy sigh. He had not slept well. He unlocked the combination lock on the case, unloaded the papers. Zempfke brought a steaming mug of coffee.

"I couldn't get through all of this," Monty said, handing Zempfke some of the papers from the case. "But here's a rough draft of a reply to Senator Root. Shape it up and get it typed, please."

"Aye, aye, sir."

"I'll try to get to the rest sometime today. Anything hot?" He sipped the coffee.

Zempfke had already gone through the morning's batch of papers. He knew what was hot.

"This," he said, peeling a radio message from the pile. It was a copy of the ALNAV announcing the Selection Board. Monty skimmed through it, restudying the document.

"And this," Zempfke said, handing Monty a thick sheaf of papers held together by a strong metal binder.

Monty skimmed the top page. On the surface, it seemed a minor matter. Six months ago, Monty had put in a request to the Pentagon Building Manager's office, to erect a glass partition between the desks of two of his officers. The partition was to provide minimum telephone privacy, the glass so that if one man had to go to the head, the other could watch the classified papers on his desk, saving the trouble of putting them all away and locking the files. A clear partition was not standard. Therefore, it had been disapproved. Moreover, erecting the partition involved moving a floor telephone outlet, which was in the way. That meant coordination between the carpentry shop and the telephone division, apparently a task beyond the capability of the building manager. But this minor matter had become, for Monty, a kind of Mount Everest. He had sworn that he would see the partition in place before his relief arrived. He had resubmitted the request, again and again, through Navy, Department of Defense and the Pentagon housekeeper, General Services Administration. Now, once again, it had been disapproved.

"Find out who's in charge down there," Monty said to Zempfke. "I'm going down, in person, today and see them. If I have to, I'll drag a carpenter up by the collar."

"While you're down there," Zempfke said with the air of a man dealing in lost causes, "you might want to talk to someone about the cleaning. I don't have enough rank. They didn't clean the Admiral's office over the weekend again. Have a look."

Monty went into the Admiral's office. By Pentagon regulation, Rear Admiral Starr was a P-3 executive, entitled to 300 square feet of space, drapes, wall-to-wall carpeting, a flag, large wall map of the world, couch, end table with lamp, three cigarette ashtrays (standing), chair rail and paneling beneath, and other emoluments. By some luck of the draw, one of his predecessors had obtained all that, and a trifle more, including three fine-framed prints of old naval battles—sailing vessels, firing broadsides. Except for the prisonlike view through the window, it was a livable office.

The Admiral was a cigar smoker, with a careless habit of flicking his ashes wherever he happened to be. Monty examined the carpet and the area behind the desk. It had not been cleaned.

"Did you call?" he said to Zempfke.

"Aye, sir. I got some old bitch on the phone down there. I told her the Admiral was entitled to Executive Level Cleaning, meaning, by their own regulations—General Service Administration policy—his carpet should be vacuumed *every* night. Well, she blew her stack. She said that because of budget restrictions, they were down to 450 cleaners. There are 400 flag officers in the building. Almost as many generals and admirals as she has cleaners."

"What's that got to do with it?" Monty injected.

"Well, nothing actually. She was ranting on about the help not showing up and all that. They're blacks, minimum-wage people. They can make more on welfare. I also took the opportunity to tell her *our* office hadn't been swept for at least two weeks. She said the regulation had been changed. Now, they're only going to sweep noncarpet floor areas every *three* weeks."

"I'll speak to them," Monty said, returning to his desk. "What else?"

"This," Zempfke said, handing Monty another radio message from the pile.

Monty looked at the message. It was classified TOP SECRET, and routed OP-IMMED, meaning it took priority over all worldwide Navy radio traffic, and decoding in the cryptology section. It was from a Fleet Ballistic Missile Submarine—a Polaris boat—on patrol station. It was a rare communication. Operationally, the FBM on patrol came under direct command of the Joint Chiefs of Staff, the Secretary of Defense, the President. Except in extraordinary circumstances, they maintained total radio silence. The circumstance, Monty perceived at once, was extraordinary.

The message stated:

CNO, INFO: OP-31
UNIDENTIFIED SUBMERGED CONTACT
0345 BREAK REMAINED IN CONTACT
30 MINUTES BREAK UNPRECEDENTED
CLOSING SPEED 30 REPEAT 30 KNOTS
BREAK UNPRECEDENTED LOW NOISE
LEVEL BREAK ADVISE

Monty stared at the message, pursing his lips. What did this mean? Was it a Soviet submarine? It seemed unlikely. No Soviet submarine had ever come near an FBM, even by accident.

"I figure it must have been a killer whale hoping to get laid," Zempfke said.

"Put it on the Admiral's desk," Monty replied. "Right in the center."

Zempfke did as instructed. Watching him, Monty thought: wouldn't he be astonished if I said, Chief, you're looking at a newly rich man with a crazy wife who wants me to retire and an errant boy who's dropped out of college and run off to shack up with a blonde. How's that for Captain King's morning openers?

"Captain," Zempfke said, returning. "Don't forget you've got the new man—Lieutenant Trimble—reporting in this morning. You've got to take a few minutes off to brief him."

"All right," Monty said, turning back to the stack of papers on his desk.

" I don't know where he is," Zempfke said, glancing darkly at the clock on the wall. "I gave him your instructions to report at 0630. He's probably lost, wandering around this goddamned Puzzle Palace."

Monty did not reply to this last. He was jotting reminders on a scratch pad: call University of Wisconsin, Scottie Mac-Intosh. . . .

★ 2 ★

Monty sat at his desk digging through the load of paper in his In box. The office had filled with people, the members of his tight, small team. The IBM typewriters clattered. There was a pungent smell of freshly brewed coffee.

"Excuse me, Captain," Zempfke said. "Here's Lieutenant Trimble." Monty removed his horn-rimmed glasses, looked up. Lieutenant Senior Grade Gale Trimble was standing behind Zempfke, wearing a dress-blue uniform, holding his cap in his right hand, a manila envelope in his left. He was blond, blue-eyed, young, powerfully built in the shoulders and neck.

Monty stood up, extending a friendly hand.

"Hey Gale," he said. "Welcome aboard."

Trimble shook hands firmly, smiling.

"Good to see you again, Captain," he said.

Gale Trimble had been the most promising and brightest of the younger men in the wardroom of the *Jones*. He had stood number one in his class at Annapolis and number one in Nuclear Power School. *Jones* had been his first sea duty, three years. He qualified for his gold dolphins faster than anyone Monty had ever known. Recently, Monty had put in a request for him at BuPers. There had been a snag. By custom, Trimble was supposed to do another tour at sea before getting a shore billet. But a classmate of Monty's had fixed it.

"Have a seat," Monty said.

Trimble sat in the old oak chair by Monty's desk. Monty looked at his sideburns. They were longer than he remembered. Quite long.

32

"Is your hair regulation?" Monty asked, half-jokingly.

"To the ear lobe," Trimble said, touching a finger to his sideburn. "Regulation by the latest CNO directive."

"As you can see," Monty said, letting this pass and offering the usual apology for the office, "we're a bit crowded here. It's worse down the hall where you'll be working. Look at me, I'm supposed to have an office not less than 15 by 15 feet. The problem is, the Pentagon was originally an Army installation. After Unification, the Army grudgingly made room for the Navy and Air Force, but not enough. The Army still has 33 percent of the building, the Navy 14 percent. We're all jammed in here. According to DOD regulation, we're entitled to 4,000 square feet, but we only have 3,000. So, we sit in one another's lap. But I've seen offices here with three or four captains sitting face to face. That's one of the prices you pay for a Pentagon tour. A captain may be a small god in the fleet; here, they're a dime a dozen."

"I see," Trimble said.

"Is this your first time in the Pentagon?" Monty went on in a hospitable tone.

"Yes, sir. I'm sorry I'm late. I got lost."

"Do you have a map?"

"No, sir."

"Well, you need a map, at first. Down at the Mall Entrance there's a receptionist. She has little informational booklets with maps. They are full of useful information, such as, there are 4,200 wall clocks and 685 drinking fountains. When I first came here, I got lost. Everybody does. You heard the story about the Western Union boy who got lost and came out six months later a full colonel? But the receptionist gave me a valuable tip. She said to think of the place not as Pentagon-shaped, but wheel-shaped, with concentric rims: A, B, C, D and E, and with spokes going out from the hub, the corridors one to ten. That helps."

"It does?" Trimble asked, utterly perplexed.

"The most important thing to remember," Monty went on, "is that it is almost always better to go into the hub, the A Ring, and then out again, rather than going the circumference."

Monty broke off. Without a map, it was a hopeless thing to explain.

"First thing, get a map," Monty smiled. "Then I'll show you what I mean. How about transportation? Are you squared away on that?"

"No, sir. My wife dropped me off this morning."

"Well, you can car pool it, or drive yourself. There's a Car Pool Locator in the Concourse to help you get with people who live in your area. The parking situation here is plenty tight. A privilege, they say, not a right. There aren't enough spaces. Just 10,000 for 30,000 people. But everybody is entitled to a permit. The spaces are dealt out by rank. You'll probably have to park pretty far away. Get Zempfke to take you down to the Navy Parking Control Officer. He gets his allotment from DOD parking authority or someplace—very touchy. Hang onto your permit. It's worth its weight in gold."

"Yes, sir."

"And you'll need a Building Pass. During the day, you don't need it, but between 1800 and 0600 the doors are guarded. We work pretty long hours here: 0600 to 1900. So you'll need a pass, first thing. Zempfke can arrange a temporary pass until you go down to DOD and get your picture taken."

"Sir, I just had a baby," Trimble said earnestly. "A girl."

"Congratulations!" Monty exclaimed. "Where's my cigar?"

Trimble seemed worried.

"I'm wondering when—or if—I'll ever see her again," he said.

"Oh," Monty said, sighing, leaning back in his chair. He

went on solemnly. "This tour is pretty important to your career, Gale. I had a hell of a time prying you loose. Here you'll get a chance to do some really vital work. Meet a lot of important people. Learn a lot. If you keep your nose clean, do a good job, and your Selection Board has a grain of sense, you'll leave here a two-and-a-half striper."

Trimble seemed doubtful, or disinterested.

"I think you ought to know, sir," he said, "I'm not sure I'm going to stay in. I've got a good background in nuclear engineering. The power companies are paying top dollar for that experience. My wife wants me to get out. My tour on the *Jones*—the three years at sea—just about wiped her out. She couldn't take it."

"They'll pay you a $15,000 cash bonus to ship over," Monty said. "It'd take you a while on the outside to earn that."

"I know that, sir. It's more than just money. The life at sea, I think, is just boring as hell. Besides, it's not fair to my wife. We were pretty close when we got married. I'd like us to be that way again."

Monty said nothing. He thought of Nancy. Was it this way all over? At every level?

"The housing in Washington is really steep," Trimble went on. "I won't be getting Sub and Sea pay anymore. Even with subsistence, I don't know how we're going to make it. Burn up what we saved I guess. Captain, I appreciate your thinking of me, but . . . "

What had happened to Gale Trimble? Monty thought, anger rising. Two years ago, he had been eager. Gung ho. Now he was a whiner. Turning up his nose at career opportunity.

"Lieutenant," Monty said, reprovingly. "You're in this man's Navy, you serve where you're most needed. You put your country's interest ahead of your own. Any lieutenant in the Submarine Force would give his right arm to be in your shoes . . . now, let's get down to work. I'll take a minute and explain what we do here. We are the plans and policy-making arm of the Submarine Force. We deal with weapons, strategy, tactics, budgets. Our job is to provide the Force the tools to do its job. That's not easy. Money is tight. We spend 25 percent of the Navy's money. Eight billion a year. Everybody tries to shoot us down, get their hooks into our budget. Air Force, Department of Defense, Army, our own aviation people, the carrier people, who are hurting bad. Our job is to hang onto what we have, and fight for more.

"We're a paper mill, as are most Pentagon shops. We draw up papers. We coordinate papers. We get signatures on papers. Point papers. Impact papers. Congressional mail. Memos for CNO and SecNav. We're divided organizationally into branches. Budget Branch, Electronics Branch, and so on. We have project managers for the new weapons. The fast attack class. The Turbo Electric Drive prototype. The emphasis in this shop is on work, not ceremony. By the way, the uniform here is optional. Most everybody wears mufti. You save money. If you wear your blues, they'll get shiny in the pants and elbows, the gold braid frays. Anything of an administrative nature, see Zempfke. He knows his way around. You have your pay records?"

"Yes, sir."

He opened the manila envelope.

"Give them to Zempfke. You'll get paid twice a month by check, mailed to your home, if you want. Get Zempfke to brief you on security. Our security is local. Every man is responsible for his own papers. Everything here is Top Secret. So be careful. They have people coming around at night searching offices. If they find an unlocked safe, some-body gets burned. Badly. Watch your conversation in pas-sageways and heads and use your burn bags."

"Aye, aye, sir."

"One more thing. Have you been briefed on ULMS?"

"No, sir. There was an unclassified briefing on it on the

Jones, but I was away at the time, attending an electronics seminar."

"Get Zempfke to set up a briefing. I want every one of my people completely up to date on ULMS."

"I know it means Underwater Long Range Missile System," Trimble said. "That's about all."

"It's very important to all of us," Monty said. "The future of the Submarine Force. Basically, it is an extension of the *Polaris-Poseidon* concept, with which you are completely familiar. But it is a wholly new system. Very sophisticated. Very expensive. New launching platform—twice the size of the *Polaris* hulls. New missile. 5,000-mile range. MIRV warhead. And so on. Within two weeks, I want you to know everything there is to know about ULMS. Our primary job here is to sell ULMS to anybody we can buttonhole."

"I didn't realize it was that far along."

"We're right on the verge of signing the contracts for the long lead-time hardware. . .some of the reactor machinery. After twenty-one months, we have agreement in principle from DOD, Air Force, AEC. Hell of a battle."

"I guess I've been underwater for too long," Trimble said, rising.

"Well, you've surfaced now. So get busy."

"Aye, aye, sir."

"Rest easy," Monty said. "Your wife will come around. They all get disgruntled, every now and then. She's had a baby, then a move to a strange city. But a good Navy wife learns to put up with change and temporary inconvenience, even hardship. Later, it'll smooth out. The Admiral will be on board pretty soon. Before you get caught up in your parking problems, I want you to pay your respects. Later, after you get squared away at home, my wife and I would like you to call some Sunday afternoon."

"Thank you, sir."

"No sweat, Gale. But bear one thing firmly in mind. Here, we work for the Submarine Force. We're a small voice. The aviators outnumber us ten to one in numbers and rank. So we have to yell louder, work harder."

"Aye, aye, sir."

Monty called Zempfke to his desk.

"Take Lieutenant Trimble around and introduce him to the office. Then give him a hand with his parking permit and pay records. All that . . ."

Trimble wandered off toward the door. Monty said to Zempfke:

"Find him a place to sit, get him a ULMS briefing, then we've got to give him some work, something that will give him an overall picture . . . "

"I know just the thing," Zempfke replied, with a note of relief. "You know that memo from CNO requesting an update on the Soviet submarine threat? Nobody's had time to turn the first wheel on it."

"Perfect," Monty said. "But let me see it, page by page. I don't want him to get too far into it on his own. He's a damn bright kid but he's still pretty wet behind the ears. Tell him to see me if he has any questions. I want to work on him a little bit, John. He needs a battery charge."

"Aye, aye."

By 0700 the air in OP-31 crackled. Pressure mounted. The telephone rang urgently. Monty's Branch Chiefs scurried to and fro in shirt sleeves carrying papers. The gray metal file drawers were all unlocked, open, with the red "T" warnings in place. By every officer's desk, there was a red-and-white-striped burn bag, giving the place a festive air. In thirty minutes, Admiral Starr would arrive. By then, Monty should have prepared his morning briefing, a rough outline of the week's work.

Zempfke, manning his desk opposite Monty's, called out: "For you, Captain, Line one."

Monty punched the Line 1 button, picked up the phone. "Captain King."

"Is this Captain W. M. King, Deputy Director, Submarine Warfare Division?"

The voice was a strange one.

"Yes it is," Monty replied.

"Captain, this is Captain Reginald Davis, GSA Special Police. Is there anyone else on this line?"

"No . . . I . . . *who* did you say was calling?" Monty thought he had got it right. But he had never had business with GSA police before. He wanted to be certain.

"Captain Davis. General Services Administration Special Police. Downstairs on the first floor."

"Oh yes. What can I do for you, sir?"

He stared across the room at Zempfke. The yeoman had sensed that this call was out of the ordinary. He returned Monty's stare.

Captain Davis went on. "We have a matter down here— a very serious matter—involving a man in your office. Would it be possible for you to drop down and see me?"

"What's this all about?" Monty said, lowering his voice, turning away from Zempfke, toward his desk.

"I'm afraid I can't discuss it on the phone," Captain Davis said. "We wouldn't bother you if it weren't quite serious. I'd appreciate if it you didn't mention my call around your office. Can we set up an appointment for this morning?"

"Ah . . . yes. I suppose so. Ah . . . look. Can I call you back? My boss hasn't come in. I never know what he's going to throw at me Monday morning. I'll get back to you right away."

"All right. You understand that there's some urgency in the matter?"

"Yes of course. I'll call you within the hour."

"Thank you. My extension is 77351."

Monty jotted this on his scratch pad. Then he hung up. Zempfke was still staring curiously. Monty shrugged his shoulders, returned to the pile of papers, remembering that he must call authorities at Wisconsin, first thing. There was an hour's time difference, he remembered. Only 0600 out there. He would put it off until 0830 Pentagon time.

Zempfke called out again.

"Line two, Captain. Captain Caldwell."

Monty pushed the button, answered.

"Hi, Jim. What can we do for you?"

"Can you come over here a minute? I've got something really hot."

"I'm trying to get my briefing together. . . . "

"Monty, this is really hot."

Monty inhaled slowly, thinking. Jim Caldwell, a submariner, was aide to the Secretary of the Navy, useful to OP-31 for providing unofficial intelligence on the thinking at the Department of Defense level. Often in the past, he had unofficially passed along valuable tips of trouble to come, giving Monty time to prepare.

"I'll be right over," Monty said.

He hung up, put on his jacket. He walked to the blackboard by Zempfke's desk and logged himself out with this notation: Caldwell, 77560. The blackboard had been Admiral Starr's idea. If a real crisis struck OP-31, the men who were out could be contacted immediately. Zempfke privately called it Starr's "Pearl Harbor Board."

Preoccupied, Monty went into Corridor C hurriedly, straight into the path of a yellow electric messenger scooter. The driver slammed on his brakes, rang the bell on the handlebars, then struck Monty. He angrily turned on the driver.

"Why don't you watch where the hell you're going?"

There was a yellow flashing light on the scooter. The

driver had not been exceeding his speed limit of five miles an hour. He politely informed Monty of this.

"I'm sorry," Monty conceded. "It was my fault. I wasn't looking."

"Do you want to file an accident report?" the driver asked.

"No. No. It was my fault."

He hurried on, turning into Corridor 6, going out, toward E Ring, VIP country, where CNO and SecNav had their plush offices overlooking the grassy Mall and the Potomac River. Along the E Ring wall, there were huge, gray models of aircraft carriers, battleships, cruisers and destroyers enclosed in clear plastic exhibit boxes. The walls were hung with oils of past Secretaries of the Navy, many bewhiskered and somber. Two Marines in dress uniform—glorified bat-boys for CNO or SecNav—moved along the Ring, shoulder-to-shoulder precisely in step.

Captain James Caldwell, aide to SecNav, was waiting in the anteroom to his office, talking to one of his two pretty secretaries. He was a big man, built like a varsity tackle, with sandy hair going thin. Like other officers on the front row who came in frequent contact with the public, he wore a uniform, ribbons, silver *Polaris* patrol pin, with gold stars. From Academy days onward, Jim Caldwell and Monty King had been friendly competitors. In Submarine School, Monty stood Number 3, in his class, Jim Number 4. Monty had always thought of Jim Caldwell as the "man to beat." It would be so on the Selection Board. The odds against both of them being picked by the same Board in June were large.

"Hi, Monty. Coffee?"

"No thanks. I just had a cup."

They went into Jim's office. It was large, clean and plush, better than Admiral Starr's, infinitely superior to Monty's. The sun was rising through the window.

"I want to show you something off the record," Caldwell said, digging into his In box. He picked up a piece of paper.

At the upper left-hand corner, there was the blue seal of the Department of Defense. The paper was stamped SECRET in block red letters.

"Budget directive from OSD," Caldwell said gravely. "A very, very large cut."

He passed the document to Monty, who skimmed it quickly. "Effective immediately, all departments will . . ." he read, then his eyes dropped to the amount. $10 billion total, $3 billion from the Navy. Exactly as Nancy had predicted! He returned the paper, feeling suddenly shaky and sick.

"Ridiculous," he sighed. "Absolutely ridiculous."

"My reaction, exactly," Caldwell said. "I would say, off-hand, there goes your ULMS. Straight down the tube. Along with a lot of other things."

"The hell you say," Monty shot back. He picked up the paper again, reading more carefully, looking for hedges, what-ifs, or other loopholes. There were none. It was an order, a direct, unequivocal order. "They can't do this. They're crazy. We'll have to lay up half the ships in the Navy."

Jim was right, he thought. ULMS was vulnerable, terribly vulnerable. Controversial. Expensive. The contracts not yet signed. Easy to chop. And with it, my Legion of Merit, and maybe my stars. Twenty-one of the hardest months of my life, crucial career months, down the drain. Shit!

"This is going to tear the Navy apart," Caldwell said sadly.

"They *can't* make it stick," Monty said defiantly.

"I'm afraid they're going to really try. They ran on an antimilitary platform. They got elected. Now . . . "

"But . . ."

"The carrier people are already bled dry—there's not a dime you can cut."

"I know . . . but . . ."

"They'll be on the offensive by 0800."

"This is really crazy. Madness!"

"It sure comes at a bad time for you and me. Another twelve short weeks and our Board would be done. Now, if we're not careful, you and I will be caught in the middle of a vicious new paper war. A lot of people will get hurt. Fatally, career-wise."

"Well, the hell with that," Monty replied. "I'm not going to let them shoot down ULMS, I'll tell you that. The Submarine Force needs ULMS. The country . . . "

"Cool off, Monty," Caldwell broke in, patronizingly. "You've got to stop being so emotionally involved with that weapons system. I may be your competition, but I'm also your friend of thirty years. Zimmerman and Starr have used you . . . You stepped on enough toes already pushing ULMS. Don't let them steam you up all over again. Lay back, play it cool. You get one shot at the Board. A lifetime in the Navy, one shot. All right, so ULMS goes down the tube. You don't get your gong. You still have as good a chance as any one of us. Rollow's your buddy, for God's sake. He thinks you're CNO material. Get your stars. Later you can get the ULMS ball rolling again."

"You mean you're going to lie back and play dead until June?" Monty said icily. "To avoid mashing toes? You'd let ULMS go down the drain without lifting a finger?"

"Don't give me that sanctimonious flag-waving, Monty King. This is Jim Caldwell. Your buddy. You can't snow me. You know goddamned good and well you were riding ULMS for two stars. All right, go on riding it. I'm going to play my own game the way I see it. But you've got no right to imply my way is more morally despicable than yours."

Feeling a wave of rage, Monty turned, walked to the door.

"You people in OP-31 are too specialized," Caldwell insisted, voice climbing in pitch. "Too parochial. If you're going to be Flag Rank, you've got to take a broader view of the defense establishment."

"Blow it out your ass," Monty said, slamming the door behind him.

★ 4 ★

Going back toward OP-31, Monty suddenly changed his mind, detouring by way of Flag Plot. This was CNO's special combat command center, with maps displaying U.S. and Soviet naval vessels and communications link-ups to friendly forces. He showed his ID card to the Marine on duty at the door, then went in to study the maps, noting the position of the FBM that had sent the contact report, the position of other U.S. nuclear submarines and surface forces. Then he hurried back to OP-31.

He made his way into the office, toward his desk, noting the Admiral's door was shut. Was he here?

Yes, Chief Zempfke signaled with his eyes, and a slight tilt of the head toward the door. Monty walked to the door, put his eye to a tiny peephole, which, like a fish-eye lens, provided a wide-angle view of the interior of the office. The Admiral kept his door closed to seal out the noise of the outer office. He had weak kidneys, and often went to the head by way of a door leading directly from his office to the C Ring passageway, without informing them. They kept track of his comings and goings, without disturbing him, through the peephole.

Monty could see him, wearing a gray tweed suit, standing, looking out the window into the bleak space between C and D Rings. His back was to the peephole. There was a cigar in his ashtray, smoke curling upward.

Behind Monty, Zempfke spoke:

"Captain, I just got a call from Warrant Officer Collins in CNO's office. He said CNO had asked for that updated

44

Soviet submarine threat paper—the one we gave to Mister Trimble—this morning. He wants it yesterday."

"Oh, hell," Monty said, turning to face his yeoman.

"He needs it by 1700 tomorrow for a special JCS meeting," Zempfke went on. "The Lieutenant's got a lot of personal paperwork to do, I don't see . . . "

"Who else can we give it to?"

"Everybody's up to their eyeballs."

"Well, tell Trimble to drop everything and get on it. His personal affairs will have to come second. Tell him to see me within the hour. I'll help him get it going."

"Aye, aye, sir. And, sir, will you ask the Admiral to please sign that stuff he's got on the desk? He's had some of it four or five days. Two or three are overdue. . . . "

"I'll get on him. *If* I can nail him to his chair."

Monty knocked, pushed open the door.

"Admiral?" he said.

"Come in," Starr boomed, without turning.

Monty walked into the office, respectfully, and, except for his short sleeves, a bit formally. Starr was only five years his senior but Monty thought of the Admiral as one of a prior generation. The World War II generation. Starr had graduated from Sub School in time to fight the entire submarine war in the Pacific. He helped commission a new boat in 1941, then made seventeen war patrols on her and others, operating out of Pearl Harbor, Perth, Australia, Midway, Guam and the Philippines. He had won two Navy Crosses, a Silver Star and a Bronze Star, a Legion of Merit and two Letters of Commendation.

Starr was famous, in Navy circles, for two achievements. In 1939, when he was Midshipman Regimental Commander, he heard the famous Orson Welles radio show which gave the impression that Martians had landed on earth and were advancing on Washington. Without hesitation, Starr had mobilized the Midshipmen on the Parade Ground, resolutely prepared to march to the defense of the Capital. In 1945, when the last great Japanese warship, the super-carrier *Yamato*, broke from her berth in the Inland Sea, in a suicidal one-way dash to Okinawa, Starr had made the initial contact report off Kui Suido which enabled four other Fleet Boats to close in and kill her off. He was the last of the old breed sea dogs, serving his final tour. Behind his back—never to his face—he was known as "Twinkle" Starr.

"Good morning, Admiral," Monty said. "I hate to start off ruining your day, but I was just over in Jim Caldwell's office. Some very bad news is on the way."

The Admiral glanced warily at Monty, cutting in. "I've been in this insane asylum two years. I've yet to hear a single piece of good news. What is it now?"

"Sir, he showed me a DOD budget directive. A $10 billion budget cut—servicewide. The Navy's share will be $3 billion. It is not a drill, but a direct order."

The Admiral sat down, squinting. His face seemed puffy. He had been drinking hard last night, Monty thought.

"They're full of shit," the Admiral said quietly.

"Caldwell said he thought they meant it. I read the directive myself. It's emphatic."

The Admiral said nothing in return, sitting stonily, staring at the door to the corridor. Zempfke entered the office, bringing the Admiral's coffee mug, setting it on the desk. Then he checked the Admiral's Out box. It was empty.

"What do they expect us to do?" the Admiral said, at last, shrugging his shoulders helplessly. "It's impossible, that's all."

"Yes, sir," Monty said. "That's what I thought."

The Admiral sipped his coffee, frowning, lost in thought. Monty ventured: "ULMS may be in trouble."

"Nonsense!" Starr exclaimed, slamming the desktop with his open palm.

"Caldwell said, quote, 'There goes your ULMS, right down the tube,' unquote."

"He did, eh?" Starr asked, raising his bushy left eyebrow.
"Yes, sir."

"Whose side is *he* on?"

"I'm not sure anymore."

Admiral Starr licked his lower lip. "They're going to get
one hell of a fight," he said, as though there were nothing
he relished more this morning. "A goddamned good run for
the money."

"And, sir, did you see that contact report?" Monty asked,
leaning over the Admiral's desk, sifting through the papers.

"Yeah, I saw it," Starr growled. "Faye's got his nerve,
breaking radio silence to send in a thing like that. What do
you think?"

"I don't know, sir. It was pretty vague."

"Probably a whale," the Admiral said.

"I'm sure Faye thought about it pretty carefully," Monty
replied. "He's not one to go off half-cocked. Very cautious
type."

"That's true," Starr said, picking up the message, reread-
ing, holding the paper almost against his nose. He was
short-sighted in the extreme, yet he refused to wear glasses.
He laid the message aside. He changed the subject abruptly.

"I see where your Board's been announced. Don't worry.
Don't waste any sleep."

He fished through the papers in his attaché case, with-
drew one and went on:

"Here's a rough draft for your gong. Get it smoothed up
and typed and I'll sign it and get it in your jacket. They're
not going to push submarines around again this year, by
God. If they try, they're going to get a good fight from me.
I'll blackball every man they put up. There's going to be
plenty of horse-trading this time, believe me."

He passed Monty the paper.

"Read it," he said, gruffly.

Monty read:

"For exceptionally meritorious service as Deputy Director,

Submarine Warfare Division, Navy Department, from——
to——, Captain King has consistently displayed maturity,
keen judgment and professionalism in the conduct of the
often difficult affairs of this office. Captain King made
significant contributions to the urgent and complex formula-
tion of division plans and policies under extreme pressure.
In particular, he is responsible, to a large degree, for the
acceptance within the Navy Department, and higher echelons in the Department of Defense, of the Navy's proposed
Underwater Long Range Missile System (ULMS). During
this tour, Captain King has worked unstintingly in behalf of
ULMS. . . . He was instrumental in . . ."

"Fill in the rest," Starr growled self-consciously. "You
know how I get tangled up with words. You know what to
say."

"Thank you very much, sir."

"Forget it."

"But, sir. What if they cancel ULMS?"

"They won't."

Monty turned to leave, folding the paper carefully.

"Wait a goddamn minute," Starr said suddenly, snapping
a finger, then pawing through the papers on his desk. He
lifted the contact report and waved it in the air, then rushed
on with a note of triumph. "Monty, this goddamned thing
may be heaven sent."

"Sir?"

"The contact. It may be just what we need to head off
this budget cutting farce—have we got anybody close by?"

"Yes. A nuke, eight hours way."

"We'll send him to investigate. Anybody else in the area?"

"Three other nukes within a day and a half."

"We'll send them too."

"But Admiral, they're in the middle of an antisubmarine
warfare fleet exercise."

"Screw that."

"But, sir . . ."

"We want this to look important."

"Yes, sir. But . . . "

"No buts, Monty."

The Admiral drained his coffee quickly.

"I'll be in Flag Plot," he said. "Get over to see Zimmerman and see if he has any ideas . . . call Buzz Creighton. . . ."

"Sir," Monty said. "Don't you think we better query Faye before we crank up all this effort?"

"That's how we got the shit kicked out of us at Pearl Harbor, Monty," the Admiral replied with gravity.

"But, sir . . . can you at least take a few minutes to get some of this paperwork cleared away?"

The Admiral scowled at the papers on his desk.

"Sign my name if you have to," he said. Then he steamed out from the office with the cigar, now dead, jutting rakishly from his mouth, like the bowsprit of a clipper ship. Damn the torpedoes, Monty thought uneasily, full speed ahead.

★ 5 ★

Monty returned to his desk, carrying the Admiral's paperwork. He jotted the names Creighton and Zimmerman on the reminder pad, beneath Wisconsin, MacIntosh and Captain Davis. Then he divided the Admiral's papers into piles, attending first to the congressional mail with the pink buck slips. By CNO regulation, congressional mail would be answered within five working days. Two letters were already a day late. He read the replies carefully, like an editor, making sure they were soundly argued, that the grammar and spelling were perfect, that the typing was neat and clean. Then he signed the Admiral's name.

At 0800, he paused to telephone Buzz Creighton—Richard

Creighton—Washington Representative for New England Shipbuilding. NES, as it was known in the Submarine Force, was a large bureaucracy, almost like a branch of the Navy, administered mainly by retired submarine officers, like Buzz.

The line rang. A pleasant voice answered.

"Good morning. General Nucleonics."

General Nucleonics was the parent company for NES, a defense conglomerate, with aircraft, electronic, missile, space, submarine, oceanographic, and data systems divisions. It ranked near the top of the dozen largest defense contractors which did a third of all the Pentagon's business.

"Captain Creighton, please," Monty said.

"Thank you. I'll ring Mr. Creighton's office."

Richard Creighton was a classmate of Monty's. He was one of the keenest, most resourceful and decisive men Monty had known in the Navy. He had stood Number 3 in the class at Annapolis and 1 in Sub School. Later, he had been one of the first to enter Zimmerman's nuclear-propulsion program, one of the first to command a nuclear submarine. He had been "early-selected" for captain. He might have been early-selected for rear admiral, but he retired on twenty years' service. He was a devout Catholic with six children. His wife, Carolyn, needed his firm hand at home, and extra money to educate the children. Admiral Fitzgerald, a submariner whom Creighton had served, now retired and a director of New England Ship, had arranged the Washington Rep's job, at a salary of $25,000 a year. With Navy retirement pay, Buzz made $35,000. It was Buzz Creighton who first suggested to Monty that, if he were passed over for Flag Rank, he come to work for NES as an ULMS project manager.

"Mr. Creighton's office," a pleasant female voice answered.

"This is Captain King. Is Captain Creighton in?"

"Yes, sir, Captain. One moment please."

Buzz Creighton came on the phone almost immediately.

"Hello, Monty. It must be ESP. I was going to call you. I think I know why *you're* calling."

He probably did, Monty thought. General Nucleonics had an amazing intelligence-gathering network.

"The word landed here this morning," Buzz went on, speaking guardedly and generally. "Like a thermonuclear bomb. The top management is taking it very seriously. They're worried about you-know-what. They've got a task force of doubledomes coming down on the oh-nine-hundred shuttle for a strategy session. Can you have lunch with us at the Army-Navy Town Club?"

"Ah . . . I'll try. . . . We're up to our armpits . . . "

"It's important," Buzz said, leaving no doubt.

"O.K. I'll make time."

"How's your transportation situation?"

"Lousy," Monty said.

It was impossible for him to get transportation from the Pentagon Motor Pool in the basement. The 145 official cars were reserved for Pentagon personnel officially classed as VIPs—Flag Rank or GS-16 or higher. There were 700 VIPs in the Pentagon. If he drove the VW to town, his space might be gone when he rereturned. A round-trip cab fare was ridiculously expensive.

"I'll send a car and driver to pick you up," Creighton said. "Mall Entrance. Twelve hundred."

"O.K., Buzz."

"By the way," Buzz said, lowering his voice. "If you've got any of our stock, don't panic. Our financial people are fore-casting a drop this week—when the rumors start—but hold on. When we get this mess cleared up, it'll come back strong."

Monty felt suddenly queasy. *Goddammit!* he thought. I *am* a stockholder. Or Nancy is. Did Buzz know Nancy owned the stock? Acting on inside information like this *must* be against the law. How could Buzz be so casual about it? He decided he would let it pass without any comment.

When Monty hung up, he found Lieutenant Trimble standing at his elbow with a white Navy tablet and pencil. He was in shirt sleeves now, ready for work. He did not appear overjoyed.

"Sit down," Monty said. "Sorry to hit you with this on your first day, but it's top priority. A CNO special. You see how it goes here? Your first day, you're preparing a memo for CNO."

"I read the request from CNO," Trimble said. "It seemed pretty vague. Can you give me some idea of how you want me to get into it?"

"We always begin these Threat papers with a capsule historical summary," Monty returned. "Label it *Background*."

"You mean a whole history of submarines? Back to Simon Lake and all that?"

"No. No. A capsule of World War II."

"Why?"

"Why?" Monty repeated. "Because that's the way it's always been done here. Dig in the files. There are plenty of summaries. Go down to the Pentagon library. They've got 250,000 volumes down there."

"But I don't understand. He seems to want an order-of-battle type . . ."

"Just do as I say, please. We don't have time in this shop for debates. Our job is to supply facts."

"But Captain," Trimble insisted, "you can't expect me to do something intelligently unless I know why I'm doing it."

"All right," Monty said impatiently. "Every chance we get in this shop, we remind people of two things: One, the importance of the submarine. What a tremendous job we did against the Japanese. How close the Nazis came to winning the war with the U-boat. Two, how big the Soviet submarine Navy is now. We put in the Japanese stuff because the carrier admirals kept it out of all the histories of World War II—Admiral Samuel Eliot Morison and so on—

and nobody's ever really appreciated what the submarine did, or what it might do in the future. Does that answer your question, Mister Trimble?"

"Yes, sir. It most emphatically does."

"I told you our job here was to sell submarines. The carrier people sell carriers. The Army sells rifles and jeeps and tanks. The Air Force sells airplanes and missiles. You're learning your first lesson. The Pentagon Indian is a salesman, first, last, always. You tell them how effective your product has always been...and why you need more in the future."

"I understand that, sir."

"Just remember the guy in the Army uniform and the Air Force uniform doesn't give a damn about your problems," Monty went on. "There's just so much money to go around. Everything costs billions. He wants every dime he can lay his hands on. He'll cut your balls off while you're not looking. And that goes for our carrier people, too."

"Yes, sir."

"This is a kind of combat . . . just like your *Polaris*."

"I understand."

"All right. Put in there we had only 200 Fleet Boats against the Japanese. We lost 52 boats. But we sank 6 million tons of Jap shipping—more than the carrier task forces, Army Air Corps, mines, natural disasters and everything else combined."

"I see," Trimble said, making notes on the pad.

"That's the kind of stuff we want people to remember," Monty said. He added: "Besides, Admiral Starr likes to see that up front. He was a part of that and it means a lot to him. CNO was out in the Pacific, too. He was on a carrier, but he'll remember. You have to keep reminding people, all the time. Now get started like that. If you need any help, Zempfke knows the score. He was out there too."

"Aye, aye, sir."

Watching Trimble hurry off, Monty thought: When was

he born? 1944 or 1945? He was just a little older than
Mike and Paul. He probably didn't know anything about
World War II. It meant nothing to him except words in a
book, or action on film. It was like talking about World
War I during World War II.

He looked at the clock. 0830. Time was spinning by. It
was time to call Wisconsin, go see Admiral Zimmerman
and Captain Davis. He put on his jacket, logged himself
out on the blackboard with a simple Z. There was no need
to put down the telephone extension. Everyone in OP-31
knew it by heart. As Zempfke often chided, OP-31 didn't
go to the head without calling Admiral Zimmerman.

Monty went into the passageway, walking swiftly toward
A Ring where, he knew, there was a public phone booth.
The booth was occupied. Monty waited, pacing, going to
the window of A Ring, looking down on the inner courtyard of the Pentagon. It was daylight now. The inner court
was a parklike area with grass and shrubs and walks and
benches. In the summer, the snack bar in the center was
open. Many people ate lunch outside, basking in the sun.
Monty had never had time for that.

He returned to the booth. Now it was empty. He went
in, closed the folding door, placed the call, charging it to
his home phone. A pleasant man in the university security office named Jim Olsen answered. Monty explained
the problem, giving the information Nancy had obtained.
While Monty held on, Olsen went off to check his files. He
returned to report he had nothing.

"I wouldn't worry about it, Captain King," Olsen added.
"There are hundreds of these runaways and dropouts nowdays. Routine for the course. The other night, the dean told
us they're more or less figuring it's going to take the kids five
or six years to get through college, counting dropout time.
They all do it."

"It's my wife who's worried," Monty pressed.

"That's understandable."

"Is there any way you can check on the girl?"

"You don't know her name?"

"No."

"Let me see what I can do for you, Captain. I was in the Navy in the war. World War II, I mean. I'm still a Navy man at heart. I won't hold out much hope, but let me check further and call you back."

"Well," Monty said, taken aback by this sentimentality. "I'd sure as hell appreciate it."

After giving his office number, he hung up feeling uplifted. There was at least one man out there in the heartland who still had respect for the military, he thought. Should he call Nancy and reassure her? No. Mr. Olsen might strike out. Better to wait.

Nancy King woke up with the telephone ringing in her ears. Paul! she thought. She reached for the phone on the bedside table, glancing at the clock. It was eight-thirty, later than she had slept in years.

"Nancy?"

It was Alma Caldwell, Nancy's junior-college roommate, friend, fellow Navy wife. Nancy pulled herself up on the pillow, forcing herself awake, energy into her voice, feeling ashamed for lying abed so late. She said cheerily:

"Good morning."

"It's a lousy morning," Alma replied grumpily. "Raining cats and dogs." She paused, then asked in a more cheerful tone, "Did you hear the news?"

"Yes," Nancy said. "Jim called Monty last night from the Pentagon."

"What a lucky break for Monty that Fred Rollow is president," Alma said. "Well, it's Commissary day, remember?"

"Oh yes," Nancy lied. It had slipped her mind. Every three weeks, she and Alma bought groceries and supplies at Fort Myer, then had lunch. Nancy had not even prepared her list.

"I've got a problem," Alma went on. "I can't get the car started. The battery's dead or the wires are wet or something. Do you think you could drive?"

"Of course. Let's see, how'll we do this. . . . "

"You pick me up. We'll go to the Commissary, then back to your house, unload your stuff, then we'll come here, unload mine and have lunch. How's that?"

"Fine."

"I hate to make you do the driving."

"I owe you. . . . "

They concluded the arrangements. Nancy got up, looking forward to the day, getting out, having a good, long talk with Alma Caldwell. She would understand, completely, Nancy was sure.

She slipped off her nightgown, pausing to observe, and appraise, her figure in the full-length mirror. As a teenager, when she first met Alma at Calvert Hall, Nancy had been an exceptionally pretty and wholesome girl with long, silky, blonde hair, wide-set blue eyes, a perky freckled nose, clear, taut skin, and a good, firm bust, like her mother. Now her hair was streaked with gray. There were tiny crow's feet near the corners of her eyes. Her bosom had sagged. But her tummy was still flat, her legs and thighs, in spite of three children, trim. She had lost a little weight since she stopped menstruating. Today, she weighed exactly what she had weighed in high school—107. She had not let herself go like a lot of Navy wives who turned to booze to fill in the empty nights.

She dressed warmly, in a tweed suit. In the kitchen, waiting for the coffee to perk, she turned on the radio—a morning talk show—for company, sat at her desk, making the grocery list. When the coffee was ready, she put the list in her purse and moved to the table in the breakfast nook in a multipaneled bay window overlooking the back yard. It was a dismal day. A queer, greenish light bathed the dead grass in the back yard.

Nancy hated the house, the neighborhood, Glen Pines. It was a new subdivision in Annandale, one of the many little Virginia towns that had sprouted up around the Pentagon in the last decade or two. The house was flimsily built, piratically overpriced. The builder had cheated them on the insulation. It was damp in winter, too warm in summer. There were no trees. She had no real friends in the neighborhood. Most were transient military—Army, Air Force, Marine Corps, Navy. A few GS-15–level civil servants. Four of the twenty-six houses in the subdivision had been broken into within the past year, two in broad daylight, or so Nancy had heard from the woman next door, a mousy, fearful gossip.

In the front foyer, she got her camel's-hair coat and umbrella from the closet, pausing to look through the arch into the living room. It was cozy, homey, furnished with hand-me-downs from her family and Monty's, all redone. The retirement home would be smaller, she thought. The baby grand would have to go. Paul didn't play it anymore anyway, now that he had his frightful guitar. The piano might bring $200. Or more.

She went into the raw, cold drizzle to the Olds wagon in the drive. The seat was cold, her breath made clouds of fog. She got the engine going, then the heater, backed out and went out to Braddock Road, a main artery leading to the Washington Beltway. She followed the Beltway clockwise, through Fairfax and McLean into Maryland, turning on River Road toward Bethesda-Chevy Chase. The drizzle had stopped. The traffic was heavy—late-rising civilians going to their jobs. She turned into Wilson Lane, passing

Landon, an expensive private school, where the two older
Caldwell boys had gone. Two blocks further, across Bradley
Lane, she turned into the long pebble drive.

The Caldwells' home was a lovely old Georgian brick
colonial, built in 1870. When Jim's grandfather had ac-
quired it, the place had been a country estate and farm,
far from downtown Washington. It was verdant, rolling
countryside, where the Chevy Chase Fox Hunt had been
founded. After his retirement from the Navy, Jim's father
had sold off much of the land to developers, keeping only
the original house and two tree-shaded acres, which he
passed along to Jim and Alma. This gift had given the
Caldwells an economic edge on most Navy families. By
renting the place when they were not in Washington, they
had always had extra money to send the children to private
prep schools, to join the Chevy Chase Club and have a full-
time servant.

Nancy parked in the circular drive behind the Caldwells'
station wagon, went up the brick walk between the solid,
waist-high English boxwood, to the front door, painted
black. She raised the brass knocker—shaped like an anchor
—and let it fall once.

Alma swung open the door. Her blue eyes twinkled
happily. She might have just walked off the paddle tennis
courts at the Chevy Chase Club. She wore a cashmere
sweater and a tweed skirt to her knees, low-cut suede shoes.
Her hair was short and streaked, the latest style. Her skin
was, as always, remarkable. Not a line, a wrinkle. She
looked every inch an Admiral's wife, Nancy thought.

"Come in and have some coffee, dear," she said. "This
is really ridiculous, your coming all the way over here in
this weather. I'm terribly sorry."

She kissed Nancy on the cheek.

Nancy followed her into the large center hall. The house
was furnished with sturdy, traditional pieces, now slightly
threadbare from the wear and tear of four children, many

tenants, and all the dogs, cats and other pets. They went back into an enormous old-fashioned kitchen which Alma had refurbished after the last tenant. It now gleamed with new appliances, a double, stainless-steel sink. There was an artificially low ceiling with built-in lighting behind frosted panels. Alma poured coffee into dainty cups, then they sat at the round table in the center of the room.

"I hardly slept a wink," Alma said, stifling a small yawn. "When Jim got home from the Pentagon, he wanted to have a drink and talk, analyze the members of the Board and all that. I got a second wind . . . "

She went on about the Selection Board members, listing those who she believed thought well of her husband, those who might be a problem. She believed the pros outweighed the cons, that Jim would be selected, that she would shortly be an Admiral's wife. A lifelong dream realized. Nancy felt sorry for her. If Jim didn't make it, it was going to be a staggering blow for both of them, especially Alma. She felt a sudden compulsive urge to break in and shock Alma with her not inconsiderable news.

"Paul has disappeared," she said.

"What?"

"He dropped out of school. His landlady said he ran off with a blonde hippie."

"When?"

"Last week."

"Why didn't you call me?"

"I didn't find out until day before yesterday."

"Where is he?"

"I have no idea. Monty's calling the school to see if they can help."

"My Godfrey," Alma said, letting out a deep sigh. Then she looked darkly at Nancy, as if to say: it was foreordained. However, she said, "Oh, he'll show up. I wouldn't worry. From what I read, it's routine."

"Until it happens to *you*," Nancy said, sharply.

"Yes . . . "

"I hope to God he isn't on drugs," Nancy said. "I don't think he has the right temperament. He's the type to get addicted."

"Oh pshaw!" Alma said.

"I wouldn't worry if it were Mike," Nancy said. "He's got Monty's inner toughness. Paul's always been so—so impressionable, easily led. I still think the trouble in Charleston came because he was so suggestible."

"He fell in with that horrible girl," Alma said.

"That's what I mean. Maybe this girl's another."

"Oh God! Let's hope not."

"What Paul needs is firm guidance from his father," Nancy said, turning the conversation to her decision. "A couple of years together under the same roof. Paul's really never had a strong male figure around to emulate. The whole time he was growing into teenage, Monty was away on the *Jones.*"

"Yes, I know. But—he's twenty years old."

"It's not too late. At times, he seems very much a child."

"They all do, at times," Alma agreed.

"If Monty is selected for Flag Rank, he'll have to go back to sea."

"Not necessarily."

"With our luck."

Alma looked at Nancy with surprise. "What are you getting at, Nancy?"

"I want Monty to retire. Right now."

"*What?*" Alma shrieked. "Retire? With the Board meeting in twelve weeks? Nancy, you're putting me on."

"No," Nancy said solemnly. "I've never been more serious in my life."

"You're upset about Paul. I don't blame you. . . . "

"It's *not* just Paul, Alma. I made up my mind a long time ago. During Christmas. When Paul was home. I have a good many reasons."

"What would you live on?"

"We'd live in a less expensive area. We have some money put away. Investments. I'm not worried about *that*."

"But . . . "

"I want a *husband*, Alma."

"What would you do with Monty around the house all day?" Alma said. "He's still in his prime. The Navy's his whole life. You'll suffocate. He'd drive you crazy. Or you'd drive him crazy. I couldn't imagine a life with Jim around the house all day."

"That's the conventional view."

"You can't put Paul and Monty under the same roof . . . "

"Why not?"

"It's too late."

"Who says?"

"Ask anybody . . . "

"I'm tired of accepting other people's advice, Alma,' Nancy insisted. "All my life, I've been the dutiful, uncomplaining Navy wife, doing what I was told. Now, for once, I'm going to do what *I* want to do, what *I* believe is best for me, and Monty and Paul."

Alma's eyes fell to the empty coffee cup.

"More?" she said, picking up the cup.

"Half."

While Alma poured fresh coffee, Nancy went on compulsively:

"I want to spend the next twenty years—if we live that long—finding out what life is. Up to now I've been going from pillar to post without rhyme or reason, waiting on shore. . . . Alma, I don't know a thing about myself or, really, a thing about Monty. I don't even know why I'm supposed to be living. But there just has to be more to life than *this*."

"I don't think you're very likely to find out about life by resigning from it," Alma said, returning with the coffee "Even if you *could* find out about it."

"I'm not resigning from life," Nancy retorted. "I'm facing up to life for the very first time. The Navy isn't real life, Alma. It's escapism. We're like children, in school. All these rules and regulations . . . customs. Everything taken care of, if you fill out the forms in triplicate. I want to find out about myself, my husband. I want to forget all this and begin all over."

"In a cozy rose-covered cottage?" Alma asked, ironically.

"Perhaps."

"And a perfectly gorgeous sex life, too?"

"Why not?"

"Oh, Nancy. That's a fantasy."

"It doesn't have to be."

"You and Monty had your kicks . . . "

"That's not true," Nancy said, angrily. "We've had a perfectly miserable sex life. Absolutely miserable."

"What? Now, that's hard to believe. Jim and I always thought you and Monty were the perfect married couple."

"Outwardly," Nancy said bitterly.

"Well . . . " Alma began, self-consciously.

"He hasn't slept with me for *thirteen* months. Look at me! Am I all that repulsive?"

"No. Of course not.

"If Monty and I could start over, on a normal, intelligent level, I know our whole life could be quite different—wonderful."

Alma stared silently into her coffee.

"Did I tell you what happened on our honeymoon?" Nancy raced on.

"Yes, of course . . . "

"No. I mean the real part."

"What real part?"

"The sex. Or rather, the lack of it."

"Well, no. Actually you . . . "

"Let me tell you. Maybe that's when it started, for me. After the ceremony in the chapel, you remember, we went to that big old hotel down at Old Point Comfort, Virginia?"

"Yes, you told me," Alma said, eyes glancing at the kitchen clock.

"I didn't tell you what really happened," Nancy went on urgently. "It wasn't glorious, at all. The Army had all but taken over the hotel. We went up to the room. It was shabby. It smelled like stale whiskey. I felt good . . . eager. I wasn't afraid at all, the way mother said I would be. I wanted him very much. He went out to get a bottle of champagne. I took off my things. He came back. We got in bed . . . Monty was eager too. There was a lot of confusion . . . he was premature . . . that's understandable. But just as I got ready, the damned door flew open and here was this Army major standing there with a Val-Pac over his shoulder. Alma, I could have died. I slid to the floor behind the bed. Monty jumped up and said what the hell . . . ? It turned out to be a mix-up at the desk. They had assigned us the same room. We bolted the door, but were so shook, we couldn't do anything anymore. Not even in Williamsburg where we moved the next morning. We never did get it right. Monty was always so early. I was uptight. I didn't have an orgasm until six months later . . . the night of the Submarine School graduation party . . . remember? When we all got high as kites? That was the first time. That was the night we made Joanie, by accident. My *first* orgasm . . . "

She paused, remembering the ghastly night Joanie was born in the sub-base infirmary. She alone with the stupid Navy doctors. Monty on the West Coast with his stupid submarine. The twenty-two hours of labor. The breech birth. V-J Day in the infirmary.

"But what's so unusual about that?" Alma asked. "Most of us had trouble making a sexual adjustment. Did I tell you about *our* honeymoon?"

"Wait till I tell you the rest," Nancy said.

"We better get going," Alma said, again glancing at the clock. "Otherwise we'll never get finished today."

★ 7 ★

Monty mounted the stairs to the fifth floor of the Pentagon, following Corridor 6 out to the E Ring, to an office just above CNO. However, on this floor, the E Ring was not plush country. It was drab like most other corridors. He went to office 5E665, where the door sign read:

NAVAL SHIPS SYSTEMS COMMAND
DEPUTY COMMANDER FOR NUCLEAR
PROPULSION
VADM. S. M. ZIMMERMAN

He opened the door and walked into a small anteroom. There were two civilian secretaries and a female yeoman working at desks. The anteroom was large and airy, with two windows overlooking the Mall Entrance below. It was decorated with dozens of framed color photographs of nuclear submarines going down the launching ways, steaming at sea, or near ice, or moored in Holy Loch, Scotland; Rota, Spain; Guam and Hawaii. There were also exact scale models of all the types of nuclear submarines ever built mounted on chrome stands, like those in Monty's den.

"Good morning, Captain," the yeoman said, brightly.

"Is the boss in?" Monty said, nodding his head toward the closed door.

"Yes. He's looking for you."

The yeoman opened the door into the inner office and said:

"Admiral? Captain King is here."

Monty heard the Admiral's high-pitched, raspy voice: "Send him in."

64

The yeoman nodded solemnly to Monty, holding the door, standing to one side. Monty could see the Admiral beyond her, some distance away, sitting at a huge desk in the middle of his huge office. He was small, silver-haired, beak-nosed. He wore a light gray suit and a shirt that seemed too large at the neck. He was busy going through papers. He did not look up when Monty entered.

Vice Admiral Zimmerman was one of the most astonishing characters Monty had ever met or served. During World War II, he had been a faceless engineer in the Electrical Division of the Bureau of Ships. After the war, he had taken an interest in nuclear technology. With the help of an unorthodox team of Navy engineers, he had developed a nuclear power plant for submarines. When his name came before a Flag Rank Selection Board, he had been passed over because he was too specialized. Buzz Creighton, then one of his right-hand men, had secretly mobilized a risky press crusade to "save" Zimmerman and his team. It worked: Congress climbed on the bandwagon, demanding Zimmerman be promoted, his brilliant team kept together, or else the entire promotion list would be denied. The Navy reluctantly yielded, forming a new Selection Board specifically to select one captain "skilled in nuclear engineering." Zimmerman. It was the only time since the Selection Board system had been instituted in 1916 that a decision had been overturned.

In the ensuing years, after his nuclear power had revolutionized the Submarine Force and the Navy, Rear Admiral Zimmerman had again been promoted by edict of the Congress. In addition, he had been showered with special medals created by the Congress. He had been written about endlessly in the press, magazines and books. Now in his seventies, he was still on active duty, a kind of *éminence grise,* all the mandatory retirement regulations having been waived by the Congress. In Monty's mind, Zimmerman, for whom he had once worked as aide, ranked somewhere between Einstein and God. He was certain that when the military history of the times was written, Vice Admiral Zimmerman would emerge as *the* towering figure, like Admiral Sims and General Billy Mitchell of bygone times.

"I see your Selection Board's been announced," the Admiral said without looking up. "I'll get a letter to them if you want. But it may do more harm than good. There are still a lot of bastards around here that hate my guts."

Monty hesitated, not knowing what to say. The Admiral spoke the truth. In spite of the good Zimmerman had done the Navy, there were many senior Flag Officers who despised his methods, his arrogance and brilliance and who were jealous of his fame and popularity in Congress. He was not a member of the inner club. Far from it.

"They want me out of the way," the Admiral said, looking up with defiance. "They think they have people who can fill my shoes. The stupid bastards don't realize I've just started. . . . They think you can do a thing like this with *routine* methods. If I'd followed routine methods, I'd still be waiting for an authorization to obtain my first dollar. Does that make sense?"

"Yes, sir, Admiral," Monty replied crisply.

It was a familiar refrain. There had been a time when Monty would have taken issue with the Admiral, but over the years, he had gained an important insight into the man's character. Those who were not 100 percent in his favor, the Admiral considered mortal enemies, to be verbally flogged at every occasion. It was easier, Monty had found, to let the Admiral run on.

"You tell me what to do about the letter," the Admiral said. "I won't be hurt if you don't want it."

"Sir," Monty responded delicately. "I . . ."

"Dumb bastards," Zimmerman went on. "They'll pick the stupid ones. In a bureaucracy, mediocrity rises to the top.

That's a law, absolute as Murphy's Law, or Parkinson's Law. If we could fire every third person in this building, maybe we could get something done. Does that make sense?"

"It certainly does, Admiral," Monty agreed heartily.

"I'm trying to fight a technological war with the Soviet Union," the Admiral said. "But I'm caught up in a paper war with the Department of Defense. Studies! Look at this! If we let those bastards have their way, when war comes, the only thing we'll have to throw at the enemy is paper."

He jumped up agitatedly.

"I am *bombarded* with esoteric studies from DOD," he railed, turning churlishly toward Monty. "It reminds me of Count Uvarov, the Minister of Public Instruction in the reign of Alexander the First of Russia. Are you familiar with him? He wrote brochures in French, corresponded with Goethe on Greek subjects in German, and discoursed on Slavic poetry of the fourth century. Someone said to him: 'We've got our hands full fighting wild bears, Mr. Minister. Can we dispense with ballads about the gods of Samothrace?' Monty, DOD is full of Count Uvarovs, dilettantes, writing memos. Do you realize I now have to go through fourteen separate command echelons to get a simple valve approved?"

"Yes, sir," Monty said, wondering where the Admiral had come across the obscure Russian Count. In his railing against his supposed enemies, the Admiral frequently dropped in such nuggets. Some of his detractors had said they were supplied by the Admiral's wife, a brilliant student of philosophy and history.

Monty waited patiently for the Admiral to wind down so that he could convey the news from Caldwell's office. But he showed no sign of letting up.

"Monty, I'm an old man. I'll tell you, frankly, I'm tired. I feel . . . I feel as though the Department of Defense is a greater threat to this country than the Soviets will ever be.

They've got to be stopped. I tell you this from ... from the bottom of my heart. I know they say I'm a publicity hound. I don't want publicity."

He returned to his desk, opened a drawer, took out an old logbook with yellow pages. He held the book in his hand like a missal, opened to a mark and said: "In the old days when I was a young officer traveling through Kingston, Jamaica, I saw an inscription on the floor of one of the transepts of the Spanish Town Cathedral. The inscription was for Colonel John Colbeck of the British Army. It said: 'With great applause, he departed this life ye 22nd day of February, 1682.'"

The Admiral looked at Monty earnestly, and said: "I thought it would be good to have the same said of me when I leave. I have tried all my life to act so as to merit such 'applause.' But I'm sure there are plenty of those bastards in DOD who will be happy to accord me applause—when I'm gone."

He grinned, replacing the book. Monty returned the smile, uneasily. He had never heard the Admiral speak of death, or its possibility. Even in jest. But he was growing impatient. The Admiral was wandering, wasting time. With a sudden jolt, Monty asked himself if the old man was getting senile.

"There is nobody who could have done this job—the nuclear engineering job—except my team," the Admiral went on. "We did it against the opposition of the Navy, DOD—everybody! The important thing to keep in mind is that the job is *not* finished. It's far from finished. Give those bastards in DOD a single opening and they'll tear down all the work I've done for the last twenty-five years. Does that make sense?"

Monty let this question pass, now taking the conversation to the matter for which he had come.

"Admiral. This morning we received unofficial word that DOD is requesting a $3 billion budget cut in the Navy.

We felt, that among other things, ULMS might be vulnerable. Admiral Starr suggested that I liaison with you as soon as possible."

"I heard about it," the Admiral said, somewhat indifferently.

"Well, sir . . . "

"Don't worry about it."

"But, sir. I . . . "

"What's the status of the ULMS contract for the long lead-time hardware?"

"It cleared CNO and SecNav two weeks ago," Monty said. "It's somewhere over in DOD."

"Did you write a press release to go with it?"

"Yes, sir. A one-paragraph statement with the amount, $150 million. I gave it to Chinfo. I don't know what happened after that. It was supposed to be cleared through DOD and then, ultimately, released, as I understand it, through Congressman Magruder's office."

"I want you to get that press release out of DOD by Wednesday," the Admiral said, with an inscrutable smile.

"You mean before we know the contract's signed?" Monty asked.

"Yes."

"But, Admiral . . . "

"The best defense is a strong offense," Zimmerman said.

"Yes, sir."

"All right. We're going on the offensive. That press release will serve as a lightning rod. If there is any real opposition to ULMS on the DOD level, that's good intelligence. We'll smoke the bastards out. Then we'll know who the enemy is and gear up. If, on the other hand, the release is cleared, it's a good sign ULMS is safe. Neither the Navy nor DOD will back down, kill or cut back ULMS, after they have taken a public position in its favor and let Chairman Magruder publicly identify himself with it. Does that make sense?"

"Yes, sir, Admiral."

"I've been around this building a long time, Monty. Bear one thing in mind. You and I can spend half our lives sitting in committee meetings or writing papers, but I'll tell you this: most of the real policy in this building is made over press releases, usually in a flap, shooting from the hip. You can't hedge a press release. There's no in-between position."

"But Admiral," Monty protested. "The contract. How do we get the contract signed?"

"Let the lawyers worry about contracts," Zimmerman said vaguely. "We got to grab ours while the grabbing's good. How the hell are they *not* going to sign a lousy contract if they've already put out a press release?"

"They may try to coordinate them," Monty said doubtfully.

"You're giving them too much credit," Zimmerman said. "The left hand never knows what the right hand is doing. Haven't you learned anything in twenty-one months in the Pentagon?"

"Yes, sir. But . . . "

"Then we exploit that well-known fact."

"But this is a new ball game, Admiral. The new budget directive . . . "

"*What* new budget directive?" Zimmerman asked with mock innocence. "I haven't received a new budget directive. Have you received a new budget directive?"

"No, sir. Not officially."

"Then officially, we don't know anything. It'll take it a week to filter down to our level. So, meanwhile, we're going about our business. Get that press release out. Once they commit to long lead-time hardware, there's no turning back."

"But, sir. ULMS is a whole weapons system, not a simple . . not a new valve. I'm sure they'll want to review . . . "

"In the meantime," Zimmerman said, ignoring Monty, turning back to the papers on his desk, "I've been talking

to Chairman Magruder. He's not very happy about the
budget memo. No one bothered to ask his opinion. You
remember once, years ago, someone offered him the job
of Secretary of Defense? You remember his reply? He said:
'I'd rather be Secretary of Defense from here.' Well, he's
going to show this new bunch where the real power lies.
On Thursday, he's called a hearing to look into the Soviet
naval threat. You people be prepared to appear up there
in uniform. Open session. Meanwhile, I'll touch base with
Buzz Creighton. They're concerned, too."

"Yes, sir, Admiral," Monty replied, feeling a sudden lift,
now regretting his rash thought that Zimmerman might be
senile. He was still a crafty curmudgeon, a consummate
bureaucrat. The Chairman of the House Armed Services
Committee, Magruder, had not called that hearing. Monty
was certain that Zimmerman had arranged it. An ace
in the hole.

Monty hurried on to his next two appointments. He walked
down to the fourth floor, then took the escalator to the second,
getting off by the Mall Entrance Reception Desk. The woman
who had taught him how to navigate the Pentagon was
there, sitting at a desk behind a paneled counter. There was
a vase of fresh flowers on the desk, lending a cheery note
to the drabness. Remembering Lieutenant Trimble's need
for a Pentagon map, Monty stopped at the desk to ask for
a guide book. Smiling, the receptionist provided one, then
launched into her ritualized briefing, as though Monty were
a newcomer.

"Thanks," Monty broke in. "I know my way around. This

is for one of my men who just reported on board."

He went toward Corridor 7, flipping through the pamphlet. It had not been changed in twenty-one months. There were the same awesome figures: "200 acres of lawn ... 17 miles of corridors ... 30,000 cups of coffee, 6,000 pints of milk and 5,000 soft drinks prepared and served by a restaurant staff of 600 persons dispensed in two restaurants, six cafeterias, nine snack bars ... a post office handling 1 billion items of mail a year ... a city within a city."

He stuck the pamphlet in his pocket. He turned in Corridor 7 toward A Ring, then descended an escalator to the first floor. Here, the symmetry of the layout was disturbed by the pedestrian ramp leading up to the second floor. He was momentarily disoriented. Then he found the office he sought. The sign said:

> GSA ROOM 1A331
> BUILDING SUPERINTENDENT
> MR. MARVIN C. KOONTZ

He opened the door and walked in. It was a large room, with many girls working side by side at desks. Two older women were staring into space, doing nothing. Monty thought: fire every third person, improve efficiency. Then maybe the Admiral's office would be cleaned properly. He announced himself to the receptionist-secretary, adding: "I'd like to see Mr. Koontz."

"May I say what it's about?" the girl asked, with a doubtful look.

"It's about ... a partition and a cleaning problem."

"Mr. Koontz is in a meeting," she said. "Perhaps his deputy, Mr. Greene, could help you?"

"OK. Fine." In the Pentagon, the deputies, not the chiefs, got things done, Monty told himself. The chiefs spent all their time in meetings.

"Will you have a seat please?"

He sat down, eyes roving the bulkheads. On one he saw

a row of pictures. Former building managers, displayed like the paintings and photographs of former CNOs and Sec-Navs on the fourth deck. On other bulkheads there were many framed awards—for safety records, efficiency, economy. There was an "idea" box for suggestions on ways to do things better and cheaper. Above it was a large picture of a GSA employee who had won last month's award—$500. He was a black—James O. Roberts. Curious, Monty leaned forward to read the citation:

"Mr. Roberts receives this month's GSA achievement award for the following money-saving idea: there are 7,748 windows in the Pentagon, each with a venetian blind. As in any office or home, venetian blinds get dirty and break. The blinds must be washed, a large task. Mr. Roberts conceived the idea of automating the washing of venetian blinds. He devised an automatic system, not unlike an automatic car wash installation, onto which the blinds could be hung, thereafter traveling through a series of automatic processes: washing, rinsing, drying. This system, which was installed recently in the Pentagon Venetian Blind Shop, enabled a reduction in staff from ten men to two. It also speeded up the process so that every venetian blind in the Pentagon can now be washed once a year on a regular, systematized basis. Mr. Roberts is to be congratulated for his ingenuity."

Monty sat back, thinking that the idea was good, certainly worth $500, if they had been able to cut the Venetian Blind Shop by eight men. Now maybe his own ragged venetian blind would be refurbished. Zempfke had not even bothered to call about that. The secretary interrupted his thoughts. The deputy, Mr. Greene, was free.

Mr. Greene occupied an office five times the size of Monty's. It was carpeted. There was a couch, table lamp, and a green telephone with five or six buttons. On the wall were aerial photographs of various government buildings —places, Monty assumed, where Greene had served. The office appointments indicated that Mr. Greene was a GS-16 or above, equivalent to Flag Rank.

Mr. Greene was young, perhaps thirty. He had long, well-trimmed hair and sideburns. There was a printed card on his In box that said: "The secrecy of my job doesn't permit me to know what I'm doing." He got up, enthusiastically, shaking hands as though he were genuinely pleased to see Monty. A regular Rotarian.

"What can I do for you, Captain?" he said affably.

Monty explained his business. Since Mr. Greene out-ranked him, he was respectful—frequently inserting the word "sir"—and made it clear that he was representing Rear Admiral Starr. Mr. Greene listened with apparent interest and attention. But when Monty had finished, he took the floor with a counter-presentation:

"Captain King, I appreciate your problem. I hope you also appreciate mine. I'm trying to make do here on a budgetary ceiling, just like everybody else. Our total work force, the housekeeping unit, has been cut back to 750 people. We're making do now with 450 cleaners and 300 other people. We used to have a dozen girls, just to answer the telephone complaints. Now we're down to four or five. You can't imagine how pressed we are. What a mammoth job this is. Do you realize, just for example, the problems of garbage and trash? Just one small item. Every week we collect 4½ tons—repeat tons—of coffee grounds from the sink slop rooms where you people leave your private coffee grounds. I'm not even talking about the snack bars and cafeterias and private dining rooms. That's almost half a million pounds of *private* coffee grounds a year. I've got to keep two men on day shift and two men on night shift just to empty those GI cans. Now, I also have to get rid of 8 tons of classified trash a day and 11 tons of nonclassified trash. It costs us $150 a day just to haul the non-classified trash away. A hundred tons of trash a week! You want a wall partition installed? Then you should know the

Carpentry Shop is down to fifty-five carpenters. Only fifteen of whom are assigned full-time to partitions. They're six months behind! I've got Flag Officers calling here four, five times a day. That's why your request has been deferred. And our Carpentry Shop must, by custom, service the White House. Did you know that? Right now our carpenters are doing a job over there—converting the basement swimming pool to a new press room. I'll bet you didn't know that, did you?"

Monty did not. Nor did he much care. Mr. Greene was giving him the usual Pentagon sales pitch: desperate need, no money. It was just like OP-31. Everyone in the Pentagon, it seemed, was by necessity a salesman. Mr. Greene pressed:

"We're down to seventy electricians, twenty plumbers, and twenty sheet-metal workers. We used to paint the walls every five years. Now we're stretching out to seven. You know what happened to us last Friday? We got a pigeon in the air-conditioning system. You think you have problems? I had to put six men to work tracking down that damn pigeon. They sneak in under the eaves and get into the system. But I don't have the sheet-metal workers to close up the eaves. Nor the roofers. I've got 2½ million square feet of slate roof I'm responsible for. Now, ever since the march on the Pentagon, when we had those troops stationed on the roof . . . do you realize what they did to my slate with their heavy boots? A quarter of a million in damage. No provision in the budget for new slate. I've only got two qualified slate men to replace slate. Try to find a good slater these days! We can't keep up with it. Next thing you know, the roof will be leaking!"

He said the last as though it were Armageddon. Monty shifted uneasily in his seat, opened his mouth to bring the conversation back to his business, but Mr. Greene rushed on:

"If you think that's a problem, listen a minute. Consider my lighting problem. I've got 1,125,000 fluorescent tubes in this building, at a cost of one dollar each—we're 99 percent fluorescent. Now, Captain, let me tell you a fluorescent fixture is not a permanent fixture. In other words, it burns out. I used to have twelve lampists, who did nothing but go around changing tubes. These twelve men could only keep up with *half* the service calls. In other words, they were falling behind by a factor of 50 percent. Now this force has been reduced to 3.4 people. There is no way we can keep up. Little by little all the lights are burning out in this building. We're sliding into a major catastrophe. How are you going to get your work done if you don't have light? You've got terrific travel time involved in these service calls. I can't get good people. We conceived a program in this office which I call 'Group Relamping' whereby we would take whole sections of the building at a time and change the tubes in one fell swoop, saving terrific travel time. Besides, it's more orderly to do it that way. But we couldn't fund it. We don't have the people. We're spending a half million a year on new tubes as it is."

He threw up his hands as if to say: "What can you do?" Then he added darkly:

"And the terrazzo floors are beginning to crack. The vinyl is holding up all right, but we can only wax it every ten to thirteen weeks, which is not enough. Now what was your problem again, Captain?"

Mr. Greene was apparently finished. Monty heard himself repeating his complaint, but his spirit was no longer in it. Mr. Greene had deflated him. He felt that to press his case would be to impose a silly request on a desperately overworked office. They would make do without the partition. Maybe they could sweep the Admiral's office themselves. He left the office thanking Mr. Greene for the information, wishing him luck. He went back into the corridor wondering how long the great huge monster, growing darker by the week, could stagger on.

★ 9 ★

Monty walked on, watching the office numbers. The sign on the second office below Koontz's said:

ROOM 1A313—GSA

SPECIAL POLICE DETAIL

MAJOR C. M. ROBERTS, CHIEF

CAPTAIN R. DAVIS, DEPUTY

He opened the door to find himself in a miniature police station. There was a policeman—black—sitting behind a counter, manning a switchboard and a radio.

"Can I help you?" the policeman said.

"I have an appointment with Captain Davis," Monty replied, giving his own name and rank.

"Down that hall, second office on the left."

Monty walked down the hall to the second office, a small cubicle, with a desk, four chairs and a ground-level window, with heavy steel bars, opening onto the inner courtyard. There were two men in the room. One a white civilian; the other, Captain Davis, a black, wearing a GSA police uniform: white shirt with gold captain's bars, gold badge, blue trousers, pistol in a holster. There was a police radio mounted on a shelf over the desk turned low.

"Captain King?" Davis said, standing.

"Yes," Monty said.

Davis put out his hand. He was an older man, with white, kinky hair, a thin gray mustache, a genial Uncle Tom disposition. Monty shook hands awkwardly.

"This is Mr. Lambert from the Building Commandant's

office," Davis said, turning to the man who was sitting in the corner. Lambert appeared to be about fifty-five. He wore a brown suit, brown tie. He seemed cold, or bored, or both. He stood and shook hands.

They all sat down, Monty somewhat uneasily, noting the open folder on Davis' desk. Davis spoke:

"I'm afraid we have some bad news for you, Captain. After a rather lengthy investigation, we have conclusive evidence that a man in your office has been forging S-3 parking permits."

Monty was momentarily stunned by their seriousness over such a small matter. Surely they were kidding?

"Who?" he said, already knowing the answer. There was only one would-be artist in OP-31.

"A chief petty officer. John M. Z-E-M-P-F-K-E. Serial number 873-35-0943."

Monty bit his lower lip.

"This has been going on for some time now," Davis went on. "A very, very clever forgery. Here, take a look at this."

He passed Monty an S-3 permit from the folder. Monty looked at the front and back. If it was a forgery, it was indeed clever.

"We get a lot of this," Captain Davis went on, less formally. He handed Monty another S-3 permit. "See that one? It's amateurish."

It was. The wavy blue lines forming the background of the permit behind the large black S-3 were crudely etched.

"That's your typical forgery," Davis said. "We get a couple of dozen of those a year. But your man, Zempfke—am I pronouncing it right?—he's something else. He's a real pro."

Monty did not reply. He was hovering between laughter and disbelief.

Davis, proud of his detective work, rambled on:

"This is the toughest forgery case we've ever come across in this office. When we picked up the first bad permit, I alerted the whole force. All 300 men in the Special Police Detail. Then we put my special team on it. Then we found out he was forging these things and giving them to the other chiefs. We've got it all. Chapter and verse. Here, this is a list of men he gave them to, with dates, and so on. We were on top of it all the way."

Davis proudly handed Monty a list. There were six names, chief petty officers, with Pentagon office numbers. The evidence was thorough, explicit, damning.

"We might never have solved this case if we hadn't had a break," Davis went on. "One of the petty officers in one of the offices found out that his friend was using forged permits and he got jealous. So he wrote us an anonymous letter, fingering your man, Zempfke. After that, we called in Mr. Lambert for assistance."

He turned to Mr. Lambert, who cleared his throat in a stagey way and said: "I'm with Commandant, Counterintelligence. CID. We put a tail on Zempfke and a tap on his home telephone."

"How long has this been going on?" Monty asked, wondering what private secrets of OP-31 may have leaked to Lambert. The Army. OSD.

"Two and a half months," Lambert said.

"My men are not trained in that area," Captain Davis said, as if to explain why another government agency had been called in.

Lambert went on, again clearing his throat. "Actually, by OSD regulations, we're required to step in on cases like these—routinely. A forged parking permit tells us a man is dishonest. It's a tip-off. One of our jobs is to be sure he's not also violating the National Security Act—selling secrets to a foreign government."

Monty caught his breath.

"I'm happy to report that Zempfke is in the clear on that score," Lambert went on. "But, you're going to have to take your own disciplinary action in regard to his security clearance. You can't keep a man in a position of trust with highly classified information when you know he's forging parking permits. Zempfke has the highest clearances."

"But Mr. Lambert," Monty said, anger suddenly rising, "Chief Zempfke is one of my best men. I've known him for fifteen years. He's vital to our operation."

"I'm sorry," Lambert said, without seeming to be. "Regulations are regulations."

"But you'll destroy his career if we . . . "

"*He* should have thought of that," Lambert said, indifferently. "I'm only doing what the book says."

"Well, for God's sake," Monty shot back. "It's only a stupid parking permit . . . "

"It's a violation of GSA Regulation 41-CFR 101-19.310," Captain Davis said pompously. "Quote, 'Permits may not be copied or duplicated under any circumstances.' Unquote."

"You're making a mountain out of a molehill," Monty said. "This man has served his country brilliantly for thirty years. He was decorated in World War II . . ."

Monty stopped. The two men were staring at him stonily, obviously unimpressed. They were proud of their detective work, and intent on hanging Zempfke.

"Sir," Monty said, turning to Lambert. "May I ask exactly what your jurisdiction—your legal jurisdiction—is in this matter?"

"Certainly," Lambert said, clearing his throat again. "The Pentagon is designated as an Army facility, falling under command of the Military District of Washington. MDW. The building Commandant, as you know, is an Army Colonel. Colonel Demerest. As with any Army facility, we have a counterintelligence division. CID. I am chief, CID, Pentagon. I work for Demerest. So, in a legal sense, we have prime investigative authority for any violation of law that may occur on the premises."

Monty frowned, digesting this.

"Now," Lambert went on, "as with most military buildings under MDW jurisdiction, the bulk of the routine police work is carried out by GSA police, like Captain Davis and his men. This saves us having to put a lot of MPs in here. GSA has responsibility for such things as guards on the doors, keeping an eye on those so-called protesters outside, parking control, routine theft, and so on. Technically, his chain of command is back through GSA, to GSA headquarters. But we work together in an informal arrangement."

He smiled at Davis.

"But who brings the actual legal proceedings against Zempfke?" Monty asked. "You or Captain Davis?"

"Captain Davis. Since this is basically a parking matter, not a security violation case. In security violation cases, my division brings charges."

"I see," Monty said.

"We'll want to make the formal arraignment before the U.S. Magistrate day after tomorrow," Captain Davis put in. "I assume you'll assist us by bringing Zempfke down. The court convenes down the hall, Room 1A474, at 1000."

"Look, you guys," Monty said, earnestly, "is there any way we can avoid that? If I promise to discipline . . . "

"I'm sorry, Captain," Davis said. "The machinery is in motion. There's no way to stop it. It's a tough break, but don't take it personally. It's not the worst thing that's happened around here, believe me. I've been here on the force for twenty years. I've seen everything. Suicides. Numbers rackets. Dope rings. Psychos. Knife fights. Whiskey bootlegging. All the misdemeanors and felonies of any town with a population of 30,000. We still have an unsolved murder in North Parking. Found a guy in the trunk of his car. Whenever you get this many people under one roof, you're going to have a certain amount of this. Even if we're all cleared for security. We've got these damned war protesters outside and bomb threats. . . ."

★ 10 ★

Nancy swung into her driveway. The back deck of the wagon was loaded with Commissary grocery bags, twenty altogether, three weeks' food and supplies for the King and Caldwell families.

"When we retire," Nancy smiled at Alma, setting the brake, "at least I'll have a man around the house to bring in the bags."

"Oh, stop that nonsense," Alma said. "Anyway, you wouldn't be going to a Commissary."

"Yes we would. Wherever we settle down, it'll have to be near an active military base. We'll use the BX and the Commissary. Save 18 percent on food. That's part of my economic plan."

They each carried one of Nancy's bags to the front stoop. Nancy unlocked the door, pushing it open warily. She hated to come back to an empty house. She was certain that one day she would come home and surprise a burglar—or a rapist.

Returning to the car for a second load, Nancy got the morning mail from the rural box by the curb. Among the junk, she spotted a letter on Naval Academy stationery from Mike, or as he had printed on the back of the envelope: Midshipman William Montgomery King III. After they finished unloading Nancy's bags from the car and stored the frozen food and meats in the freezer, they paused to rest in the living room. Nancy read Mike's letter.

Dear Mom and Dad,

Great news! Our Company has won the Regimental Competition with a near-perfect score of 3.9. This means *we* will select the Color Girl for June Week. And what that really means is that as Company Commander, *I* will do the choosing. Naturally, it will be Judy Ridder. Make plans! ! ! In addition to that, we get a long—a very long weekend this week. I may get home for a visit Wednesday night—staying till Saturday.

Well, by my calculations, I have two months, four days and sixteen hours before we toss our white hats into the air. To say that I can hardly wait to receive my ensign's stripe, to take my oath of office, to go to Sub School and sea, even knowing that I'll be "George" in the wardroom, is to drastically understate my frame of mind. Judy's too. She is looking forward to you-know-what beneath crossed swords.

All the talk here for the last week has centered on the wonderful essay in this month's *U.S. Naval Institute Proceedings* by Captain Robert J. Hanks, entitled "Against All Enemies." Have you read it yet? He says, in essence, that it is high time the men of the Armed Forces stood up on their hind legs and talked back to the many critics of the military. He says the antimilitary talk and demonstrations have come to the point that the country is seriously endangered, that if the erosion of confidence in the military continues, it could so seriously weaken the country that it might be violently overthrown by revolutionaries. Our mission, the military mission, is to prevent this. To speak out, now, in our own defense. He reminds us—rightly I think—that in the oath we take, we swear to defend the country against *all* enemies, both foreign and *domestic*. (Hence the title.)

I couldn't agree more. Most everybody here in Bancroft Hall feels the same way.

I read another article just the other day in the newspaper, about how the military academies—Annapolis, specifically—are turning out vacant-minded good-looking yes men who will go on mindlessly perpetuating The

System. (The Armed Society, he called it.) This article was slanted and full of factual errors. The reporter didn't know a thing about Annapolis, and how it has changed in the four years I've been here. There was nothing about the new majors—literature, economics and political science. Or that a midshipman can now work toward a liberal-arts degree. He didn't mention the fact that there are thirty-eight blacks here now. The press never points out the good things.

By the way, Dad, did you hear that there will be even more changes next fall? The curriculum will be expanded to include twenty-four majors—seventeen of them non-engineering! The seven old departments will be expanded to eighteen—and eleven of these will be chaired by civilians! ! ! The Superintendent told us last week in chapel that he intends to prove that love of country and dedication to its service can exist side by side in the same institution with academic freedom and excellence. He also said:

"You can't have it both ways. You have to stand up and be counted. Either you're with us and believe in preserving our society or you don't belong here."

I've got to run to a formation. See you Wednesday!

Best love,
Mike

Nancy finished the letter feeling impatience and despair. She passed it to Alma, who read swiftly, and then said: "You should be very proud."

"I'm not," Nancy said desperately. "I feel sorry for him."

"Sorry? Why Nancy!"

"There's my own life, repeating itself," Nancy said gloomily. "Don't you remember, Alma? June Week? Jim and Monty, sneaking over to Calvert Hall? All those passionate love notes and stolen kisses? We were like four people from the pages of a Victorian novel. Blind. Naive. Brainwashed.

Thrilled by Tarawa, Saipan, Guam . . . the President, ex-
Navy . . . even Churchill. It was unreal, Alma, and you
know it as well as I do. Now I see Mike and Judy, going
the same way, like my mother and father, yours and Jim's,
Monty's."

The telephone rang.

"Paul!" Nancy said, jumping up, rushing to the kitchen.

It was not Paul. It was Scottie MacIntosh, the stock-
broker, a classmate of Monty's and Jim's who had retired
years ago, and who had done well with Navy clients. One
of his specialities was New England Ship.

"Nancy? How are you? I was trying to reach you earlier."

"Sorry, Scottie. This is Commissary day. Alma Caldwell
and I were over at Fort Myer, stocking up."

"I hear Monty's Selection Board has been announced."

"Yes."

"I wish you all the luck . . . "

"You should have stayed in," Nancy said sarcastically.
"Then you could have the pleasure . . ."

"I thought of that this morning, and how glad I was I
didn't, thank you. I know what you're going through, or *will*
be going through."

Not I, Nancy thought.

"Anyway, I called to ask if you'd seen what's happening
to your stock?"

"No, I haven't," Nancy replied, casually, covering her
sudden anxiety.

"It's down four points. There are rumors all over town
that the new crowd really intends to make good on the
campaign promises. That there may be a budget cut . . . "

Ha! Nancy thought, triumphantly. Just as I thought.
Then uneasily . . . , but four points! Four thousand dollars!

" . . . but I can't believe they're really serious," MacIntosh
went on. "You know how these things come and go over the
years. All the new boys come in there intending to econo-
mize. Well, anyway, between you and me and the gatepost,

I talked privately to Buzz Creighton today. He says to hang on, it's only temporary. They've got some stuff in the works this week—he wouldn't say what—to offset the rumors. By the end of the week, he thought, the stock would climb back and close strong. You know what Bernard Baruch said. Buy when the stock's falling, sell when it's going up. It takes nerves of steel. But he did all right."

"How far does Buzz think it will drop?" Nancy said, lowering her voice, turning her back to the living room.

"He has no way of knowing. Two, three more points, maybe. Then . . . "

"What is your advice?"

"Hang on. Very definitely, hang on."

"All right. But keep me posted."

"Yes, ma'm."

Nancy hung up slowly, thinking. She had confidence in Scottie. There had been ups and downs before. Some really scary times. But his advice had always been sound. She would watch it closely, as she had in times like this in the past.

"Who was that?" Alma asked, when Nancy returned to her chair in the living room.

"My financial advisor," Nancy said vaguely.

"Oh," Alma said.

"He says there're rumors going around that the defense budget will be cut."

"They're always cutting the defense budget."

"Yes. But I have a feeling this might be something big. Serious. The administration is pledged to . . . "

"Campaign oratory," Alma said blithely.

"If they do," Nancy said angrily, "you know what will happen. They'll lay up more ships. But they won't cut the commitments. That means the ships left in commission will have to do twice as much work. And that means the crews will not get any leave or liberty. They'll be at sea all week and then refitting and replenishing all weekend. They'll kill the new military pay raise and the plans for new base housing. They won't let dependents go overseas."

"You really are negative, aren't you?"

"Yes, I am," Nancy sighed wearily. "The Navy's been on a wartime footing ever since V-J Day. They still are. If they cut the budget, it will be even worse. What kind of life is that to look forward to?"

Alma looked silently at the floor. She would be happy enough, Nancy thought, if Jim went back to sea. It seemed to make no difference. Or maybe she *preferred* him away.

"We better go," Alma said at last. "My frozen stuff's going to melt."

They returned to the car. Driving along the Beltway toward Bethesda, Nancy felt a compulsion to go on about the early days of her marriage.

"Don't you remember those days in New London after the war?" she began. "When we all thought we were settling down for a long, lovely time of peace? Spelled both ways, by the way. But the men all spent the first six years at sea. Even when Monty lucked out and got that job as aide to ComSubLant, he was gone all the time, at sea. Alma, we all grew from girlhood to womanhood—twenty-one to twenty-seven more or less—without a man. What kind of marriage is that? It's a miracle any of us stayed together . . . never mind sexual adjustments. All that idle time. You remember Sue Byerston and Christine Kane and Jocelyn Kirk? I know! It was my luck for Christine and Jocelyn to pick *my* shoulder to weep on. What misery! The carrying-on right in the home! God!

"It took a will of steel to stay faithful. Did I tell you what happened to me one day? Monty was Exec on the *Irex* then. Admiral Starr was his C.O. They went off on a long exercise. You remember that point of land where the Thames runs into the Sound? Monty and I had a little going-away ritual. I would take Joanie down there and wave goodbye. That day, I remember, it was freezing cold. When I got home, I found the basement flooded. A faucet had burst. The furnace was out. The temperature was falling. I was frantic. I couldn't get a repair man—naturally. I called you and Jim. No answer. Then I called Joey and Tom Kemp. Luckily Tom was in port, didn't have the duty . . . "

"Yes," Alma said with an impatient sigh, "you told me . . ."

"I didn't tell you the *real* part," Nancy went on. "I told you this morning I never really told you all the truth. Well, Tom came in foul-weather gear. Joey took little Joanie home to keep warm. Tom fixed the faucet and relit the furnace. Then, in the kitchen, he asked me for a hot toddy. Then two. I had one myself. It was so damned cold in the house. He made a *pass* at me, Alma. Right in the kitchen. And, you know, to tell the truth, I was . . . well, honestly, I was so grateful to him. I . . ."

"Nancy King! You didn't . . . ?"

"No. Of course not. I was never once unfaithful to Monty. But, I was tempted. Later, I felt sick about it. Here was Monty, gone two hours, and me . . . The point I'm trying to make is I can understand what happened to Sue and Christine and Jocelyn and all the others. Peyton Place! That's a Mother Goose story compared to New London."

"Tom Kemp was a Don Juan," Alma said, grimly. "Or at least he fancied himself one."

"You know from experience?"

"Yes," she said. She did not elaborate.

"Monty would come home," Nancy rushed on, "and we had all the normal impulses. Like they used to say, the *second* thing he did was set his bag down. But he was always in such a hurry. I'd get all steamed up and he'd be premature. And then he'd want to go to sleep right away, or else he'd worry I wasn't satisfied. It was terribly frustrating. But, then, the second night, he was not so interested. Even in the very early days. Then all those wardroom parties and stupid formations at the club—Alma I hated

those dumb affairs they staged for Navy wives, didn't you—
and then I'd get tired. We could never get on the same wave
length. Sometimes I think Monty was eager to get back to
sea . . . just to avoid climbing in bed with me for another
frustrating battle."

"Nancy! What nonsense. Didn't you ever *discuss* it with
him?"

"How would you discuss a thing like that? Lieutenant,
permission to have an orgasm, sir? Granted."

"But if you had a real problem . . . "

"I don't know *who* had the problem. Monty or me."

"Well, we all . . . "

"Do you honestly suppose they had a girl in every port?"

"No."

"I used to think that. I had wild fantasies. I would think,
he's shacked up in Norfolk or Philadelphia or Key West
with some tramp. That's why he isn't interested in me. Or
maybe he has clap, or worse. Did you ever see that movie
Captain's Paradise with Alec Guinness? He commanded a
ship on a regular weekly schedule between Gibraltar and
Africa someplace, and he had a *legal* wife in both ports.
Very funny . . . except when I saw it, I got *really* paranoid."

"We all have . . . at times."

"Then I began to think, seriously, there was something
really wrong with me. I couldn't sleep. Maybe I was a latent
nymphomaniac, Alma. I really *enjoyed* sex . . . "

"Why didn't you tell me you were going through all this
mental agony?"

"Because I was too embarrassed."

"What is a friend for?"

"*You* never mentioned sex after you got married . . . "

"I guess I was too embarrassed, too."

"Did you have the same . . . ?"

"Precisely."

"Then you may be interested in something I read recently
at the Armed Forces Medical Library," Nancy went on,

lowering her voice. "It was an unpublished doctoral thesis by some psychologist named Brainard Douglas. He had studied three Navy families. He called them "maritime" families. Going back three generations. He called them Family A, B, C. No real names. But, damned if I didn't think they resembled a lot of people we know. He said, in brief, maritime families are hung up, sexually. The hang-up is passed on from generation to generation. He argues, basically, that the progeny of the maritime male seeks escape to sea and that the female, usually a maritime daughter, seeks an absentee mate for a husband because she, in reality, is marrying her absentee father, who had rejected her. . . . No, wait, that's not exactly right. Her father is absent at sea. She feels rejected. So, to retain her father's love, she marries a man like him. But she can't really have him. That would be, as Douglas says, psychic incest. So . . . "

"Nancy, for God's sake!" Alma broke in disgustedly, "you've been reading too damned much garbage. Your mind is completely preoccupied with sex. I've never heard such nonsense. These damned psychologists . . . "

"It's a good paper, Alma. Have you ever read anything good on the Navy wife?"

"No. But it *can't* be any good. Otherwise it would have been published."

"Well, that's true. Still. Let me tell you his main point. The main point is that maritime families tend to *seek* situations where there can be little sex because they're afraid of sex for deep-seated reasons."

"I'm not afraid of sex, I'll tell you that," Alma insisted. "So that shoots that down . . . "

"You may be the exception that proves the rule."

"You're not really serious, are you Nancy?"

"Not really. I mean, I haven't bought it completely. But it makes you stop and think."

"Hmmmmmmm."

"I didn't tell you the worst part."

"Worst part of what?"

"The New London time."

"All right, tell me the worst part, then."

"One night in the house on Bluff Road, I was lying there by myself—you remember Joanie had her own room then—and it was very hot. An August night, I remember. Monty was at sea. He'd been gone five, six weeks on Fleet Exercise, the time they sank all those carriers. I was lying there and I started thinking about him, trying to remember, very specifically, his body. I was really in heat, in more ways than one. Actually, I'd been reading a sexy novel, *Forever Amber* or something like it. And . . . oh, Alma. It's terrible. I shouldn't . . . "

"Go on," Alma said. "Get it out of your system."

"All right. I hope you don't think . . . well anyway. I was thinking about Monty and got *very* excited. And I did it to myself."

"Is *that* all?"

"Well yes. No. What I mean is, I really, really *enjoyed* it, Alma. I . . . I . . . took my time, you know. Very slow. And then it built up . . . and oh, God! It was incredible."

Alma said nothing. She fixed her eyes on the highway.

"Did you ever . . . ?" Nancy said hesitantly.

"Yes," Alma said.

"After that," Nancy said, "I did it all the time. I mean . . . a *lot* of times. Until Key West, I remember."

"Hmmmmm."

"Now, you can see why I really thought there was something wrong with me. Seriously wrong."

"That doesn't mean there *was* something wrong. You were lonely."

"People can change," Nancy said.

"Of *course* they can change."

"That's my point. I want to start all over again, from scratch."

★ 11 ★

Admiral Starr fixed Zempfke with his squinty eyes and
graveled: "If we were at sea, I'd have you flogged and keel-
hauled. You dumb sonofabitch, you've disgraced all of us.
The Submarine Force—OP-31—the Navy. What the fuck
did you do it for?"

Monty sucked in his breath. Zempfke, standing at attention before Starr's desk, turned ashen.

"Sir, it was a joke."

"A joke!" Starr exploded.

"Yes, sir. We were at a party one night. I was making
some caricatures and Chief Brown—in OP-34—says to
me, Zempfke, I bet you couldn't draw an S-3 parking permit.
I said that would be easy. It was. I did the first one right
there at the party. And then Brown got this funny look
and said, 'Why the hell should we park in W-N and walk
three-quarters of a mile to the building when Zempfke can
draw us all an S-3 permit?' Well, that was supposed to be
funny. I mean, we were all bombed. So Brown says, 'We
can all sleep a half hour later in the morning.' Everybody
chimed in saying, yeah, yeah. Then Chief Warner—he's
in OP-05—said I couldn't do them skillfully enough. We'd
never get away with it. Well, that was a challenge, you
see? Then when I did, Warner said, hell we wear uniforms
and the people in S-3 don't, we'll get caught. So we worked
it out, we wouldn't wear our hats, and with overcoats, we'd
look like everyone else in S-3. So that's how it got started."

"Well, shit," Starr said, sullenly. "Nobody there stopped
to consider what might happen if you did get caught?"

"I don't think anybody thought we would get caught."

"Well, you're caught."

"I never dreamed CID might get in on it," Zempfke said, with no trace of his old cockiness.

"Well, they did, and your ass is in a sling," Starr rumbled. "All of you. I swear to God, Zempfke. . . . "

"There was some natural resentment at the bottom of it," Zempfke went on. "Admiral, the Pentagon is bad duty for a Navy chief. We can't live on our pay, even with the housing subsidy. Most of the guys are moonlighting—driving cabs at night. On the base at New London, I had a parking place right by the pier."

"That's not got a goddamned thing to do with it," Starr said. "You broke the law. You've exposed all of us."

"I'm sorry, sir. Honest to God, none of us ever took it seriously. It was just a little game."

"Well, get out of here, Zempfke," Starr snarled. "Get out of my sight. Go home until you receive further orders."

"Yes, sir, Admiral."

Zempfke turned on his heel and left the room. Monty took another deep breath and said to Starr:

"You were pretty hard on him, Admiral. The guy has knocked himself out for us—fourteen hours a day—these last few months. He's right. It's bad duty for a chief. Anywhere else, they run the base. They have their deals going. Here, they're just shit—real Indians. There's got to be some way we can get this thing squashed."

"Don't be a fool, Monty," Starr said, eyes squinting. "Don't you realize this thing is made-to-order for the press? I can see the headline already: THE GREAT PENTAGON FORGERY CAPER. They'll make us all look like idiots. Anytime they can ridicule the Pentagon, they will. And remember this, my friend. The slop bucket's going to fall on you. If a ship runs aground, they don't hang the duty officer, they hang the captain. You're the one who's looking right into the teeth of a Selection Board. This stupid deal could blow your whole career."

"But, Admiral . . ."

"Monty, I've sat on those Boards. I know what happens. You got ten, fifteen people, some you never heard of. Just names. All the jackets look equally good. You've got to eliminate. So, they get picky . . . and how the hell can I defend *this*?"

Monty felt a chill.

"What you've got to do," Starr said, standing up, squinting over the desk toward Monty, "is protect your ass. See if you can get him transferred out of here this morning. Then, when he comes up before the judge, he won't be attached to OP-31. He'll be in transient barracks at Anacostia, or some goddamned thing. The Navy Gun Factory. Anyplace. Then, next thing you do, lift his security clearance. We can say the instant this thing hit us, we took prompt action. That'll look good on the record."

"But Admiral, that'll ruin him. And how can I get him transferred today?"

"Ruin him?" Starr shot back. "What the hell do you care. He didn't think twice about ruining you. Call that buddy of yours in BuPers. Get busy."

"Yes, sir, Admiral."

"By the way," Starr said smugly. "I ordered those four nukes to close in and start a search for that unidentified contact."

"Yes, sir."

"As soon as you get Zempfke squared away, get on that ULMS press release. That's a good gimmick. The old bastard hasn't lost his cunning, has he? Good man to have around in a fight."

"Yes, sir, Admiral. Are you sure you don't want to reconsider lifting Zempfke's security clearance? That's so drastic."

"What did the CID man tell you? What if he comes poking around here to see what kind of disciplinary action we took? What if the sonofabitch puts another tap on our phones? You lift that clearance and notify CID immediately."

"Yes, sir, Admiral."

"I know what I'm doing, Monty."

"I'm sure, sir," Monty said quietly.

Monty went to his desk. He called Yeoman Armbruster, Zempfke's assistant, to his desk. Armbruster was a frail young man with effeminate hands, and a soft, babylike face, who had routinely come to OP-31 a year ago. Monty had been told that he was an excellent organ player, that he sang with his church choir.

"Zempfke's leaving," Monty said to Armbruster. "Until we can dig up a replacement, you'll be acting chief."

"Aye, aye, sir," Armbruster said, sadly. "He told me about it."

"All right. Keep it to yourself. We don't want a lot of unnecessary scuttlebutt. If anybody asks, say he took some emergency leave or something."

"Yes, sir."

"You'll be collecting the burn bags and locking the files," Monty said. "I don't want any goofs. Triple-check everything before you leave, O.K.?"

"I have a check list," Armbruster said. "I will triple-check. Shall I sit at Zempfke's desk, sir?"

"Yes."

Monty picked up the phone to call his classmate in BuPers, the same who had arranged Trimble's assignment. Waiting for the connection, Monty became aware that the Lieutenant was now standing by his desk, holding a manila folder. The line was busy, Monty hung up.

"Excuse me, Captain," Trimble said, looking somewhat at sea. "They told me Zempfke just left on emergency leave. He was in the middle of helping me on this Threat paper."

"Oh yes," Monty said. "By the way, I've got you a map."
He reached in his pocket, gave Trimble the pamphlet.

"When we get a minute, I'll show you what I mean about the wheel concept," Monty said. "Meanwhile, I better give you a hand on the paper. Have you got anything for me to read?"

"I did the World War Two part," Trimble said, offering the folder. Monty took it, removed the papers: two pages of handwritten history on white Navy tablet. He read swiftly.

"That's good," Monty said, returning the folder. "You turn a nice phrase. By God, I'm glad to have someone around here who can write a clear, incisive sentence. You may find yourself very popular."

"Where should I go from here?" Trimble said.

"Give it to Armbruster for typing, then go on with the background. Sketch in the history from 1945 to, say, 1955."

"Any special reason for those dates?" Trimble asked, earnestly.

"Yes, 1955 was the year the first nuclear submarine got under way. It was the beginning of the new era. But, there was a ten-year period in there, when we were still messing around with diesels. Sit down."

"Yes, sir," Trimble said, sitting in the oak chair.

"Give it a couple of pages."

To save Trimble time, Monty sketched in the post-war, pre-nuclear power history. Yeoman Armbruster broke in.

"Admiral Zimmerman on Line two, sir," he said.

Monty reached for the phone, then changed his mind.

"Tell him I'm out," he said to Armbruster. "I'll call back in a minute."

"Aye, aye, sir."

"So," Monty resumed, "when Korea came, we got some money. Everybody got money. We had money coming out of our ears. So we went ahead with the *Tang* class—new boats. But they were an utter disaster."

Monty paused, remembering his own service on the *Trigger,* sister ship of the *Tang.*

"Two years, most of it spent in Navy yards, trying to make the ship seaworthy," he said grimly.

"Yes, sir," Trimble said. "And, sir, what about the Russians during this period?"

"I'm coming to that, right now. Ever since they were wiped out by the Japanese at Tsushima Straits in 1905, the Russian Navy had been a zero threat. A joke. A few old broken-down cruisers and half-assed sailors. They had a little Submarine Force. Couple of hundred coastal submarines which Stalin used to protect the seaward flanks of the Army. They were actually under Army command. There was no real Navy command—no maritime vision. Moreover, the Russian naval picture has always been complicated by geography. They don't have natural warm water ports. They had to grab a window on the Baltic, and then a window on the Black Sea. Actually, our own Admiral John Paul Jones helped them in the Black Sea."

"I've read about that," Trimble said. "I know the early history pretty well. By the way, sir, did you know that John Paul Jones was ridden out of Moscow on a rail for shacking up with a ten-year-old girl?"

"He was framed by jealous Russian admirals," Monty replied.

"I don't think that's been proved."

"Well, the hell with that," Monty went on. "Now, when the Russians came into Germany at the invitation of General Eisenhower, they overran some Nazi submarine building yards. They picked up thirty brand new U-boats and all the factory machinery and the German technicians. They took these back to Russia. That was the beginning of the Soviet Navy as we know it today. That was the beginning of the real threat. We've never pinned this down, but I also believe they got some Nazi submariners. . . . We do know positively they got those thirty Type XXI boats. Now, in reality, overnight technically, they had a better Submarine Force than we did. Better than our Fleet Boats."

"But they didn't know how to use them?"

"Well, yes."

"Then it wasn't really a threat."

"Not really. Not then. But wait . . . "

"And they had the problem of geography."

"Yes. The other problem of geography is that it is a long way from Russia to the United States. I'm sure you've studied that? Those U-boats didn't have the range to come here from Russia and stay any length of time and get back. Plus the fact the bases were vulnerable in the Baltic and Black Sea and even in Vladivostok on the Sea of Japan. They would have to come and go through very narrow straits, choke points as they call them today. So, in order to use these boats against us effectively, they'd have to have forward bases like the Nazis did in France and so on. They'd have to first overrun Europe. But we're getting far afield here."

Trimble had caught up with his notes. He waited, pen poised on the tablet.

"What's important," Monty said, "was the Russians put these German technicians to work and built a whole flock of new submarines, Chinese copies. By the time we got the *Tang* launched, they had built fifty new Russian-made copies. So, with the ones they captured, they had eighty modern submarines."

"I noticed in one paper about the time of Korea, it says 300 Russian submarines."

"That included the 200 old coastal boats."

"Why did they include those?"

"To make the total look impressive, Trimble. Eighty doesn't sound very impressive—even though Hitler launched World War Two with only fifty-seven submarines. It's part of the numbers racket around this building. You couldn't get people stirred up about eighty Russian submarines. Especially with the geography problem. Plus the lack of combat experience. The Navy was fighting for its life against the Air Force. The Air Force was taking all the money to build the B-36—remember the Billion Dollar Blunder? If there were no Soviet naval threat, then how would the Navy get any appropriations?"

"Yes . . . well, it seems devious . . . dishonest."

"I repeat, Lieutenant, the Navy was fighting for its life. The Air Force had managed to get the first super-carrier canceled. We were putting all our eggs into one basket: strategic bombing. SAC. Curtis LeMay. The powers-that-be in the Navy—Admiral Radford, Arleigh Burke—thought that was suicidal. If they hadn't exaggerated the Soviet submarine threat, risked their own careers, where would the Navy be today? All during the Cold War—Korea, Suez —the Navy, the aircraft carrier, has proved to be indispensable."

"What was the position of the people in the Submarine Force?" Trimble asked. "They must have known the Russian Submarine Force was a joke."

"Their position was, in one word, silence. We wanted money for the *Tang*-class boats. When we got the *Tang*, and it turned out to be a lemon, we needed money in a hurry to do something else. That's where Admiral Zimmerman and nuclear power comes in. . . . "

"Captain," Armbruster called from his desk. "It's Admiral Z again on Line two. His yeoman says he knows you are sitting at your desk. You better pick up . . . "

"And how does he know?" Monty said irritably, picking up the phone.

"They say Zimmerman can see through concrete and steel," Armbruster replied.

"That I don't doubt," Monty said. Then to Trimble, "Put that down on paper and see me later today. But don't put in any of the politics. Just the hard facts. Numbers."

Monty answered the phone.

"What's the status of the ULMS press release?" Zimmerman asked, curtly.

"Sir, I haven't got to it yet," Monty replied, guiltily.

"What the hell are we paying you for?" Zimmerman demanded, half-jokingly.

"Sir, you're not paying me very much. And I can't be two places at once."

"Well, you better drop everything else and get on that press release."

"Yes, sir, Admiral. Right away."

Admiral Starr came from his office, dead cigar between his teeth.

"You got that letter lifting Zempfke's security clearance for me to sign?"

"No, sir."

"We better get it worked up on the double."

"But . . ."

★ 12 ★

"I'd like to see Captain Kemp," Monty said to the receptionist-secretary in Chinfo—the Navy Chief of Information's Office.

"May I say who's calling?" she replied.

"Captain King, OP-31."

"Oh yes," she said, vaguely, then buzzed her boss on the intercom.

Tom Kemp, the Deputy Chief of Information, came immediately from his office. He was a short, stocky man, with a thick neck and a bald head. A suave glad-hander and ladies' man. Monty remembered. He wore a uniform, dolphins. At Annapolis, Kemp had been the yearbook editor. After the war, he had published several popular books on submarine exploits. They were considered laughable by most submariners, but they had earned Kemp much money. One had been made into a movie starring a well-known Hollywood he-man. Kemp had been technical advisor on the movie. In the gossip columns, he had been linked with a starlet. Thereafter, he had become an information specialist.

"What can I do for you?" Kemp said, inviting Monty into his enormous office, shutting the door behind them. "Would you like coffee?"

"No thanks," Monty said, sitting down in a pull-up chair. The office was decorated with many large color photographs of Navy ships, aircraft, submarines, plus pictures of Sec-Nav, CNO, Deputy CNO.

"I guess you got the word on the Selection Board?" Kemp said, smiling broadly.

"Oh yes," Monty replied, returning the smile. But he thought: did Tom Kemp really believe he had a prayer of being selected? If so, it was wildly misplaced optimism. His books, the movie, the gossip columns had destroyed him professionally. Didn't Kemp realize that Chinfo was a burial ground, like the Office of Naval Intelligence?

"We need some help," Monty went on, turning the conversation away from the Selection Board. "You remember that press release we sent through here a few weeks ago? The ULMS long lead-time hardware contract?"

"Yes," Kemp replied, still smiling. "I saw it."

"Do you know what the status is?"

"It's over in DOD somewhere, I believe."

"I'd like to try to dynamite it out of there this week."

Kemp's smile disappeared. He was suddenly grave. He said earnestly, "I'll give it a try, but I don't hold out much hope. You can't rush those people anymore. Trying to get something through there these days is like pulling teeth.

They've got about five thousand people down there, an incredible bureaucracy. Everybody has to initial everything. You know what I mean? Especially new contracts. They've been sitting on all the contract releases . . . BuShips, Bu-Air, BuOrd, BuDocks. . . . We hear they're taking another look at the budget. The guys in the press room say they think something big's in the wind."

"They've had it over a month," Monty pressed.

"Haw! That's nothing!"

"I've got orders to get it out this week," Monty said impatiently. "If I have to, I'll hand-carry it through. But I have to know where to start. Can you find out where it is right now?"

"Are you going to hand-carry it right to SecDef?" Kemp said doubtfully. "He personally approves every press release."

"Yes—if necessary. Why the hell should he object to a press release? We got budget approval for the contract. It's a piddling little thing . . . 150 million dollars."

"Let me see what I can do," Kemp said, again smiling. "I'll get back to you this afternoon."

"All right," Monty said, rising to leave. "By the way, when are you people over here going to get some favorable publicity for the Navy? Everything I read is antimilitary, downbeat. . . . "

Captain Kemp's face took on a blank look, as though he had been slapped in the face.

"You guys don't realize the problems we're up against," he said, with a grave expression. "These reporters, young guys, they're a different breed. Long hair, mod clothes, pot-smoking. They come in here *looking* for trouble, Monty. Hell, in the old days, we had the press room eating out of our hand. Most of the reporters and editors then were veterans of World War Two. Lot of ex-Navy types. Promilitary. They were happy to give us a favorable ride. We'd give them an exclusive tidbit every now and then to keep them happy. A junket every now and then. But these kids nowdays. . . . Jesus! They don't even *remember* World War Two. They want to *dismantle* the military. Well, I'm not telling you anything new. You read the papers."

"Yes. But I don't understand their attitude. If they succeed in dismantling the military, the Russians will take over. Don't they understand that?"

"They don't believe that, Monty. They believe if we disarm, the Russians will too."

"That's ridiculous. Naive. How could they possibly believe that?"

"I told you. They're a different breed."

"Then they ought not to be reporters. Don't the publishers understand what they're doing to the country? Can't you get to them?"

"I'm in New York three or four days a month calling on publishers."

"What do they say?"

"Monty, you must understand. Publishers don't *form* opinion, they *mirror* it. There's a prevailing antimilitary wind in the country. You saw what happened in the elections. It's not popular to be promilitary. So, most publications bend with the prevailing wind. I can't get anything pro-Navy in any of them except *The Reader's Digest*. Most places I'm greeted with suspicion."

"A bunch of gutless wonders," Monty said with a weary sigh.

"It's a miracle to me they haven't jumped on ULMS," Kemp said. "Which raises a point. I'm not sure it's so damned wise to get out that press release. You might very well stir up a hornet's nest. You might be better off more or less down-playing ULMS, sneaking it by, so to speak. You're likely to trigger . . . "

"Zimmerman wants it broken loose."

"Oh. Well, I guess he knows what he's doing. It's really astonishing to me the way he's still a hero to the press. It's the neatest high-wire act in history. He's spent billions on new weapons, and yet, he can do no wrong. They think because he blasts DOD every now and then on the Hill, he's antimilitary. On their side. Meanwhile, he sits over there, designing ever more lethal submarines. One of these days, they're going to take a close look at him. Then. . . . "

"Well, don't you point the finger," Monty said.

"Come on, Monty," Kemp said in an injured tone. "Whose side do you think I'm on?"

"I was only kidding," Monty said.

They walked to the door.

"How's the family?" Kemp said, again affable, oily. "Nancy? The boys?"

"Fine. Fine. How's Joey?"

"Busy with women's lib."

"You're kidding? Joey?"

"She doesn't have anything else to do."

"You writing any more books?"

"No. The book publishers don't want promilitary books either. They don't sell anymore. If I knew something about ecology, I could get a pretty good deal."

"Tommy this and Tommy that," Monty said, shaking hands.

"Exactly," Kemp replied.

Monty returned to OP-31. It was 1155. In five minutes the New England Ship car and driver would be downstairs. He looked in the Admiral's peephole. The office was empty.

"He's back in Flag Plot," Yeoman Armbruster said, adding: "You have a bunch of telephone calls, sir. Captain Caldwell. Captain Pendleton. Captain Crimmons. Captain Rush in BuPers. And, you had a long-distance call from a Mr. Olsen at the University of Wisconsin."

"Oh?" Monty said. "Get Olsen back for me, will you?"

While Armbruster placed the call, Monty worked through the papers on his desk, remembering then, he must draft a letter lifting Zempfke's security clearance. He took the bulky policy book from the bookshelf, thumbed through it, searching for a model letter.

"Mr. Olsen on Line one," Armbruster called out.

"Thank you," Monty said, picking up the receiver, punching the Line 1 button. "Captain King," he answered.

"Captain King? This is Jim Olsen in the security office at University of Wisconsin. You called this morning in reference to your son, Paul King?"

"Yes," Monty said.

"Well, we don't have any positive information on your son's whereabouts," Olsen went on. "There's nothing in the file on him. But we've done some checking around for you. We believe we know the name of the girl with whom he is believed to have left. Would you like that information?"

"Yes, of course," Monty said.

"According to both their friends," Olsen said, "her name is Linda Adams. Our records show her as a sophomore. Age twenty. Liberal arts. Exceptional student. Five feet four, one hundred ten pounds. Blonde. Blue eyes. Distinctive birthmark on upper right thigh. Last known local address 106½ Parker Avenue. The landlady there says she is no longer living at that address. She left no forwarding address."

Monty scribbled this information on a pad.

"Her parents are divorced," Olsen went on. "She's in custody of her mother, Mrs. George Adams, 11678 Lake Road, Springfield, Illinois. We called her. She was not aware that her daughter had withdrawn. She could provide no useful leads."

"I see," Monty said.

"Her number is area code 217-529-4162 if you want to call her and coordinate."

"Yes," Monty said. "That's a good idea."

"You may be interested to know that Linda Adams was —is—described as being very active in the ah, dissident element on campus. Antimilitary. Antiestablishment. She has been identified with the most extreme militant elements. Our information is that she was very active in various demonstrations."

"I see," Monty said.

"I'm afraid that's all we have here," Olsen said. "You probably know that the federal government maintains a file on these kids—individuals of interest—in Washington. In your position, I'm sure you must have contacts in the FBI and Army. If you want to run it out further . . . "

"Yes," Monty said.

"The Army has a big file," Olsen went on. "The Office of Naval Intelligence has limited files. Just between you and me, we cooperate with them."

"I see," Monty said, jotting ONI, FBI and Army on his pad, thinking: I might call Frank Byerston, a classmate in ONI.

"That's about it, Captain."

"Thank you very much, Mr. Olsen."

"Anytime."

★ 13 ★

The New England Ship car—a black Cadillac limousine—was waiting for Monty at the Mall Entrance. The driver opened the rear door ceremoniously, as though Monty were CNO. A lavish expense, Monty thought, climbing in. They could have sent a Chevy at a third the price. Now that he was a substantial stockholder, he ought to write the chairman of the board. No. He would write nobody. Furthermore, he must do something about the stock, today. He had intended to call Scottie MacIntosh. . . .

They crossed the Potomac River, zipped past the Mint

and Washington Monument, the White House. In twelve minutes, the driver pulled up at the side entrance of the Army-Navy Club, an old ten-story red brick structure, known facetiously as "The Old Indian Fighters' Club." There were four or five other limousines double-parked.

Monty found his host, Buzz Creighton, along with two strangers, waiting at a table in the large third-floor dining room. Buzz was dressed in an expensive gray pin-striped suit. In spite of the gray hair, beautifully groomed, he seemed boyish. Eager. Energetic.

"Hello, Monty," he said affably, rising, extending a hand. He turned to the two strangers. "May I present Mr. Richtor and Mr. Cramer from our New York office. Gentlemen, this is the Captain King I told you about."

Monty shook hands with the New York men. They were pale-faced, small in stature. The General Nucleonics doubledomes, Monty thought. Both wore dark suits, Italian shoes.

"Will you have a drink?" Creighton asked.

"No thanks," Monty said.

"I asked Tony de Lucca to join us," Creighton said, "so we could coordinate. . . . There he is now."

Anthony de Lucca, potbellied and black-haired, came toward the table. He was Chief Counsel for Congressman Magruder's House Armed Services Committee. He had grown up in Magruder's district, Groton, across the river from New London, entered local politics after law school. According to what Monty had heard, de Lucca had delivered the Italian and Polish vote for Magruder, thereby earning the Chairman's undying gratitude. Now he served as eyes and ears for Magruder, a man of immense power. He was a captain in the Naval Reserve, active in Navy League affairs, a special friend of the Submarine Force.

"Hello, Tony," Buzz Creighton said, rising again.

"Hi, Buzz," de Lucca said. "Hi, Monty."

Creighton introduced the New Yorkers to de Lucca. Then

de Lucca settled his great bulk into a chair. To the waiter he said: "Bring me a double vodka martini with onion."

The waiter brought the drink. They commented on the weather. The New Yorkers complained that the shuttle flight had been jammed, the air turbulent. De Lucca said nothing, sipped his large martini, then ordered a second. Creighton took orders for food on a chit. Monty ordered a shrimp salad. When they were well into the meal, Creighton turned the talk to the purpose for which they had assembled.

"It appears," he said, "that these people are really much more serious than we ever believed."

The New Yorkers nodded in gloomy unison.

"Have you seen what happened to our stock?" Creighton went on.

"No," de Lucca said. Monty looked on, trying to seem casual.

"It dropped seven points this morning," Creighton said. "That's a loss of twenty million in our capital structure."

Monty was not sure what this meant. But seven points meant seven thousand dollars for the King family.

"It's eating into our capital structure," the New Yorker, Cramer, said. "It's got to be stopped—now. We've got to protect our stockholders."

De Lucca nodded. He was now working on his third double martini.

"*Every* defense stock is plunging like mad," Creighton said.

"If it keeps up," Cramer said, "it's going to wreck the *entire* economy. The institutional buyers, the foundations, mutual funds, insurance groups, are pulling out of the defense sector. Do you know what that means?" He looked directly at Monty.

"No, sir," Monty replied.

"It's going to touch off a major market slide," Cramer said. The other New Yorker, Richtor, nodded. "A very deep slide. It will trigger a recession six months from now, perhaps a hair-curling depression. Money will be tight again. Credit will dry up."

"Tens of thousands of skilled workers will be thrown out of jobs," Richtor put in. "Maybe hundreds of thousands. The entire defense industrial base will be uprooted."

"They just can't get away with it," Creighton said. "So, gentlemen, let's get our ducks lined up. Monty, I understand from the Admiral, you're trying to get the ULMS press release sprung?" Creighton spoke of Zimmerman as though he were the only admiral in the Navy.

"Yes," Monty replied.

"And you've got the Soviet Navy hearing laid on?" Creighton said to de Lucca.

De Lucca nodded, finishing off the martini in one large gulp. He wiped his mouth with his napkin and said in his deep voice, "The Chairman's itching to take those people apart. They put out that directive without even telling us. He's having lunch with them tomorrow. There's going to be hell to pay all over the Hill. We're going to call them to testify next week."

"What about the press release, Monty?"

"I don't know. Tom Kemp says DOD's sitting on *all* the contract releases."

"He's too negative," Creighton said.

"As I understand it," Monty said, "the release is to be the lightning rod. If it gets hung up . . ."

The New Yorkers listened, with eyes intent.

"That's right," Creighton said. "But if it gets through, we're home free. And by the way, Monty, if it gets sprung, we can provide all the backup help you need with our PR department."

"Which brings to mind another idea, Buzz," de Lucca said, ordering another martini. "When we get that release broken out, I think it would be a good occasion to stage a kind of appreciation dinner for the Chairman. At the Sub Base Officers' Club, or someplace. I'm thinking of a formal dinner with a lot of VIPs. Maybe SecDef, SecNav, CNO, Zimmerman, members of our committee, chairman of the AEC, maybe the membership of the Senate Armed Services Committee, the New England members anyway. Special entertainment: the Navy Band, the Air Force Strolling Strings, maybe the Marine Corps Drum and Bugle Corps."

Creighton nodded. De Lucca went on:

"We've been getting a little political pressure. We're not worried, you understand, but after the election last fall, we've got to be prudent. There's a young lawyer up there, a conservationist, antimilitary type, who's running hard. He has a lot of support among the young long-hairs. They've been conducting a voter registration drive that . . . well, they're pretty energetic. They've even got high school kids working for them. We've got the hard-hat support in the shipyards, of course, but the lawyer has stirred up a lot of damned housewives about the pollution in the Thames River. He's got a pseudo-scientific committee up there measuring the river for *nuclear* pollution—from the boats going in and out of the yard. We're not really worried, as I say, but the release gives us a good opportunity to restate and reemphasize exactly what the Chairman has done over the years by way of defense contracts for his district."

"Of course," Creighton said.

"We need somebody to pick up the tab," de Lucca said, nursing his fourth martini fondly.

"Don't worry about it," Creighton said. "Leave that to us."

"Good," de Lucca said.

Monty groaned inwardly. The Navy, he knew, would have to provide transportation for all this brass, a vastly complicated undertaking. Plush aircraft, controlled by the Air Force Special Air Mission at Andrews Air Force Base, operating on tight, tricky schedules. A thousand telephone calls, anxious moments. Most of the load would fall on OP-31. . . . Without Zempfke . .

"Don't worry, Monty," Creighton said, smiling as though he had been reading Monty's mind. "Our PR department can do the heavy hauling."

"Good," Monty said. Then to de Lucca, "When would this be?"

"I don't know," de Lucca said. "We'll have to work up a date. Everything depends on the release."

"Yes," Monty said, turning to Creighton. "Tom Kemp raised a point that may be worth considering. He says we've been lucky the press hasn't jumped on ULMS. He said maybe we ought to try to sneak it by."

"That's why Tom Kemp is in Chinfo," Creighton sneered. "We need that contract broken out to stop this stock slide. He wouldn't understand that. The press isn't going to jump on ULMS. For one thing, we've got the Admiral, a secret weapon. He's still got plenty of IOUs all over town. For another, the General Nucleonics advertising department places a lot of advertising."

"I see," Monty said, not certain what he meant about the advertising. De Lucca nodded silently, now eating a steak with large bites.

"They haven't jumped on submarines *yet*," Creighton smiled.

"That's true," Monty said.

"The press doesn't know anything about submarines," de Lucca said. "We need that release as a peg for the appreciation dinner." He was now glassy-eyed. He slurred his words. How would he work the rest of the afternoon? Monty wondered.

When the luncheon broke up, de Lucca invited the group to join him in the first-floor men's bar. All declined. Creighton escorted Monty downstairs to his car. In the elevator he said, with a smile:

"I see your Board's been announced."

"Yes," Monty replied. It was a damn good thing Buzz

Creighton was not among the competition. He would be picked without hesitation, leaving one less vacancy.

"I can't say that I wish you well," Creighton went on, still smiling. "We want you at New England Ship—provided, of course, we don't lose ULMS. You understand that, I'm sure?"

"Yes, I understand. No ULMS, no job."

"So," Creighton said, leading the way to the car, "assuming the worst about the Board, this week, what's good for New England Ship is good for Monty King and vice versa. A hell of a lot depends on you, personally, Monty. We can lay all this on, but you've got to move the ball. You're the quarterback, right in the pit."

"I'd do my damnedest for ULMS—job or no job," Monty replied. "You know that."

"I knew you would," Creighton said, shaking hands.

Riding back to the Pentagon in the solitude of the large rear seat, Monty thought again of the stock—this time with a chill. If it were known he owned it—or Nancy owned it —in pushing hard for ULMS, he could be charged with acting in his own financial self-interest. A hell of a position. If the Board found out. . . . Goddamn! Nancy had exposed them seriously.

★ 14 ★

"I always thought of Key West as an exotic place," Alma Caldwell said to Nancy. "Mysterious . . . Hemingway . . . smugglers . . . deep-sea fishing . . . the Little White House . . . "

They sat at Alma's kitchen table having a lunch of vegetable soup and crackers, tossed salad with diet dressing.

"So did I," Nancy said, bitterly. "Until I *got* there. I remember how much I was looking forward to it. Monty's first shore duty. We would live on a cozy little base where it would be safe and convenient and congenial. The life I remembered as a little girl growing up. Officer's country, unauthorized personnel keep out. Filipino mess stewards, all that. Monty was to be an instructor at the Sonar School."

"Yes, I remember."

"We'd moved thirteen times in the first year and a half ... seventeen times up to the point Mike was born. Key West was the eighteenth move. By then, the furniture was a shambles. Scarred up, the china all chipped. Alma, do you *know* where Key West is?"

"In the Keys. Just below Miami."

"That's what I thought. Well, we had the old Ford then. Joanie was going on five. Mike was still in diapers. I was five months gone with Paul. We spent the night in Miami with Pete and Lizzie Kane. Then we took off. We drove. And we drove. And we drove. Key West is 150 miles southwest of Miami. Out in the damned ocean. It was about 115 degrees in the shade. The car boiled over. Joanie and Mike were hot and tired. We ran out of diapers ... Mike had a touch of diarrhea. As Monty said, we got about twenty-five miles to the diaper on that trip. God! When we got there, the grill was solid with crushed mosquitoes! And the Navy had run out of mosquito-control money!"

Nancy spooned her soup.

"Key West was awful," she went on. "A dirty, dingy Navy town, full of taverns and Negroes. More Negroes than I've ever seen anywhere. The base is tiny! We drew a house— an old wooden frame thing that was filthy. The screens were ripped. It was so humid all the time, my hair was always a mess. We didn't have air conditioning. Nobody had air conditioning in those days. And the water! They had to bring the water down from Miami in a pipe which was not buried, but lying above ground. The sun blazing on it for 150 miles. By the time it came out of the tap, it was almost boiling. And *bugs!* Ugh . . . roaches, ants, rats, palmetto bugs. We had to keep everything in our tiny little refrigerator . . . even the cereal."

"Would you like more soup, Nancy?" Alma said, rising.

"No thank you," Nancy said. "Here. I can put my bowl in the sink. Stop waiting on me.

"Then Monty was gone all the time, anyway. Shore duty! What a joke!"

"I'll bet the fishing was good," Alma said, hopefully.

"I hated it," Nancy said. "I went once. They had a boat . . . the Officers' Club boat. The day I went it was rough and I got terribly seasick. I was sunburned. We didn't catch a damned thing except a couple of bonitos. They're not good eating. I never did go fishing again. By then I was out to here with Paul and it didn't seem a good idea to go out in a pitching boat."

"No," Alma said. "Would you like coffee?"

"Please."

"And then, poor Joanie," Nancy said, with a catch in her voice.

"You told me about that," Alma said, setting the coffee on the table. "Did I show you my new needlepoint?"

"I don't think I ever told you the *whole* story," Nancy said, with a far-away look in her eyes. Alma, standing behind her, laid a hand on her shoulder.

"Don't," she said. "You're just raking up all the bad memories. Trying to justify . . . "

"No. I'm trying to be fair. Truly I am. It's just that I can't seem to remember anything good."

"Monty's first command."

"That took him away again—for months and months. That's all his first command meant to me. He was not home when Joanie was born. He was not home when she died.

"And when Paul came, three weeks later, Monty was back at sea again. He was never with me when I gave birth to any of the kids."

"I know that. Would you like a tiny bit of lime sherbet?"

"Yes, please. A *tiny* bit."

Alma got the sherbet from the freezer, dished out two servings.

"I said a tiny bit." Nancy smiled wanly. She glanced at the clock. "I really must get home soon. Paul may have been trying to call."

"Don't gobble the sherbet, you'll get a headache."

"I was never so glad to get out of a place in my life," Nancy said. "You just don't know how lucky you were to draw Hawaii."

"Oh, it wasn't all *that* great."

"I *dreamed* of going to Hawaii."

"It had its good points. But it was humid too."

"And then everything was going to be so much better." Nancy went on grimly. "Monty drew the *Trigger*. New construction. Back to New London for the umpteenth time. Korea—remember? All the Navy money? Fabulous new boat, all that."

"You had a lovely cottage in Mystic . . . "

"Poor Monty. He was so frustrated. That lemon. They limped from one Navy yard to another. Boston. Philadelphia. Norfolk. Charleston. Laid up, month after month, rebuilding those damned engines. And I was left in New London with Mike—he was walking then—and Paul all colicky. . . . "

"Nancy, stop it! That was so long ago. Why do you torture yourself like this? Try to think of the good things . . . the happy times. . . . "

"What good things?"

"Your friends."

"I didn't have any real friends."

"That's not true, Nancy. Remember the Commissioning parties, the Wardroom parties? Nancy, we were young and gay. We had a ball."

"Maybe you did, but I hated those drunken brawls. Monty lived in mortal fear that something drastic might happen. You remember what happened to Pete Kane in Philadelphia at his Commissioning party? The crew got wildly drunk and tore up a tavern. Pete got blamed. It was a wonder he ever made captain."

"He drank too much. You can't compare . . . "

"Alma, have you stopped to consider what this Selection Board might do to *our* friendship?"

"What do you mean . . . ?"

"I mean what if Jim is selected and Monty isn't? Or vice versa. Do you think we could go on being friends?"

"Certainly. You learn to accept . . . "

"Be realistic, Alma. Try to imagine the situation."

"I wouldn't let . . . "

"Yes, you would, Alma. If Jim failed and Monty made it, you'd be bitter."

"Oh, Nancy, I've learned to take things as they come."

"Not this, Alma. I don't want to lose you as a friend. You're the only really true friend I have. What is life if you don't have a friend?"

"We'll still . . . "

"The other night," Nancy went on, "I was lying on the bed reading. All at once, this weird feeling came over me. Alma, it was really scary. I had this picture in my mind of the universe, as though I were looking down on it from an immense height. From space. It was enormous, beyond comprehension. Thousands of billions of stars, this whole huge thing, *existing*. And I thought: how did it get here? I mean, Alma, *who* put it there? And if you say God put it there, then I say *why*? And if God put it there, who is God? Where did God come from? I started thinking about that, and I got really frightened. And then I started thinking: what a brief, truly brief, fleeting thing is life. My life. I felt desperate. Thinking of all the things that I had missed. The opportunities lost. Wrong choices. Mistakes. Loneliness. . . . "

"You've got to stop thinking about those things," Alma said, gently laying her hand on Nancy's arm.

"But I *want* to think about them. Do you think about them?"

"Not if I can help it. It's too scary."

"It's frightening."

"Nancy, as an old and true friend, let me give you a piece of advice. You've been running on in a negative vein for three hours, raking up a lifetime of grief and trouble. I think you're terribly upset about Paul and the girl, more upset than you'll admit to yourself. Now you come on with this ridiculous malarkey about not standing for Selection. Retiring! I don't care if Monty *is* competition for Jim. I can't stand by and let you do anything this foolish. You're in no shape to be making big decisions like this. At the very least, Nancy, you ought to go get some professional advice."

"You mean a . . . a . . . ?"

"I mean a psychiatrist or some kind of professional. No intelligent person these days would make huge family decisions like these without outside help. You won't listen to me. So . . . "

"You know what Monty thinks of headshrinkers. He'd be appalled. He wouldn't . . . "

"If for no other reason, you ought to get some help—professional advice—on Paul. Before he gets deeper into trouble."

"I suppose you're right. But who? Where?"

★ 15 ★

"That's damned good," Monty said to Lieutenant Trimble, returning his two pages of post-war submarine history. "Crisp. Right to the point."

"Thank you, sir," Trimble replied, smiling. "Now maybe I can get something to eat. By the way, sir. Are you a member of the Pentagon Athletic Club?"

"The Officers' Athletic Center," Monty corrected. "Yes. Last year I wrenched my back lifting the damned lawnmower out of the station wagon. Slipped a disc. The people at Bethesda Naval Medical Center advised me to swim. So I took out a membership and swam during my lunch hour. It's the best athletic club in the world, I'm told. A real bargain. Ten-dollar initiation fee and five dollars a month dues. No waiting period—if you're assigned to the Pentagon. And, speaking of food, they've got the best food in the Pentagon in the grill over there. Are you a swimmer?"

"No, sir. But I like to work out in a gym . . . weight-lifting and so on."

"That's good. You'll like it over there. It's a nice little break from this madhouse. I enjoyed it. I wish I had time for it now."

Trimble rose, holding his manila folder.

"Where do I go from here?" he asked.

"Sit down," Monty said, stealing a look at his wrist watch. "I can spare a couple of minutes right now, while the Admiral's out."

Trimble sat down, pen poised on his note tablet.

"All right, let's see. We're done with the diesel era, so move it right into the nuclear-powered era. About the time of Korea, they found out how to produce uranium in quantity and to make a bomb with much less. So, we had uranium available for other purposes, like submarines. Point out that nuclear power brought on the real revolution in submarines. With a piece of uranium the size of a baseball as a power source, we were able to build the world's first *true* submarine. Range limited only by the endurance capability of the crew. No need to surface to charge batteries. High-speed performance submerged. Nuclear power increased the effectiveness of the submarine by a factor of roughly 100 over the *Tang* class. We proved that in fleet exercises. Start this section with a line or two about Admiral Zimmerman."

"Why introduce personalities into a history?"

"Because we sell Zimmerman the way we sell submarines."

"Sir?"

"We use the Admiral as a selling tool on the Hill. The way toothpaste advertisers use celebrities to endorse their product on TV. Admiral Zimmerman has credibility. A lot of people on the Hill—including Congressman Magruder —believe he's a deity unto himself. He's done a lot of people on the Hill favors—putting defense installations in their district and so on. Anyway, he deserves credit. Nobody else could have given us the nuclear-powered submarine so quickly and so perfectly done."

"I see. And how, sir, am I supposed to separate the real Admiral Zimmerman from the legend?"

"You don't have to go into all that."

"You know him very well?"

"Yes. I worked directly for him about six months over in the old Main Navy Building, as sort of an aide—before I went out to Idaho to Nuclear Power School."

"Did you get the famous Zimmerman interview?"

"Oh that was a lot of crap—exaggeration in the press. Basically, he's a very kindhearted guy. Heart of gold. He likes to put on a tough act—it served him well—but . . . "

"I saw him from a distance, when he came on the *Jones* one time. After you left."

"You'll meet him soon enough."

"Is it true the Selection Board originally passed him over because he was a Jew?"

"Oh—I don't know. I think it may have entered into it."

"I heard at the Academy that his class—1922—was really anti-Semitic. There was a guy named Kaplan, who stood Number one. They say he was so hated they perforated the page in his yearbook so that guys could tear it out easily."

"That story—unfortunately—was true. But the Navy's changing. It takes time—generations—to break down that kind of prejudice. Anyway, Zimmerman really put the Submarine Force on the map with the *Nautilus*."

"You served on the *Nautilus*, didn't you?"

"Yes. Briefly. For a year, right after Nuclear Power School. The *Nautilus* was a kind of seagoing post-graduate school in those days. Zimmerman was reeducating us to nuclear power, running everybody through his school and a tour on *Nautilus*. It was remarkable, really, the way he got control of the Submarine Force. He got himself authorized to screen all the people . . . pick the submarine captains . . . the whole damned works. Tough! Jesus. To graduate from Nuclear Power School, you had to take a fourteen-hour examination, created by Zimmerman. He's a perfectionist."

"Were you on *Nautilus* when she first got under way on nuclear power?"

"Yes. January 17, 1955. I was communications officer, among other jobs. I sent the message to ComSubLant: 'Under way on nuclear power.' Pretty historic. That was quite a few years back, by golly. That first year on *Nautilus* was incredible. The brass we took to sea on demonstration rides! Sixty-eight members of Congress, 186 admirals and

various SecNavs and SecDefs. I remember once we had a
four-star admiral on the bow planes, a three-star admiral
on the stern planes and a two-star admiral at the helm!
One of the seamen, who had been displaced, looked at
the two-star admiral and said: 'Well, by God! They always
put the junior man on the helm.' "

Monty laughed hard at the recollection. Trimble smiled,
thinly.

"Anyway," Monty went on, "I'm wandering again. Let's
see. Put down Zimmerman. *Nautilus* under way, the date.
A line or two about her voyages beneath the Arctic ice
pack—making that vast, hostile part of the world a routine
operating area for submarines—and then get right ahead
to the first production-line nuclear-attack subs. The *Skate*
class: *Skate, Sargo, Sea Dragon, Swordfish* and *Swordray*."

"*Swordray* was your boat, wasn't it?"

"Yes, sir," Monty said. "My first command. Fantastic
boat. 'Fandamntastic,' as we used to call it. Amazingly reliable. We never had a reactor failure. Not even an alarm.
In one exercise, we sank 200,000 tons of combatant naval
vessels: destroyers, cruisers, aircraft carriers. Old Admiral
Willoughby was furious."

"Yes, sir. Did you make a polar voyage?"

"Yes. We surfaced through a polynya at the pole. But
Skate did it first. By the time we came along, it was routine.
Under-ice operations were routine—once we got the upward-
scanning sonar and the reliable gyro compasses. That was
a great era, too—lot of fun. The wives weren't too happy.
We spent a hell of a lot of time at sea. A *hell* of a lot. All
the surface ships wanted to exercise with us. The ASW
people—Hunter-Killer groups—so they could learn how to
deal with a nuclear submarine."

"Did they learn?"

"We helped a little. But they had a hell of a time. We
could drop down below 1,000 feet and hide beneath the
thermoclines and we had such terrific escape speed, ma-

neuverability. However, those first boats *were* a bit noisy . . . the steam turbines made a terrific racket at full speed. The ASW people could pick that up. Anyway, that's that. After that, do the Russian part. How the Russians got the nuclear-powered submarine.

"Sir, can you give me some background on that?"

"A little. But, my memory is tricky. There's a Captain Frank Byerston over in ONI who can give you chapter and verse. A real expert on Soviet submarines. He's a classmate. Good Joe. Tell him I suggested you call him."

"Captain Byerston?"

"Yes. Extension 77550."

"Yes, sir."

"All right. Picking up the Soviet story. They had already decided to put the main naval effort into submarines, as we discussed this morning. No carriers for them. They thought carriers were vulnerable in a nuclear-weapons age. There's a quote from Admiral what's-his-name, the Soviet CNO, saying carriers are obsolete. Frank Byerston can give you that, probably off the top of his head. Anyway, let's see. Oh yes. The Defense Minister, Zhukov, the big hero of Stalingrad, was opposed to spending a lot on the Soviet Navy. Gave it a hard time. But he got fired around 1957, I think. And Khrushchev, who was the real power about that time, put a big push behind the Soviet Navy. In 1959, you may remember, the Soviet Navy sent a nuclear-powered ice-breaker, the *Lenin,* to sea. It had three reactors. They cut their teeth, nuclear-powerwise, with the *Lenin.* Then a year or so later—Byerston can give you the exact date—they built three what we now call November-class nukes at the yard in Severodvinsk on the White Sea. We picked them up with the U-2."

"Where, sir?"

"Severodvinsk. S-E-V-E-R-O-D-V-I-N-S-K. But that's not important. The first November boats were 328 feet, displacing about 3,500 tons, powered by a single reactor, more powerful, I believe, than those in our *Skate*-class boats. The first Novembers were *faster* submerged than our *Skate*-class boats."

"I didn't know that."

"But they had plenty of reactor trouble. They were always breaking down at sea, always being towed. Reminded me of our *Tang*-class diesels. . . ."

"How fast were they?"

"About twenty-eight knots submerged. Maybe a bit faster."

"That's amazing."

"It certainly was. What was amazing was how fast they got a nuclear-powered submarine after *Nautilus*. They trailed us by, let's see, only five years. A lot of people thought it would be years and years, ten or fifteen, before they got an atomic submarine. Even Zimmerman."

"But you say they were not very reliable."

"That's right. They had plenty of technical trouble. They didn't have a Zimmerman in the Soviet Navy Department . . . a technical perfectionist. Anyway, the November class was a tremendous achievement for them. You see, with a nuclear-powered boat, they overcame their built-in disadvantages of geography. Be sure to emphasize that. You don't have to refuel a nuclear boat except every few years. So they didn't need to overrun Europe and have sub bases in Brest. They could now make the round trip to the United States with ease, and stay as long as they liked—as long as they had sufficient food for the crew. In theory, they could deploy a force of nuclear-powered submarines against us before the outbreak of hostilities, have it in place, in the open ocean, beyond the narrow straits—choke points —and we'd have a hell of a time finding them. I mean, it was the obvious, perfect weapon for them."

"Yes, sir. Really much more valuable to them than us."

"In a way. Yes."

"I was just thinking, sir. Maybe it was a mistake for us to ever build a nuclear-powered submarine."

"*What?*"

"I mean, sir, when Zimmerman built *Nautilus*, it was like *proving* it could be done. I mean, we proved to the world —including the Russians—it was feasible. Then we touted it as a terrific achievement, calling attention to it. So maybe the Russians began thinking about it more than they might have otherwise. I mean, Khrushchev. I once read somewhere that the biggest security leak on the atomic bomb was actually using it at Hiroshima and Nagasaki. That proved it would work. So the Russians started right in, building their own. In a way, the submarine thing is the same."

"Lieutenant Trimble," Monty said, coolly. "That's the most asinine thing I've ever heard. You seem to imply we have a monopoly on brains, that the Russians are dolts and copycats. Don't fall into the trap of underrating the Russians, scientifically. Look at Sputnik. They were first to orbit a man around the earth. Haven't you ever heard the saying that if a weapon *can* be built it *will* be built?"

"No, sir."

"Well, burn that into your mind."

"Yes, sir. Captain."

"Look at it this way," Monty went on. "Suppose we had reached your decision—I mean, we decided not to build *Nautilus* because it would be telling the Russians, look, here's a beautiful weapon for you. And then, just suppose, there had been all the time a Russian Zimmerman over there, plugging away. Then, suddenly, they unveiled a nuclear-powered submarine and we didn't have one to match it. The best way to kill a nuclear-powered submarine is to send another one after it. All right, Lieutenant, then where'd we be?"

"I don't know, sir."

"Up shit creek without a paddle. That's where. Now, get out of here and get something to eat. I've got work to do."

"Yes, sir."

★ 16 ★

Yeoman Armbruster sang out: "Admiral Zimmerman on Line one, Captain."

Monty set aside the tablet on which he was drafting the letter lifting Zempfke's security clearance. He answered, "Captain King."

"Monty? Can you come over here right away? A friend in DOD just tipped me off. That ULMS press release just ran aground."

Monty felt his stomach drop.

"Yes, sir. On my way."

He logged himself out on the blackboard and hurried off to the fifth floor. It was late—already dark outside—but Admiral Zimmerman's anterooms were humming energetically. The Wave yeoman escorted Monty into the Admiral's office. He was in shirt sleeves, on the telephone, apparently talking to a congressman or a senator. His tone was polite, deferential, as it always was when he talked to important people on the Hill. Monty sat down on a chair.

When Zimmerman hung up, he seemed depressed. Defeated. He turned to Monty and spoke wearily.

"Sorry to interrupt your work. Will you have an apple? Candy?"

The Admiral shoved a silver tray toward Monty. It was stacked with apples and hard candy in cellophane wrappers, a few hard-boiled eggs. Monty chose a piece of hard candy. Zimmerman leaned back in his swivel chair, put his shoes on the edge of his desk, hands behind his head. Monty noted a hole in the elbow of his right sleeve. The Admiral was famous for his frugality—both with Navy funds and his own.

"This bunch is serious," he said speaking sourly, turning down a corner of his mouth. "We've got a very large problem in OSD. I'm told they're going to ask for a complete review of the submarine program. And maybe tomorrow afternoon."

Monty was dismayed. The Admiral paused, frowned.

"The sonsofbitches!" he shouted, slamming his palm on the desk. He swung his feet to the floor. Then he got up and sat on the edge of his desk, swinging a leg back and forth.

"All right," he went on in a calmer tone. "We've got a *real* fight on our hands. Maybe the hardest yet. We have a new man in the front office. He believes he has a mandate from the people to cut the military budget. We've got to stop it, for the sake of the Navy, the country. He doesn't know his ass from first base about how to cut a budget or about submarines. So, he'll turn to his Systems Analysis for facts and figures, advice and opinion. Does that make sense?"

"Yes, sir, Admiral."

"Then the real enemy, our target, is Systems Analysis. Our job is to discredit—*destroy*—Systems Analysis. Put it out of business. Then we can deal with the new man on even terms."

Monty looked at Zimmerman doubtfully. The Admiral held up his hand like a traffic cop.

"Wait a minute," he said. "Let me tell you something. You and your contemporaries take Systems Analysis for granted. It's there—so it must be dealt with, rationally. But what you do not seem to understand is that it was *not always there*. It can be removed."

"But, Admiral . . . " Monty interjected.

"When that man from Detroit came down here to be Secretary of Defense," the Admiral went on, "he was going to straighten out the Pentagon once and for all. The press built him up as a whiz kid. He would knock heads, put computers to work. He would teach us all about cost effectiveness—show us how to get more bang for the buck, with Yankee ingenuity and Detroit production know-how, with modern accounting principles, with Systems Analysis. He would eliminate duplication. He would save the taxpayer billions.

"When he got down here, he called me over for lunch. We talked. I told him what was wrong with the Navy. The technical bureaus. That no one man was accountable for a project. That the men were rotated every two years. That in many cases, the men were not technically qualified. That all of us technical people were crushed by layers and layers of administrators, committees, boards. That the only way to improve the system was to select qualified engineers and keep them on the job until the project was completed and make them totally responsible. Like I've done here. That no committee, no board could ever see a technical project to completion, that in the final analysis, technical achievement was a matter of individual talent, accomplishment and responsibility."

Monty reached forward, selected another hard candy. He was bone tired. The arguments were familiar. What Monty wanted to know precisely—and urgently—was how the Admiral proposed to "destroy" Systems Analysis.

"Well," the Admiral went on, "he listened, but he didn't grasp. You understand? Instead of doing something about the personnel problem as I recommended—the technical personnel—he created a whole new bureaucracy—Systems Analysis. He brought all those whiz kids down here. With their computers. Stupid questions. Memos. Studies. Before he came, DOD consisted of a mere 1,500 people. When he left, seven years later, there were tens of thousands. An army of mental midgets, telling us what to do. Just look how the DOD phone book has grown. He insulted Flag

Officers, behind their backs, to their faces. He pissed on decades of military experience. He gave orders directly to ships at sea, bypassing CNO."

The Admiral paused to pick up an apple and bite into it with his front teeth, like a chipmunk. Monty's eyes were riveted on him, wondering when he would come to the point. The battle plan.

"And what has been the end result?" the Admiral went on. "Disaster. Every new weapon we proposed has been delayed from one to four years. We have thrown away our submarine lead. We're throwing away our ICBM lead. Our Navy is staggering along, making do on obsolete weapons, while the Soviets surge ahead, creating the best Navy in the history of the world. The cost of defense has doubled. What weapons we do get—years behind schedule—are costing three, four, five times what they should have. Monty, the man was a fraud, a rainmaker. He has done more to jeopardize this country than any man in its history."

Monty inhaled, slowly filling his lungs. These were strong words, even for the Admiral. He glanced at the clock.

"Does that make sense?" the Admiral asked.

"Yes, sir, Admiral. I understand perfectly. I'm not sure what *I* can do about it. But I understand."

"Any man with the proper determination can change the world."

"Yes, sir," Monty said doubtfully.

"Systems Analysis must be *destroyed!*" the Admiral said again, eyes blazing. "Can't you people see that? You've got to de-fang that monster before it eats us alive. Destroys our country."

"Yes, sir," Monty said. "But . . . "

"Back in 1947, what the Navy feared most about unifying the services," Zimmerman went on, "was the creation of a General Staff mentality, a single-service, a single-minded strategy, like the old German General Staff. The Navy argued against putting all our eggs in one basket. Rather, it favored flexibility and versatility in strategy so we didn't turn up with another Maginot Line that could be overrun."

"Yes, sir, of course."

"When the Congress voted unification, it specifically set up the Department of Defense as a loose organization, in which no single mind—or concept—could prevail. With checks and balances on the power, like the government as a whole. It was *designed* to prevent a General Staff concept. The Department of Defense would *not* tell the three services in detail and specifically what weapons it would buy and how. The Department was supposed to be a policy-making group, a small group, which would iron out differences between the services, set the defense budget, military strategy. We worked that way for a dozen years—not always perfectly, I'll be the first to admit, but we got the job done. You see?"

Monty nodded affirmatively.

"Well, that jerk from Detroit was power mad, a maniac. Under the guise of saving money, he used Systems Analysis as a tool, a way of imposing *his* absolute control and ideas on the military. A General Staff mentality. If he could dictate weapons, then he could dictate strategy. Does that make sense?"

"Yes, sir."

"He's gone now, but Systems Analysis remains. It has grown. It is, in effect, a General Staff, running the entire military-industrial establishment. It has, in reality, more power than the White House. It ignores Congress. It has more power and say-so in shaping decisions concerning naval weapons than you or I or CNO or SecNav. Isn't that true?"

"Yes, sir," Monty replied, not wholly certain the Admiral was right, but, at this late hour, not wishing to argue or prolong the discussion.

"They are not only telling us what ships to build, they are telling me what *pumps* and *valves* to put in the reactor compartment. Do you realize that?"

"Yes, sir."

"Isn't that a General Staff concept? Isn't that kind of rigid ukase what led Germany to lose World War One? Destroyed the German Submarine Force in World War Two?"

"I suppose so, sir."

"Contrary to the wishes of Congress—the ultimate civilian control of the military?"

"Yes, sir," Monty replied.

"You see how Systems Analysis has intimidated us? We're running so scared, so negatively, that we're like children—trying to hold onto the little we have with desperate little measures. Like a ULMS press release. When you're finally reduced to that point, Monty, you're in real trouble. Now they say they want to cut the budget even further—but we're not going to let them do that."

Monty sat up straight, sucking on the hard candy. The Admiral, he sensed, was getting to the point, the meat.

"We're not going up there hat in hand again. Remember, Monty, the best defense is a strong offense. We're going in there and destroy the credibility of Systems Analysis, once and for all, and not only that, we're going to ask this new Secretary of Defense for an *increase* in submarine production."

"Admiral, sir," Monty said, disbelieving. "You can't be . . . "

"I have never been more serious in my life."

"But, sir. They'd think we were crazy."

"Not when we finish," the Admiral replied firmly. "Not after we've shown them how Systems Analysis has crippled the Navy, criminally endangered the national security, driven so many of our best people into retirement . . . reduced this country to a *second-rate* naval power."

Monty stared at Admiral Zimmerman, holding his breath.

"And, Monty," the Admiral said, voice falling to a low pitch, "I'm depending on you to help me. I can't depend on Starr. He's too impulsive. Playing war games in Flag Plot! This is not his cup of tea."

Monty swallowed the remnant of the hard candy. He felt a knot growing in his stomach.

"I know what you're thinking," the Admiral went on in a kindly tone. "You're thinking this could cost you your stars. That I'm using you. True?"

"No, sir . . . " Monty faltered.

"Let me tell you something," the Admiral said, leaning forward over the desk, speaking earnestly. "From the day you set foot in the Naval Academy, you were trained in courage, in duty, honor. To put the interests of your government before your own personal interests. Damn the torpedoes. Don't give up the ship. Now, Monty, in real combat, courage comes easy. There is the enemy. You command from the bridge. You attack—or you resist attack, to your utmost ability. You don't have a choice, really. Here, in Washington, courage does not come so easy. The issues are never so clear-cut as kill or be killed. You can fog them up with a memo. You can evade, hide behind the classic bureaucratic on-the-one-hand and on-the-other-hand. You can go along, follow the path of least resistance. Don't rock the boat. I have seen thousands of people perform that way in a bureaucracy. They rise, too. Up and up. Two stars. Three. Four. But that is why we have such utter mediocrity in our high command!"

The Admiral slammed his palm on the desk again. Monty shifted in his chair, waiting.

"But," Zimmerman went on, "what about self-respect? Do they sleep at night, knowing they are not doing their best for the Navy? Their country? Do you think they sleep?"

"I don't know, sir," Monty replied.

"Hypocrites!" the Admiral snarled. "Goddamned hypocrites. Why live at all? What has their life counted for?"

Monty remained silent, eyes on the Admiral.

"I had to make a decision years ago," the Admiral said, voice again going to a low pitch. "If I had laid low, gone along with the system, I might have got a shipyard command, an easy berth, serving out my time, building up retirement pay, then I might have gone off to live a quiet, blissful life, spared being dragged through the press and Congress. Let the *Nautilus* go down the drain. Nobody cared. I was trying to help them, and they wouldn't even listen. Then one night, I thought long and hard about courage. . . . "

"Admiral," Monty cut in suddenly, "you can depend on me to do what you think is best for the Submarine Force. The Navy. That's what I'm here for. It's my duty. I'll do my best, come what may."

Monty stood up, and approached the large desk, offering his hand, as if to seal a deal. The Admiral shook hands, limply and hurriedly, as though he found human touch embarrassing or distasteful. Monty picked up another hard candy and left the office, going through the passageways, the throngs who were leaving the building, work done, or set aside for another day.

★ 17 ★

As Nancy walked into her front foyer, calling out as always to scare off burglars and rapists, she heard the telephone ringing. She ran down the hall to the kitchen. It was Scottie MacIntosh.

"Nancy? I've been trying to reach you."

"I've been out again," she replied, feeling guilty. What if Paul had tried to call?

"The stock closed down nine points," Scottie said in an apologetic tone.

"God!" Nancy gasped. Nine points. Nine thousand dollars.

"I think that is probably the worst of it," MacIntosh went on. "I talked to Buzz again. He seemed absolutely confident that whatever he has in the works will pull it back by the end of the week."

"I see."

"My advice is still to hang on. You've got plenty of paper profit. Room enough to absorb a swing like this."

"All right," Nancy replied. She would have to discuss it with Monty. It was his money, too. She rang off, feeling downcast. The equivalent of half a year's pay, down the drain.

For the next hour she busied herself with make-work. She polished the silver picture frames on the piano. She wrote a letter to her younger sister who lived in Seattle. She reread Mike's letter, wincing. Then she got out the standing rib roast and prepared it for the oven. From now on, she thought with satisfaction, she would no longer be in competition with those fabulous cooks in the submarine wardrooms.

The sun set, bringing on the most uneasy time of day for Nancy. The hours between sunset and seven, when Monty usually came home, were the hours when, by her reckoning from newspaper accounts, most violent crimes were committed. She rechecked the locks on the back door, then the front, snapping on the front-stoop light. Then she turned on lights all over the house and sat in the wing chair by the fireplace, picking up her needlepoint. The telephone rang again, shattering the stillness of the house. She leaped up, hurrying to the kitchen, lifted the telephone from the cradle. It was a woman's voice, strange, loud, clear.

"Mrs. King? This is Mrs. Adams—Linda's mother."

Linda? Nancy thought. Linda Adams? She sat down on her desk chair in confusion.

"Who?" Nancy asked.

"I'm Linda's mother. I assume Mr. Olsen at Wisconsin called you? He called me this afternoon and said he had talked to you. That we might want to coordinate."

"Mr. Olsen?" Nancy replied.

"Oh," the woman said. "I thought they called you. He said . . . "

With a rush of mental images, heaping atop one another, Nancy realized who was calling. It was the girl's mother. Paul's girl.

"I'm sorry," Nancy cut in. "My husband was to telephone the university. He's still not home from the office. I didn't know the outcome. Is there some word?"

"No," the woman said. "Have *you* heard anything?"

"Nothing," Nancy sighed.

"I'm terribly upset," the woman was saying, with what Nancy believed at first was a slight lisp. Then suddenly, she was reminded of Sue Byerston . . . the slurry way she talked after two martinis. So, Mrs. Adams was a drinker— an alcoholic—like Sue? Perhaps that explained Linda. Unhappy home, no love, taking Paul away. . . .

"I can't blame you for being upset," Nancy replied, knowing her words were hopelessly inadequate. "So are we."

"Linda's never done anything like this," the woman went on, slurring her words slightly. Her accent was Midwestern. Nasal. Yet, it seemed, well-bred. "She has always been very sweet, very . . . what shall I say? Innocent and unworldly. Last year, she was on the dean's list. Do you have any idea where they might be?"

Nancy bridled at the implication It was Paul's fault. Paul had deflowered her poor little Linda.

"Of course not," Nancy replied coolly. "Frankly, I was

stunned when I heard Paul had left with a woman. He's very shy with girls."

"I would hardly call Linda a woman," the voice said, with an ironic laugh. "A twenty-year old student. Well, that's neither here nor there, anyway. The thing is, what do we do? Do you think we should notify the police or the missing-persons bureau?"

Nancy pondered this. She was unwilling to commit herself, plan a course of "coordination," until she had talked to Monty. She did not know what he knew. Perhaps, by now, he had some ideas.

"Why don't I have my husband call your husband when he comes in . . . after dinner?"

"I don't have a husband," the woman said.

Nancy thought: A widow? Divorcee? A fatherless child. That could explain a great deal about Linda.

"Oh, I'm sorry," Nancy said. "In that case . . . "

"We were divorced five years ago. Fred ran off with his secretary. He lives in London."

Nancy felt the woman wanted to say much more, as though the saying of it could shed some light, or reinforce her position, relieve her of blame. But, though she was curious, Nancy did not really want to hear a tale of divorce.

"He doesn't see much of the children," the woman went on. "Especially Linda, who no longer speaks to him. She was very bitter about it." She seemed proud of that fact.

"Yes, I can understand that," Nancy said.

"He has to pay the tuition by the terms of our property settlement," the woman continued. "But I don't know what happens now . . . the legal side of it. I suppose she forfeits her education, don't you think?"

"I don't know, really . . . " Nancy replied. She knew nothing about divorce settlements. No one she knew well had ever been divorced. Navy people really couldn't afford divorces, although she had heard the rate was going up, as everywhere. A divorced officer had no chance to advance. That was an unwritten rule of the Selection Board. If you couldn't advance, you couldn't afford divorce. Wishing not to be drawn deeper into the woman's intimate affairs, she added: "Where do you live, Mrs. Adams? What's your number?"

"Springfield." She gave her number.

Springfield, Nancy thought. Missouri? Capital of Missouri? Lincoln's tomb? Not in Missouri. As if reading her thoughts, the woman said:

"Illinois. *Not* Missouri or Massachusetts."

"Oh," Nancy said, sheepishly, jotting this down, growing anxious about the cost of the call. In their family, long-distance calls were rare, always terse, businesslike and only for conveying vital news. Births. Marriages. Deaths. If this woman was divorced, she must be hard up for money. How could she be so casual on long distance?

"You're Navy, I take it?" the woman went on.

"Yes," Nancy said.

"Fred was in the Navy during the war. A lawyer. Judge Advocate's Office. He went in a JG, came out a Commander. He didn't see any combat, but he certainly took to the Navy. He was stationed at the Great Lakes Naval Training Center. I don't think he ever saw a ship. . . . "

She said the last derisively. Yet, hearing this, Nancy's view of the family changed radically. She felt a bond, a kinship. Anybody who could rise from JG to Commander in two or three years—even in wartime—must be brilliant, competent, rich or politically well-connected. Perhaps there were two sides to this divorce. Maybe the woman had a serious drinking problem. Nancy felt herself instinctively siding with the husband.

"Well . . . " Nancy put in.

"Linda wrote me about Paul," the woman went on. "I feel I almost know him. She says he is very talented musically and very *creative*—the photography."

"Yes," Nancy replied. "He has a strong creative streak." Probably inherited from Monty's mother, Nancy thought.

"I think Paul has a powerful hold over Linda," Mrs. Adams said.

Nancy laughed into the phone at this suggestion, but inwardly she was growing impatient and angry. Again, the implication was clear: whatever was done, it was Paul's fault. Again, she came to her son's defense.

"Knowing Paul, I think it was probably the other way around."

"Linda is easily led," the woman rejoined.

"I imagine there is much we don't know," Nancy said judiciously. "Shall I have my husband call you later? I've got to get dinner on. And I'm beginning to worry about your phone bill."

"Well I'm worried about my daughter," the woman replied, with a reproving tone. She added: "All right, thank you. And please call collect if you hear anything at all. Any time of night."

Nancy resented the "collect." If there was news, she would call at her own expense. But she let this pass, ringing off politely, yet insistently.

Returning to her chair, Nancy was suddenly reminded of Alma Caldwell's advice. Get professional help. But whom? To her knowledge, no one she knew was seeing, or had ever seen, a psychiatrist. In the Navy, that could ruin a career, no less than divorce or alcoholism. She remembered the name Brainard Douglas, author of the unpublished doctoral thesis on Navy wives. Might he be in the Washington telephone book?

She returned to the kitchen, to her desk, where she kept the thick phone book. Yes. His name was there, followed by an M.D., which meant, in all probability, he had gone from psychology to psychiatry, medical school. He was legitimate. She jotted his office and home numbers on a scratch pad. Then she returned to her needlepoint.

★ 18 ★

It was dark and cold and raining hard when Monty left the Pentagon. He opened his umbrella, put his head down, and hurried over the dimly lit pedestrian ramp toward South Parking. On the way, he passed the encampment of protesters. These were young antimilitary pickets who, each night, came from their tents to stand behind police barricades and jeer at the people leaving the Pentagon. A dozen of them were standing in the rain, holding a poncho over their shaggy heads.

"Make love," a young man called to Monty.

He hurried to the VW, parked in the S-3 section, lane 11, reserved for small cars. By now, the lane was deserted. He unlocked the door, climbed in and drove off, swinging into the cloverleaf, and then onto Shirley Highway, a massive ten-lane Interstate. Thirty minutes later, at 7:10, he pulled into his driveway.

On the stoop, beneath the overhang, he paused, brushing the water from his coat, scraping the mud from his shoes on the mat. He pushed the lighted doorbell. Through the two small leaded windows in the door, he saw Nancy in the foyer. She peeped out, smiling recognition, then undid the chains and bolt and swung open the door.

In the foyer, he gave his wife a peck on the cheek. She took his raincoat and said: "The girl's mother, Mrs. Adams, called."

"Did she know anything?"

"No. Nothing."

"I found out a little about the girl," Monty said, going to the kitchen. "God, that smells good. I'm starved. What is it?"

"Roast beef."

"Good. The girl, Linda, is a protester type. A radical."

The highball glasses, ice bucket, tongs, jigger and the fifth of Scotch—Old Scott, a four-dollar Commissary special —stood on the sideboard, where Nancy had arranged them. Monty carefully poured a level jigger for each glass, then added plain water. They went to the living room, Nancy bringing a silver tray with Brie and Camembert and smoked oysters. Nancy recounted her conversation with Mrs. Adams.

"Did you have a rough day?" she asked.

"Yes," he said, sipping the drink, thinking of Zempfke. Then the stock. He said, "Honey, what the hell are we going to do about that damned stock. I didn't get a chance to call Scottie. If anybody found out . . . "

"Did you see what happened to it today?"

"I heard it was dropping."

"Nine points. Nine thousand dollars."

"Wow!" Monty said. "But what are we going to do?"

"Scottie called and said hang on. He said Buzz Creighton said it would come back by the end of the week."

"Naturally he'd say that. God, honey, do you realize I could be hanged for this?"

"Why? Nobody knows but Scottie. The stock's in a street name."

"What does that mean?"

"It's being held in the name of a brokerage house."

"You mean it's not actually in your name?"

"No."

"Why didn't you tell me that? I've been worried sick."

"You didn't give me a chance."

"Well. . . . "

"There's nothing to do but hang on. We can't sell out now and lose nine thousand dollars. That'd be crazy."

"I suppose so. Look, honey. It's your money. You do what you think best. All right? Hell, I'm all involved in a damned fight in the office which could affect the stock. I can't be directly involved. That would surely be unethical."

"All right. I heard there might be a budget cut."

"There might be. A big one."

"I told you so. Now, what's going to happen to the Navy?"

"I don't know. God, a terrible thing happened today. The police called me down and told me they'd caught Zempfke forging parking permits. Starr blew his stack and kicked him the hell out of the office. Now he wants to lift his security clearance."

"For forging a parking permit? That's ridiculous."

"The Pentagon police are making a federal case out of it."

"Anything to shaft the Navy."

"Poor Zempfke. This is going to finish him."

"Can't you help him?"

"I don't see how."

"You've *got* to help him, Monty."

"Starr's afraid it might get in the papers."

"And you'd be blamed?"

"Sort of. Oh hell, let's not talk about it. What kind of day did you have?"

"Interesting."

"What did you do?"

"I met a very charming older man, gray-haired, but European. Very suave. We went to Chez Vendôme for lunch. Very good Rhine wine. Then he invited me to his hotel to see his etchings."

"Sure."

"He found me very interesting. He asked my opinion on things. He thought I had a youthful figure."

"Swell."

"It was nice to have *somebody* make love to me."

"All right. You win."

"Actually, it was Commissary day. I had a nice, long chat with Alma."

"What did you talk about?"

"Oh, just girl talk."

"You didn't say anything about . . . ?"

"Yes, I did. I told her what I hoped you'd do."

"Nancy! You shouldn't have."

"Why not? I have a right."

"She'll tell Jim and he'll spread it all over. You could ruin . . . "

"She will *not* tell Jim."

"How do you know?"

"Because she's my best friend."

"I wouldn't count on that. Jim Caldwell is playing it *very* cool. He wants those stars so bad he can taste them."

"It makes me *sick*. Listen to you. You're all poisoned."

"Now, honey—cool down. You only get one crack . . . "

"Oh shit!"

She jumped up and went to the kitchen to serve the dinner. They ate in silence. When the dishes had been cleared away, Monty said:

"I'm sorry, honey. I was out of line."

"I'm sorry, too."

"Maybe he'll call tonight."

"I hope so. I keep having this mental picture of him lying in a road someplace, a ditch. Dead."

"Don't. I'm sure he's all right."

"When we find him, we've got to get some professional help, Monty. A psychiatrist."

"What he needs most is a good talking to. A firm hand."

"No. I think he better have professional help. And don't worry. I won't spread it around."

"I didn't . . . "

"I won't even tell Alma. Although she was the one who suggested it."

"We'll talk about it later—when we find him. Hell, he might be in better shape than both of us."

"Perhaps."

They returned to the living room.

"I'd like to go over the finances with you in detail," Nancy said.

"What finances?"

"Our retirement finances."

"Can't we do that tomorrow night? I've got a huge load of paperwork. Tomorrow . . . "

"It's always tomorrow. I've lived my whole life waiting for that glorious, wonderful tomorrow."

She sat down, picked up her needlepoint. Monty worked for two hours in the den, going carefully through Admiral Starr's paperwork. When he emerged, Nancy had gone to bed. He shut off the lights, turned down the heat and went to the bedroom, snapped on the bedside light. Nancy was crying.

"Turn off the light," she sobbed, angrily.

He turned the light off, sat down on the bed, put his hand on her shoulder.

"All right," he said, "let's talk. Come on, we'll have some coffee in the kitchen. . . . "

"No!" she said, voice low. "Get out. Get away from me. You don't want me. Leave me alone."

"Nancy, for God's sake."

"Go back to your damned papers and leave me alone."

They heard the soft chimes of the front door bell.

"Who in hell . . . ?" Monty said.

He went into the front hallway, snapped on the front-stoop light, peered through the little window. He could see two shapes, backs of heads. Unfamiliar. Then, at the window, full-face, a young boy, familiar dark eyes.

Paul!

My God! Monty thought, undoing the chains, the bolt, swinging open the door. There, in the light of the stoop, he saw an astonishing sight. Paul, with a scraggly beard, hair down to his shoulders, wearing beads, some kind of Indian outfit, with an enormous A-frame pack on his back.

Standing beside him, a girl with long blonde hair, low-slung bell-bottom slacks and corduroy jacket, wearing granny glasses, and though soaking wet and bedraggled, strikingly beautiful, eyes round behind the glasses, and blue and deep. She too had an enormous pack on her back.

Linda! he thought.

Monty stepped back. The two young people walked boldly into the foyer, wearing leather sandals, dripping water in little pools on the tiles. The girl looked around inquisitively, blinking against the glare of the light. Then wordlessly, they shed the packs, stacking them against the wall.

Nancy rushed up the hallway.

"Paul!" she cried, throwing her arms around his neck, kissing him. "You're soaked. Get out of those clothes. Where have you been? Why didn't you call?"

Paul said nothing. His eyes traveled to the tile floor, the pools of water.

"I'm Linda Adams," the girl said.

"I know," Nancy replied coolly. "Your mother called."

"How . . . ?"

"It's a long story. You can call her after you change into dry clothes. Chop, chop. Hot showers, before you both catch your death."

Paul leaned to pick up his pack. He seemed to lose his balance, and half-fell, in slow-motion, against the wall, as though he were drunk. Linda leaped to grab him, a lithe, graceful motion.

"Come on, love," she said in her husky voice. Then she picked up both packs, half-hanging each on a shoulder. Monty moved to help, but she said: "That's all right. The one balances the other."

Nancy led the way down the hallway. At her bedroom door, Nancy stopped. "You can use our bathroom," she said to Linda. "Paul can dress in his room."

"That's all right," Linda said in the strange, husky voice. "I better look after Paul. He's coming off a bummer."

"A what?" Nancy said.

"Don't get uptight," the girl said. "He'll be all right."

"What's the matter with him?" Nancy said coldly.

"He had a bad trip. Please, if you don't mind, the packs are heavy."

Nancy led the way to Paul's room. It was just as he had left it at Christmas. Twin beds, primly made. The photographic gear—developing tank, enlarger—in the corner. Some of his better pictures hung on the wall, supported by tiny clamps. Linda dropped the packs. Paul sat down on the bed, humming inanely. The girl put both of her hands in his soaked, matted hair and said: "We're safe now, Paul."

Paul nodded silently. Nancy looked on.

"Thank you," Linda said to Nancy. "This is very nice."

Nancy went to the hall closet for soap and towels. While she was rummaging, Linda closed the bedroom door. Monty came from the foyer. He looked at the closed door, then at Nancy.

"What's wrong with Paul?" he said.

"He's drunk," Nancy said. "At least, I *hope* he's drunk."

"He looks like he's been drugged."

"Or . . ."

"I'll get some coffee," Monty said.

Nancy returned to the bedroom. The girl was kneeling on the floor by the packs, unbuckling the straps, pulling the filthy clothes out, strewing them on the floor. Paul was lying back on the pillow, eyes on the ceiling.

"Do you have a washing machine?" the girl asked, pulling her hair from her eyes.

"Yes," Nancy said.

"Good. Everything is filthy. I was going to go to a laundromat, but we didn't have enough money."

"You could have called," Nancy said. "Me, or your mother."

The girl stood up, took the towels, placed them carefully on the bed by Paul's feet.

"Has he been taking drugs?" Nancy said to Linda.

"Yes."

Nancy's heart thudded. She felt panicky.

"What kind?"

"Acid."

"What?"

"Acid. A kind of LSD . . . but, we got some bad cubes, I think. In Indiana. You can't trust what you get on the road. I should have known better. Paul was in bad shape. Paranoid. He tried to jump out of a window."

Nancy looked down at Paul. My God in Heaven! She ran to Monty in the kitchen.

"He's in some kind of drug shock," Nancy said, trying to stay calm. "She said he'd been taking acid. LSD. Tried to jump out of a window."

"God," Monty said.

"Monty, please be gentle with Paul. We don't know what we're into now."

"I know."

Monty carried two cups of coffee to the back hall. The bedroom door was closed again. He tapped on it with his foot.

"Yes?" the girl answered.

"Coffee," Monty said, forcing cheer.

"Just a minute," the girl sang out in her husky voice.

The door opened. The girl stood there, with a look of surprise. She was naked from the waist up. Her long blonde hair fell forward, partially hiding her firm, full, youthful breasts. Stunned, Monty offered the two cups, one in each hand, keeping his eyes level on the girl's face, determined not to look at her breasts.

"Excuse me," she said. "I thought you were leaving them on the floor. Thank you." She took the cups unsteadily, closing the door with her bare foot. Monty heard her say: "Paul? Paul? Here, love. Drink this coffee. Sit up. . . . "

Monty went back to the kitchen.

"We better call a doctor," Nancy said.

"Could a doctor give him anything that would help?"

"I don't know. Go ask Linda."

Monty returned to the door, knocked. He could hear the shower running. The water stopped. He knocked again.

"Yes?" she called.

"Do you think we should get a doctor?" he called through the door.

"No. No." Her voice was louder, closer.

She opened the door again. She now wore two towels, one around her waist, one around her bosom, ingeniously knotted. Her hair was wet, plastered to her cheeks and shoulders. Monty looked at Paul. She had removed his wet clothes, laid a towel over his waist. His eyes were closed. The room was a shambles of clothes, thrown everywhere.

"He's had a tranquilizer," she said, taking another towel, fluffing her hair. "That's all a doctor would give him. He'll be all right."

"Did he really try to jump out of a window?" Monty said.

"Yes," she said. "A bad scene. *Very* bad."

"Has he tried to do that before?"

"I don't think so. He said not."

"Where have you two been?"

"On the road. Hitching rides."

"What are your plans?"

She looked at him thoughtfully.

"My plans are to try to stop you from building ULMS."

"ULMS! What the hell do you know about ULMS?"

"A great deal," the girl said, defiantly.

She leaned down and fished through the pile of clothes on the floor. She held aloft a cloth banner with neat, black lettering. It said:

FUCK WAR

"How do you like that, Captain King?"

Monty stared at the banner, the girl, speechless. She

tossed the banner aside, then picked up a thin, cotton dress. She slipped it over her head. The towels fell away. Monty saw the birthmark on her upper right thigh—an irregular brown spot, the size of a half dollar. Then the brief dress fell to mid-thigh, covering her.

"It's clean," she said. "I was saving it."

She rummaged on the floor, found her beads. She put these over her head. They lay in between her breasts.

Nancy came from the kitchen.

"She says he doesn't need a doctor," Monty said to Nancy. "He's had a tranquilizer."

"He'll be all right," Linda said to Nancy.

"Take your things to the guest room," Nancy said to the girl. "I'll look after Paul. Monty, get me some pajamas. Then, Linda, you call your mother."

"I'd better look after Paul," the girl said. "If he wakes up, he may not know where he is. He may be afraid."

"Let's take that chance," Nancy said firmly.

"All right," Linda gave in.

"Call your mother," Nancy said. "There's a phone in our bedroom."

Linda went into the bedroom. She returned a moment later.

"There's no answer. She's probably stoned—passed out. I've never been able to call her after nine o'clock. By then she doesn't know whether she's coming or going."

"Well, call her first thing tomorrow."

"All right," Linda said, yawning, going to the guest room.

Nancy put the pajamas on Paul, covered him with a blanket. Monty shut off the hall lights and locked the front door again. Then he joined Nancy in the bedroom.

"We're going to get professional help," Nancy said. "Tomorrow."

"I guess we better."

"Poor thing. I left the light on, in case he wakes up."

"Good."

They got undressed and into bed. Monty snapped off the bedside light.

"You know what the girl told me?" he said to his wife. "She said she was here to stop me from making ULMS. Can you beat that? She's got a banner . . . "

"Ridiculous child. Aren't you going to kiss me goodnight?"

He kissed her lightly, then rolled over, dead tired. In a moment they were both asleep.

Monty dreamed that he was being pursued by the un-identified submerged contact. It was a nightmarish chase, through the deeps, without letup, each moment bringing a new crisis. Then, suddenly, he was wide awake, aware of a monumental din. Nancy awoke too, calling out: "What in the world?"

Monty shook his head, bounded from bed. It was the piano. Someone playing loud, a deafening noise.

"Paul!" Nancy said, leaping up, pulling on her house-coat. "My God!"

They ran down the hallway, stumbling in the dark. The girl, Linda, rushed from the guest room, naked, colliding with Nancy in the hall. She was shouting: "Paul! Paul!" Monty snapped on a light.

"Get your *clothes* on," Nancy hissed at the girl.

Paul was seated on the piano bench in pajamas, playing furiously. Nancy turned on a lamp. Monty came behind her, stopped, stared at this long-haired creature who was his son, bent over the keyboard, playing maniacally. Jesus H. Christ! he thought.

Linda raced into the living room, shouting: "He's trip-ping again. Paul! Paul!"

She rounded the piano bench and clutched him from behind, holding him. Nancy cried again at the girl: "Get out of here. Let him go." Then to Monty, "Make her . . . "

Nancy ran behind the piano, tearing the girl's arms from Paul. Paul, bent to the piano, went on playing, as though entranced. Then, suddenly, he stopped, got up, walked around the piano toward his father. He was steady now. Nancy and Linda watched from behind the piano. Monty looked at his son and said: "It's late, Paul. Why don't we all go to bed?"

"Get away from me . . ." Paul shouted at his father, backing. "Get away from me. . . ."

His eyes were black with terror. Monty raised a hand, unconsciously, an offer of help.

Paul flinched, stepping backward, as though warding off a blow.

"Stop him," he shouted. "Stop him . . . the fucking bum . . . fucking bum is trying to kill me . . . kill me. . . ."

Monty stepped forward.

"Fucking bum . . ." Paul shouted again.

He spit in his father's face. Monty reeled back, overcome by rage. He swung. His fist smashed into Paul's jaw and nose. Paul sank to his knees, blood running from his nose to the carpet. Monty stood over him panting, heart thudding, palms wet.

"You creep," he said, spitting the words. "Don't you call *me* a bum. And don't you ever use language like that in front of your mother."

"Monty!" Nancy cried out. "Monty! Get away. Get away."

She ran to Paul. With Linda's help, she picked him up and half-dragged him back to his bedroom. When they were gone, Monty went into the kitchen and poured a strong drink. He drank it down straight, coughing as the fluid burned to his stomach. Then he felt a pain in his back. The disc.

"My God," he said aloud, staring down into the sink. "What have I done?"

★ Book III ★

Tuesday

★ 1 ★

Admiral Starr, wiggling a dead cigar between his front teeth, fixed Monty with a squinty stare and said:

"You look like you got run over by a truck."

"Yes, sir," Monty replied. "I was up late. Paul came home unexpectedly from college."

"Why?"

"He dropped out."

"That's par for the course, these days. You don't get the tuition refunded?"

"No, sir."

"Is your back acting up on you again?"

"Yes, sir. I . . . I slipped on the wet grass, running into the house last night."

"Oh. Well, take care of your health. Your back goes . . . that's all she wrote. You're no good disabled."

"No, sir."

"You see this report from *Sargo*?" the Admiral said, pawing through the papers on his desk. He passed a radio message to Monty. It was from the nuclear-attack sub *Sargo*, SSN 583. It read:

> ARRIVED AREA BAKER-SIXTEEN AT 1945 Z BREAK
> COMMENCED SEARCH BREAK NO CONTACT BREAK
> ANTICIPATING RENDEZVOUS WITH SCULPIN AND
> BARB AND TULLIBEE NEXT FOUR HOURS BREAK WILL
> COORDINATE SEARCH. BT

"I'll have to get over to Flag Plot and help with the search," Starr said. "You hold down the fort."

"Sir, you haven't forgotten the SecDef meeting at 1400?"

"No. I'll be available for that."

"We're sort of shorthanded. Watson's in New London. Pierce called in sick. Cosby's on annual leave. . . . I don't even have an assistant briefer."

"What about your new boy, T . . . Tasker?"

"Trimble, Admiral. But he's green. . . . I've got him working on a Threat paper."

"What else?"

"Sir, I've been thinking," Monty said. "It seems to me that lifting Zempfke's security clearance is an overly harsh measure. Do you know what's involved? We've got to send copies to every branch of the government. FBI. CIA. Army. Air Force. DOD. A dozen others. Then you get in this fantastic legal proceeding. Under the law, he's entitled to a hearing to contest it. We have to spend hours and hours. And then, Admiral, he's not really been found guilty of anything yet. He hasn't even been formally charged. It seems to me we could at least wait until after he appears before the Magistrate tomorrow. Otherwise, we're in the position of declaring a man guilty before his trial. I think it might even be unconstitutional. We don't have a damned thing in writing from Lambert, the CID man. Just an oral deal. So . . . "

"Oh, hell," the Admiral grumbled. "All right."

"We can take another look at it tomorrow," Monty went on. "Besides that, sir, I'm plain running out of time."

The Admiral fixed Monty with a squinty stare again. Then he snapped his fingers.

"I think I've got it," he said. "Call up the Bethesda Naval Medical Center. Get him over to a headshrinker. Tell the shrink Zempfke's been working fourteen hours a day . . . he cracked up. Did this thing. Then maybe we can get him off with a medical . . . "

"Sir, I don't think . . . "

"Do as I say, Monty."

"Yes, sir, Admiral."

"What else?"

"That's all for the moment, Admiral. Would you please take time to go over some of these papers?"

"All right."

Monty returned to his desk, walking stiffly, favoring his back.

Yeoman Armbruster called from his desk.

"Sir, Captain Caldwell on Line two."

Monty, standing by his desk, punched the Line 2 button, glancing at the wall clock. It was 1030. He was already dead tired. He had not slept well. Despite five cups of coffee, he could not think clearly.

"Captain King," he answered, curtly.

"Monty? Jim Caldwell. Would you mind telling me what the hell's going on? My boss just landed on me with both feet."

Monty sat down gingerly. He replied:

"All I know is that when I got in this morning, I got instructions from Admiral Zimmerman's office to prepare for a meeting with OSD at 1400—to review the submarine picture."

"Did he coordinate with anybody at all?"

"As I understand it," Monty said carefully, "he cleared it direct with CNO."

"Why didn't he clear it with *this* office?" Caldwell asked in an injured tone.

"I don't know. Maybe he's holding you in reserve."

"He *can't* go on making these end runs, dammit. The Secretary's furious. He's *got* to stay in channels."

"Jim. Be reasonable. You know Zimmerman as well as I do. He doesn't even know what a channel *is*."

"It's time he learned."

"It's a little late for that."

"How did the meeting come about? Did Zimmerman propose it?"

"I'm not sure," Monty evaded. "We had a press release over in OSD on the ULMS long lead-time hardware. It went aground in Systems Analysis and then the upshot was SecDef called for the review. I assume he wants the full picture before he O.K.'s the release. Who knows? We cleared that press release with your office."

"Yes, I know."

"Why don't you tell the Secretary that and explain that it got hung up in OSD and SecDef called this meeting."

"His nose is still going to be out of joint. From now on, I wish you people would make an effort to keep us informed. It would make my life a hell of a lot easier."

"O.K., Jim. Sorry."

Monty hung up. He had not been entirely frank with Jim Caldwell. Part of Zimmerman's plan, as the Admiral had explained it to Monty earlier that morning, was to bypass SecNav's office, to save time, to avoid a possible roadblock. Perhaps he had other reasons, personal or otherwise.

Another phone call. It was Art Pendleton in the Office of Congressional Liaison. Art, a classmate, was the deputy. His boss, Admiral McInnerney, was one of the Navy's most adroit diplomats and artful persuaders. He had served on the Peace Negotiating Teams in Asia, the Middle East, and with the oily NATO brass at SHAPE. Now he was wining and dining senators and representatives, adroitly coordinating Navy business with the Congress. He had, among other gifts, a cast-iron stomach. Or so Monty had heard.

"Monty, I hate to gig you," Art Pendleton said, "but you've got some congressional mail overdue."

Monty felt a sinking sensation. His eyes went to his attaché case, the unedited, unprocessed mail with the pink buck slips—all overdue. It was the first offense for OP-31.

"I'm sorry, Art. We got hit with a bucket of shit yesterday. A SecDef-level briefing today at 1400. My people got the stuff all ready for you. I just didn't have time to look at it. It's my fault."

"I was sure it must be something special," Pendleton said. "But you know how the Admiral is—what the policy is. If we didn't keep a tickler file here, if we let it all begin to slip, everybody would fall behind, and then . . . "

"Yeah, I know," Monty said. "Look, I'll have it in your In box by six o'clock, without fail."

Monty remembered with a jolt that Admiral McInnerney would sit on his Selection Board. He did not know Mc-Innerney except by reputation. Art Pendleton was a competitor for selection. If Art was so inclined, he could report Monty's lapse to his Admiral, perhaps with profit to himself. But, no, he thought, how could he think such petty thoughts?

"That'll be O.K., Monty. Thanks a lot. Sorry to bother you."

"No sweat," Monty replied, hanging up, feeling that he had failed an important duty.

Captain Howard Shanks ambled into the office. He was a tall, gaunt man, an aviator, with deep green eyes. He was Deputy Director, OP-34, the Strike Warfare Division, which served the carrier forces much as OP-31 served the Submarine Force. Shanks was an articulate salesman for the aircraft carrier, a tough opponent in a debate—or a budget fight.

"What's this we hear about a SecDef-level submarine review?" he asked, the smile vanishing. "Nobody coordinated with us or OP-03."

"It's a Zimmerman special," Monty said.

"Well, to hell with that," Shanks said. "We've heard about the budget cut. And now, here you are making an end run to SecDef."

"SecDef called the meeting. . . . "

"You've got to coordinate with OP-34 and OP-03. We're going to present a unified picture."

"It has nothing to do with the budget cut . . . "

"You'll be up there selling submarines."

"We're going up there to answer questions."

"You're going up there to sell him ULMS, Monty, and my boss is going through the overhead."

His boss, Director OP-34, was Admiral Bascum, another aviator. Damn, Monty thought. When Zimmerman started making waves, it rocked the whole Navy Department.

"Well . . . " Monty began, wondering how best to placate Shanks, to protect OP-31. There was no time to coordinate with OP-34 and OP-03. There was barely time to pull together the paperwork they needed for the 1400 meeting with SecDef. Yeoman Armbruster interrupted again.

"Admiral Leggett's office on Line one."

"Excuse me," Monty said to Shanks, picking up the phone. Admiral Leggett was OP-03, Deputy Chief of Naval Operations for Fleet Operations and Readiness, the next echelon up, boss of both OP-31 and OP-34. Leggett, an aviator, was new in the job. Monty had never met him, never briefed him. He, too, would serve on the Selection Board. Monty answered the phone crisply.

"Monty? Paul Crimmons here."

Captain Crimmons, another aviator, was Admiral Leggett's Chief of Staff. Like Shanks, he was a classmate. Yet another competitor. He was a good man. Monty had got to know him well on this tour.

" . . . listen, can you fill me in on what's going on? The Admiral just got word from OP-34, Admiral Bascom's in a real swivet."

Admiral Starr came out of his office, cigar jutting. He looked at Shanks with an exaggerated scowl.

"Lock up the papers," he said, turning to Armbruster. Then he punched Shanks playfully in the ribs.

"Who let a brown-shoe aviator in here?" Starr asked, winking at Shanks.

Shanks smiled respectfully. Admiral Starr would sit on

the Selection Board, casting an equal vote with his boss, Admiral Bascum. Monty talked on the phone to Crimmons, explaining carefully, diplomatically.

"Sir," Shanks said to Starr, "my boss asked me to come over and find out what you people are laying on with SecDef this afternoon."

"It's a Zimmerman meeting," Admiral Starr said, winking again. "It's been cleared down through CNO."

Shanks nodded.

"Anything else?" the Admiral added.

"No, sir. Thank you very much, sir."

Shanks turned and walked smartly to the door.

"How do you suppose that tall drink of water ever squeezed into a fighter plane?" Starr wondered aloud. Then to Monty: "You didn't tell him anything?"

"No, sir," Monty said, following Starr into his office. "Sir, Admiral Bascum called Admiral Leggett and accused us of making an end run to SecDef. Leggett blew his stack, according to Crimmons, and wants a meeting at 1100 with all of us to go over the whole Navy picture. Crimmons said Leggett said *nobody* in his division was going direct to Sec-Def, without first touching base with his shop. Moreover, he wants a unified picture going up to CNO to SecNav to SecDef . . . "

"There's no time for all that," Starr replied angrily. "Did you tell him it was a Zimmerman special?"

"Yes, sir. Crimmons reported Admiral Leggett to have replied 'fuck Zimmerman' and 'Zimmerman isn't running the Navy.' And so on."

"Well, shit," Starr snarled. "We better keep him happy. He's new on the job and nervous. Always was a goddamned old lady. . . . We are all going to be in a goddamned meeting one day and the whole country's going to go right down the tube."

"Yes, sir."

★ 2 ★

Lieutenant Trimble came into the office, carrying his manila folder. He wore a mod, double-breasted jacket and a wide tie, gray flannel slacks and loafers.

"Good morning, Gale, how goes it?" Monty said, glancing uneasily at the clothing. "By the way, we're very short-handed today. I'm going to need you for a briefing at 1100 with OP-03 and then at 1400 with SecDef and Thursday morning on the Hill—Congressman Magruder's committee. See how you get around in this place?"

"Yes, sir. But how am I going to finish?"

"You'll just have to work twice as hard," Monty smiled. "How's the family?"

"Not too good, sir," Trimble frowned.

"What's the problem?"

"I got home very late last night. My wife didn't like being by herself. There's a lot of crime in the neighborhood. She was scared."

"I see," Monty replied.

"She wants to get a house way out in the suburbs, but we can't afford that."

"Oh. Yes. Well . . . let's see what you've written."

Trimble passed four sheets of hand-written copy to Monty. He read swiftly.

"Good . . . excellent," he said to the Lieutenant.

"I couldn't boil it all down into two pages."

"That's all right," Monty said, returning the paper. "This is damned good. Best stuff anybody's ever put together around here."

"Thank you, sir."

"Have you studied the Pentagon map?" Monty asked.

"Some. But I got lost again today. Wandered into the Hall of Heroes, by mistake. That's quite an impressive exhibit."

Monty remembered his first visit to the Hall. It was a walled-off section of A Ring, one of the few sightseeing exhibits in the building. There were Medals of Honor under glass, huge blow-ups of the medals against purple drapes, dramatically lighted, and polished panels with the names of all Medal of Honor winners on little brass plaques.

"I had no idea 3,000 men had won the Medal of Honor," Trimble went on. "How many submariners?"

"Seven."

"I noticed, too," Trimble continued, "the Pentagon walls are covered with damned fine combat art. I'd like to bring my wife down here sometime and show her. She's an artist."

"I didn't know that. My mother used to dabble."

"She's quite talented," Trimble said proudly. "It just popped out about two years ago. She took it up to pass the time in Charleston and turned out to be damned good."

"I don't know exactly who owns the Pentagon art," Monty said. "There's a plaque on the wall down in the Mall Corridor that explains the origin of it all. It says the Army wanted to send out about forty artists during the war, but Congress refused to appropriate the money. So, *Life* magazine hired about twenty of them and paid to send them into combat, then had first publication rights to the pictures. So, maybe *Life* still owns them—or maybe *Life* gave them to the Department of Defense. You're too young to remember the combat paintings in *Life,* I suppose?"

"Yes, sir."

"Well, let's get back to your paper," Monty said, turning to business. "Now that you've dealt with the U.S. and Russian nuclear-powered attack-class boats, go ahead now with the Polaris concept. Tell how both we and the Russians got into that evolution. Do you want me to thumbnail that for you, too?"

"If you don't mind, sir," Trimble said.

Monty said to Armbruster, "Hold my calls for five minutes, please."

Trimble took out his pen, prepared to make notes.

"All right," Monty said, leaning back in his chair, clasping his hands behind his head. "Here we go. To give a little historic perspective, start out by saying the original concept of firing a missile from a submarine goes back to World War Two, the Nazis again. They didn't get far with it, but one must assume the German submarine technicians the Russians got knew about it, and took the idea to Russia. You know, of course, that the Nazis perfected the first long-range missiles. First, the V-1 air-breather, a pilotless aircraft. And second, the ballistic missile, the V-2. Both were fired against London. . . . "

"I'm familiar with that, sir."

"Well, we and the Russians divided up the German missile technicians after the war. We got Wernher von Braun and his bunch, but the Russians got a lot of missile people *and* missiles."

Trimble jotted notes.

"Right after the war, the U.S. Navy got hold of some of the old Nazi V-1s, the little pilotless drones. Somebody on the ComSubLant staff with far-out ideas dreamed up the concept of firing the V-1 from a submarine. They renamed it the *Loon* and messed around with it for years. The *Loon* grew in size and then became the *Regulus*. We converted a couple of Fleet Boats to fire *Regulus*. They had ungainly topside hangars that could hold two birds. But that was a dead-end program. The birds burned liquids . . . jet fuel. . . . It was just too dangerous to store jet fuel on a submarine, you see?"

"Yes, sir," Trimble said, bent over his notes.

"The other thing was, the program wasn't well-funded," Monty continued. "Back in those early days, the Air Force was top dog, with SAC—the Strategic Air Command. They claimed they could win any war with massive retaliation. Manned bombers. Nobody believed in missiles. Not even the Air Force. Even so, the Air Force was opposed to our *Regulus*, small as the program was. The Air Force didn't want the Navy getting into any weapons that might be called *strategic*. You know, long-range, anticity weapons. . . . "

"But what about aircraft carriers?"

"In those days, aircraft carriers were permitted by the Air Force strictly for *tactical* missions. You know, small wars, and so on. The Joint Chiefs of Staff never did assign the carriers important Russian targets. They assumed the carriers would be too vulnerable to get near Europe, or the planes from the carriers couldn't get through. Anyway, you'll hear about carriers at 1100 in the OP-03 briefing. You'll see the competition we're up against around here."

Trimble looked up and waited.

"To go on with the sub-missile thing," Monty continued. "As I said, *Regulus* was a dead end. O.K., meanwhile, as you know, the missile was coming into its own. The early liquid-fuel rockets, *Atlas, Titan, Thor* and *Jupiter*. They were all pretty crude and unreliable and very dangerous to have on board a ship with all that volatile, exotic fuel. The early ones were always blowing up down at Cape Canaveral. So for a period of about five years, it didn't look like the Navy could ever get seriously into the long-range missile picture. The Air Force had cornered the deterrent market again, so to speak. Then, we got the real breakthrough of the solid propellant missile—*Polaris*—which was safe enough to put on a ship. The advantages of putting a solid propellant missile on a nuclear-powered submarine were so obvious and overwhelming that not even the Air

Force could oppose the system. So, with *Polaris*, the Navy, for the first time, got its toe into the long-range strategic deterrent door. We mated Zimmerman's nuclear brainchild with missile technology—and, of course, the Submarine Force really came into its own. It became a significant part of the deterrent, which had been, up to then, an Air-Force monopoly. In fact, the Navy even helped the Air Force. A slightly larger version of *Polaris* became the second-generation Air Force ICBM. The Minuteman."

"I know about that, sir. They taught us that at Annapolis."

"Good. All right, where was I? Oh yes. The *Polaris* missile came along so fast, we didn't have a nuclear-powered missile-firing submarine—a launching platform—to go with it. So, for the first one, they sliced a *Skate*-class attack boat in half—the *Scorpion*—and inserted the *Polaris* missile compartment and renamed it *George Washington*."

"I didn't know that."

"Yep. That's how they got the first one. Of course, they went right into production after that, and built forty more *Polaris* boats, each with the capability of carrying sixteen missiles with a warhead of one megaton . . . I'm sure you know all this. But be sure to put in that the *original Polaris* had a range of only 1,500 miles. Then came the improved *Polaris* missile, with a 2,500-mile range. *Polaris* A3. We had them on *Jones* when you were there, didn't we?"

"Yes, sir. The A3."

"And now, today, we have *Poseidon* to replace the A3. *Poseidon* has a 2,800-mile range. Each *Poseidon* carries ten MIRVed warheads. Always explain what MIRV means: Multiple Independently Targeted Reentry Vehicles. Throw in a further line to explain this means all ten warheads in each *Poseidon* can be targeted to separate targets—or, of course, the same target."

"Yes, sir," Trimble said, jotting.

"Put in also," Monty went on, "that only thirty-one of the

total forty-one *Polaris* boats were converted to *Poseidon*. Explain that the total force will carry thirty-one boats times sixteen missiles times ten warheads, which is a total warheadage of 4,960. You'll get to know that figure very well around here. We use it ten times a day, one way or another."

"I never stopped to think of it in terms of aggregate warheadage," Trimble said. "Five thousand warheads! What do we need all that for?"

"We'll get into that later today . . . keep your ears open. Meanwhile, let's wrap this up. I'm running out of time."

"Yes, sir. Sorry."

"Now, the Russians," Monty went on, staring at his desk top. "In the 1950s, while we were fooling around with the old *Regulus* concept, they were doing the same. But they stuck with it longer and built nuclear-powered boats for their pilotless drones, or as we call them now, cruise missiles. The subs were called, by ONI, *Echo* class. They appeared about the same time as the *November*-class attack boats. Each *Echo* carries eight *Shaddock* cruise missiles. That's a lot of firepower. The reason we believe they stayed with this old bird was to use *Echo-Shaddock* against our surface forces—aircraft carriers—in event of war. They now have thirty nuclear-powered *Echos*. Quite a fleet."

"Are they still building them?" Trimble asked, looking up.

"Not that we know," Monty replied. "All right. In addition, the Russians started messing around with ballistic missiles. The first nuclear-powered ballistic-missile sub was called, by us, *Hotel*. It carried only four Sark or Serb missiles with a range of about six hundred and fifty miles. The *Hotel* was, obviously, the first crude counterweapon to *Polaris*, but with only a fourth the number of missiles of less than half the range. They only built ten *Hotels* . . . not enough to mount any kind of serious threat against our cities. Got that?"

"Yes, sir. Ten *Hotels* with four Sark or Serb missiles. Range six hundred and fifty miles."

"Good," Monty said. "Then, in 1968, they surprised hell out of us. They suddenly showed up with almost an exact copy of *Polaris*, years before ONI thought they would. Or even Zimmerman, I should say, especially Zimmerman. We called their copy of *Polaris: Yankee*. Same size, shape as *Polaris*. Carried same number of missiles—sixteen. So far they have turned out twenty-five *Yankees*. We believe they are building to a force of at least fifty."

Monty paused, waiting for Trimble to catch up with his notes.

"Sir," Trimble said, in a moment, letting his pen rest. "To recap. The Russians have, or will have, a total of ninety nuclear-powered missile submarines. Fifty *Yankees*, thirty *Hotels* and ten *Echos*."

"Yes. They have some old diesel-powered cruise-missile subs too. But we don't include those because of the range factor. They might be used against European targets, but all that gets too complicated for this paper."

"And we have thirty-one *Polaris-Poseidon* and ten old *Polaris* boats. A total of forty-one."

"That's right. And then comes ULMS."

"But, sir," Trimble said, with a puzzled frown. "Frankly, I don't understand. If we already have five thousand independently targetable *Poseidon* warheads, why do we need ULMS? Isn't this enough?"

"Lieutenant," Monty broke in sternly. "That is *one* question we never ask in this office. I'm sorry I haven't had time to explain . . . give you an adequate briefing on ULMS. After you get it, you won't ever ask that question, believe me. Now . . ."

"Sir, I realize that yesterday you told me to burn into my mind the phrase, 'If a weapon can be built, it will be.' But I can't help but wonder. I mean, sir, as the senior, most experienced submarine force, we're continually providing an example, a lead for the Russian submarine force, aren't we? I mean, first we get nuclear-powered attack boats, then they come up with *November* in response. Next we put cruise missiles on our boats, then they come up with *Echo*. Then, with *Polaris*, we go to ballistic missiles. Then they come up with *Hotel*, and then an exact copy of *Polaris: Yankee*. In every instance, it seems to me, these new weapons are more valuable to the Russians than to us. Now, if we proceed with ULMS—"

"Wait a goddamn minute, Lieutenant," Monty broke in, raising his hand. "Suppose we decided *not* to build ULMS and they went ahead anyway? Then just were would we be?"

"Up that same creek without a paddle?"

"Exactly."

"But—"

"I don't have time to argue with you, Lieutenant."

"Yes, sir. But one more question, sir. What am I to do in these briefings today and Thursday up on the Hill? I don't really know a damn thing."

"Lieutenant Trimble," Monty replied, with half a smile. "You will carry my briefing charts, my easel and my pointer. While I am making the presentation, you will change the charts and stand there looking very, very bright. If anybody directs a question to you, you defer to me. Don't worry. In SecDef, they never ask questions. Note this fact well. The Pentagon briefer always has an assistant. It goes back to a selling principle in civilian life, I believe. Two salesmen are always better than one. The theory is, one salesman wouldn't lie in front of another. Shall we say, the practice promotes credibility?"

"I see, sir," Trimble said, rising, frowning, returning to his office.

★ 3 ★

In the Pentagon telephone book, under the heading, "National Naval Medical Center, Psychiatric Division," Monty spotted the name "Rosenwall, Marvin W., Captain, USN." A lucky break, he thought. Rosenwall had made a long cruise with Monty on the *Jones*, to study crew habitability. Monty dialed his extension. A female voice answered.

"This is Captain King calling. May I speak to Captain Rosenwall please?"

"This is Captain Rosenwall's secretary," the woman replied. "The Captain's in a meeting. I'll have him return your call as soon as he's free. Is it a personal matter?"

"No, no," Monty replied hurriedly. "It's official . . . Navy business."

"Can you give me some idea?"

"Miss," Monty said impatiently. "I'm Deputy Director, Submarine Warfare Division, Navy Department. We've got a very serious official problem. My boss, Admiral Starr, insists that I talk to Captain Rosenwall immediately."

"One moment please," the woman replied.

"This is Captain Rosenwall speaking."

It was a clear, precise voice. Monty remembered Rosenwall well. Young. Very young. Dark. Penetrating eyes. A New Yorker. No sense of humor.

"This is Captain King calling. Monty King. You remember me?"

"Of course, Monty. How are you? *Where* are you?"

"I'm in the Pentagon. OP-31."

"Well, what can we do for you?"

"We've got a hell of a problem over here," Monty said. "We need some help—yesterday."

"Yes?" Rosenwall replied, drawing the word out slowly, conveying that he was not a man to be rushed.

"You remember Zempfke? My Chief Yeoman?"

"Yes I do. Very well. He typed those reports for me . . . very efficiently, very creatively, I thought."

"Yes . . . well . . . " Monty hesitated, remembering the stupid report on the bulkhead colors, and the other non-sense that had occupied so much of Zempfke's valuable time and had even fascinated Zempfke. "Well, confiden-tially, Zempfke's got himself in trouble over here . . . a long story . . . but he's being arraigned before a U.S. Magistrate or whatever tomorrow, and my boss, Admiral Starr, felt it would be helpful if you people could take a look at Zempfke before we get down there and, ah, say he's over-worked, or whatever. He's been working fourteen hours a day under pressure in this shop. Admiral Starr feels he cracked up. You understand?"

There was a long silence. Then Rosenwall replied un-hurriedly: "What did he do, exactly?"

"Like I say, it's a long story. Briefly, he forged a Pentagon parking permit."

Rosenwall laughed explosively. Then he said, "Is that all?"

"Captain, that's a very serious offense."

"Twenty years at hard labor in Portsmouth prison?" the doctor said airily.

"No. But it's serious. Actually, there are several permits involved—a big case over here. I don't have time to go into the whole deal, but—"

"How would a negative psychiatric report help Zempfke?"

"Well, if he could claim . . . if you could testify . . . "

"Monty," Rosenwall cut in suddenly, "do you realize how

serious a negative psychiatric report could be? On Zempfke's whole psychic structure? I thought you were his friend."

"Well I *am*, goddammit," Monty said. "I've been looking after him for fifteen years. I just can't understand why . . . you don't seem to realize this is damn serious—for the Navy, Defense Department, everybody. They might spread this thing all over the newspapers."

"Who?"

"GSA or somebody. The police who cracked the case."

"You sound paranoid, Monty. Are you sure it's Zempfke you want to help? Or is it Admiral Starr?"

"Zempfke, dammit," Monty said angrily.

"I saw him working under pressure for long periods," Rosenwall said coolly. "I thought he was one of the most cheerfully agreeable yeomen I ever encountered in the Navy. A trifle cocky, but most of your men were, as I recall. I imagine, apart from the legal complexities, it might be very difficult—"

"What legal complexities?"

"Monty, you must understand, we have our own channels and routines and policies, just as you have over there. We go by a book too. In the first place, in order to undertake this, I have to have a piece of paper from you—a bill of particulars. We just don't undertake psychiatric examinations unofficially, or during our lunch hour. Then this must be followed up by an examination of the man, his family —I assume he's a family man—and his superiors. It's complicated and time-consuming. You are dealing with a man's professional career and possible separation from the service and his retirement status and all that. You just don't run out and declare a man emotionally unstable for duty—not anymore."

"You couldn't just talk to him, say, once?" he asked.

"That wouldn't help—Zempkfe *or* Admiral Starr. There are enormous follow-up complications when you initiate a step like this, Monty. Believe me, I know. We have enough *legitimate* cases coming through here. My God! Sometimes it seems to me the whole middle-management of the Navy Department's emotionally strung out . . . cracking up, as you say. Can't you go to CNO or someone and make a special pleading in his behalf?"

"No. Right now, it's in civilian hands. A civilian court."

"Well . . ."

"There's nothing you can do?"

"I'm sorry," Rosenwall replied. "Not unless—"

"Oh, never mind," Monty said sharply, hanging up.

Monty stood up creakily, like an old man. His back throbbed. He stood for a moment, hands pressing on his sides, back ramrod straight. The pain eased. He stared into the bleak concrete wall.

"Excuse me, Captain," Armbruster said, behind him.

Monty turned.

"Sir, there're some men out here from the Building Manager's office. Would you believe, they've come to install that partition?"

Monty stared at Armbruster in disbelief, then toward the door. There were three carpenters and two telephone men waiting. The chief carpenter, a kindly gray-haired man, with a fine hammer hanging from a loop in his coveralls, walked over and handed Monty a piece of green paper. It was a GSA work authorization.

"You asked for a partition in here?" the chief carpenter asked, looking around. Monty read the work authorization swiftly.

"I did," he said. "But they told me—Mr. Greene told me —it had been disapproved."

"That was yesterday." The chief carpenter smiled.

"I don't get it," Monty said.

The chief carpenter lowered his voice and said in a confidential tone: "They went over the budget last night. They found out we were not spending our partition authorization fast enough . . . that we'd have a surplus at the end of the fiscal year. If we don't spend it in the next ninety days, we'll get our budget cut for the next fiscal year. So, now we've got a big push—a crash program—to burn up all the partition money. You know how it goes."

Yes, Monty thought. He knew. But this was no day for carpenters.

"Couldn't you reschedule us for another day?" He asked. "We're up to our eyeballs in urgent work."

"I'm afraid I can't do anything about it, Captain," he replied. "Everybody has the same complaint. Would there ever be an ideal time?"

One of the phone men—apparently a junior supervisor —stepped forward. He, too, offered a work order—yellow. As he explained it, there was no way they could postpone the telephone installation either. The approval had come down, like a Supreme Court decision. It could not be countermanded. The junior executive now seemed compelled to brief Monty on Pentagon phones in general.

"Sir," he said, "our goal in the Pentagon is to provide twenty-first-century telephone service in the twentieth century. We have the largest electronic switching system in the world downstairs, handling well over 200,000 calls a day on 94,147 individual stations, connected by 100,000 miles of cable, with merely eighty-five operators. We invite you and your personnel to inspect our installation at any time."

"But—" Monty interjected impatiently. He had no time for a telephone briefing, a sales pitch. The important thing was to get rid of all these people and to get the work finished.

"With this equipment"—the junior executive rushed on —"we've managed to hold the Pentagon telephone bill to a mere 13 million dollars a year. I don't know if you realize that one-half—repeat one-half—of all the telephones in the Pentagon alone are moved every year—14,000 changes. We've got fifty-five men in the building just moving phones."

He paused, staring at Monty, awaiting some reaction, as though he had just imparted the most important fact in history.

"There are 10,000 changes in the telephone book every month," he went on. "Only a dozen years ago there were only 18,000 phones in the whole system."

"I can appreciate that," Monty said, suppressing his impatience. "Meantime . . ."

The young man eagerly went on to tell Monty about the eighty-five separate Wide Area Telephone Circuits—WATS —and the Automatic Voice Network—AUTOVON—connecting all the U.S. military installations.

Monty found himself giving in, agreeing, agreeing. Yes, it was amazing telephone service. Yes, the record of malfunction was minimal. Amazing. Yes. Yes.

"Sir," the salesman concluded, "you're familiar with the trouble they're having with telephones in Manhattan?"

"Yes, yes," Monty said impatiently.

"Then you can appreciate the kind of service we provide for the military. Now, sir, if you'll give us some room, my men will be in and out with a minimum of interruption. Just show us where you want the phones moved to. . . ."

"How long will they be out of service?" Monty asked.

"An hour. Two at the most."

"All right," Monty said, yielding to the implacable weight and momentum of bureaucracy. It would take him two hours to get Greene on the telephone and cancel this long-sought project. Greene would not understand. It was easier to go along.

The carpenters and phone men set to work. Immediately, there was a din of hammers and saws. All the phones went dead.

★ 4 ★

Nancy awoke suddenly, propping up on her elbows. The sun beamed brightly through the windows. She looked at the clock. She had overslept two days in a row. She lay for a moment, listening, remembering. Paul. Monty. The fight. The drugs. She could hear the clothes dryer tumbling, the kitchen radio turned to a hard-rock station. Linda must be up, she thought. Taking over my house. And Paul? What about Paul? She lay back, chewing a knuckle, remembering the scene, the blood. Then she got up quickly, pulled on her housecoat, brushed her hair.

In the back hall Nancy paused, staring at the door to Paul's room. It was shut tight. She went into the kitchen, turned the radio down, then peeped into the laundry room. Linda, wearing the thin little dress and granny glasses, was transferring damp clothes from the washer to the dryer.

"Good morning," Linda said cheerily. "I hope you don't mind . . ."

"Not at all," Nancy said coolly. She felt guilty for oversleeping, resentment that the girl was washing Paul's clothes. "How is Paul?"

"Better."

"Is he up?"

"No. He's awake, but he's still in bed."

Nancy returned to the kitchen, poured a cup of coffee. Dishes, coffee cups and the frying pan were stacked neatly in the sink.

"I had some breakfast," Linda explained, coming into the room. "I was starved."

Eyeing the girl's dress, Nancy said, "Don't you have a

bra?"

"I don't wear bras."

"I see," Nancy said. "Have you called your mother?"

"No. It's an hour earlier out there. I thought I'd wait until she's up. She sleeps late."

"I see. All right. Now, if I may, I'd like the answers to some questions. Why did you and Paul leave school? What did you mean, you've come here to stop my husband from building ULMS?"

"I've come here to join the Committee for the Eternal Vigil."

"The *what*?"

"The protest group at the Pentagon. I am a member of the Wisconsin University chapter. We raised money and stuff. Now I'm going to put in my three months on the picket line at the Pentagon."

"You're a radical . . . a Communist?"

"We are certainly *not* Communists."

"The protestors at the Pentagon are Communists."

"Who told you *that*?" Linda laughed.

"My husband."

"He's wrong."

"They fly Russian flags," Nancy said.

"That doesn't mean they're Communists," Linda said.

"What is your relationship to my son?" Nancy said, fighting to keep her voice level and cool. "Are you going steady or engaged or what?"

"We've been living together, but we don't plan anything definite. Not now."

"How long have you been living together?" Nancy asked, forcing strength to her voice.

"Since Christmas."

"Where?"

"Oh, with some kids. Eight of us got this house."

"A commune?"

"Sort of. Not exactly."

"Is that where Paul started taking drugs?"

"No. Before . . ."

"How long?"

"Oh, four or five months, off and on."

"And you? Do you take drugs too?"

"No. Not acid. A little grass occasionally."

"Marijuana?"

"Yes."

"But it's illegal."

"Of course it's illegal."

"Where does Paul get the money for drugs?"

"He works."

"Works? Doing what?"

"He plays lead guitar with a group . . . a little acting . . ."

"Acting?" Nancy asked doubtfully. "Paul, an actor?"

"Yes, he's . . . we've played a few bit roles."

"What kinds of bit roles? What are you talking about?"

"We made some porno movies."

"Some *what*?"

"Pornographic movies. Skin flicks."

Nancy felt the blood draining from her face.

"Don't get uptight," Linda went on. "It means nothing to us. It's an easy way to pick up a hundred bucks for a couple of hours' work. Everybody does it."

"Do you mean *nude* movies?" Nancy asked, voice wavering.

"More or less," Linda replied.

"What goes on in these movies?"

"Everything."

"Dear God," Nancy sighed, lifting her hands.

"What's the harm?" The girl shrugged. "I mean, they show these flicks to a bunch of dirty old men—in those cheap downtown places."

Nancy felt faint. She got up, put bread in the toaster, busied herself getting out the butter and strawberry jam.

"Are you pregnant?" Nancy asked the girl.

"No," she replied. "Of course not."

"You take precautions?"

"The pill."

"Well, young lady, in our opinion, Paul needs professional help. This morning I'm going to call a psychiatrist and make an appointment."

"You better ask him first. It wouldn't do any good if he objects."

"I don't care what *he* thinks."

"I think you better. It's time you started caring what *he* thinks."

"What do you mean?"

"Just what I said."

"How do you know so much?"

"Paul's told me everything."

"Well, all right then, what *does* he think? Why has he taken to drugs? Why has he quit school?"

"He wants to do his own thing."

"And what might that be?"

"Live his own life."

"Well, he can start right here, in his own home. Soon. My husband's planning to retire. We're going to move to a smaller town with a college. Then my husband can help Paul find himself."

"That's ridiculous."

"Why is it ridiculous?"

"It's the worst thing you could possibly do. It means you still don't trust him to think for himself. You want to go on keeping an eye on him. Don't you understand, he's bitter about his father? Paul is a pacifist. He despises everything you and your husband represent."

"Pacifist!"

"Yes. You made a terrible mistake, after the Charleston thing, sending him to military school."

"What do you know about Charleston?"

"Everything. Paul told me."

"*What* did he tell you?"

"That he got in some silly little trouble with the pigs. He got busted. And you and your husband panicked— worrying about your own reputation and Navy career—and you never gave him a chance to work it out for himself. Just shipped him off to that place for emotional cripples."

"It wasn't *silly* little trouble. He was running around with a bad crowd. Hoodlums. Sneaking the car out. Drinking. And then the breaking and entering. He needed to get away from them, to a place where there were regular hours and routines, and plenty of older men to supervise him. His father was away a great deal of the time, on *Polaris* patrol. That was a large part of the problem."

"Why did his father say he had brain damage?" Linda said.

"For a while, my husband had the idea that I had had too much anesthetic at Paul's birth," Nancy replied. "It was a popular theory at one time. Something he read in a magazine, I think. But I never seriously believed it. On the contrary—"

"You know that Paul heard him say it?"

"Yes. That was unfortunate."

"To say the least," Linda said.

"Raising two teen-age boys with an absentee father is not an easy task," Nancy said defensively.

"And, naturally," the girl pressed, "he's also bitter about the way his father doted on Mike. Mike this, Mike that. What an obtuse thing to do. Really medieval."

"Mike was the first-born, or, rather, the oldest boy. It's perfectly natural for a father . . ."

"It was stupid! Haven't you read anything at all? Paul has felt it since he was a small boy."

"Monty tried—"

"Well, in my opinion, it's much too late now. Paul's twenty years old. He's going out on his own. You and your husband will have to adjust to your own guilt."

"What about his college?" Nancy asked.

"He doesn't care anything about that now," the girl said. "It was another thing forced on him, because it was the thing to do in your circle. He wants to spend some time thinking it out."

"But he'll be reclassified, drafted—"

"Oh no. He's going to Canada."

"Canada! That's illegal! He couldn't ever come back. We're not going to let him—"

"I don't think you have anything to say about it anymore," Linda said, leaving the room.

★ 5 ★

Paul came from the bedroom to the kitchen, wearing levis, a buckskin jacket, scuffed boots. His dark eyes were clear and lively, but his nose was swollen, Nancy saw. She reminded herself that she must be calm, dispassionate, yet firm.

"Good morning, Mother," Paul said, going to the table and kissing her on the forehead. "I'm sorry about last night."

"I'm sorry too, Paul. Let's just forget it."

"All right."

"Your father loves you very much," she said.

Paul sat down.

"Would you like some breakfast?"

"Just coffee."

Nancy poured him a cup of coffee.

"We both love you very much and we want to help you any way we can," she went on carefully. "How do you feel today?"

"Fine."

"You shouldn't—"

"I thought you said we'd forget it."

"Last night, yes. But I want to talk to you about drugs in a larger context. You shouldn't—"

"Oh hell, Mom. Don't get uptight. I'm not a drug problem."

"But—"

"I'm not hooked. I can take it or leave it."

"You should be very careful, Paul. I've read you could go into permanent shock. A psychotic—"

"Come on now. You mean because I was born with brain damage?"

"Your father didn't mean that, Paul. He had no idea what he was talking about. I'm sorry . . ."

"I was only putting you on."

"Paul, I want to talk seriously. There are some things you should know. Your grandmother, Monty's mother, was a strange person. You don't remember her, I'm sure. But she was moody . . . creative. A poetess. An insomniac. I personally believe that she was a bit schizophrenic. I've read that if you have those kinds of genes, you're especially vulnerable to strong drugs. More so than other people. Isn't that true?"

"Maybe. There's not much reliable data. I don't think anybody knows."

"I think I should tell you she didn't die of a broken heart."

"I never believed that. My theory was she committed suicide."

"That's true," Nancy said, disguising her surprise. "After your grandfather was killed in Manila, she went into a depression and never pulled out. She jumped from the New London bridge. The police were very good about it —they kept it out of the papers. Very few people know the truth. But I thought you should know. You are very much like her in many ways. Not that I think—"

"I'm not going to jump off a bridge."

"I didn't mean to imply—"

"Of course you're implying."

"Linda said you tried to jump out of a window."

"She did?" Paul asked, looking up in surprise. "That can't be true."

"I'm only repeating what she said."

"She likes to be dramatic at times. *Melo*dramatic."

"Still . . ."

The telephone rang. Nancy answered. It was Scottie Mac-Intosh.

"Nancy?" he said, in a low, uncertain voice. "I thought I'd better call. The stock opened sort of soft. It's down another five points."

"Dear God," Nancy said, inwardly reeling. She sat down at her desk. Fourteen points in two days! Fourteen thousand dollars!

"I frankly don't know what to say," MacIntosh went on. "I'm shocked."

"Me too," Nancy said.

"All I can do is repeat Buzz's advice," he added. "He ought to know what he's talking about."

"I certainly hope so."

"Why don't we watch it today and see what happens? It's *got* to come back."

"All right. One more day."

She hung up slowly, feeling helpless. Tonight, she and Monty must sit down and decide what to do. They couldn't go on drifting. *He* would have to make the decision. She returned to the table, putting that from her mind.

"Now the next thing is this," she said to Paul. "I simply cannot understand why you despise everything we—this family—stands for. For generation upon generation, both sides have served their country, at considerable personal sacrifice, including some lives. Your great-great grand-father was killed . . . your grandfather . . . my brother . . ."

"Mother, please don't recite a litany."

"Don't interrupt your mother when she's talking."

"I'm sorry to interrupt," Paul returned defiantly, "but I

don't want to hear all that again. It's not my bag. You've got Mike to carry on your damned selfless tradition."

"It has *not* been an easy life," Nancy went on. "I have been by myself a good deal. I've tried very hard—"

"And don't give me the 'they-also-serve-who-only-stand-and-wait' cliché."

"Paul! Don't talk that way to me!"

"I thought you wanted to talk seriously?"

"Another thing I want to clear up"—she pressed on—"is the Admiral Farragut Academy. We did not send you there because we were afraid of our reputation. We sent you there in your own best interest."

"It was a mistake."

"I have never claimed to be omniscient. But you can't go through life holding a grudge against us because we did what we truly believed to be in your own best interest at the time. Would that be fair?"

"No."

"Nobody's perfect."

"Well, that's for damn sure."

"You will find life a bit complicated as you get older."

"You're not going to do your Polonius thing, are you?"

"No, Paul. I'm trying to talk sense to you. I want you to understand that your father and I want to do what is right for you. We're not going to stand aside and watch you destroy yourself, with drugs or . . . or . . . with undesirable companions."

"You mean Linda?"

"Not specifically Linda. Anybody. But speaking of Linda, I wouldn't say she's the most stable person I've ever met, would you?"

"I'm not sure what stability means exactly, or even if it is a desirable criterion."

"She strikes me as immature."

"On the contrary . . ."

"Well, be that as it may," Nancy interrupted. "I understand she's leaving, going to picket the Pentagon. What I want to talk to you about is our immediate plans. Your father is considering retiring shortly. We will move to a smaller town where there is a college of some sort. I want you to come home with us, be a day student and, if God's willing, we can all begin again on a different footing. I want you to get to know your father, Paul. He has his faults, he's not a genius, but he is a fine, decent, intelligent man. He has much to give you."

"I'm sorry, Mother," Paul said. "But you'll have to exclude me from your plans. The vine-covered cottage bit. I do not want to withdraw from the world. I want to go into the world. I've had it up to here with theory and books. I want to get out there and feel it, touch it with my hands, and observe it and smell it and then see what I can do to help fix it. Not Linda's way—I don't believe in that. Violence breeds violence."

"What is it you want, Paul?"

"I don't know yet."

The telephone rang again. Nancy answered. It was Alma Caldwell, who asked cheerfully, "What's new?"

"Paul's home," Nancy said, staring across the room at her son. "We're having a little chat. Can I call you back later?"

"Oh, I'm so glad for you, Nancy. Is everything O.K.? Is he all right?"

"Yes. Fine."

"Good. Talk to you later."

Nancy hung up, returning to the table.

"You're not serious about going to Canada, are you?" she said to Paul.

"I'm dead serious."

"But you're evading your responsibility."

"Which responsibility?"

"Your responsibility to serve, at least briefly, your country. Every generation—"

"Every generation has lived by myths handed down by the previous generations, and look what's happened! Look at your country. I'll not contribute myself or money or anything to the military machine that is choking the lifeblood from this country. *You* may think it wrong to go to Canada, but I don't. It's what I must do—what I'm going to do."

"You'll be branded a criminal. Your whole life will be destroyed."

"So be it. So it goes."

"We're not going to stand idly by and let you do this to yourself."

"There's not a damn thing you can do to stop me. Unless . . . I suppose you could call the FBI. Tip them off. But, you don't know where I'll be crossing the border. It's a big country out there."

"Paul, don't be arrogant."

"Then you stop being didactic."

"I'm not being didactic. But when a person would debase himself to the extent of *fornicating* before a camera in order to get money for drugs, don't you think he may need help?"

Paul blushed. "It was just a caper," he said.

The telephone rang again.

"Damn!" Nancy said, going to answer it.

"Congratulations," a female voice said. "You have been selected from among hundreds of your neighbors to win a prize of a one-year subscription to *Ladies' Home Journal*, provided only—"

"No!" Nancy cut in. "Stop calling here, do you understand? I want my name taken off those lists. Right now. If you don't—and if you don't do it this minute—I'm going to sue you!"

"But, Mrs. King—"

"Right now, I said." She hung up angrily, reminding herself again she must remain calm. She returned to the table, directly to her main point.

"Really, Paul," she said, "you seem lost. We want to help. Would you consent to our getting professional advice?"

"What sort of advice?"

"A psychiatrist."

"I've already spent a good deal of my time in introspection," Paul replied, with a thin smile. "I've taken courses in psychology. I've read a good deal. I have two good friends who are psych majors. We talk—"

"I don't mean fraternity-house psychology," Nancy said. "I mean the real thing. A professional."

"I don't think I need it."

"I think you do. God knows, everybody needs insight."

"Including you?"

"Including me. As I said, I'm not perfect, not omniscient."

"What would Dad say?" Paul went on, smiling ironically "I thought he held psychiatrists in utter contempt."

"He's agreed."

"I'll tell you what," Paul returned, still smiling. "If you two agree to go, then I'll go. How's that?"

"I don't think your father . . . "

"He may need it more than anybody else."

"I'll speak to him."

"When?"

"Now. I'll call him."

"All right."

She returned to the phone, dialed Monty's office. There was no ring. The phone line dead? She dialed the main Pentagon switchboard—LIberty 5–6700—and asked for Monty's extension, 54127.

In a moment the operator said: "I can't get that extension to ring, miss. Hold on a minute."

A supervisor came on the line.

"Trying five-four-one-two-seven again," she said.

Nancy waited. The supervisor said, "I'm sorry, miss. That extension seems to be temporarily out of commission. I've reported it. Will you try again in an hour?"

She hung up.

"The line's out of order," she said to Paul. "But I'm going to make the appointment anyhow."

"This sounds like fun," Paul said, still smiling.

Monty, Admirals Zimmerman and Starr, and Lieutenant Trimble, who carried the briefing charts and easels, arrived at the Secretary of Defense's office at 1330, half an hour early. They took seats in a small anteroom, decorated in Williamsburg style. Admiral Zimmerman took a small volume of essays by Montaigne from his pocket and started reading. Admiral Starr lit a cigar and stared intently at the ceiling. Lieutenant Trimble leafed through a stack of military journals—*Ordnance, Marine Corps Gazette, Aerospace* —on the coffee table. Monty found an old dog-eared copy of a news magazine featuring the new Secretary of Defense and the Deputy Secretary of Defense on the cover— two heads with long necks sprouting from the center of a jocular painting of the Pentagon, from which poured forth miniature tanks, submarines, jeeps, helicopters, aircraft carriers. There was a yellow slash across the cover and these words: "THE MILITARY INDUSTRIAL ESTABLISHMENT: Time for a New Look."

He leafed absently through the magazine, feeling better now, clear-headed and confident. To get away from the din in OP-31, where the carpenters made it impossible to work, he had spent the lunch hour in the Officers' Athletic Center. First, he had taken a long swim to ease the tension in his back. Then he had a cheeseburger in the grill where, in peace and quiet, he had reviewed the problems at home.

From this distance, they did not seem insurmountable. To-night, he had decided, he would have a good, sensible talk with Nancy, then a tough talk with Paul.

He read the cover story on Secretary Allen and Secretary Hawkins. Allen was a management genius who had left the nation's largest defense appliance conglomerate, General Electronics, to serve the new administration in this "man-killing" Cabinet post. He had put one condition on taking the job: that he be allowed to name his own deputy. This turned out to be young, muscular, gruff-talking Roger Haw-kins, who had served Allen as hatchet man at General Electronics, where the two executives had worked as a team, "like binary stars," moving up through the executive suite. The two men, the story said, would bring new economies to the Pentagon, with a sweeping reorganization of the Pentagon's upper-echelon management, and a "new, hard look" at duplicate weapons systems which cost the taxpayers billions upon billions.

The same old story, Monty thought, laying the magazine aside. A cliché! Each new Defense Secretary who came to office had the same goals, same statements, the same opti-mistic send-off in the media. But, after a few weeks, each came face to face with reality: there was no way to cut the budget. The problems, the complexities, were overwhelm-ing. Each man left office dispirited, defeated, broken physi-cally.

At 1445, the door to the Secretary's inner office burst open. An Air Force group, a half-dozen men, ranking from three stars to bird colonel, all in uniform, wearing caps with lightning on the bill, ribbons on their chest, came out seem-ingly troubled. Among the group, Monty recognized a colonel whom he had met and debated in budget meetings. He was from the Air Force Office of the Director of Operations, Strike Force Division, a specialist in strategic missiles: *Minuteman* and the *Minuteman* follow-on, ICM. He was competition for ULMS—in spades.

The colonel walked directly to Monty. He lowered his voice. "Have you been up against that bastard?" he asked.

"No," Monty said. "This is our first trip."

"I hope you do better than we did," the colonel said, shaking his head in a woebegone way. "Tough," he added. "Real tough."

Then he was gone. The appointments secretary said, "The Secretary will see you now."

They went into the office. It was an enormous, low-ceilinged space with pale blue carpeting and leather furniture, and a huge walnut desk that had once been General "Black Jack" Pershing's. The blue walls and carpeting, together with the many line drawings of old naval battles, gave the office a nautical air, reminding Monty of SecNav's and CNO's offices.

It was not the Secretary of Defense, Hamilton Allen, sitting behind Pershing's desk, but his Deputy, Roger Hawkins, whom Monty recognized from the news magazine's cover drawing. He was in shirt sleeves, a cigarette dangling from his mouth. He didn't seem young. He seemed mid-fifties or more. But why was Hawkins sitting at Allen's desk?

Hawkins stared at them with an inscrutable expression. He was, Monty thought, incredibly ugly. His face was acne-scarred. He was tough-looking, like a factory foreman. He made no effort to greet them. He merely pointed to a corner by a couch. Zimmerman led the way there silently.

"Hey, you," Hawkins said, suddenly and gruffly. Monty turned. Hawkins was looking straight at him, with expressionless black eyes. "Come here."

Monty walked to the desk. Hawkins smiled, looking to Monty like a death mask, a skull, with his incredibly short iron-gray hair.

"Sir?" Monty inquired warily.

"What's your name?"

"Captain William Montgomery King, sir."

"I got a postcard this morning in the mail," Hawkins graveled, picking up a picture card. "Listen to this, Captain King." He read the short message: " 'Dear Mr. Hawkins. I saw your picture in the paper the other day. You must be the ugliest man to hit Washington since Abe Lincoln. If I saw you coming down our road, I'd dive in our tornado shelter. Haw! Haw! Give 'em hell, as they say. Don't let those military dandies give you a snow job. Sincerely, Larry Weinhurst, Jennings, Kansas.' "

Hawkins looked at Monty, smiling again, like the skull He said, "That's a voice from the heartland. From the grass roots."

Monty was monumentally baffled. Why would this hideous man deliberately call attention to his ugliness?

Lieutenant Trimble set up the two easels in the corner indicated by Hawkins. He arranged the charts. The overlay on one easel said: "The Enemy Threat." The other read. "ULMS." Admiral Starr pulled chairs around facing the easels, like a miniature theater. While this was being done, another man, Dr. Ralph McMillan, Director of Systems Analysis, came from the anteroom. He was gray-haired, rumpled, with the usual baggage of the academician: tweeds, pipe, bifocals.

McMillan, whom Monty had faced often in Pentagon meetings in the past, was a career military-scientist with a Ph.D. in nuclear physics. His background was well known. He had arrived on the military scene two decades back, a young genius of thirty, one of the brightest and most practical of the legions of scientists recruited by the Pentagon to help guide it into the thermonuclear, jet and space age. He didn't have the mind of an Edward Teller or John von Neumann but he was an able weapons man. He had made military science a career, serving first on the Department of Defense Scientific Advisory Committee, then as the Navy's Chief Scientist and, finally, Director, Systems Analysis.

"Mr. Secretary." McMillan bowed politely to Hawkins, then to the others, holding his pipe aloft. Zimmerman scowled. To him, McMillan was the enemy to be destroyed, the scientific advisor to be discredited.

"Have a seat," Hawkins said to McMillan, coming from behind the desk with a shuffling walk, shirttail hanging out in the back. "Allen's having lunch with Congressman Magruder in the dining room, but we'll get started anyway." Then, turning directly to Zimmerman, he said, "The way we work here, Allen and I are interchangeable."

Hawkins walked to the easels. He scowled at the charts and then Trimble.

"What's your name?" he said to Trimble.

"Lieutenant Gale Trimble, sir."

"Well, pack up your charts."

Hawkins turned to Zimmerman again and said, "I've had enough horseshit briefings in the Pentagon. We'll just sit down here, face to face, and talk straight facts."

Monty looked first at Zimmerman, then Starr. Both Admirals were now seething. Trimble seemed angry. He packed up the easels and charts. They took seats as ordered, Monty easing himself gently into a chair.

"What's the matter, got a cob up your ass?"

Monty opened his mouth to reply but Starr rose to his feet and said curtly: "Captain King has a temporary back strain, Mr. Secretary."

Hawkins laughed and said, "Fairly common ailment in the Navy, I hear, with all that bungholing at sea!"

Admiral Starr glared at Hawkins. For a moment, Monty thought he might swing at the Deputy Secretary of Defense. But he held himself in control.

At that moment, Secretary Allen came from the door to his private dining room. He was tall, silver-haired, impeccably dressed in a tailored, dark blue suit, expensive tie, gleaming black shoes. He carried himself with an air of command, yet he smiled graciously and immediately greeted the Navy group like old friends, shaking hands all around, like a politician, repeating each man's name.

He said genially to Zimmerman, "Chairman Magruder just told me he's planning a hearing with you people Thursday morning on the Soviet Navy."

"What?" Hawkins exploded. "That's the first I've heard. Who cleared *that*?"

Allen, still smiling, turned his eyes toward Zimmerman.

"That's right," Zimmerman said defiantly. "Noboby cleared it. When the Chairman of the House Armed Services Committee calls you down for a hearing, you don't *clear* with anybody."

"The hell you don't," Hawkins said briskly. "You clear all congressional appearances with this office. That goes for *you* and everyone else."

Zimmerman glared at Hawkins.

"Is that clear?" Hawkins demanded of Zimmerman.

"Have you discussed this with Magruder?" Zimmerman replied, apparently equally unimpressed by Hawkins.

"Hell no! Why should I discuss anything in *my* department with that senile old drunk?"

"Shall I quote you?" Zimmerman said sarcastically.

"Look, Admiral," Hawkins retorted, "I didn't come down here to shovel shit with people like you. I came down here to get work done, to straighten out this goddamn mess."

Monty sucked in his breath slowly, keeping his eyes on the pale blue carpet. This was a tragically wrong note on which to launch a briefing upon which so much was hanging. He looked at Starr. He seemed ready to explode.

"Gentlemen," Secretary Allen said, with a genial smile, "I'm sorry I can't stay for your meeting. I have a meeting at the White House with the President. However, I want to leave this distinguished company with a thought. Nobody in this administration has come down here to seriously undercut the effectiveness of the military. On the contrary, the President has pledged to maintain the strongest and most effective military establishment in history. He has a mandate from the voters to bring the military budget into reasonable line. I believe I need not remind you that military costs since World War Two have been something on the order of *two trillion* dollars. Don't get me wrong. I'm not a dreamer. It was, of course, necessary to spend some of it. I understand quite well it was the price of maintaining freedom. But, gentlemen, it is incumbent on us now to *realistically* assess the Soviet military threat, if humanly possible, their intent, and finally, our ability to cope. We must evolve a military strategy of, not parity or superiority, but rather, what the President calls *sufficiency*—a realistic deterrent. Thank you for your time. I know that you and Mr. Hawkins will arrive at a solution here that is satisfactory to all. Good day."

Smiling, gracious, the Secretary departed from his office by the private elevator leading to the basement and his private limousine.

Monty turned to face Hawkins, reordering his thoughts and ideas, tactics and strategy. This, clearly, was no ordinary man, no ordinary Pentagon briefing. Hawkins might just be the first civilian to impose his will on the Pentagon, without killing himself. Zimmerman's strategy to discredit McMillan and Systems Analysis was a foolish hope. They might all be lucky to get out alive.

★ 7 ★

Hawkins got up, walked to his desk, picked up a piece of paper and returned to his chair. Monty followed him with his eyes.

"What's this shit about a ULMS press release?" Hawkins smiled sarcastically at Zimmerman. "Did you think we'd be naive enough to fall for the old press-release gambit? Did you really think you could sneak this by me?"

"The long lead-time hardware for ULMS was approved by your predecessor and the Joint Chiefs of Staff and the Congress," Zimmerman began. "We—"

"Fuck the Joint Chiefs of Staff, my predecessor and the Congress," Hawkins shot back, black eyes narrowing. "You heard Allen. We're reassessing the whole picture. Nothing that was approved in the past remains approved. Not a single nut or bolt. Is that clear?"

Hawkins turned to Monty.

"Is that clear?" he said again.

"Yes, sir," Monty replied lamely. Inside, he felt his stomach falling wildly, like an elevator out of control. Twenty-one months' work—everything—going up in smoke. He looked at Zimmerman. The old Admiral was glaring at Monty, as if to say, where is your courage?

"The Air Force wants a new intercontinental missile to replace *Minuteman*," Hawkins grumbled on. "*And* they want a new bomber to replace the B-52. You want ULMS. *Why* do you want ULMS, Captain King?"

He looked directly at Monty.

"Sir, because of the war in Southeast Asia, all our new follow-on weapons systems were delayed, postponed. There wasn't enough money—"

"You got money to MIRV *Polaris*. You've got thirty-one *Polaris* boats with sixteen new *Poseidon* missiles, each with ten warheads. That's five thousand separate warheads. Enough to blow Russia off the map all by yourself. The Air Force has MIRVed *Minuteman*. They've got three thousand warheads. That's a total of eight thousand warheads, not counting the bombers."

"But, sir—" Monty began.

"And *that* seems a sufficiency," Hawkins went on. "If you people had your way, you'd want fifty thousand warheads, wouldn't you?"

Monty sucked in his breath again, looking directly into

the skull-like face, the black eyes. He thought: grab the ball and run. He replied: "Mr. Secretary, the Russians have a total of two thousand land- and sea-based missiles aimed at us. This is an unprecedented threat to the survival of this nation. For the first time in modern history, the United States is vulnerable to total destruction and conquest by an enemy."

"What makes you think the Russians would want to conquer us?" Hawkins broke in again.

"Sir, the Soviet Union is pledged to enslave the Free World," Monty replied.

"Who says?"

"The intelligence community. Everybody . . . "

"Intelligence community?" Hawkins sneered. "A bunch of washed-out career guys sitting on their fat butts, picking their navels, building empires. Listen. Intelligence said that when we put our troops into the Bay of Pigs, the Cubans would rise up and overthrow the government. What bullshit! There are 100,000 people in intelligence in this town. They have naturally institutionalized the Soviet Threat. If there were no Soviet Threat, they wouldn't have a job."

"Sir," Monty replied evenly, "everything I've seen in twenty-five years of naval service leads me to conclude that the Soviet Union is bent on conquering the Free World. Nikita Khrushchev said: 'We will bury you.' That, it seems to me, is crystal clear."

"Peasant braggadocio," Hawkins scoffed. "They wouldn't be idiots enough to start a war."

"I hope not," Monty said. "But you don't defend your country on the basis of hope. You have to prepare for the worst contingency. Otherwise, sir, you could have another Pearl Harbor."

"All right," Hawkins said. "Tell me, why do you want ULMS?"

Monty hesitated. The long, formal presentation that he

had given so many times, listing all the advantages of ULMS, would not do. They would have to go straight to the point.

"Sir, to put it as simply as I can," he replied, "when it was conceived, *Polaris* was the near-perfect weapons system. It gave us an added, seaborne dimension to our deterrent: the classic Third Force. To wipe us out, the Russians would first have to track and find every single one of our *Polaris* subs in the vastness of the oceans. That meant they had to have nuclear-powered attack submarines. They didn't have them. All right, they started building them. We extended the range of *Polaris* missiles, from fifteen hundred miles to twenty-five hundred miles. That meant we could stand farther back from Russia. We had millions and millions more square miles of ocean in which to hide. But now they have built more and more nuclear-powered attack submarines to go after *Polaris*. We need to draw back farther. ULMS will have a range of five thousand miles. That means we can fire from almost any spot on the globe. It means the problem of finding us will be complicated by a factor of tens of thousands—"

"In recent years," Admiral Zimmerman cut in, "the Soviet Union has become a major sea power. On all fronts, they are placing a major effort in sea power. Their surface Navy is one of the best and most modern in the world. The merchant marine fleet is growing by tens of millions of tons every year. Oceanographic research. Education. They are turning out tens of thousands of marine engineers. They have achieved maritime vision—"

"Admiral," Hawkins said, turning stonily to Zimmerman. "I've been hearing that propaganda about the Soviet Navy from the day I set foot in this place. I've heard it from the Joint Chiefs of Staff and CNO and I'm sick of hearing it. It's a lot of goddamn bullshit, and you know it as well as I do. What I want to talk about here, specifically, is ULMS. Now the Captain here says he needs ULMS because the Russians are building more and more nuclear-powered attack submarines. He wants to complicate their job by drawing back, having more range. The implication here is *Polaris-Poseidon* is getting vulnerable. Isn't that what it boils down to?"

"Any intelligent discussion of the problem," Admiral Zimmerman broke in agitatedly, "must begin with a grasp of the total Soviet maritime effort. This is what Dr. McMillan and Systems Analysis have been blind to for all these many years. He and his so-called experts have been sitting back smugly, like technological deities, deprecating the Soviet Navy, delaying all our new weapons proposals year after year, forcing us to undertake pointless paper studies, while the Soviets have surged ahead in quantum leaps technically—"

"Aw, shut up, Admiral," Hawkins said, waving a hand insolently. "Turn off that stuck whistle."

Monty glanced at Zimmerman. He was ashen-faced. His eyes flamed with rage.

"All right, Captain King," Hawkins said. "How many submarines do the Soviets have that can come after *Polaris-Poseidon*?"

Monty hesitated again, thinking carefully. Before he could reply Zimmerman broke in again.

"They have three hundred seventy-five submarines," he said. "They are producing nuclear submarines at a faster rate than we are. That's because Systems Analysis delayed our new design submarines for four years, fighting us with paper studies. Systems Analysis made us throw away our submarine lead, the only weapons lead we had. . . . "

Hawkins ignored Zimmerman, keeping his eyes on Monty.

"Of the three hundred seventy-five Soviet submarines in commission," Monty said, "about two hundred and fifty are attack submarines."

"But most of those are old diesels," Dr. McMillan put in from his chair, puffing on his pipe, "without range or endurance. The threat boils down to their modern, nuclear-powered attack submarines."

"You can't simply dismiss two hundred and ten diesels," Zimmerman cried out. "For Christ's sake—"

"Shut up," Hawkins shouted at Zimmerman. Then to Monty: "What's your opinion?"

"Sir," Monty replied, "under certain circumstances, the diesels might have limited use. The main threat is the forty nuclear-powered attack submarines."

Zimmerman glared again at Monty, who added: "And, of course, the *rate* at which they are building new nuclear-powered attack submarines."

"But we don't *know* that they will continue to build at that rate," McMillan said from his chair, calmly. "Years ago, when the first Russian jet bombers appeared, the military *assumed* they would be built in quantity. This is what I call the 'worst case' analysis. The military always assumes that the enemy will do more, that his weapons are better that his will perform flawlessly, while ours may fail. Now, in spasm reaction to the bombers, we spent literally tens upon tens upon tens of billions—no way to accurately measure the cost—to build an air-defense network, whole new fleets of interceptors, antibomber missiles, a vast defense complex. And on top of that, we rushed the B-52s into production as a counterweapon and built six hundred of them at a cost of—who knows? Billions. Now, the fact was, the Russians never did build their bomber in sufficient quantity to threaten us. Just a few which they cleverly let intelligence find and photograph."

"I remember that very well," Hawkins said glumly. "I was on the Defense Industrial Advisory Committee in those days."

"The same thing happened with the next-generation weapon, the ICBM," McMillan went on, between puffs on the pipe. "When Sputnik orbited, the military went into another spasm. They *assumed*, from Sputnik, the Soviets had an ICBM capability. Again, the 'worst case' analysis. So we go into crash production of a whole family of ICBMs —*Atlas, Titan,* then *Minuteman.* The military propagandists spurred this on with alarmist cries of 'missile gap.' The Russians were outpacing us. Well, as it turned out, they didn't produce the ICBM, after all. Not then. You remember, we discovered there wasn't a missile gap?"

"Yes, I remember quite well," Hawkins said.

"Another fifty billion," McMillan said.

"Well, that's not going to happen again," Hawkins said, lighting a cigarette. "That's what we're here to prevent. Spasm reactions."

"I fear we may be getting into another one here," McMillan said.

"They have two thousand missiles aimed at us," Zimmerman said to McMillan icily.

"*Now* they do," McMillan said. "But if we hadn't crashed in with our ICBMs, maybe they wouldn't."

"The history of warfare proves that if a weapon *can* be built, it *will* be built," Zimmerman returned, voice rising. "It's just a goddamn good thing we did what we did, otherwise this country—"

"Admiral," Hawkins said turning to Zimmerman, "when I want your opinion, I'll ask for it. Now, Captain King, suppose we take a look at those forty Russian nuclear-powered attack subs you claim are making *Polaris-Poseidon* vulnerable. What's your opinion of them?"

"Well, sir," Monty began slowly.

"They are marvels of technology," Zimmerman said suddenly, standing. "A fantastic scientific breakthrough. A miracle of—"

"*Admiral!*" Hawkins said angrily.

"Wait a minute," Zimmerman shouted, rushing on. "I want to speak. These technological meatheads in Systems Analysis—"

Hawkins jumped up, waving a finger at Zimmerman.

"Sit down, you old goat!" he shouted. "Unless you want me to throw the whole bunch of you out on your ass."

Monty sucked in his breath again. No, no, no, he said to himself. This was wrong, wrong. They couldn't outshout Hawkins. They had to deal with him calmly, technically, point by point. But now, strangely subdued, Zimmerman resumed his seat, staring blankly at the carpet.

"Go on, Captain," Hawkins said quietly, sitting down again.

"Sir," Monty said, "the earlier models were crude, like our first boat, *Nautilus*. They had a lot of reactor breakdowns. They've improved technically. The most recent boats we believe have achieved a reduction in quietness."

"What's the significance of that?" Hawkins asked.

"Sir," Monty said, "quietness is, or is becoming, the decisive factor in submarine-versus-submarine warfare. We've had breakthroughs in the range of sonar listening gear. Some sonar now has almost as much range as radar. You measure the superiority of a submarine in many ways. But, to put it simply, the fastest boat making the least noise is the best weapon. A submarine commander who has the quietest boat will pick up the enemy first, and, therefore, have the advantage of surprise in a submerged attack. If the boat is quiet *and* fast he definitely has the superior edge. He can maneuver into attack position, or if necessary, evade, or escape rapidly."

"How do we stack up quietness-wise?" Hawkins said.

"We believe our boats are twice as quiet," Monty replied.

"Making ours twice as good?" Hawkins asked.

"Well, sir . . . "

"Overall technically," McMillan broke in, "we figure that our boats are *three* times as good as those of the Soviets. Maybe more."

For the first time, Admiral Starr injected himself into the proceedings. Rising to his feet, he boomed out: "Mr. Secretary, I don't know if you've been briefed on this or not. I assume you have. But yesterday, one of our *Polaris-*

Poseidon boats picked up an unidentified contact on patrol station. It is the first time any *Polaris* boat has encountered a contact on station. I'm not talking about going in and out of Rota and Holy Loch and Guam, I'm talking about on the high seas. Now the commanding officer, a cautious man, reported to us that this unidentified contact had been tracked with quote unprecedented low noise level unquote. We sent a search group of four attack nukes into the area. We haven't found her yet. We believe she represents a fantastic increase in performance."

Oh my God! Monty thought. This was even worse! There was not the slightest shred of proof the contact was anything solid, absolutely nothing to support Starr's contention. Hawkins was not going to swallow that.

"Admiral," Hawkins sneered to Starr, "you wouldn't bullshit me, now would you? My briefer told me about that contact yesterday, but he understood it had been dismissed as a whale or something."

"We haven't dismissed it, Mr. Secretary," Admiral Zimmerman put in heatedly. "And under the circumstances, I wouldn't want to risk dismissing it."

"You mean you seriously credit that report?" Dr. McMillan asked, eyes wide.

"Do you want to go on record discrediting it?" Zimmerman countered, with a sneer. "Another brilliant opinion from Systems Analysis?"

"What I fear, Mr. Secretary," McMillan said calmly, "is we're in the making of another spasm reaction. The Russians simply couldn't have created an improved submarine without our knowledge. We have SAMOS reconnaissance satellites orbiting their shipyards and naval bases with cameras that can pick up a golf ball on a tee from fifty miles up. We have a worldwide underwater hydrophone detection net—SOSUS—keeping track of each and every one of their submarines. We've got our own attack submarines shadowing theirs. We've got long-range antisubmarine aircraft and the whole United States Navy keeping an eye out. It's impossible—"

"And that's what they said at Pearl Harbor," Starr said bitterly to McMillan, taking his seat again.

Admiral Zimmerman jumped up from his chair. He struck a pose of defiance and shouted: "*I* built the American submarine force. But I'll tell you this. Today I would rather command the Soviet submarine force! And for this we can thank Systems Analysis . . . "

His voice trailed off in mid-sentence. His face went blank. Both hands clutched at his chest. Then he groaned and fell forward on the carpet, face down.

"Admiral!" Monty cried out, jumping to his feet.

Monty knelt on the floor over Zimmerman, giving mouth-to-mouth resuscitation. He was not certain this was proper first aid for a heart attack, but it seemed better than nothing. As their lips touched, Monty could taste age and decay.

"Here's the Max Cart," Monty heard Admiral Starr say somewhere behind him.

Three medics in white jackets were coming into the room, pulling a wheeled stretcher fitted with an oxygen tent and other first-aid gear. One medic knelt immediately beside Zimmerman, tore his shirt away from his heart and plunged a hypodermic needle straight in. Then Monty felt Starr's hand on his shoulder, pulling him away. Monty rose slowly, feeling an agonizing stab in his back.

In a moment, they had lifted Admiral Zimmerman to

the stretcher, clamped on the rubber oxygen mask. One of the medics said, in a low voice, to Monty: "Fifth one this week."

"Where are you taking him?" Monty replied.

"Intensive care. Army Dispensary. Concourse."

"I'll go," Admiral Starr said to Monty. "You wind it up here, get back to the office and keep an eye on things."

"Aye, aye, sir."

When the stretcher was gone, Monty looked around the office. Trimble was standing somberly by the cases containing the charts and easels, waiting for instructions. Hawkins and McMillan were some distance away, by the window, conferring in low tones. Monty walked over and said to Hawkins: "Sir, with your permission, I'll return to my office."

"Tell your Lieutenant to go on," Hawkins said. "I want to talk to you a minute."

"Aye, aye, sir."

After Monty dismissed Trimble, McMillan came over and took him by the elbow.

"That's a tough break," he said. "I don't wish that on my worst enemies."

"He's had one before," Monty said.

"I know," McMillan replied. "I rather imagine this may be the end for him professionally. The end of an era."

"He's tough as an old turkey," Monty said.

"But getting senile, I think," McMillan replied. "Or paranoid, or both. I guess you submarine people will have to do all your own thinking now."

Monty did not reply. He felt suddenly drained. He wanted to get away, back to the office where he could think.

"Sit down a moment, Captain King," Hawkins said. "I'm sorry this happened. He's done a lot for the country. But . . . I was just beginning to feel you and I were getting someplace. We'll set another time to get back to all this. As you can see, we've got a big job to do here. I want to dig into this submarine thing pretty deep. You seem like a reasonable man. I don't think you lied to me—"

"Sir," Monty said, indignation rising. "I don't—"

Hawkins held up his hand. "Captain," he went on, "one of the plans we have in the works is to revamp the Navy promotion system. We need new vitality in the upper management levels of the Navy. Most of those old sea-dog admirals they've got running the place are too brass-bound, too inflexible. Especially that carrier crowd. They've had a strangle hold on the Navy too long. Like the battle-ship admirals. We're going to break that up. We want to reach down and pull up younger people, the best talent we can find. What's wrong with a forty-year-old admiral? Put them in management harness like competing vice presidents and see what we come up with. We need energy, ideas, young Turks. Naturally, with submarines taking 25 percent of the Navy's operating budget, we feel submariners ought to have a larger voice in management. But we don't want any more Billy Mitchells or Sidney Zimmermans. No zealots. We want people with a balanced corporate view, so to speak. Not only of the Navy itself, but the other services, the economy, the needs of the country as a whole, with the military requirements balanced off against the requirements for health, education, welfare and other vital elements of society."

"Yes, sir," Monty replied, outwardly calm. Inwardly, he was trembling. Here, after twenty-five years, ten thousand "aye, aye, sirs," the impossible dream of Flag Rank was being offered on a silver platter. He had but to go along to get along, to zip by Caldwell and Shanks and Crimmons and the whole Year Group. Flag Rank, and perhaps more. A huge shake-up in the Navy high command. Monty King, rising overnight to CNO. All the power and the glory, and the means to bring change and improvement, in his hands. Plus the perquisites: private airplanes, luxurious quarters, servants by the dozen.

"You think that over, Captain," Hawkins said.

"Yes, sir."

"And we'll get together later."

"Aye, aye, sir," Monty replied, rising.

"Hold on Monty, I'm going your way," McMillan said.

They went into the corridor.

"Looks like you've got the big one right in the palm of your hand," McMillan said, lighting his pipe as they walked along.

Monty said nothing. He was thinking back to the meeting. He stopped, turned suddenly to McMillan and said, "I wanted to ask you something personal, Ralph."

"Sure, Monty."

"In the old days, not so long ago, you were a big weapons man. As I recall, you helped Zimmerman push the Reactor Program through the Office of Naval Research and the Atomic Energy Commission General Advisory Committee. You got Edward Teller and John von Neumann behind the program."

McMillan nodded thoughtfully, closing his eyes, as though trying to recall a bygone time. Monty went on: "Now, I know you're wearing a different hat, and part of your job is to nit-pick for SecDef, but I got the impression in there today that you had, more or less, *philosophically* changed your stripes."

"I think that may be true," McMillan said, nodding.

"Why?"

McMillan shifted his briefcase and studied Monty's face.

"It's a long story, Monty. I've had the advantage of a broader viewpoint, perhaps. The overview as they call it. All the new proposals land on my desk. Everything from a new Army mess kit to . . . to ULMS. What I have seen is a kind of mad momentum. For twenty years now, we have assumed the worst possible case, the greater-than-expected threat. The best brains in this country have been applied, with singular dedication, to creating every conceivable kind of weapons system . . . growing, on an exponential curve, in sophistication and complexity, generating a need in the Kremlin for the same mad momentum, and Monty, it finally occurred to me that, honest-to-God, the more we did, the more we increased our *in*security. As Allen said today, we have spent two trillions of dollars since World War Two and we are less secure now than we were then. I think it was that simple idea that started me thinking. And then I thought, it is a case of *reductio ad absurdum;* we have engineered ourselves almost to a point of no return. And I say to myself, there must be a systems analyzer in the Kremlin, a man just like me, thinking exactly the same thing—maybe he is trying to reach me by ESP—and I think: if only we could sit down and chew the fat for a couple of hours, we might dismantle this monster before it devours the whole of civilization."

Monty nodded thoughtfully. Then he said half-jokingly: "But I was told the Russians want to conquer the world."

"That may no longer be a valid assumption," McMillan said seriously. "They have plenty of problems. The bunch in there seems stable to me, level-headed. They're not Stalinists or revolutionaries. They're . . . businessmen. Damn near capitalists."

"But what about China?"

McMillan chuckled. "We're like a weapon in search of a mission, aren't we? If the old assumptions about Russia are no longer valid, then we need a new enemy, right? Right. China is the Russia of the 1950s. The new myth. If China did not exist, the military-industrial complex would have to invent her. Be reasonable, Monty. How can China possibly pose a serious threat to the United States?"

"If she put an effort into a *Polaris* system, she could. With only a dozen boats, she could threaten our cities— most of the population."

"She wouldn't do it."

"Why?"

"Because Russia would invade and destroy her, I expect."
They walked on.

"Why are you so down on submarines these days?"
Monty asked. "You used to be our strongest supporter. You
know damn well how cost-effective the *Polaris-Poseidon* and
ULMS are. Why are you road-blocking us?"

McMillan stopped.

"Because, Monty, the way you people are moving, driving, it seems to me you're trying to corner the whole
deterrent structure. If we went along with your ULMS
program, unreservedly, a fleet of fifty new boats with five-
thousand-mile missiles, MIRVed with ten warheads, it
would gobble up the entire defense budget, and you know
it. You remind me of the Air Force in the early 1950s, when
they argued that air power alone—bombers and nuclear
weapons—was a sufficient deterrent. Remember Curt Le-
May and the old SAC arguments? Bomb them back to the
Stone Age? Now, it seems to me, the Navy used to argue—
in the days before *Polaris-Poseidon* and ULMS—that we
shouldn't put all our eggs in one basket, right? That we
needed a mixed deterrent, a flexible deterrent, that a single-
deterrent structure was a Maginot Line concept . . . dangerous, perhaps fatal. Right?"

Monty said nothing. McMillan went on.

"So now *you* people have got to be restrained. If we can't
dismantle our arsenal, declare an end to the arms race, well,
at least we're going to have what the Navy always argued
for: a mixed deterrent. ICBMs. ULMS—maybe. Maybe even
a supersonic bomber. A variety of weapons, a good mix, but
in rational quantity. Not an overwhelming superiority but,
as Allen said, a sufficiency. Well, here's my corner."

"I'll be seeing you," Monty said.

"By the way, Captain King. Which submarine force would
you rather command? Theirs or ours?"

★ 9 ★

"You're driving too fast," Nancy said to Paul, as he swung the station wagon off the Beltway to the ramp leading to Fairfax, Virginia.

"Oh, Mother, relax."

It was dark now. They were in rush-hour traffic.

"Turn right at the next corner," she said, pointing.

"Who *is* this guy anyway?" Paul asked.

"His name is Brainard Douglas," she said. "Very brilliant. He was a Navy psychiatrist. Then he retired for some reason. He works now as a civilian in the Pentagon someplace. He just takes a few patients these days, in the evenings, to keep his hand in."

So Dr. Douglas had informed her on the telephone, when he reluctantly made the appointment.

"Mental moonlighting?" Paul asked.

"He's giving up his dinner for us," she said.

"How did you get on to him?" Paul asked.

"I read a paper he wrote some years ago. Here it is. Turn in here."

Paul swung the car off the road into the parking lot of the Fairfax Medical Clinic, a low-slung red brick building. They went inside, into a small reception room with half a dozen red and orange plastic chairs. There was no one behind the frosted glass receptionist window. A small sign said: AFTER SIX RING BELL

Nancy pushed the button. In a moment, a man came from the back hall. He was tall and thin, and much younger than Nancy had expected. He wore rimless glasses and a rumpled gray suit. He had a heavy five o'clock shadow.

"Mrs. King?"

"Yes," Nancy said.

"I'm Brainard Douglas. And this is Paul?"

"Yes," Nancy said.

He shook hands. His hand was cold. His grip hurried and weak, Nancy thought.

"I'll talk to Paul first," he said. "Please make yourself comfortable."

"All right," Nancy said in momentary confusion. She hadn't expected to be excluded.

She took off her coat and sat alone in a hard chair. She read magazines, skimming, unable to concentrate. Then she got up and scrutinized the oil paintings on the wall. They were surrealistic, globs of paint, beyond comprehension. Time dragged. Thirty minutes. One hour. An hour and fifteen minutes. Then Douglas returned, followed by Paul, who seemed in a fey mood. He winked at his mother.

"All right," Douglas said to Nancy. "Will you come with me, please?"

Nancy followed Douglas down a long hall, green-tiled, like a hospital corridor. There were more incomprehensible paintings on the walls, and names of doctors in gilt on the closed doors. His office was a Spartan room with a small, modern desk, two pull-up chairs, bright fluorescent overhead lights. There were no paintings. no books, no couch. On his desk were the remains of a sandwich and a paper cup of coffee. The room was stuffy, too hot. Dr. Douglas offered a chair, then sat down. The overhead light reflected from his glasses in miniature.

"Before we begin," Douglas said, "an administrative detail. As I understand the arrangement, I'm to see both you and your husband. I work days in the Pentagon civilian dispensary. I have a free lunch hour tomorrow if your husband would like to drop down to my office."

He passed a card to Nancy.

"I haven't spoken to him yet," she said, putting the card in her purse.

"Oh? You indicated there was an emergency. I've adjusted my schedule accordingly."

"I tried to call him," she replied. "The phone was out of order. Then he has been in a high-level meeting all afternoon. I'll speak to him when he gets home tonight."

"Good. I believe I told you, I'm not looking for new patients."

"Yes, I know. I appreciate your making time for us."

"Your son, Paul, is an extraordinary young man," Douglas went on, in a low, unemotional tone, "with extraordinary insights into himself. I really have the feeling you're blowing this thing out of proportion."

"What do you mean?" Nancy broke in. "He ran away from school with this girl; he came home high on drugs; he tried to jump out of a window. Now he wants to run away to Canada—"

"You're overreacting."

"They've been acting in dirty movies to get money for drugs," she went on, gripping the arms of the chair tightly.

"I wouldn't worry about the drugs," Douglas replied. "I don't think it's a serious problem at all. It's been my experience that the kids get seriously hooked on drugs when they're depressed. Bored. Indecisive. Lacking in motivation. But Paul is very well-motivated. He has a good grasp of himself."

"He's a child. Under the influence of that girl . . ."

"I don't think so."

Nancy stared at Douglas. This whole thing was a mistake, she thought. What had happened to her judgment? This man was Navy, civil service, bound to be incompetent. Why hadn't she checked around, called a talented civilian?

"He's definitely not suicidal," Douglas went on.

"How do you know?" she asked. "The girl said—"

"I can't be absolutely certain," Douglas replied. "But it's my best judgment."

"After one hour and fifteen minutes?"

"Mrs. King," Douglas said, with a pained expression, "I remind you again that I am not seeking patients. You called me. I tried to refer you elsewhere. Now, if you're going to challenge my professional judgment, then I think we might as well break it off here. Right now."

There's no time for that, she thought. By the time she found another man, Paul might be gone.

"I'm sorry," she said. "But, if you could have seen him last night . . ."

"You realize, of course," Douglas went on, ignoring this, "your plan to bring him home again is completely unrealistic?"

"Why?" Nancy asked, feeling a chill.

"He doesn't need you—either of you. What he needs, and he understands his own needs quite well, is to get out, away, and learn to survive within his milieu. Not merely to survive, but to prevail."

"I don't understand."

"You've pampered him, showered him with material things, objects. He wants to assume responsibility for himself. That's when real maturity begins."

"Maturity?" she retorted, sarcastically. "He wants to run off to Canada. That's not maturity. That's *avoiding* responsibility."

"He doesn't believe in the draft."

"You mean you condone—"

"I didn't say I condoned it. I'm trying to give you his point of view."

"Well, it's ridiculous."

"Let's say, Mrs. King, it's complicated," Douglas went on. "And it's going to take a little time to unravel all this. Whether or not he goes to Canada, or to Timbuktu, is irrelevant. The central point is that he wants to get out from under your domination, fend for himself, learn, entirely on his own, how to make his own way. I am in agreement on this central goal. The problem with our whole society, fundamentally, is child pampering. Children are mothered to death."

"But what about his education. How can he—"

"The kids stay in school too long. Today, they know more when they get out of high school than we knew when we got out of college. He doesn't feel books and theory will help him anymore right now."

"But he *has* to get a degree. You can't get a job without a college degree. What is he going to do?"

"I don't know. But let *him* decide that."

Nancy inhaled, then sighed.

"Now, the other thing I want to ask you," Douglas went on, "is about this notion you have about your husband retiring."

"It's hardly a notion."

"Well, your plan, or whatever you call it. Why?"

"Because I want a father for Paul . . ."

"It's too late for that."

". . . and a husband for myself."

"I looked him up in the Navy Register," Douglas said. "He seems well-qualified for Flag Rank."

"I don't want him to stand," Nancy said. "I've seen too many good people ruined."

"Does he have an outside job lined up?"

"Yes, but—"

"Mrs. King, really, you can't be serious about this. How can you expect a man who has been intensely active all of his life to suddenly retire at age forty-six? What would he do around the house all day?"

"Talk to me."

"But—"

"And do all the things he promised. Travel, and . . ."

"But . . "

". . . make love to me."

"Hold on a moment, please—"

"He hasn't slept with me for *thirteen* months," she hissed.

"Well now," Douglas said calmly. "Let's just slow down a minute and take a look at that."

"All right," Nancy said. "Why won't he sleep with me?"

"I can't answer that as yet," Douglas said. "Tell me, generally, what kind of sexual history have you and your husband had? Good, bad, indifferent?"

"I don't know . . . bad, I guess. Indifferent."

"Infrequent intercourse?"

"Yes. I—"

"May I ask," Douglas said, "are you still menstruating?"

"No."

"Before that, were you on the pill?"

"No. I was advised not to. We have a history of blood clotting."

"I see. And now, you feel sexually energetic?"

"I don't know . . ."

"I mean by that, you feel a stronger sex drive than heretofore?"

"Yes. I suppose so."

"In this retirement plan, do you anticipate a more robust sex life with your husband?"

"Yes . . . I think so, I hope so. Naturally—"

"Begin again? And get it right this time?"

"You could put it that way."

"You realize that, too, may be unrealistic?"

"Why should it be? I've been reading—"

"I don't think people can change basic instincts," Douglas said, again folding his hands on the desk top. "Generally, I find, people pick and choose one another, initially, for a good reason. They establish a relationship, a set of ground rules, operating behavior, and in spite of all you read, it is extremely difficult, perhaps impossible, to readjust. You might, conceivably, engineer a euphoric second honeymoon, but I fear it might be short-lived. You'd have to cope with the added problem—huge problem—of your husband being around the house all day, feeling castrated and useless—"

"Castrated!" Nancy cried. "I'm not a castrating woman."

"But you may well be a very selfish person," Douglas said, fixing his eyes on Nancy.

"Selfish? I've wasted my whole life, living on promises, waiting for Monty, giving my all to my children, the damn Navy. Really, Dr. Douglas, the one thing you *can't* say is that I'm selfish. That is ridiculous!"

He opened his center desk drawer and took out a paper.

"One of my colleagues," he said, passing the paper across the desk to Nancy, "has made an interesting study of what he calls the post-menopausal sexual renaissance. Very good paper, in my opinion. Breaks a lot of new ground. Take it with you. Read it. Keep it. In essence, he claims that many women—those who haven't already been on the pill—feel, during the post-menopause, a sudden heightening of sexual drive, due to the release from fear of pregnancy."

Nancy accepted the paper. It was a Xerox of an article from a psychiatric magazine.

"It may apply in your case," Douglas added. "These are powerful forces. Very powerful. They lead us, at times, to create some pretty extraordinary mental fantasies. And that's what we must deal realistically with here. For openers, I merely want to prevent you from structuring what may turn out to be a catastrophic situation with your husband."

"Catastrophic!" she echoed, in a hollow voice.

"It might destroy both of you. If you persist, I could very well imagine a situation where your husband might feel totally suffocated and just up and walk out on you. It's happened before."

"But there's more to it than sex!" Nancy cried.

"Perhaps."

"I'm lonely," she said, lowering her voice. "I'm bored."

"But fundamentally—"

"Oh, what a lot of garbage!" Nancy hissed, standing up. "Pure garbage. You're telling me I want my husband to retire because I want to make love day and night."

"I didn't—"

"And that's all you people . . . all you ever think about is sex."

Dr. Douglas rose behind his desk. He said calmly, "It's much more complicated than sex, Mrs. King. We've only begun. But let me say this. I'd rather see you go out and have an affair with somebody else than force your husband to retire."

★ 10 ★

In OP-31, Monty's desk was piled high with paper work. Half a dozen important documents. Routine mail. Congressional mail. Radio messages. He pushed it all aside, sat down wearily. Yeoman Armbruster brought him the afternoon's accumulation of telephone messages. Buzz Creighton —Urgent. De Lucca—Urgent. Frank Byerston, ONI. Jim Caldwell—Urgent. Captain Shanks, OP-34—Urgent. Crimmons, OP-03—Urgent. Tom Kemp—Urgent. Art Pendleton —Urgent. Chief Zempfke. Monty laid them aside.

"Captain Pendleton on Line three," Armbruster called out from his desk.

Monty picked up the telephone.

"Monty? I hate to bug you again about that congressional mail, but the old man is getting impatient. You said you'd have it on my desk by six."

"I'm sorry, Art. We spent the whole afternoon in SecDef's office. I just got back. I'll get it to you within the hour. Honest to God."

"No later?"

"Right."

"Then I'll wait around."

Monty hung up. He dug the overdue congressional mail from the pile, signed Admiral Starr's name without reading over the letters, saying to himself: God, don't let there be any mistakes.

"Captain Caldwell on Line two," Armbruster called.

"Monty? Jim here. What the hell went on this afternoon? I heard Zimmerman and Hawkins got in a fist fight."

"No, no," Monty replied. "It was a tough meeting. Zimmerman got worked up a little and had some kind of attack. I don't know exactly what it was. Heart maybe. They took him to the Army Dispensary down in the Concourse. Starr's still down there, so I don't know . . ."

"I hope it's nothing serious," Caldwell said.

"Me too," Monty replied, glancing nervously at the clock. "Look—"

"By the way," Caldwell said, "I heard Paul came home from school."

Damn! Monty exclaimed to himself. Damn Nancy for blabbing.

"I hope everything works out all right," Caldwell went on. "I guess it's Standard Operating Procedure these days for kids."

"Yeah," Monty cut in. "He'll be all right. Look, Jim, can I call you later? We're in a flap over here."

"Sure, Monty. Call you tomorrow."

Monty hung up, thinking, Damn! Damn!

"Captain Creighton on two," Armbruster called.

Monty picked up the phone again.

"Monty? Buzz. Listen, what the hell happened to Zimmerman?"

"I'm not sure, Buzz. Off the record, I think he had another heart attack. Maybe very serious."

"God!"

"It was a real tough meeting, Buzz."

"What happened?"

"I don't have time to talk right now. Can I call you back tonight or tomorrow morning?"

"I'll be out with the New York brass tonight. What, in a word, is your assessment?"

"Trouble."

"Big trouble?"

"Very big."

"Have you seen what our stock did today?"

"No," Monty replied, feeling a chill.

"It closed down another seven points," Creighton said. "Down sixteen points in two days. Monty, we've got to get on the stick. We've got to turn this thing around."

"Right," Monty said.

"Everything is riding on you, Monty."

"I know, I know," Monty cut in impatiently. "If you'll let me get off this damn phone, I'll try to think of something to do."

He hung up.

"Sir," Armbruster called out. "I've got Chief Zempfke holding on four."

Zempfke! He snatched up the phone.

"Sir?" Zempfke said. "I hate to bother you. I know you're busy. I was sorry to hear about Admiral Zimmerman. But . . . ah . . . sir . . . my wife and I got to talking this afternoon. She said she thought maybe I ought to get a lawyer before I went down to that judge tomorrow. I was wondering what you thought about that, sir. And if you thought I ought to, where can I get a good lawyer?"

Dammit, Monty thought. It was too late. Why hadn't he thought of this before?

"Ah . . . John . . . " he began.

Admiral Starr, chewing a dead cigar, steamed into the office. His bushy eyebrows were scowling malevolently. He came directly to Monty's desk and said: "Get off the damn phone. Come in here. We've got work to do."

"Sir," Monty said, holding a hand over the mouthpiece. "I've got Chief Zempfke on here. He wants my advice on getting a lawyer for tomorrow."

"Zempfke!" Starr exploded. "Screw Zempfke! Let him get his own lawyer. Get off. Get in here."

He went into his office, slamming the door behind him. Monty said to Zempfke:

"Chief, the Admiral wants me. Look, there's no time to dig up a lawyer. You get in here tomorrow morning by 0900, with a good haircut and shined shoes and all your medals. The best thing you can do is get a good night's sleep."

He hung up, went immediately into Starr's office. The Admiral was sitting behind his desk, puffing furiously on the cigar.

"Sir," Monty said, "I've got to get the overdue congressional mail to OLA . . . "

"Screw them," Starr said. "Don't you know we're in trouble?"

"Yes, sir. But—"

"I want you to drop everything else," Starr graveled on. "Everything. Turn all your other work over to somebody else."

"Sir, there *isn't* anybody else."

"Tell Armbruster to get on the horn. Get everybody back here. Declare a state of national emergency."

"Yes, sir."

"Monty, you saw that sonofabitch. He *caused* that heart attack. He deliberately tried to kill that poor old bastard."

"Sir, how *is* the Admiral?"

"Bad. Bad attack. They took him to Bethesda Medical Center. The doc told me they could probably save him. But he's finished. No more Pentagon. We've got to carry on,

Monty. If you want your goddamn two stars, we've got to save this program. Save everything!"

"Yes, sir."

"That goddamn sonofabitch. He's *crude*."

"Yes, sir."

"An alley fighter. All right. If that's the way he wants it, we'll show him how to alley fight. We'll make him rue the day he ever came down here. You don't speak to Flag Officers like that!"

"No, sir. But—"

"This Magruder hearing is absolutely vital," Starr rushed on. "With or without Zimmerman. We'll get up there and—"

The door opened. Yeoman Armbruster peeped tentatively into the office.

"What do you want?" Starr bellowed.

"Sir, Captain Kemp from Chinfo is out here. He's been calling all afternoon. He says it's really urgent."

"I'll bet," Starr growled. "O.K. Tell him to come in."

Tom Kemp came into the office smiling genially. To Monty, he said, "Don't you fellows ever answer your phones?"

"We've been busy," Starr graveled. "What do you want? Make it quick. We've got work to do."

"Sir," Kemp returned. "Captain King asked me this morning to look into the ULMS press release. I have some information I want to pass on."

"What is it?" Starr said, puffing on the cigar.

"We hear the release is right on Hawkins' desk," Kemp said.

"Well, for Christ's sake!" Starr shouted at the ceiling. "That's *news*?"

"We were up there this afternoon on it," Monty explained quickly.

"Oh," Kemp returned. "Sorry . . . "

"Thanks all the same," Monty replied.

"The other thing is this," Kemp went on. "I've had a fellow, a reporter, in my office all afternoon. One of the old hands, used to work as a regular in the Pentagon press room. Now he's a wire-service feature writer. Ex-Navy. Very reliable. Wants to do something positive about the Navy. Submarines. I thought if you could spare the time, you could give him a little background sales pitch on ULMS. It wouldn't hurt . . . "

"Not a prayer," Monty said. "We haven't got time."

"Wait a minute!" Starr said, squinting craftily at Kemp. "You're sure this fellow is reliable?"

"Yes, sir."

"What's his name?"

"Mark Spaulding. He wrote a book on submarines, *The Silent Service*."

"I saw that book," Starr said. "That was a good book."

"No literary masterpiece," Kemp said, "but solid."

"Yes," Starr said. "Well, go get him. We'll talk to him."

"Now, sir?"

"Yes. Right now."

"Aye, aye, sir."

Kemp left the office immediately. Monty turned to Admiral Starr and said: "Sir, you know you're not supposed to talk to the press without a DOD clearance. What are you going to talk to this reporter about?"

"The contact," Starr said, relighting the cigar.

"You mean you're going to leak . . . "

"I mean I'm going to shove it right up Hawkins' ass. Scare hell out of everybody. It'll be in the papers tomorrow. Then Thursday morning, we have the hearing. A perfect one-two punch."

Monty sat down wearily. He ran a hand through his hair.

"Admiral," he said, "I'm not going to let you do this. Sir, you're playing with dynamite."

"Come on, Monty. Put your courage where your principles are."

"Admiral . . . sir . . . this is reckless. That man, Hawkins, all those people up there, are too sophisticated for an old gambit like this. We've got to fight them some other way. A new way. Get some new arguments. New approaches. Win them over inside, not outside. If you do this, you're going to infuriate them."

"Good."

"How do you know you can trust this reporter?" Monty pressed. "He might shaft you."

"You heard Kemp. If he shafts me, I'll shaft Kemp."

"But, sir. Kemp is just trying to butter up this guy. Get him an exclusive, or something. You don't know the motives in Chinfo."

"You want your ULMS?" Starr asked, voice low, squinting.

"Yes, sir."

"This is the only way to get it. Just scare the pants off everybody. You watch . . ."

"But, sir. Getting down to basics. We don't even know if it *was* a contact."

There was a knock on the door.

"Come in," Starr bellowed.

Tom Kemp entered the office, trailed by an older, grayhaired man wearing a cheap gray suit. He was florid-faced, vaguely familiar. Kemp made the introductions, then Starr invited Spaulding and Kemp to take seats. Monty got up to leave.

"Stick around, Monty," Starr said.

"Aye, aye, sir."

"Weren't you on the *Nautilus*?" Spaulding said to Monty, in a hoarse, whiskey voice.

"Yes."

"I made the first press trip on *Nautilus*," Spaulding said. "Some years ago."

"Yes," Monty said, now remembering Spaulding—a much younger Spaulding. "I was on board."

"I read your book," Starr said, cutting in. "You're a friend of the Submarine Force."

"Yes," Spaulding said, obviously much pleased at the reference to his book. "Fine outfit."

"You're goddamn right," Starr said. "Well, we might have a story for you."

"What are the ground rules for the interview?" Kemp said pompously. "On the record? Off the record? Background? What?"

"For background," Starr said, looking at Spaulding. "And if you quote me directly, I'll cut your goddamned balls off."

Kemp said to Spaulding, "Is that O.K. by you?"

"Sure," Spaulding said, taking out a notebook and pen. His fingers trembled.

"No notebooks," Starr said, waving his cigar at Spaulding. "All right."

"I'm going to read you a Top Secret radio dispatch from one of our Polaris boats," Starr said. He took the crumpled message from his jacket pocket, read it in a somber voice. Monty watched as Spaulding's eyes grew wide.

"You understand the significance of this?" Starr said.

"Yes," Spaulding replied, gripping the arms of his chair, crossing his legs nervously.

"All right," Starr went on. "We've sent a search force of four attack boats to verify this and track it down. I'm in constant touch. I can't give you any details—all this is classified—but I want you to know we take an extremely serious view of it."

"Yes," Spaulding said. "Does it mean the Russians have a breakthrough? A new class of attack submarine? A super-quiet boat in commission?"

"You can speculate however you wish," Starr said cagily. "I wouldn't deny anything you've said."

"And," Spaulding went on, "our *Polaris* boats might be vulnerable?"

"I'm not denying anything," Starr said.

Spaulding whistled beneath his breath. "You say you've sent a search force?"

"Yes."

"Can you tell me what they've found?"

"No. That's classified."

"I see. But . . . Admiral, years ago, when I was covering the Navy regularly, I understood you people built a kind of underwater radar-sonar net. SOSUS? You could actually develop sonar signatures for each individual Soviet submarine and track them and know pretty much where all the boats were at any given time. I was asked by CNO at the time not to write about that, in the national interest. I didn't. But can you tell me, off the record, whether or not you picked this boat up on the SOSUS net?"

"I can't talk about the net," Starr said. "That's Top Secret."

"I see," Spaulding said. "But—"

"Let me say this," Starr went on. "That net—if it exists— would necessarily have built-in weaknesses. Sound waves are not solid and reliable like radar waves. You get a lot of background noise in the water—shrimps whistling and so on—and sound varies according to the salinity content of the water, temperature, bottom characteristics, and so on. So even if there were a net such as you describe, and I didn't say there was, it couldn't always be perfect. Stuff could slip through."

"I see," Spaulding said. "What about our SAMOS satellites? I understand they orbit the Soviet shipyards. You'd pick up a new class sub on the building ways, wouldn't you?"

"Not necessarily," Starr said. "What if they built it beneath a shed? A camera can't look through a roof, can it?"

"But at the fitting-out docks?" Spaulding asked.

"They can be covered over, too."

"I see," Spaulding said, nodding thoughtfully.

"I didn't say *positively* they had a new class boat," Starr went on. "I'm just telling you what it says in the radio message." He tapped a forefinger on the message.

Spaulding nodded, waiting.

"Is that a story for you?" Starr asked, grinning with satisfaction.

"It certainly is," Spaulding said.

"You've heard of ULMS?" Starr pressed on.

"Sure," Spaulding said.

"We need ULMS," Starr said earnestly. "We need more range on the missiles so we can stand back farther from the Soviet Union and make their job of finding us that much tougher."

"I understand the ULMS concept," Spaulding said.

"This," Starr said, tapping the radio message, "makes ULMS an urgent requirement, if we are to maintain the credibility of the seaborne deterrent."

"I can certainly see that, Admiral," Spaulding said. "This is a frightening development."

"Not *frightening*," Starr corrected. "But something to be concerned about. Something every American man, woman and child ought to know about."

"I'll see that they do," Spaulding said, grinning through yellowed teeth.

"You smoke cigars?" Starr said, affably, leaning forward to offer his cigar box.

"Thank you," Spaulding said, taking one.

"How about some coffee?" Starr asked. "Then we can really talk submarines."

"That would be fine," Spaulding said. "Black, please."

"Monty," Starr said expansively, "ask Armbruster to bring our friend some coffee."

Monty left the office to relay this request to Armbruster. Pouring the coffee, Armbruster said: "Sir, Lieutenant Trimble's been trying to find you."

"I don't have time to see him right now," Monty said.

"Sir, I think you better."

"Why?"

"I just have a feeling, that's all."

"Is there a problem?"

"I think there is."

He went into the Admiral's office with the coffee. Monty hurried to his desk, pressed Trimble's button on the office intercom.

"Sir?" Trimble answered immediately.

"You looking for me?" Monty asked.

"Yes, sir."

"Can it wait?"

"No, sir."

"Come on up then."

"Yes, sir."

Trimble appeared in the doorway almost at once. He carried his overcoat over his arm. He approached the desk resolutely.

"Sir, I just wanted to tell you my wife called. She heard a noise. She's afraid. So, I'm going home . . . "

"What?" Monty replied incredulously. "We've tons of paper to get out of here tonight."

" . . . and, sir, I'm not coming back."

"What do you mean, Lieutenant?" Monty said, stung.

"I'm not staying. I'm resigning my commission."

"But you can't do that!" Monty replied angrily.

"Yes, sir," Trimble answered gravely, "under the law I can."

"But, why? You've got the world—the whole Navy—by the ass!"

"Sir, please don't insist on asking me why."

"Bullshit. I want to know."

"Because, sir. I don't agree with you and the Admiral about anything you are doing here—the need for ULMS, the magnitude of the Soviet submarine threat, or anything else. I don't want any part of OP-31, now or ever."

★ 11 ★

Monty swung into his driveway at seven-thirty, a half-hour later than usual. It was raining hard and cold. He paused a moment in the car, telling himself he must leave the office behind, stay off the telephone, give all his time and attention this evening to Paul and Nancy.

He got out of the car gingerly, favoring his back. He walked slowly and carefully up the flag walk to the front stoop, noting that the station wagon was not in its usual place beneath the carport. Yet the house was brightly lit. When he opened the door, he was overwhelmed by loud music, coming from the kitchen. He hung up his coat and walked down the hall calling above the music: "Anybody home?"

Linda appeared in the kitchen doorway, wearing slacks and a blouse. She raised her hand, making a V with her fingers.

"Hi," she called.

"Hello," Monty replied. "Where are Paul and Mrs. King?"

"They've gone to the doctor," Linda said.

"*What* doctor?" Monty said.

"The shrink."

"Oh . . . oh yes," he said, remembering his commitment from last night.

He went into the kitchen. Linda followed, turning down the radio. He took the Commissary Scotch from the cabinet and measured a jigger, poured it into the glass. On second thought, he made himself a double.

"Would you like some cheese and crackers with that?" Linda asked.

"Yes," he said. "Thank you."

He took the drink into the living room. There was a fire blazing. He stared into it for a moment, then sat down. Linda brought the cheese and crackers on a silver tray. She glanced at the fire.

"I love a fire, don't you?"

She looked at him, head tilted slightly, lips parted. She was, Monty thought, truly beautiful. Behind the granny glasses, her blue eyes were wide-set, intelligent. She reminded Monty of Nancy, somehow. Years ago. In another life.

Monty sat down, leaned his head back, letting the cool liquid trickle down his throat. He felt peace settling over him, the drab, gray image of OP-31 receding. He closed his eyes and then he remembered her strange statement from last night.

"What did you mean," he said, "when you said you were coming down here to help stop me from building ULMS?"

"I'm joining the picket at the Pentagon."

"You are?" he said wearily.

"I am."

"That's not going to stop us from making ULMS."

"If we don't stop it here," she said, eyes growing hard, "we'll do it someplace else. We'll blow up the New England Shipyard."

"Don't be ridiculous."

"I'm not being ridiculous."

"What do you know about ULMS anyway?"

"Everything."

"Who told you?"

"I make it my business to study every new major weapons system," she said smugly. "We get copies of congressional testimony. I read your testimony last year. And Admiral Zimmerman's—the original Dr. Strangelove."

"And why do you oppose ULMS?" Monty asked, thinking now of Zimmerman. He must call the hospital and see how he was getting along.

"Because it will bring on another idiot cycle in the arms race," she said, suddenly vehement. "If *we* build it, *they'll* build it. Then they'll build more nuclear-powered attack submarines to hunt our ULMS, and then we'll build more nuclear-powered attack submarines to kill their ULMS or their attack submarines. In a few years, the oceans will be swarming with hundreds and hundreds of nuclear-powered submarines—each one of them contaminating the water with nuclear radiation. The radiation will soon kill all the phytoplankton that put oxygen into the earth's atmosphere. In ten or fifteen years, we will all die from lack of oxygen."

"Oh nonsense!" Monty replied, sipping his drink. "What will you kids think of next?"

He made a mental note to check on phyto-plankton. If they were to be attacked with this new argument, they would need counter-facts. Statistics. Then he told himself: Stop. I'm not going to argue ULMS tonight. I must find out what I can about Paul.

"Young lady, if you don't mind, I'd rather not argue deterrents tonight. I'd like to talk about Paul. Can you tell me why he's left school? What's eating him?"

"That's very complicated," she said, resting her head on her fist, staring into the fire.

"If I understood him better," Monty said, "maybe I could help him. He's a complete mystery."

"He's bitter," she said.

"Bitter about what?"

"The world . . . the country . . . the mess your generation is leaving us."

"He's never said one word to me."

"You never had time to listen."

"That's not true."

"You were never home."

"That was not my fault. It's the way of life."

"He's bitter too, that you're a . . . a war lover."

Monty bristled. "I am *not* a war lover. I have spent my *entire* life . . . my whole career . . . working to prevent war.

So that you and Paul and your generation could grow up in a better place . . . a safer place."

"Something must have gone wrong," she said.

"There was no war." He corrected himself: "No *major* war."

"But you created a war society. The economy, the whole country turns around the arms race—"

"I'm not going to debate all that with you, Linda," Monty cut in harshly. "I want to know about my son."

"I'm trying my best to explain," she said coolly.

"Well, don't try to explain my son in the context of an arms race. That's absurd."

"He's bitter about Mike, too," she said.

"What about Mike?"

"He doesn't like what you've done to Mike."

"Mike is fine. What the hell—"

"Paul says you never gave Mike a chance . . . an opportunity to think for himself. You've turned *him* into a war lover. You really want Paul to be another one. But he isn't. He's very much his own person."

"Mike chose a military career entirely on his own," Monty said, coldly. "I had nothing whatsoever to do with it."

"That's hard to believe."

"Is it so very, very wrong for a boy to grow up emulating his father?"

"It's not that. It's the brainwashing. You brainwashed Mike. Like, I knew this ex-priest at school. He grew up in a strict Irish Catholic family. He went to parochial schools. Then to an all-boys' high school, with Jessies for teachers. Then straight to the seminary. He says he never had a chance to think for himself. It's the same thing."

"What Mike chose to do is beside the point. I want to talk about Paul. What else is he bitter about?"

She stared into the fire.

"He says you have no respect for him. That you laugh at his talent."

"I have *never* laughed at his talent. Never once. Precisely what talent do you mean?"

"His creative streak. The photography. The music."

"I brought him a camera and a developer from Scotland," Monty said. "Very expensive gear."

"Would you like another drink?" Linda asked.

"No thank you."

He was a one-drink man. But, he reconsidered, what the hell? He said: "On second thought, yes, please. A double."

She jumped up, took the glass to the kitchen. Monty waited, thinking about Paul's talent. In truth, he did not think Paul was very talented. Linda returned with his drink and sat by the fire.

"Why does he take drugs?" Monty asked.

"For release . . . the same reason you're drinking that whiskey. It's the same thing."

"I don't try to kill myself. Tell me about that."

"Oh," she said vaguely. "We were in this . . . we stopped in this place we knew about."

"Where, exactly?"

"Oh . . . ah . . . Lancaster, Pennsylvania."

"What happened?"

"We got some bad acid. Paul tripped out. Then he went wild. He got paranoid. He thought the pigs were coming in to bust us. So he jumped up on the window sill and was going to—he thought he had wings, you know? But I grabbed him."

"I see," Monty said, remembering, with a jolt, his mother and the bridge in New London. "What else can you tell me about him?"

"I think the main thing," she said very slowly, "is that he is bitter about the way you treated your wife."

"*What?*" Monty said, sitting up quickly, spilling some of the liquid. "What the hell do you mean?"

"I really shouldn't talk about it," she said, staring at the fire. "You should ask him yourself."

"I want to hear it from you. *Right now.*"

She stared at the fire. Then she spoke in a low voice.

"The way you've run around on her."

Monty slumped back in his chair, closing his eyes, fighting down the rage. Well, Jesus H. Christ, he thought. Jesus H. Christ.

"It's a *lie*," he said.

Linda said nothing.

"The lowest, most cowardly thing he could have said," Monty went on bitterly. "I never *once*—in all my life—never so much as *looked* seriously at another woman. He must be really crazy to make a charge like that."

"He was pretty positive about it."

"Based on *what*, for Christ's sake?"

"I don't know. The way of life maybe. Stories he heard from the other Navy kids. Isn't it true that a sailor has a girl in every port? That's what I've always heard."

"Some do. Some don't. In that respect, it's no different from any other walk of life."

"You've been away from home a lot."

"It's a lie," Monty repeated. "Just a goddamn, fat, dirty lie."

"He told me that you always turned down the shore jobs to go to sea."

"That's not true either," Monty said. "I went where I was told. We've had a personnel problem in the *Polaris* program. We had a critical shortage of good people. Many of the officers have spent years at sea. Everybody had to do double duty. Not just me."

He fell silent. How could he explain all that?

"He says he's never even seen you kiss your wife," Linda went on.

"That can't be true either . . ."

" . . . that you are cold, indifferent. Never home."

Monty drained his glass. His head throbbed. Goddammit, he thought. Goddammit. How . . . He said suddenly: "It happens that Nancy and I don't believe in public displays.

That's the way we were raised. But I love my wife very much. She loves me very much."

Linda turned her face to Monty. She smiled enticingly, again parting her lips. Her eyes doubted.

Monty went on. "Paul is really not qualified to . . . love can express itself in many ways, not just sex."

Monty stared morosely into the embers. He had to get off this subject before he really blew his stack.

"Did you ever get your mother on the phone?" he asked Linda.

"Oh, yes. This morning. She said she was going to send me some money. She wants me to buy a plane ticket and come right home."

"I think you probably should do that. It makes more sense to me than picketing the Pentagon."

"Well, not to me. I have an obligation to those people, the cause."

Monty heard the car in the driveway. Nancy. And Paul! He sipped his drink, listening to the front door, the footfalls in the foyer. Linda sat silently, staring into the fire.

Nancy came into the living room in a rush. She seemed pale, Monty thought. Upset. Her eyes were angry. He raised his glass in greeting, forcing a grin.

"Well," Nancy said coolly, hands on hips. "Isn't this a cozy little scene? Are we having a party?"

"We were talking about Paul," Monty said wearily. "Where is he?"

"Going to his room," Nancy said, staring at Linda.

The girl got up and went to join Paul. Nancy brushed her hair back and said: "I need a drink. Badly."

"How did it go?" Monty said, getting up slowly. He kissed her on the forehead.

"Not very well, Monty. I believe I made a mistake. I got the wrong doctor."

They went into the kitchen. Monty made Nancy a strong drink. She got out the food for dinner.

"What did he say?" Monty asked.

"He blamed it all on *me*," she replied scornfully. "Said I was selfish."

"Blamed *what* on you?"

"Everything," she said, taking out the pots and pans with a clatter.

"Well, that can't be . . . "

She turned on her husband.

"After one hour with Paul," she said angrily, "he had the gall to tell me there was no drug problem, no chance of suicide, and that Paul was *maturing!*"

"Maturing?"

"The idiot," she seethed. "Monty, are you aware that your son plans to run off to Canada to evade the draft?"

"No! Nobody told me that. What—"

"And that doctor more or less condones it."

"I don't believe it."

"Here," she said, digging into her purse. "Here's his card. Paul wouldn't go unless we both agreed to go. So you go see him tomorrow in the Pentagon and hear it with your own ears. Believe me, it's quite an education."

"It's crazy," Monty said, turning the card over in his hand.

"It is. After dinner, I want *you* to take Paul aside and have a very tough talk with him, Monty. To hell with Brainard Douglas and all his garbage. We'll settle this ourselves. You're *not* to let him go to Canada."

"Of course not."

"We've got to keep an eye on him every minute," she said darkly. "Not let him out of our sight. From what I understand, the LSD in his system can boil up again and bring on another trip."

"It can?"

"Yes, and you tell him that Linda has to go home tomorrow."

"Right."

★ 12 ★

They ate dinner at the dining room table in stony silence. After Nancy and Linda had retired to the kitchen to do the dishes, Monty invited Paul to the den. He would be firm, yet unemotional, dealing with his son legalistically, as he might deal with an enlisted man on report, facing a Captain's Mast.

Monty closed the door, switched on the desk light. To Paul he said politely: "Have a seat."

Paul sat on the couch. Monty sat at the desk, ramrod straight. While Paul lit a cigarette, Monty examined his son. Not in years had he really looked at Paul closely. His skin was clear, no sign of the acne that had once marred his face and neck. His eyes seemed stronger. Clear. The beard was a joke. It would take years before it amounted to anything. The long, dark hair seemed filthy, a rat's nest.

On the whole, Monty thought, he was not a prepossessing figure. There was no strength of character evident. On the contrary, he gave the impression of fragility. Something that might blow away in a strong gale. And yet—this is my flesh and blood, Monty thought. My son. He felt, inexplicably, a surge of compassion.

"That was good pie," Monty began.

Paul said nothing. He inhaled on the cigarette.

"Well, Paul," Monty went on, "let's dig in and see what we can come up with. O.K.?"

"O.K.," Paul said, looking directly at his father.

"Your mother and I are not perfect," Monty said. "We have many faults. We have tried, very hard, to do everything we could for you and Mike."

He broke off, thinking. No. Don't prattle on about how hard they worked, sacrificed. That was self-pity.

"Never mind that. I would like to know, if I may, why you are so bitter. Is that too much to ask?"

"No," Paul said, tapping the cigarette into the ashtray on the coffee table. It was a cross-section of a 4-inch shell, honed by the machine shop in New London, a relic from the early days when Monty smoked.

Paul cleared his throat, holding a fist to his mouth.

"I don't want to be any trouble for you," he said. His voice, while deep, seemed uneasy, fearful. "I just want to go away and do my own thing."

He stopped. Monty felt disappointed. The answer seemed trite. He said: "You didn't answer my question. Tell me why you're bitter. That's what I want to know."

"It'd take all night," Paul said, smiling thinly.

"That's all right. I've got all the time in the world. I want to get into it. You said—"

"What's the point?" Paul broke in, leaning back, crossing his legs. "We could talk all night and you'd never understand."

"I am here because I want to *try* to understand," Monty said, coolly. "You may think I'm stupid, but I deal with some fairly complex matters."

No, he said to himself. That was not right either.

"I don't think you're stupid. But you can't understand. Like, right now. I feel like I'm in the house of an enemy."

Monty felt anger rising. But he said: "We're your friends, Paul. We care more about you than anybody on earth. You and Mike. Your mother has been almost out of her mind ever since she heard you left school. . . . You must understand that we love you."

Paul looked at the floor.

"That's not what I mean," he said.

"Go on and explain."

Paul inhaled deeply on the cigarette.

"You are high in the Establishment," he said. "A Captain. Soon you'll be an Admiral. Then you may be CNO. We believe—I believe—the military establishment is the . . . the enforcing arm of a Fascist society . . . America. The armed society. The country is a military arsenal. To maintain it, to make the weapons, people here and all over the world are exploited. People in Bolivia are starving. Right here, our own migrant workers—slaves. The blacks—trampled and suppressed. I was brought up to care for my brothers. I was taught not to kill, not to exploit. But ever since I can remember, you and your classmates have been killing innocent civilians all over the world. Tens of thousands—"

"I have *never* killed," Monty cut in urgently. "I am opposed to war. We—my classmates—are all opposed to war. War is unthinkable."

"You seek war so you can get fast promotions," Paul returned quietly. "Decorations, medals."

"No, son. That's not true. Honest to God, it's not true. Please believe me. I don't know a single man who . . . oh, I know two or three gung-ho types who've always believed in a preventive war. But 99 percent of the people I know oppose war."

"I mean *un*consciously."

"I don't understand."

"Deep inside, you feel frustrated. You're bound to be. You spend your life in an outfit dedicated to war, to eulogizing war, and the heroes who fought it. Jones. Farragut. Dewey. Nimitz. Halsey. Howard Gilmore . . . "

Monty inhaled, then sighed.

"Son," he said. "I am very glad I have never fought or killed. I believe that, *because* I never had to fight, I did my job well. My contribution was worth something to the country. Certainly, during the years, people have been killed. In Korea, the Middle East, Southeast Asia, but most of us were not even involved in that. They were . . . unfortunate sideshows. Our main job was to see that the really big killing—the ultimate killing—did not take place. It hasn't. That's because we kept the country and our deterrent strong. We must go on being strong. Certainly, being raised in a Navy family, you can understand that?"

Paul said nothing.

"You blame the sideshows on us," Monty went on, "when it was the Russians—the Communists—who provoked every incident in the Cold War, beginning in Berlin, before you were born, when we had the airlift."

"The Russians didn't start the Cold War," Paul said. "We did."

"Who told you *that*?"

"We studied that in Contemporary History."

"You mean they taught you *we* started the Cold War?"

"Provoked it."

"Oh hell," Monty sighed. "That's not true, Paul. It's simply not true. I have been here, on the scene. I know."

"The military crushes the blacks," Paul went on, stubbing out the cigarette. "And the students on campus . . . anybody who dares raise a voice against the Establishment. If the military had its way, it would shoot anyone who opened his mouth in protest. Look at the way the Navy has dealt with the Norfolk Seven."

"Those men were subversive," Monty retorted. "Mutinous. They were *in* the Navy. Subject to Navy Regs, Rocks and Shoals. You can't let a bunch of subversives in your own service publish an underground paper ridiculing you. That's stupid. If they didn't like the Navy, why didn't they get out?"

"Because they were signed up for six years. Forced into the Navy by the pressure of the draft when they were eighteen years old. Now they're doing twenty years each in Portsmouth because they dared raise a voice . . . dared say they had been denied freedom."

Monty fell silent. He had defended the Navy's action in the case of the Norfolk Seven, but privately did not agree with the court-martial punishment. It had been too harsh. Better, he had thought at the time, simply to give the men a dishonorable discharge and get rid of them. Now, inevitably, they had become martyrs. But this matter was irrelevant.

"Anyway," he said to Paul, "what is your concept of freedom?"

"Freedom, to me," Paul replied, after a slight pause, "is the right to grow up and do what I please. The right to serve or not serve the military, for example. As it is, I have no choice. It's serve or go to jail. Freedom is the right to study what I want. Not what some idiot administrator who is out fund-raising and recruiting athletes and angling for a better job tells me I should study to get a degree. Freedom is being able to smoke or drink what I please, of doing what I want to my body or my mind, without a pig arresting me. Grass. Acid. Freedom is the right to assemble, for whatever purpose, whenever I please with my contemporaries, to listen to music, or, if I want, to take off my clothes and go naked. Freedom is the right to use whatever language I please, any words that come to mind. Fuck. Shit. Piss. Freedom is the right to face my black brothers without feeling shame."

Monty drew in his breath slowly. He was surprised. He had not thought Paul capable of marshaling and articulating his ideas. It was the longest sustained comment from Paul that Monty had ever heard. He replied, in a subdued tone: "But freedom goes hand in hand with responsibility, Paul. In our society, we abide by the will of the majority. We have laws—"

"Neither we nor the blacks have any say in the law-making process," Paul broke in, lighting another cigarette. "The law-making process is controlled by the Establishment, the military-industrial-scientific-congressional complex, which exists to oppress the deprived and to deny them help."

"I wonder if you have considered this, Paul. Before you can ever achieve the kind of freedom you want, you better make damn certain you have a strong military to protect whatever kind of country you come up with. Otherwise—"

"No!" Paul said firmly, waving the cigarette. "Dad, you don't understand. Freedom will begin only when we've dismantled the military machine. The military is the enforcing arm of the Establishment. The mailed fist. When that is removed, then we will have the beginnings of freedom."

"Paul," Monty broke in urgently, "if you dismantle the military machine, you'll have Russians sitting in the White House. Can't you understand that? You can't . . . you can't leave a power vacuum. The Russians only understand force. They move in every time. For example: The British are dismantling their military machine—for economic reasons. They're going broke and can't afford it. They just pulled their fleet out of the Indian Ocean. You know what happened? The Russians moved *their* fleet in. Now they will dominate that area. Doesn't that one small example tell you anything?"

"Yes. That they are provoked by *our* Navy. If we didn't have such a huge Navy, they wouldn't feel compelled to have one. If we disarm, they'll disarm. Dad, listen. It is no longer a matter of filling power vacuums. That's an archaic, short-range view. It's a matter of human survival. Our munitions plants are chewing up the raw materials of the earth at a fatal rate. They are polluting the streams, rivers, lakes, oceans and the air we breathe. They are killing the phyto-plankton in the oceans vital for putting oxygen into our atmosphere. They are cutting down the trees which provide oxygen. In another twenty or thirty years, man will destroy himself—not with nuclear weapons—but by the contaminating inputs of the military-industrial system which is making the weapons. The Russians must understand this. Without firing a single nuclear bomb, you will destroy the planet."

Paul fell silent, puffing on his cigarette. Monty, sitting quietly, turned Paul's argument over in his mind. He regarded his son with new-found respect.

"Paul," he said, "as I have grown older, taken on more responsibility, I find the world an incredibly complex place. When you are younger, everything seems so simple and clear. All right, we are cutting down the trees that provide us oxygen. So you say, simply, stop cutting down the trees. But, why are we cutting down the trees? To make room for apartments so people have a place to live. All right, there are too many people. Stop having babies. But, now you're meddling with a basic biological instinct of man. Plus, you have an enormous religious problem—Catholicism—the Pope, who believes birth control is murder. To go on: we also cut trees down to make way for highways. All right, you say, stop making so many cars. We're not only losing life-giving trees, we're pumping tons of exhaust into the atmosphere. But how can you stop making cars? The entire economic structure of this country—steel, Detroit, the financial centers—is now underpinned, more or less, by the auto industry. Stop making cars and you'll bring on a depression that will make your hair curl. So, you see? When you get older, you learn that when you try to pull a single thread, you run the risk that the whole sweater will unravel."

"But what's to happen then?"

"I don't know, Paul. I honestly don't know. I have no solutions to these problems. I hope somebody has. Maybe over in HEW. I have all I can do in OP-31 to keep people from . . . to keep my little operation intact. Believe me."

"Man will destroy himself," Paul repeated morosely.

"Maybe so," Monty said. "But I think not. I hope not."

It would obviously take most of the night if they continued in this vein, Monty thought. The ground to cover—endless. The complexity of the ground—infinite. And they were clearly approaching that ground from diametrically opposed routes. He said suddenly: "Paul, I'll tell you what I'll do. I'll make a deal. Rather than jumping around like this, what do you say we go at it systematically? Let's spend, say, a week on this. You draw up a list of areas for discussion. Then we'll take them one at a time. You bring your ammunition and I'll bring mine. Then we'll have it out. What say?"

A monumental job, Monty reflected. First, proving the Soviet Union started the Cold War, and then provoked the sideshows, kept the Free World off-balance, in turmoil around the periphery, and still had, as a national goal, an ideological goal, world revolution, enslavement. It would be an orderly way to proceed, he thought, just as they might in OP-31 with a point paper, a disagreement on strategy or a weapons system. Make the assumptions, prove the case. Yes, it would be a monumental job, but something that might really help Paul. Something he owed his son as a father.

"I won't be here long enough for that," Paul replied. "And even if I were, it would be a waste of time. You have your views; I have mine. I can see, they're completely irreconcilable."

Monty smoldered at this rebuff. With an effort, he kept his voice even.

"No views, Paul. Facts. We'll deal in facts. You haven't given yourself a chance. You've never exposed yourself to the other side of the case, have you? You've just blindly accepted everything those radicals have told you."

"And you've blindly accepted everything your Fascist bosses have told *you*," Paul replied calmly. "You've never exposed yourself to my point of view, have you?"

"My bosses are *not* Fascists," Monty said. "And what do you mean you're not going to be here that long? You're not going anywhere."

"I'm going to Canada."

"Don't be absurd. You're not going to Canada."

"I'm going to Canada," Paul said, with defiance in his eyes. "You can't stop me."

"If you evade the draft, you'll be a felon."

"I don't give a damn."

"What's the matter? Are you yellow? Afraid to go into the Army?"

"I am not cowardly," Paul replied calmly. "I am quite willing to die for what I believe in, just as you are."

He fixed his dark eyes on his father. Monty felt a certain steely power in that statement.

"Dad, you face facts. There is a *real* revolution in this country. There's no turning back from it now. We believe there *must* be revolution if mankind is to survive. You people won't listen. Well, we're going to *make* you listen. If it takes violence, or whatever. We will not be repressed. When we say, 'fuck war, fuck the killing, fuck the military machine,' we mean just that. Fuck it. And we believe morality is on *our* side. We are the new crusaders. You are the enemy. Every one of us is willing to die for that belief."

"You're all fools," Monty exclaimed agitatedly. "You're suckers. You're just playing into the hands of the Russians, the Communists. They're fomenting all this unrest, can't you see that?"

"Oh, Dad!" Paul exclaimed, with exasperation. "That's *such* a tired, old, patently false idea. You're so Communist-oriented, you can't conceive that there may be other ideas abroad in the world to threaten you. You're like a battleship admiral, clinging to old shibboleths, dredging up yesterday's enemy, yesterday's clichés, yesterday's solutions. You're the classic military mind."

Monty let this pass. He turned the conversation.

"Paul, why do you take drugs?"

"Because I can't stand the sadness I see around me. I have to get away from it. I feel pity for the people who are dying—the kids who get shot on campus, the starving—I want to help but I can't. Not yet. So, I get it up to here and I have to trip out."

"Paul, you can't go through life carrying the burden of everyone's sorrow. The world is immense sorrow. You need to . . . to get your mind off it. Try not to think about it. Do something. Get back to your education. Get busy. Make something of yourself. If you want to help people, be a doctor or something. Get yourself in good physical shape. You'll ruin your mind."

"I can take drugs or leave them," Paul said. "I have a good tolerance for acid. We got some bad stuff on the road. That was a lesson. After this, I'll be certain what I'm buying."

"You're going on with it?"

"When I feel like it. *If* I feel like it."

"You're going to destroy your mind."

"I won't be that stupid. But what if I did? What's the difference? You believe I'm brain-damaged anyway."

"Paul! I do not think you're brain-damaged," Monty shot back. "I'm sorry as hell. It was stupid. There was nothing to base it on. We were shocked by the trouble in Charleston. I suppose I felt compelled to find a clinical reason. I couldn't concede to myself that I might have done anything wrong—that I might not have been the best possible father. I'm truly sorry . . ."

He broke off.

"That's O.K., Dad," Paul responded, in a friendly tone. "I worried for a while. I mean, the Charleston thing did seem crazy. I thought maybe . . . you know. But then, after a while, I figured it out."

They both fell silent. Paul lit a cigarette. Then Monty said: "Another thing, Paul. Ask yourself if this girl, Linda, is good for you. I have seen relationships between two people that were destructive. This may be one of them."

"We don't have a formal relationship," Paul explained. "I mean, there's nothing permanent about it. She has some things she wants to do. I have some things to work out for myself."

"A good woman, in a positive, constructive situation, can be an immense help, an indispensable help, for a man going through life. But you can't just pick up—you have to have assurances, legal bindings—speaking of which, I want to bring up one last subject before we break off. Earlier to-night, Linda told me that one reason you were bitter about life was that you thought I was running around on your mother—"

Paul jumped up instantly, wide-eyed, shocked.

"No, no!" he shouted. "That's not true! I *never* said that . . . I never believed that . . . she's crazy! She's blown her mind. Oh, shit!"

He sat down again, seemingly awash with despair. "My God, Dad," he said. "I'm sorry. Honest to God, I didn't say that. Nothing like it. I don't believe it. She's crazy. She's always doing things like this."

"An *agent provocateur?*" Monty asked.

"Yes," Paul said. "I suppose you could call her that. You see, she thinks all men are philanderers. I think it comes from her father. He was messing around with his secretary. They ran off. She *hates* the secretary. One time Linda wrote a whole bunch of love letters to her father in a different handwriting and then left them for the secretary to find. Her idea of a joke. She has this monstrous father hangup. You can see, the way she goes for older men."

He stopped, turning his eyes away.

"Paul," Monty said carefully. "Did you come home by way of Lancaster, Pennsylvania?"

"No. We came through Cumberland, Maryland."

"I see."

"Why?"

"Oh, nothing. I was just curious."

"I should never have brought her here," Paul said. "I'm sorry."

"It's true, Paul," Monty went on, "I've been away from home a great deal of my life. I now blame myself for many things that have gone wrong. It's also true, as I'm sure you know, that most sea-going men have affairs here and there. None very serious. One-night stands. Maybe a week's fling.

But the men always go home again. You have very few divorces in the Navy. It's the nature of the beast, the life. However, I'm the exception to that rule. There have been plenty of chances, believe me. But Paul, I have never slept with another woman. I have never even so much as held hands with one. I want you to understand that and believe it."

"I believe you, Dad," Paul said plaintively. "I really believe you. It occurred to me, but I've never said anything to anyone. Besides, I don't think you're the Don Juan type."

"My fellow officers think I am a sanctimonious prig," Monty said. "Well, so be it. Maybe I'm just undersexed. I don't know . . ."

Paul lit another cigarette, His eyes were fixed on his father.

"I love your mother very much," Monty went on. "We don't believe in mooning around in public, but there has never been an instant in the last twenty-five years that I ever regretted marrying her or thought I might find a better deal."

"I understand," Paul said, voice wavering. "Dad. I know this must have hurt. I'm truly sorry. Linda must be really crazy to do a thing like this. I—I can't stand to think that because of *me*, you were hurt. I don't want to hurt anybody."

He broke off, covering his face with his hands, quietly sobbing. Monty, feeling a powerful surge of compassion, got up, walked to the couch, put a hand on Paul's shoulder. The touch magnified the compassion. This, he thought, is my flesh and blood.

"Come on, son. Let's go to bed and get some sleep."

"Go on," Paul sobbed into his hands. "I *can't* go . . . not yet."

"Well, good night, Paul. Wherever you go, wherever you are, please remember that your mother and I love you very much. The front door is always open to you—no matter what. I brought you into the world, gave you life. That imposes an obligation on me that transcends . . . that is larger, even, than the ideological chasm between us."

He left the room, closing the door behind him, going into the living room, shutting off all the lights but one, biting his lip.

★ 13 ★

Nancy lay on the bed, hearing Monty's footsteps in the hallway, watching the door. He came into the room with a deep sigh and went directly to the bathroom where he took two aspirin.

"What happened?" she asked, when he came back into the room. "How did it go?"

"I think your friend Douglas may be right."

"*What*?" she cried, rising from the pillow.

"Now calm down, honey," Monty said. "Paul is a very intelligent boy, deeply committed to his point of view. Quite sincere. I'm now convinced he has will and strength of character. But he is thoroughly radicalized. I tried to talk sense to him, but it was a complete waste of time. There's no point in trying that approach anymore. He's a . . . I was going to say Communist . . . but I think a more accurate word would be revolutionary."

Nancy kept her eyes fixed on Monty.

"Oddly enough," Monty went on, "I think he's going to turn out all right. God knows, there's little reason to think that now. But I feel, instinctively, that someday, somewhere, he'll snap out of it."

"I don't understand," she said. "Did you give him a good talking to or not?"

"We had a good exchange of views."

"I mean, did you tell him he had to stay?" she asked, voice trembling, anger rising.

Monty frowned and said, "I agree with Douglas. There's not a prayer of keeping him home. There comes a time, honey, when you can't do a damn thing. That time, I feel, has arrived. He's twenty years old. We've got to let go, hope for the best. Politically, he's a basket case, a shambles. But I feel we've given him something good—the proper standards and values. Someday he will come to his senses and fall back on these. And then . . ."

Nancy seethed. What was this? Monty had not talked to Paul at all. They had been in there all that time talking politics! Ridiculous! She turned angrily to Monty.

"You *want* him to leave, don't you?"

"Now, honey . . ."

"Yes!" she exclaimed, jumping up. "That's it. You never *intended* to lay down the law."

"Honey, that's not true. I—"

"You don't give a damn what happens to him. You never did. Oh yes, the sun rises and sets on Mike. But Paul—"

"That's not true," Monty broke in sharply.

"It is so true," Nancy railed. Then grimly, "If you allow Paul to leave this house, you know what's going to happen? He's going to go straight back on drugs and—and *kill* himself. If you let him leave this house, you'll be committing murder."

"Nancy! Stop that!"

"Murder!" she repeated hysterically. "You want him out of here—out of our lives—because you're afraid that goddamn Selection Board will find out you have a domestic problem. That's the real truth, isn't it?"

"My God, honey. You can't possibly believe that. You—"

"*Shit!*" Nancy cried. She stood, hands on hips, glowering at her husband.

"Look, honey," Monty replied calmly. "I didn't get much sleep last night. I had a terrible day at the office, a real crisis. I'm doing the best I can. I'll keep on doing whatever I can reasonably do. I'll go see Douglas. Tomorrow night we'll talk some more. But meantime, I'm up to my eyeballs in trouble where I draw my paycheck. And right now, I'm going to go to bed."

He took off his clothes and put on his pajamas. Nancy sat on the edge of the bed, still glowering. She said, "There is one thing we've got to talk about before you go to sleep."

"What?" he asked, yawning, climbing into bed.

"The stock. It's down sixteen points."

"I know. Do what you want to do."

"No!" she cried. "It's *our* money. Can't you see? I don't know what to do."

"I'm sorry, honey. I'm involved in matters concerning New England Ship, and I can't, in good conscience, advise you what to do."

"The stock has no reality to you at all, does it?"

"As a matter of fact, it doesn't. It's something you keep talking about. But I've never seen it."

"I worked twenty years for that money," she cried. "Twenty years! Saving, scrimping, scheming . . ."

"You got us into it, you get us out."

She fell silent again. Then she said in a calmer voice: "What's going on at the office?"

"A big budget fight."

"What's new about that?"

"I think they really mean it this time. We had a SecDef meeting today. Zimmerman had another heart attack."

"Oh God!" she gasped. "Is it serious?"

"Yes. He's back in Bethesda."

"Another week or two and you're going to be in the bed beside him," Nancy said bitterly. "Monty, I've never seen you looking so worn."

"And Trimble quit," he went on. "Resigned his commission."

"Why?"

"Because his wife has a new baby and she's afraid to stay home by herself."

"There must be more to it than that."

"There is. He doesn't approve of what we're doing in OP-31 and he doesn't want to be part of it."

"That Barbara Trimble's a smart girl," Nancy replied. "They're getting out before they get sucked in too deep."

"If we lose all the Trimbles, the Navy's had it."

"Let somebody else worry about that."

"Oh, by the way," he said airily. "The Deputy Secretary of Defense offered me two stars today."

"What? You're joking . . . "

"Nope. He was serious. He's going to shake up the top Navy management. Sweep out the deadwood. Early-select a lot of young people. I believe if I went along with his views, I'd get two stars next week."

Nancy lay silently, considering. "What would you have to do?" she asked.

"Probably give up ULMS. How's that for a piece of irony?"

"It wouldn't work."

"What wouldn't work?"

"The promotion. Not inside the Navy. They'd say you sold out. They'd make your life miserable. You might ride high for a year, but what happens when the new team has gone back to Detroit or wherever? The Navy would send you to Siberia . . . Alaskan Sea Frontier. They'd grind you to pieces."

"Not if I were CNO."

"Oh, Monty. Dream on."

"It's possible," he said sleepily. "This new bunch . . . why don't you turn out the light?"

"Because I'm waiting for the girl to go to the guest room," she said. "She's still in Paul's room. They're *not* going to sleep together under *my* roof."

"Strange, fiendish girl," Monty said. "I meant to tell you.

You know what she did? While you and Paul were at the doctor's, she told me that the reason Paul was so bitter was that he was convinced that I was running around on you. I asked Paul about that. He denied it, and I believe the denial. He was quite upset. She's a troublemaker, it seems. Then, she said Paul tried to jump out of the window in Lancaster, but—"

In her mind, Nancy saw an image of Paul and the girl, lying naked on Paul's bed.

"That slut!" she spit out furiously. "She's a whore. Monty, we're going to get that girl out of here. Right this instant."

She stood up again, hands on hips, glowering.

"Wait a minute, honey," Monty said, sitting up. "You can't toss her out in the middle of the night. Wait till morning."

Nancy turned and said bitterly: "Why can't I throw her out? Can't you see she's ruining Paul? And trying to ruin *us*?"

"Because you're—you're too decent a person to do a thing like that," Monty replied. "It's late, it's raining . . . "

"I don't give a *damn!*" Nancy cried back.

She hurried toward the door. Monty got out of bed quickly, caught her by the arm.

"Let go of me."

"Nancy, you can't do this. You're upset . . . "

"Let go of me, I said."

"No. Get back in bed."

"Why are you protecting her?"

"I'm not protecting her, for Christ's sake."

"You *are* protecting her."

"That's ridiculous. For God's sake—"

"You're not doing a damn thing to help your family!" Nancy raged.

"I'm doing everything I know how."

"And furthermore," she railed on, "no matter what they

offer you, you're going to retire from the Navy. And I mean retire this week—and come home—and take care of your son."

Monty inhaled slowly. Before he could reply, she lashed out again.

"How do I *know* you haven't been running around on me? Everybody else does. Jim Caldwell's your best friend. He's been cheating on Alma for years. They have *never* had a satisfactory sex life. She told me all about it. Maybe Paul knows something I don't. Maybe you have a girl in every port. Maybe you have a girl at the Pentagon. Don't think I'm all that stupid and naive. I know all about how they take girls to the Marriott Motel during the lunch hour for a little sex. You haven't slept with me in *thirteen months*. So you *do* have a girl, don't you?"

"No," Monty replied solemnly. "I do not have a girl and I have *never* had a girl. I have had plenty of opportunities, but I have never cheated on you."

"I don't believe you!" Nancy cried shrilly. "You're a liar. A smoothie . . . I saw you tonight! Sitting by the fireplace with that slut! What did you do all that time?"

She did not wait for an answer. The white rage had over whelmed her. She scarcely knew what she was saying or doing. Suddenly, she tore her nightgown from her bosom, exposing herself.

"I have better tits than that slut has!" she shouted. "What's the matter with my tits? You haven't touched them in . . . I'll tell you this. No other man has ever seen these tits, Monty King. Your Linda can't say that. Now or ever . . . "

"Shut up," Monty said.

"I will not shut up," Nancy said, lifting her breasts with both hands. "What's wrong with these? What's wrong with my body? I'm too old for you. Is that it? You want to trade me in on a new model, don't you? You hope I'll leave—

after the Selection Board of course—and then you can go find your little Linda . . . "

"Shut up, I said," Monty repeated urgently. "You'll be sorry in the morning."

"I'll not shut up. I'm sick of being the dutiful little Navy wife, you hear? Those days are over. Forever." Her eyes narrowed to a squint. "No. Maybe I've got it wrong. Maybe you haven't got a Linda in every port. Maybe, by God, you're sexless. Maybe you were *born* sexless."

Monty turned his eyes away.

"Say something, you spineless bastard!" Nancy shrieked.

Monty looked at his wife and said calmly: "I think we should go to bed. Try to sleep. You're upset, and I don't blame you."

"Shit!" Nancy hissed. "Maybe you're a queer. Maybe that's why you love the sea."

"Nancy, for God's sake!"

"Maybe you're *all* queer. Queer little boys, playing with your submarines. Cooped up inside, where you never see women. Ha!"

"Nancy, I'm not going to listen to any more of this. You're hysterical. If I were keeping a woman it would cost money. You know how little I spend. You keep the checkbook—"

"Maybe she's rich. This town is full of rich divorcees and widows on the make. That's what you'd need if you made Flag Rank. A rich society bitch to entertain for you so you could make Vice Admiral and Admiral and CNO—that's what's in the back of your mind, isn't it?"

Monty threw up his hands. "Yes," he said. "Of course. If you say so."

"Ha!" Nancy shouted triumphantly. "So I wormed it out of you. What's her name?"

"Linda Adams," Monty shot back. "She's young. She's got big tits; she likes to screw; she has lots of money. How do you like that? Now all I have to do is murder Paul and she'll come running into my arms. Right?"

Nancy reeled toward the bed, delirious. She buried her face in the ·pillow, sobbing. She felt Monty's hand on her shoulder. She wriggled away, across the bed, face down.

"Try to sleep," she heard him say, as though from far away. "I love you very, very much, honey. Everything you said is preposterous, and you know it very well. This thing is killing all of us. We've got to get it resolved."

She leaned over, looked at him through misty eyes, and said coldly: "I'm serious, Monty. It's me or the Navy. Take your pick."

He shut off the light, climbed into bed. He was exhausted. Yet sleep did not come then or for many hours.

★ Book IV ★

Wednesday

★ 1 ★

The alarm tore Monty from a nightmare—a submarine imploding at great depth like the *Thresher*. He fumbled in the dark for the clock. It was the first time his mental alarm had failed him since the Naval Academy. He shaved in a fog. Remembering that he must appear in court with Zempfke, he put on his dress blues with ribbons and *Polaris* Patrol pin.

In the kitchen, he made coffee, then sat at the table waiting for it to percolate. He presently became aware that Linda was standing in the hall doorway. She was wearing one of Paul's shirts, with the sleeves rolled up. The top three buttons were undone. Her hair partly hid her face. She blinked against the glare of the light. Then she smiled sleepily and yawned.

"You're up pretty early," Monty said, eyes on her thighs.

"I'm an early riser," she replied huskily.

She came into the kitchen, barefoot, yawning again. She sat at the table, staring around sleepily. Then she said: "I'm sorry about last night."

Monty's eyes traveled to her breasts, visible through the unbuttoned shirt front. She went on: "I heard the fight."

Monty turned his eyes away. "Why did you make up that story about my running around?" he asked, voice low.

"I don't know."

"Are you trying to break up my home as well as the military establishment?"

"There's not much home to break up around here," she said indifferently. "You're too busy making war to make love."

"What do *you* know about love?" Monty asked, getting up, pouring coffee.

"Enough," she said.

"Maybe too much for your own good," Monty said, sitting down. "Or Paul's."

Linda yawned. "You'd better leave here today," Monty went on, sipping the coffee. "My wife is—"

"I know. I was planning to leave this morning."

"Linda," Monty said sternly, "I want you to answer me truthfully. Did Paul really try to jump out of a window?"

Her eyes widened, as though she were astonished by the question.

"Yes, of course."

"Where was this?"

"Lancaster—"

"Paul told me you came home by way of Cumberland, Maryland. Not—"

"Oh!" she exclaimed, with embarrassment. "That's right. I *meant* Cumberland. I don't know why I said—"

"Are you sure you're not making up stories again?"

"No," she replied gravely. "Absolutely . . . "

"All right, Linda. Now tell me another thing. Is it true that the drug can recur? I mean, that he could trip out again or whatever you call it?"

"Yes. Sometimes it comes back. Not always."

"You've seen this happen? You're positive?"

"Oh sure. *You* saw it the other night."

"He had definitely come down and then went up again?"

"Yes."

"How long can this go on?"

"Weeks, I think. Maybe longer."

"Madness," Monty sighed. "Absolute madness."

He sipped his coffee. She watched him intently.

"Why are you wearing your uniform?" she asked.

"I have an official formation."

"Formation?"

"Function . . . duty."

He poured another cup of coffee.

She asked, "Don't you ever read the morning paper?"

"I don't have time," Monty said, glancing at the clock. It was 0605, time to leave.

"How do you know what's going on in the world?"

"We have a CNO briefing at the office. We get news summaries, digests from Chinfo."

"A Navy briefing?"

"Yes."

"But what about . . . politics . . . things outside the Navy?"

"I don't have time for that."

"But—" she began, then stopped, shrugging her shoulders. She got up and went to the front door, unlocked it, brought in the paper.

"I can't wake up without reading the paper," she said. "Front to back."

"You must be very well-informed," Monty said sarcastically.

"Newspapers don't inform," she replied sneeringly. "They propagandize for the Establishment. I read them to see what the party line is for the day, much as you might read *Pravda*."

"I don't read *Pravda*."

She spread the paper open on the table, yawning again. She exclaimed: "Look at this!"

She turned the paper around for Monty. At the upper-left-hand corner, there was a two-column headline:

SOVIET SUBMARINE PLAYS
TAG WITH POLARIS BOAT

Above this, there was a smaller headline:

IS DETERRENT VULNERABLE?

Damn! Monty said inwardly. He read the story, heart thudding. It began: "A high Navy source disclosed last night that a new class Soviet attack submarine, said to be superior to any existing U.S. attack submarine, boldly challenged a *Polaris* submarine on patrol on the high seas . . . " Monty's eyes raced down the column; then he turned to the inside where the story was continued, at great length, and with photographs of an old Soviet boat and a U.S. attack submarine and the inevitable picture of Admiral Zimmerman. The gist of the story: the U.S. had "thrown away" its nuclear submarine lead, the Soviet submarine force was superior, and growing more so every week. Unless the U.S. took "drastic measures" to build ULMS, the Navy could not guarantee the credibility of the deterrent. There was a speculation that this new concern might have triggered Admiral Zimmerman's heart attack.

He set the paper aside, finished off his coffee. Linda read that part of the story on the front page, then asked: "Is this really true?"

"Is what true?" Monty said carefully.

"That a Russian submarine threatened a *Polaris* boat," she said, eyes fixed steadily on Monty. "That *Polaris* is vulnerable."

"I can't discuss it with you," Monty replied. "It's classified."

"Classified!" Linda exclaimed. "*Every*thing is classified! How can the American people make good judgments when everything important is classified?"

"The Congress—your representatives—are fully informed," Monty said.

"Oh, shit," Linda said. "They're not our representatives. They are members of the military-industrial complex. I wouldn't believe a damn thing Congressman Magruder said. And I don't believe this story. This is Navy propaganda!"

Monty got up, put his coffee cup in the sink.

"Why don't you answer me?" Linda pressed.

"I—"

"It's *not* true, is it?" she said, eyes defiant.

"Truth is—"

"It's a lie! I can tell by your eyes. It *is* a lie, isn't it?"

"I've got to go," Monty replied, going toward the front door. Linda rose and followed him. While he was putting on his topcoat, she said: "I'm very, very sorry about last night."

"All right," he said. "Forget it."

She rose on tip-toes and kissed him on the cheek, soft breast pressing against his arm.

"Goodbye, Captain," she murmured. "Please make love, not war."

★ **2** ★

Yeoman Armbruster brought Monty a mug of steaming coffee and said:

"Captain Shanks in OP-34 called."

"Get him back for me, please," Monty said.

In a moment, Shanks came on the line.

"Monty? What the hell are you guys trying to pull?"

"I beg your pardon?" Monty said.

"The morning paper. The leak."

"We—"

"Don't tell me you didn't leak it," Shanks went on. "It's got Starr's fingerprints all over it. I've heard him use the exact same language. It sounds like he *dictated* it."

"Don't be absurd."

"Admiral Bascum is furious," Shanks went on belligerently. "He thinks you're playing dirty pool. He's over with Admiral Leggett now, raising six kinds of hell."

Monty said nothing. Inwardly, he felt shame and anger.

"One more question, Monty. Are we next? Are you guys going after our carriers too?"

"Of course not. Look—"

"I just want you to know, Monty," Shanks went on. "If you try any Mickey Mouse with us, we'll ram you. It's too goddamn bad this had to happen, you know? Until this week, I thought we'd more or less created an atmosphere of trust in OP-03. You and I, Admiral Bascum and Admiral Starr, more or less working together in harness for the best interest of the Navy as a whole. But you guys have shot that down. From now on, we'll go on the premise that OP-31 can be trusted about as far as we could throw this building."

"Now wait a minute!" Monty broke in. "For God's sake don't—"

Shanks hung up abruptly. Goddammit! Monty seethed. Why hadn't he been tougher with Starr? The impulsive idiot!

He forced his mind to the urgent, overflowing paper work. Going through the morning radio dispatches, he found a message to CNO from the Search Force commander, info to OP-31 and ONI:

> BT CONCLUDED SEARCH. NEGATIVE
> RESULTS. DOUBT INITIAL CONTACT.
> REQUEST PERMISSION TO SECURE
> AND RETURN TO PREVIOUS EXERCISE.

God! Monty thought. Now what would Starr do?

"Sir," Armbruster called out. "Deputy Secretary of Defense Hawkins, *personally*, on Line one."

Monty, feeling dread, answered briskly, "Captain King."

"This is Roger Hawkins, Captain. I asked for your boss, Starr, but I understand he's not in yet. I wonder if you would mind coming up to my office?"

"Not at all, sir," Monty replied, stomach sinking.

"Thank you."

Monty logged himself out on the blackboard and walked swiftly to the office of the Deputy Secretary of Defense. A secretary ushered him into the inner office. Hawkins was sitting behind his large desk in shirt sleeves. Tom Kemp from Chinfo was sitting in a pull-up chair next to the desk.

"Sorry to take you from your work," Hawkins said affably. "But we've got a problem. You know Captain Kemp?"

"Oh, yes," Monty said, sucking in his breath, again feeling the dread. There could be only one reason why Kemp was here—the leak.

"Have a seat, Captain," Hawkins said in a friendly tone. "Coffee?"

"No thanks, sir, I just had a cup."

Monty pulled up another chair. By the ship's chronometer on the wall, it was 0710. The sun had risen.

"How's your back?" Hawkins asked.

"Better, thank you."

Hawkins, speaking calmly, went directly to the point. "Captain, one of the things we in this office are determined to do is to stop this rampant leaking to the press. I know it's almost a tradition with the military, but it's not a fair way to do business. I don't believe in washing our dirty linen in public."

Monty swallowed hard, glancing involuntarily at Kemp.

"And we don't believe in telling the Ruskies all our business either," Hawkins went on. "In our opinion, this leak is a violation of the National Security Act. The message from which it derived was classified Top Secret."

"Yes, sir, Mr. Secretary," Monty said.

"Now," Hawkins continued, glancing at Kemp, "we're all pretty certain it could not have been *you* who leaked . . . "

Watch out, Monty thought.

" . . . but we were wondering if you could perhaps shed some light on the matter?" Hawkins concluded.

Monty again glanced at Kemp. He was poker-faced, staring at the carpet.

"I didn't leak that story, Mr. Secretary," Monty said, facing Hawkins.

"I was sure of that," Hawkins replied, smiling thinly. "It's a hell of a thing to have a Top Secret briefing one afternoon and next morning, read it all, almost verbatim, in the papers."

"I agree," Monty said. "I don't approve of it."

"I thought you wouldn't," Hawkins said. "Can you shed any light?"

"Sir . . . I . . . " Monty began, not knowing what he would say.

Hawkins turned suddenly to Kemp.

"Captain, I believe you can return to your office. Thank you very much for coming up."

"Yes, sir," Kemp said, getting up quickly, with the look of a man who had been reprieved from the gallows.

"Thanks for your help," Hawkins said.

"Anytime, sir," Kemp said, hurrying for the door.

"Well now," Hawkins said. "We can talk privately. I got a copy of the radio message from the Search Force from the National Command Center. What do you think I should do?"

He held aloft a copy of the message.

"Sir . . . " Monty began.

"Whoever leaked, created a wrong, untruthful impression," Hawkins went on. "Now, if you were in my shoes, would you counterleak? Give the press a copy of this latest message?"

"No, sir."

"Why not? Isn't the public entitled to the truth?"

"Sir, I agree with you we shouldn't wash our linen in public. The leak was a mistake. The counterleak would also be a mistake. Two wrongs don't make a right."

"You realize what a dishonest thing the leak was?"

"Yes, sir."

"You condemn it?"

"I certainly do. Yes, sir."

"And wouldn't be a part of it?"

"No, sir. Not willingly."

"I'm glad to hear you talking this way, King. You seem like an honest, as well as a competent, man. That seems a rare combination in this building. Now, have you had a chance to think over what I said yesterday about improving and revitalizing the Navy high command?"

"Yes, sir. I did."

"Good. Admiral Starr is the perfect example of what I meant by the old brassbound, single-minded, war-horse Admiral. People like him have to go."

Monty sat silently.

"We know he leaked that story," Hawkins went on. "And what—"

"Sir," Monty broke in. "How do you know he leaked it?"

"It's obvious," Hawkins said. "And besides that, we have an affidavit from Captain Kemp."

"I see," Monty said hollowly. He felt sick.

"And what I want is an affidavit from you," Hawkins said, smiling.

"No," Monty said quickly.

"Now, Captain, I thought you said you'd thought over what I said yesterday. We've all got to learn to play ball. We're on the same team."

"I don't play that kind of ball, Mr. Secretary," Monty said coolly. "You're asking me to accuse my own boss of violating the National Security Act for my own personal gain."

"Your gain is incidental," Hawkins said, the smile quickly disappearing. "I'm asking you to do something in the best interest of the Department of Defense. You just said you didn't approve of the leak."

"That's right. But—"

"If you're protecting your boss because he's on your Selection Board," Hawkins went on, "let me remind you that the promotion list that Board produces must come through this office for approval. The Board's not going to promote anybody we don't approve of. I won't send it to the White House or Congress."

Monty said nothing.

"The power center is here," Hawkins added, tapping the top of his desk with his forefinger.

Monty, overwhelmed with anger and indignation, stood quickly and said: "Mr. Secretary, I'm not sure in my own mind whether this is blackmail or bribery or a combination of both. Whatever it is, I want no part of it. If I'm not qualified for Flag Rank on the basis of my twenty-five years of professional service to the Navy and my country, then the hell with it."

"Captain," Hawkins returned, "must we be so high-minded? You've been around. You—"

"Sir, I request permission to return to my office."

"O.K., King," Hawkins said angrily. "And when you get back there, tell that boss of yours I want to see him. I'm going to nail his ass to the wall."

★ **3** ★

Chief Yeoman Zempfke walked into OP-31 at 0900, as ordered. He wore his dress blues and an impressive stack of ribbons over his submarine-combat pin and *Polaris* patrol pin. His hair was neatly cut, his shoes shined. He walked to Monty's desk, head bowed abjectly.

"Good morning, sir," he said.

"Morning, Zempfke," Monty said, pushing the papers aside.

"I see they put the partition in," Zempfke said, hooking a thumb over his shoulder.

"Yes," Monty said. "Don't ask me how or why. How are you feeling?"

"Scared, sir."

"Well," Monty said, "don't worry about it. We'll go down there and see what we can do. You be damn sure to emphasize your guilt and remorse. That always impresses a judge."

"Yes, sir. I intend to do that."

"Admiral Starr on Line two," Armbruster called from his desk.

"Stand by a minute," Monty said to Zempfke.

"Aye, aye, sir."

Monty picked up the telephone.

"Morning, Admiral."

"Morning, Monty. You saw the papers? Great, eh? How are things?"

"Sir, things are not well," Monty said, lowering his voice. "Where are you?"

"I'm out here at Bethesda with Admiral Zimmerman."

"What? I thought—"

"They can't kill off this old sonofabitch," Starr said. "He's tough as nails. It wasn't as bad as we thought. He's wide awake, alert and his mind is clear as a bell. Never sharper. He's got to stay in bed a few weeks. Right now we're working out some plans for the hearing tomorrow."

"Aren't you coming in, sir?" Monty broke in.

"I'll be in around noon. What's up?"

"Well, sir," Monty began, turning toward the window, "the front office is really on the warpath—"

"Which front office?" Starr cut in quickly.

"You know, the man we were with yesterday."

"Right. That's good, Monty. Perfect. Got them off balance. If they get excited, they can't think as clearly."

"Sir, I think they're thinking *very* clearly. He called me up there on the carpet—"

"You didn't tell them anything?"

"No sir. But Tom Kemp was up there and he's—"

"He won't talk," Starr broke in again confidently. "Hell, Monty, I'm on his Selection Board."

"Still . . . sir, I think you better come right away. The man wants to see you. They're going to launch an official investigation. They say it was a violation of the National Security Act."

"I expected that," Starr said smugly. "But they're hoisted on their own petard. They claim the contact was phony. If it was phony, how could it be a violation of security?"

"But, Admiral—" Monty said, in exasperation.

"What else is cooking?"

"Sir, we have a request from the Search Group to return to its previous mission."

"No!" Starr thundered. "Keep them there another twenty-four hours. I want to be in a position to tell the Magruder Committee!"

"But they're reporting negative and raising doubt about the initial—"

"Keep them right there. Draft a message for CNO's signature. Then hold down the fort for me. De Lucca and Creighton are coming in shortly. Take care of them. See what they have cooking."

"Sir, I can't do that. Zempfke's here. I've got to take him down to the court."

"Screw Zempfke!" Starr said. "This is no time for you to show your face in a court. There might be reporters down there. Christ! We've got enough heat—"

"But—"

"No buts, Monty. This is a direct order. Do not go with Zempfke. You understand?"

"Yes, sir," Monty said, voice low. "By the way, sir, Captain Shanks called. OP-34's upset . . . "

"Screw them too," Starr replied. "Bunch of old women. Monty, we're in a fight for our lives. Stop bugging me with nits and nats. Anything else?"

"No, sir. But, sir, I think we better talk before you see the man in the front office."

"O.K., Monty. Hang in there. We've got them running scared."

"Aye, aye, sir."

He hung up. Tony de Lucca and Buzz Creighton were approaching his desk, both smiling contentedly.

"Hello, Monty," Creighton said, extending a hand. When de Lucca shook hands, Monty could smell whiskey on his breath.

"Where's the Admiral?" Creighton asked.

"At Bethesda, with Zimmerman."

"Zimmerman called me early this morning at home," Creighton said. "Isn't he amazing?"

"I guess so," Monty returned. "Come into the Admiral's office. We can talk there."

"Why the uniform?" Creighton asked.

"Oh . . . it's too involved to explain," Monty replied.

When the two visitors had gone into the Admiral's office, Monty called Zempfke to his desk.

"Chief," he said, "I can't go down to court with you. We've got a tremendous flap going here. Look, you go down there and be perfectly candid. Tell the judge how it started out as a joke—just the way you told it to the Admiral and me. All right?"

Zempfke seemed crushed.

"I'm sorry," Monty said.

"That's O.K., sir," Zempfke said.

Monty went into the Admiral's office, closed the door. Creighton and de Lucca were sitting, waiting.

"The leak was perfect," Creighton said. "It moved on the overnight wire. It was front page all over the country. It was the perfect launching vehicle for the hearing tomorrow. We've got our PR department cranked up to Xerox and mail a copy to every magazine and newspaper reporter and editor, every member of Congress, the trade press, the Navy

League—the whole list. Everybody who can do us some good."

Monty nodded.

"It's already taking hold on Wall Street," Creighton went on, enthusiastically. "The smart money is moving back in. The stock firmed up—opened very strong. It ought to rebound four, five points today, and keep on climbing tomorrow when the hearing opens."

"Let's get down to business," de Lucca said, resting his pudgy hands on his knees. "Now, Monty, here's the situation. The hearing's laid on. Zimmerman is flat on his back out of action. Next in line comes Starr. Frankly, Monty, Starr is not a good witness. He's too impulsive . . . too much of a Patton type. You know the majority of the press, these days. They're a bunch of long-haired intellectuals. They come in suspicious of the military. To impress them, you've got to be cool. Intellectual, like. You know what I mean?"

"Go on," Monty said.

"Well, frankly, Monty, you're our best witness. You've got the looks . . . the presence . . . you sort of come across with integrity and moxie . . . just the right combination . . . earnest, you know what I mean?"

"Credible," Creighton put in.

"That's the word," de Lucca said. "Credible. All right now. My plan is to have Starr make a very brief, low-key introductory-type opening, then go immediately to you—put you right in the spotlight—keep you there, and lead you, very carefully, through the key areas. You respond with understatement—always understatement. The burden of the testimony should be twofold. One—*Polaris* is vulnerable; two—we need ULMS to replace it. I'm going to stay away from everything else—the surface Navy, aircraft carriers—for the sake of simplicity, so we can concentrate on getting this one idea across. All right?"

"Do I get paid Actor's Guild rates?" Monty said sarcastically.

"Maybe more than that," de Lucca said. "I was talking to the Chairman this morning. I told him you were up for selection, when your Board meets. He was familiar with it. Zimmerman had talked to him about it. The Chairman authorized me to say that if you perform well, if we save ULMS, he'd *guarantee* your two stars. Promote you—just like we did Zimmerman. The Senate Armed Services Committee must finally approve the promotion list. The Chairman's got I O U's all over that committee. He can guarantee the list won't be approved unless your name's on it. And if Hawkins tries to intervene, he won't get a single one of his pet projects through Congress. So, that's the deal. How does it strike you, Monty?"

"Shit," Monty replied scornfully. "It's really touching, the way everybody's suddenly concerned about my two stars, my future."

"What's eating you, Monty?" Creighton asked. "You've got to get on the stick. We heard you weren't too strong yesterday with that meathead, Hawkins."

"That's not true!" Monty exclaimed angrily. "You can't brief him the normal way. He threw out the charts. He wants to talk turkey. No sales pitches—just numbers. I'm telling you, Buzz, this guy is not a meathead. You've got him wrong. Somebody is making a very large mistake."

"We've got too much money riding on this to make mistakes," Creighton replied coolly. "Hundreds of millions. I realize you're in the zone. You don't want to step on toes. But, Monty, we're in all-out war. If we don't stop Hawkins right now, today, tomorrow, we'll *all* be out of a job, out on the street selling apples."

Monty exploded. "Goddammit, Buzz, who the hell do you think you are, coming in here criticizing me? I don't give a shit about stepping on toes! I'm fighting just as hard for the Submarine Force as you are—all of you. But I think you're making a big mistake. You're not going about it right. The administration ran for office on a cut-the-military platform. They feel they have a mandate from the voters—"

"Aw, bullshit," de Lucca cut in. "They're posturing. They won on a fluke. The voters don't know fuck-all about the military, how big it should be or how small, or how much money we should spend. Allen and Hawkins are just doing all that for the record. If they meet enough resistance, they'll back off and forget it. They'll just have to go tell the voters the threat was bigger than they thought it was. Anyway, they can't get a reduced budget through the Congress. There are too many people with too much at stake."

"But the complexion of Congress is changing too," Monty said.

"Monty, let me tell you something about politics," de Lucca said. "The liberals in Congress might rant and rave about pollution and the military-industrial complex and all that shit for home consumption, but when it comes down to a vote on national security, not many of them will vote against us. The only *safe* political posture is to be on the side of a strong military. Otherwise, a political opponent can charge them with being unpatriotic, soft on communism and, believe me, that's fatal."

"So, Monty," Creighton put in, "when you get up there tomorrow, let's see some of the old enthusiasm, O.K.?"

They rose to leave. Monty escorted them to the corridor door, then returned to his desk, where Zempfke was standing, talking to Lieutenant Trimble, who was holding a batch of papers.

"Good morning, Lieutenant," Monty said coldly.

"Morning, Captain," Trimble said. "I came in to start the paperwork on my resignation. I need your signature on four of these . . . "

"I don't have time for that right now," Monty said.

" . . . and I got to talking to Zempfke here about his problem. It seems to me it's a ridiculous mountain out of a molehill. I've had a little off-duty background in law. I'm going down there to see what I can do to help him."

"No you're not, Lieutenant," Monty said. "Admiral Starr gave orders that no one from OP-31, other than Zempfke, is to go near that court."

"Why?" Trimble asked.

"There may be reporters down there."

"Since when has the Admiral become so shy about reporters?" Trimble said in a sneering tone.

"What do you mean by that, Lieutenant?"

"I read that junk in the paper this morning," Trimble replied. "You or the Admiral, or both of you, had to be the source."

"Don't be a smart ass, Lieutenant," Monty said angrily.

"You tell the Admiral you gave me a direct order not to go with Zempfke," Trimble said, "and then I refused to accept it. That'll get you off the hook with the Admiral. Your skirts will be clean."

"Now look here, Lieutenant—"

Trimble turned away and went to the door with Zempfke. Tom Kemp came into the office as they were leaving. His eyes were troubled.

"Jesus H. Christ," he said to Monty, in a low voice. "Can we talk privately?"

They went into the Admiral's office and shut the door. Monty said to Kemp: "Did you give Hawkins an affidavit?"

"A *what*?"

"He said you gave a signed affidavit that Admiral Starr leaked that story."

"I didn't tell him a goddamn thing," Kemp returned. "That's what I came to tell you."

"That sonofabitch," Monty said.

"It's the old divide-the-witnesses trick," Kemp said. "Will you please assure Admiral Starr I told him absolutely nothing?"

"Yes. You don't suppose that reporter will talk?"

"No. He won't give away his source."

"It was a stupid thing to do."

"With hindsight, I agree," Kemp said. "You *will* tell Admiral Starr I protected him?"

"Yes."

"Good. I'm going to take some annual leave, get the hell out of here until it blows over. If I were you, I'd do the same."

Then he was gone. Monty returned to his desk, sat down to tackle the paper work. Jim Caldwell came steaming into the office looking angry.

"Monty, I've got to talk to you, in private," he said urgently.

"The Admiral's office," Monty said, getting up again.

Inside, Monty shut the door. Caldwell sat down wearily and said: "You goddamn idiots! Monty, do you realize what the hell you're doing? Hawkins just called SecNav to his office. Chewed his ass out. I mean, *really* chewed his ass out. He said he knew the leak came from OP-31. He has a goddamn affidavit. A *signed* affidavit! And furthermore, he was going to clean out the Navy high command from top to bottom. And he's going to make that budget-cut stick, even if he has to mothball the whole Navy, ship by ship—"

"Now wait a minute, Jim," Monty cut in. "He doesn't have an affidavit. That's a lot of bullshit. He was going to shake up the Navy Department anyway. He's just using this as an excuse."

"But Monty—"

"I didn't leak that story," Monty said. "I didn't approve of it."

"I know you didn't leak. Starr leaked. But, Monty, you should have stopped him."

"I tried to stop him. He wouldn't listen."

"Don't you realize how badly you've hurt the Navy? Monty, the Navy is people. People are going to be hurt. Badly hurt."

"I'm sorry, Jim. Really sorry."

"No you're not, Monty. You've turned into a goddamn robot—blindly committed to ULMS, parroting Zimmerman and Starr, going for your gong and your stars—not giving a damn who gets hurt."

"That's not—"

"Monty, you're really *inhuman.*"

Caldwell turned, left the office. Monty walked to the window, slamming his fist into his hand, overwhelmed with anger and shame. He returned to his desk, telephoned Dr. Douglas for an appointment at noon. Then he put on his jacket, walked to the blackboard and logged himself out: "Traffic Court."

The telephone woke Nancy from a terrifying nightmare. She had been standing on the deck of a submarine with Monty. She had called to him, then shouted, but he had shown no sign that he heard. He had turned away, climbed down a hatch into the submarine. Then the submarine had submerged, leaving Nancy awash in a vast ocean.

She shook her head, aware of the ringing. She leaned over, groggily pawing for the phone. Her arm was sore, as though she had slept on it. Her fingers trembled. She lifted the receiver and answered sleepily.

"Nancy?"

It was Alma Caldwell. Coming awake, Nancy dragged herself to a sitting position, glancing at the clock; it was ten o'clock. Then she fingered her torn nightgown and, with a terrible jolt, remembered. The scene, the words, cut into her consciousness like a knife. My God! she thought. What have I done?

"Nancy? Are you there?"

"Yes," Nancy said hollowly, "I'm here. I'm sorry."

"Were you asleep?"

"Yes. I'm awake now."

"How're things?" Alma asked cheerily.

"Terrible."

"What happened? Is Paul—"

"Paul's all right. Paul's fine. But, Alma, last night Monty and I had a terrible fight."

Alma said nothing.

"I told him he had to choose between me and the Navy."

"You idiot!" Alma replied forcefully. "What did you do that for?"

"I don't know. I was upset. I said all kinds of terrible things."

"You nincompoop!"

"I know. I feel ghastly. Simply ghastly."

"You call him up right now. Tell him you didn't mean it. Apologize."

"I will, I will . . . "

"What brought all this on?"

"Oh, it's a long story. I took Paul to this psychiatrist—"

"Psychiatrist!"

"Now, Alma. You won't tell Jim? This is in strictest confidence."

"Of course not. Go on, what did he say?"

"Oh, a lot of things. He told me . . . He said I was acting selfishly—that I was oversexed!"

Alma laughed uproariously. Then she said: "I'm sorry. Go on."

"That was the gist."

"Well!" Alma said seriously. "You know what *I* think?"

"No. What?"

"I think he may be right. I was going to say I thought you were being selfish, *very* selfish, but I didn't want to hurt

you. In the back of my mind, I wondered if you weren't
having some kind of sex surge."

"Isn't it awful?"

"It's probably perfectly normal."

"He says it is. After the menopause."

"Really?"

"He gave me a paper about it. A scientific study."

"I'd like to read that."

"I'll give it to you. Oh, God, Alma. The things I said to
Monty."

"Like what?"

"I can't . . . I wouldn't repeat them."

"What you two need is a good long weekend in New
York."

"Maybe . . . "

"What is Paul going to do?"

"I don't know. His own thing."

"Well, that's normal, too. You've got to cut loose, Nancy.
Let him grow up."

"I suppose so."

"You always did dote on him. I've been telling you that
for years."

"It's not true."

"Oh, yes, it *is* true. My theory is you were overcompensat-
ing for Joanie."

"Well—"

"Anyway, I'm certainly glad to hear your retirement phase
is over. And, Nancy, all that crap about not being friends if
Jim makes it and Monty doesn't or vice versa. That's utter
nonsense. Win, lose or draw, I'm your friend until they
plant us in Arlington. Now, why don't you and Monty come
for dinner Saturday and bring Paul?"

"Saturday? Paul may not be here."

"Come anyway."

"Oh. I almost forgot. Mike's coming home today."

"Bring Mike. Bring anybody."

They hung up. Nancy lay back, staring at the ceiling, thinking about Dr. Douglas, his theory about psychic incest. Perhaps, Nancy thought, there was something drastically wrong with her sexually. Perhaps Douglas was right.

There was a knock on the door. Nancy pulled the sheet over her torn nightgown and replied, "Yes?"

"It's me," a husky, feminine voice called back. "I've got something for you. May I come in?"

"Oh," Nancy said, in confusion. "Yes, come in, Linda."

The door opened. Linda came into the room carrying a bed tray. On it was a glass of orange juice, a cup of steaming coffee, the morning paper, folded. Nancy stared at the tray, then the girl.

"I heard the phone ring," Linda said. "I thought you'd like an eye-opener."

Nancy looked at the girl, touched by this gesture. Now she seemed a sweet, innocent young child. She could very well be little Joanie grown up, Nancy thought. Joanie would be slightly older. Twenty-two or twenty-three. But the color was the same. The figure might well have been similar. Big-breasted, slim-hipped.

"Thank you very much," Nancy said to Linda. "It's been a long time since I've had breakfast in bed."

"You're welcome," Linda smiled. Then her face assumed a grave look. "I wanted to say how very, very sorry I am about last night. I mean . . . I hope I didn't cause the fight. I mean . . . what I mean is, I told Mr. King . . . Captain King . . . a horrible thing. I . . . told him . . . "

"I know what you told him," Nancy said, sitting up, pulling the tray toward her, slowly and with great care. This girl was a lonely, lost soul, she thought. The toughness was an act.

"Yes," Linda said. "Well . . . anyway, I'm all packed and leaving this morning. I won't be any more trouble for you."

"Are you still planning to go to the Pentagon? To that . . . group?" Nancy asked, drinking the orange juice.

"Yes, I am."

"Well, I think that's a mistake."

"I know you do."

"It's cold out there," Nancy went on. "They live in tents It's wet. You'll get pneumonia."

"It's something I have to do."

"You should go home and live with your mother."

"I can't."

"You're hurting her."

"Mrs. King, I don't want anything to do with my mother. You don't . . . you can't imagine what it was like, growing up with her. Always drinking—juiced up. She was a very, very heavy cross for my father. She has no real values. Her idea of life, her whole consciousness, was focused on fantasy and pretense—on material things: a big house in the right neighborhood, the country club, social standing, coming-out parties, dresses, the riding academy. She didn't understand anything genuine. She didn't love my father. She loved what his money could buy, including social position. But the irony was, she wasn't really accepted. Everybody saw through her, including my father. She drove him away— forced him to run off with Kathleen. She made my father go away and leave me."

She broke off, eyes filmed with tears. Nancy was touched. Who was going to help this poor soul find herself?

"I'm sorry," Linda mumbled. A tear ran down her cheek to her lips. She licked it away and managed an embarrassed laugh.

"Silly. I'm sorry. I haven't done that in a long time."

"We all need a good cry every now and then," Nancy said. "Linda, why don't you go to England and live with your father?"

"I can't."

"Why?"

"Because I love him too much. I don't want to interfere in his life. He's happy now. After all he suffered from mother, he deserves it. I would just complicate things."

"Maybe not," Nancy said. She wondered if perhaps she should write Linda's father, and explain what was going on. This child needed help, badly.

"Anyway," Linda said, "I have to do my tour in the Movement. It means a great deal to me right now."

"You could stay here," Nancy said.

"No. No thanks, Mrs. King. I appreciate the offer. I'm going to the Pentagon."

"All right. I'll get dressed and give you a lift."

"Oh, that's O.K. I can hitch."

"Nonsense. It's no trouble. When do you want to go?"

"Any time. So long as I get there before noon. By the way, when the check comes from my mother, will you return it, please?"

"Yes, I'll return it."

"Mrs. King, will you accept my apology about last night?" Linda asked imploringly. "I didn't mean to cause any hurt."

"I accept your apology," Nancy said, lifting the coffee cup, sipping. "Now run along and I'll get dressed."

Before getting out of bed, she dialed Monty's office. Yeoman Armbruster answered.

"Is my husband there?" she asked.

"No, ma'm. He's down in traffic court with Zempfke."

"Oh," she said. "Will you ask him to call me as soon as he gets back?"

"Yes, ma'm."

"I'll be out for a while. But I should be back by twelve-thirty the latest."

"I'll tell him that, Mrs. King."

"Thank you."

Nancy got up, selected a wool dress. The telephone rang It was Scottie MacIntosh, ecstatic.

"Nancy! It's going up. Opened very strong. Did you see the story in this morning's paper? That kicked it off, I'm sure. Climbed four points. Everything is going exactly like Buzz said it would. So don't worry—"

"Oh," Nancy said.

"It ought to climb right up through the end of the week," Scottie chimed in.

"Scottie," Nancy said. "I want you to sell my stock. All of it. Right now. No matter what the price."

"Nancy! You've got to be kidding. You'll take a huge loss."

"I'm *not* kidding, Scottie. Sell."

"But Nancy, *why?*"

"I have my reasons. Personal reasons."

"I can't let you do this, Nancy. I absolutely will not sell that stock."

"Then I'll have to call your boss."

"You can't really be serious?"

"I'm dead serious. Anyway, what did you say Baruch's theory was? Sell when it's going up, buy when it's falling?"

"But that's an entirely different situation, Nancy."

"Sell. Right now."

"All right, Nancy. I'll sell it. But I think you're making a colossal mistake."

"Goodbye, Scottie."

★ 5 ★

Monty found the Pentagon courtroom on the first floor, not far from the Building Manager's office. It was a large, windowless room, with six rows of hard wooden chairs and a rail, like a real court. The chairs were all full—with defendants and police. The Magistrate sat behind a judge's bench, wearing a black robe.

Monty stood in the rear of the room, looking for Trimble and Zempfke. He saw them sitting in the second row, talking in whispers. A man was standing before the Magistrate, hands behind his back. A GSA policeman was standing beside the man, speaking to the bench.

"Your Honor. The total was twenty parking tickets in a period of four months—all ignored."

The Magistrate tilted back in his chair, seemingly bored. He was a young man, with dark eyebrows and slick, black hair. When the policeman had finished presenting the evidence, the Magistrate asked the defendant, "How do you plead?"

"Guilty, sir."

"Three hundred dollars or thirty days in the federal detention house," the Magistrate said coldly.

The defendant left the bench, walked to a table at the left corner, where a clerk was sitting with a small cashbox. The defendant took out his wallet, paid his fine in cash.

"Next case," the Magistrate sang out. "Antipollution League versus the United States Government."

There was a stir in the front row. Four young men with long hair and sideburns rose and approached the bench. They were well-dressed, professional-looking. In the second row of seats, Monty saw four or five young men with long hair take out notebooks and begin jotting notes with ballpoint pens. Reporters!

"Your Honor," one of the lawyers said. "If it please the court, we have not been able to serve complaint on the defendant."

"How's that?" the Magistrate asked. "Why not?"

"Sir," the lawyer said, in a cultivated voice, "I regret to say that until the very last minute, we were involved in a nightmarish jurisdictional problem. We didn't know whom to serve and we were getting a complete runaround. We thought first to serve the Department of Defense. The legal authorities there said no, we should serve the Military District of Washington, under whose aegis the Pentagon Building comes . . . "

"Wait a minute," the Magistrate said, sitting up. "What's this case all about?"

"Sir, my client, the Antipollution League, with headquarters in Washington, D.C., wishes to sue the proper authority in the government to stop the Pentagon from polluting the Potomac River. Now, if I may go on, sir, the Military District of Washington told us that, with respect to the Pentagon Sewage Plant, they did not have responsibility or jurisdiction; it was a GSA matter. We only found this out this morning and did not have time to serve. We apologize to the court."

The reporters snickered and jotted notes.

"There's no one here from GSA?" the Magistrate asked, surveying the room.

There was no reply.

"What is the gist of your complaint?" he asked the lawyer.

"Your Honor, the gist is this: When the Pentagon was originally built in 1942, there was also built, as an outlying facility, a sewage treatment plant, a Palmer-Method chemical process facility, with a theoretical capacity of 3.2 million gallons per day, the equivalent, in capacity, for a city of 44,000. In theory, also, the plant was designed to remove 77 percent of the bacteria in the effluent. Our complaint, sir, briefly, is threefold. One, the system is now overloaded because other federal facilities are now feeding sewage into it; two, there is frequent breakdown of the equipment necessitating a partial bypass of the system and the dumping of raw sewage into the Potomac River; and, three, even when it is operating properly, my client's studies show it does not even meet the absolute minimum 60 percent bacteria removal as required by District of Columbia law.

"Moreover, they have put out a story saying that the five

tons of solids captured each week are processed as fer-
tilizer and then used by the National Park Service to ferti-
lize the grounds at the White House and Pentagon. But,
Your Honor, this is not true. They tried it experimentally
some years ago, but the grass and plants all died. In any case,
Your Honor, they are now dumping that five tons of solids
a week in the edge of the river, near National Airport, as fill,
for expansion of the airport facility, which my client also
opposes. The fill is disrupting the ecological balance of the
area. Not only that, the fill contains a high level of bacteria."

The reporters alternately snickered and made notes.

Monty sighed impatiently, glanced at the clock, listening
with half an ear to the legal proceeding. He noticed the attention in the room had now drifted from the proceedings.
The reporters stopped taking notes. One of them—a young
man with long sideburns and a full mustache who looked
not much older than Paul—turned, and eyed Monty curiously through his Ben Franklin glasses.

When the lawyers concluded their legal presentation,
they left the bench, picked up their briefcases, made jokes
with the reporters. Then the reporters filed out, chatting,
laughing—all except the young one who had been eyeing
Monty. He remained seated.

"Next case," the Magistrate intoned. "Zempfke?"

He looked about the room. Trimble and Zempfke rose,
went up the center aisle to the bench. The reporter looked
at them intently as they passed.

Captain Davis, looking grave, was already in place before
the bench, holding a manila envelope. He spoke first, for
ten minutes, giving a concise, complete history of the case,
presenting his evidence tersely and undramatically. The
evidence was massive, overwhelming, uncontestable. The
Magistrate no longer seemed bored. He listened attentively,
asked Davis an occasional question, frowned, wiped his
mouth, twirled a pencil. When Davis had finished the complaint, the Magistrate looked at Zempfke with what Monty

took to be a look of repugnance. He said: "How do you plead, Zempfke?"

"Guilty, sir," Zempfke said, adding in a low voice, "It was stupid. Silly, I'm very sorry."

"It was hardly silly," the Magistrate said sarcastically.

"I didn't mean silly, sir," Zempfke said. "I know it's serious."

"Plenty serious," the Magistrate corrected.

"Yes, sir," Zempfke said, in a low voice.

"Captain Davis," the Magistrate said, "I don't believe I have the authority to try this case. It's more than a simple parking infraction. It's multiple forgery."

The reporter who remained behind jotted notes.

"I believe Zempfke, here, ought to be bound over to a higher court," the Magistrate went on. "He may want a jury trial."

"Sir," Trimble said, addressing the bench. "If I may, I would like to say—"

"Wait a minute!" Monty called out suddenly, hurrying up the middle aisle.

Zempfke and Trimble turned in surprise. The Magistrate peered down at Monty, curiously. Captain Davis smiled faintly in recognition.

"Your Honor," Monty said. "May I say a word to the Court?"

"Who are you, sir?" the Magistrate inquired.

"Sir, my name is Captain William King, U.S. Navy."

The reporter jotted notes furiously.

"In what capacity do you address the Court?" the Magistrate asked.

"Sir, I am Chief Zempfke's commanding officer. Navy Department. OP-31."

"All right," the Magistrate said. "What is it you wish to say?"

"I would like to say, sir, that I have known this man for fifteen years. He served his country with honor in World

War Two, and for twenty-five years thereafter. He is a brave submariner, a man of highest character, integrity, dependability ,in the best tradition of the Navy chiefs—the backbone of the Navy. I have never known him to get even slightly out of line before."

Monty paused, not knowing what he would say next. The Magistrate twirled his pencil.

"Sir," Monty hurried on, "Chief Zempfke did not really intend to defraud—to do anything dishonest. It started as a joke. They were tight at a party and he was challenged to draw a permit. Well, the joke was a bad joke—he's admitted that—he's sorry. But, Your Honor, while I certainly agree it is a serious matter, sir, must it be a bad joke that will destroy his career, jeopardize his retirement rights?"

The Magistrate looked at Monty thoughtfully. Then he said: "Court recesses for five minutes. Captain King, will you come behind the bench?"

"Yes, sir," Monty said. He walked behind the bench.

"This is a case," the Magistrate said, in a low voice, "where the punishment is too harsh for the crime. But the GSA people, Captain Davis, are out for blood. Their case is solid as rock."

"I know that," Monty replied, voice low. "We don't quarrel with the evidence. My point is—"

"I know your point. You must really think very highly of this man."

"Sir, I do."

The Magistrate studied Monty appraisingly. Then he said: "All right, Captain King. These days, one rare kindness deserves another, I guess. I'd hate to see him ruined by a bad joke, too. If you assure me he won't pull any more jokes on these hard-working Pentagon police, I'll dismiss the case."

"All right. I give you my word. Thank you."

Monty passed through the opening in the rail.

The Magistrate stared down at Captain Davis and said:

"In your presentation of evidence, you stated that a wire tap was placed on Chief Zempfke's telephone and this was instrumental in preparing your evidence. Is that correct?"

"Yes, sir," Captain Davis said proudly.

"Are you aware of the federal laws on wire tapping?" the Magistrate asked.

"Generally, sir."

"Did you obtain permission from a federal judge before placing the tap?"

Captain Davis's face fell.

"No, sir. You see, Mr. Lambert, Building Commandant's office, CID, actually placed the tap. He doesnt' need permission because it was a security violation—a *possible* security violation case—and he had blanket authority—"

"But, Captain," the Magistrate said. "You're not bringing charges of a security violation. Your charge is forgery of a parking permit. So, regardless of Mr. Lambert's authority, you should have obtained a separate court authorization."

"But—" Captain Davis protested.

"If I bind him over to a higher court," the Magistrate pressed, "we'd be overruled. I haven't been overruled yet, Captain, and I certainly don't want to be now. So, we'll nol-pros this case."

"But, Your Honor," Captain Davis said. "We worked weeks—"

"Sorry, Captain, but you know the law. Dismissed. Next case."

Monty took Zempfke by the elbow and led him through the court into the corridor. Trimble came behind.

In the corridor, Zempfke turned to Monty and said, "Sir, I . . ."

"Forget it, Chief," Monty said.

Trimble came up. He said darkly, "Captain. There *was* a reporter in the room."

"I know. I saw him. In fact, here he comes now. You guys beat it. Get lost. I'll see you back in the office."

Zempfke and Trimble hurried off. The reporter walked up to Monty.

"OP-31. Is that the Submarine Warfare Division, Captain?"

"That's right," Monty said, turning away. It was noon. The civilian clinic, where Dr. Douglas worked, was nearby. The reporter followed, pencil poised on his notebook.

"I was wondering, Captain," he said, "if you could help me."

Monty stopped, turned. "As you surely know, I'm not permitted to talk with the press unless authorized by Chinfo or DOD."

"Yes, sir, I know that. But I thought maybe I could ask you something off the record."

"I don't talk off the record," Monty said. "You have my name and job. That's all I—"

"This morning," the reporter pressed, "there was a wire story on the Submarine Force . . . the Soviet contact. My editor asked me to get a new angle for my paper. Can you help me?"

"No," Monty said, adding, "I'm sorry."

"Just tell me this—was it true?"

"I'm sorry."

Monty turned, walked away. This time the reporter did not follow. After a few steps, Monty stopped, turned, and called out: "Wait—"

The reporter hurried to Monty.

"Tomorrow morning," Monty said, "there's going to be a hearing up on the Hill. Congressman Magruder's House Armed Services Committee. If you cover that, you'll get your answer . . . your truth."

★ 6 ★

Going into the kitchen, Nancy found Paul standing on his head, back braced against the wall.

"Paul! What on earth—"

"I'm meditating," he said, smiling.

She felt a sudden apprehension. Was the drug coming back? She looked into his upside-down face carefully.

"You ought to try it sometime," Paul said. "The blood runs to the brain . . . saturates the brain with oxygen. It's a great trip. Best thing in the world for brain damage."

"I'm sure."

"That was very nice of you to offer Linda a roof," he said.

"Would you please get up—sit down—so we can talk properly?"

"In primitive times, we hung from the trees upside down and talked. Why must one be erect?"

"Paul, don't be flip."

"Aye, aye, sir." He saluted upside down.

"Paul, now—"

"How does the world look to you this morning?" he asked.

"What do you mean?"

"I mean, did Douglas open your eyes a little?"

"I don't know. I'm not—"

"Part of his game plan is to provoke."

"Provoke?"

"The fight with Dad. That was good. Shook out a lot of pent-up anger and hostility. It's the first time I ever heard you fight."

Nancy blushed, sat down at the kitchen table.

"It's not normal not to fight," Paul said. "You can't bottle things up. That's dangerous."

"Would you please get up?" Nancy said.

"You ought to keep on seeing Douglas," Paul said, ignoring her request. "Ask him to put you in a therapy group. You'd get a lot out of it."

"Paul," Nancy said sternly, "I want to talk seriously to you. I can't talk with you upside down."

Paul let his feet fall to the floor. He got up, looking flushed. He kissed Nancy on the forehead. He seemed in a fey mood. She looked closely at his eyes. They were bright, cheerful. Yet, she worried . . .

"All right," he said airily. "Rap."

"Your father was much impressed by your talk last night," Nancy said. "He really admires you, Paul."

"It was good," Paul agreed. "It's the first time he ever really listened to me."

"We're changing our plans," she said. "He's not going to retire after all."

"I never thought he would anyway."

"And we are reconciled to your doing what you want to do," she went on carefully, "except for one point. We don't think it's wise for you to go to Canada."

"That's for me to decide."

"We're thinking of *your* own best interest, not ours."

"I know . . . " Paul broke off, humming, staring off at a distant horizon.

"It is one thing to be independent in your views, quite another to be a criminal," Nancy said, watching him closely.

Paul said nothing. He continued to hum.

"You ought to think about that carefully."

"I have," he said, resuming the humming.

"I was under the impression the Supreme Court had broadened the concept of the conscientious objector. If you sincerely oppose military service, there are other ways of serving the country, aren't there? I mean, running off to Canada seems a . . . a cliché. Paul, are you listening to me?"

Linda came from the back hall, dressed to leave. She was wearing corduroy slacks, cut low at the waist, a thick leather belt, a low-neck sweater, and an Eisenhower jacket, beads, and a floppy felt Australian army hat. On the front of the hat there was a large pin that said:

FIGHTING FOR PEACE IS LIKE
BALLING FOR CHASTITY

"Do me a favor, love?" she said to Paul. "Carry the A-frame out to the car?"

"Sure," Paul said, going to the back hall.

Nancy got up and closed the door. She turned to Linda, speaking in a low voice.

"Is Paul all right?"

"I beg your pardon?" Linda said.

"Is he . . . is the drug coming back?"

"I don't think so, why?"

"I found him standing on his head."

"Oh, he does that every morning."

"He seems strange to me. Euphoric . . . humming."

"Maybe he's just in a good mood."

"Oh," Nancy said doubtfully.

"He was very happy when he woke up—about your fight and all. I think he feels it is the beginning of something very good for you, you know?"

Paul opened the door. "All set," he said.

They went to the car. In the front yard, Paul skipped on the flagstones, as though playing an imaginary game of hopscotch. Nancy glanced apprehensively at Linda. She shrugged her shoulders. Paul held the door for his mother, bowing low.

"Paul," she said solemnly, "are you all right?"

"Great!" he exclaimed.

"Perhaps I better drive . . . " Nancy said.

"*Your* driving drives *me* up the wall," Paul grinned. "Get in. Relax. Getting there is half the fun."

Paul got behind the wheel, turned the radio to loud hard-rock.

"Turn that down!" Nancy shrieked.

He backed out fast, leaving the radio loud. On Braddock Road, he hummed and patted the steering wheel, keeping time with the music.

"Keep both hands on the wheel," Nancy shouted above the music. "If you had a blowout—"

He looked at her and smiled condescendingly. From the back seat, Linda asked: "Mrs. King, do you use lead-free gasoline?"

Nancy turned and said, "I don't know."

"Please do," Linda said. "The automobile engine is the greatest polluter. There are already over 100 million automobiles, and 7 or 8 million new ones coming every year. Until we get a steam or electric engine, we've got to use lead-free gas, or else in a few years we won't be able to breathe."

Nancy nodded, considering this grim possibility.

"Will you promise?" Linda pressed.

"I'll talk to my husband about it," she said, turning again to face the road.

Paul was driving erratically, Nancy thought. Too fast, too carelessly, weaving playfully through heavy traffic on the Beltway, waving to the motorists he passed.

"Paul," she said, "keep your eyes on the road. You're exceeding the speed limit."

She turned down the radio. "Did you hear me?"

"Yes," Paul said, turning the radio up again.

"Then do as I say," Nancy said, turning the radio down again.

He looked at her and said, "It's the slow driver who causes most of the accidents. Those and the drunks."

"You're driving like you're drunk," she said tartly.

"Maybe I am," he said vaguely.

Linda leaned forward and said, "Paul, are you coming up?"

"No," he said. "I don't think so."

How can he be sure, Nancy wondered.

"You're manic," Linda said.

"I know."

The car ahead slowed abruptly. Paul seemed not to notice.

"Watch out!" Nancy cried.

Paul braked. The sudden deceleration threw Nancy against the dashboard.

"Sorry, Mother," Paul said.

"I better drive," Nancy said, looking at her son with mounting apprehension.

"I'm all right. I've got it . . . we can't stop here."

Nancy sat back, watching the road, pressing her foot against an imaginary brake. Paul had always been a cautious driver, like Monty, she thought. There was something wrong. Very wrong.

Paul turned the car off Shirley Highway, into the cloverleaf leading to the Pentagon South Parking.

"There they are!" Linda said, looking at the protest camp on the grassy knoll.

Nancy turned to look. She saw five or six shabby tents, several makeshift huts. The compound was surrounded by police saw-horses. There was a police car parked outside, and two policemen lounging near one of the saw-horses, talking to a knot of long-haired, bearded protesters. A Soviet flag flapped on a short flagpole inside the compound. Nancy turned to Linda.

"Are you sure you won't change your mind?"

"Yes," Linda said excitedly, keeping her eyes on the compound until it disappeared from view.

"It's going to be very cold out there," Nancy said.

Linda said nothing. Paul swung the car into South Parking, following a lane which led toward the compound. At the end of the lane, in front of a stone wall, he stopped.

"End of the line, Valentine," he said, smiling at Linda.

They got out, Paul hefting the A-frame from the back seat.

"Thank you very much for everything, Mrs. King," Linda said, shaking hands.

"I wish you wouldn't go," Nancy said. "Honestly."

"Maybe we'll meet again," Linda replied. "Peace." She leaned to pick up the A-frame.

"Wait a minute," Paul said suddenly. "I'll carry that over for you." He turned to his mother. "Don't wait. I'll be home later."

"But, Paul . . . " Nancy said.

"I want to see the camp," Paul said. "Rap with the kids. Maybe get a little acid."

"Acid!"

"I'm only kidding."

"I wish you'd come with me," Nancy said. "How will you get home?"

"I'll hitch a ride. Don't worry."

"I *am* worried, Paul."

"I'm all right, Mother. Honest."

He picked up the A-frame, slung it on his back. They walked off, waving to Nancy.

"Paul," Nancy called out. "*Please* come back."

He waved again, cheerfully.

She got back in the car, feeling a presentiment of doom. Something dreadful was going to happen to Paul. He might really get some acid and then what would happen? She might never see him alive again. She watched them until they were out of sight. She felt an overpowering dread. I can't let him go, she thought. I must do something. But what?

"Monty," she said aloud. She would tell him. He would go to the compound and persuade Paul to come home with her.

She left the car double-parked in the lane, walked toward the Pentagon, following the signs. She entered the building at Corridor Three, having no idea where Monty's office might be or how to get there. Perhaps she had better telephone, she thought.

She wandered along the corridor, through the lunch-time throngs, looking for a public phone booth. Soon she found herself in the Concourse, the shopping mall, with department stores, drug stores, all kinds of stores. There, she found a phone, dropped in a dime and dialed Monty's office.

"He's not here, Mrs. King," Yeoman Armbruster said.

"Is he still in traffic court?" she asked.

"No ma'm. He called and said he was going to see a Dr. Douglas in the Civilian Dispensary."

"Oh, yes." Nancy remembered. She looked at her watch. It was just after noon.

"I can give you that extension, if you like, ma'm," Armbruster said.

"Yes, please."

"It's five-five-six-four-three. If you'll hold, I'll try to transfer you, but it doesn't always work."

"Thank you."

Nancy waited, hearing the clicking, the Pentagon operator coming on the line, Armbruster's polite request for a transfer.

Monty sat in a chair, facing Dr. Douglas across his clean desk top. It was a small office on the first floor, with a single window looking on the space between Rings B and C. The door behind him was closed.

Douglas took a sandwich and cup of coffee from a paper bag.

"You don't mind if I eat?"

"Certainly not," Monty said, wondering when or how he himself would find time to eat.

"I seem to be eating all my meals at my desk," Douglas said. "Everybody in this building works too goddamn hard. Cardiac cases by the score. Everybody wound up tight as a spring. Lunatic asylum."

He took a bite of the sandwich. It was ham on rye with lettuce and mayonnaise. Monty looked on, feeling hunger pains.

"Well, we better get started," Douglas went on. "I've got regular patients coming at 1300. Retirees. We counsel them, before they go off the payroll. You'd be amazed how many people go into mild shock when they retire."

"Hmm," Monty said.

"Did you have an opportunity to talk to Paul last night?" Douglas said, sipping his coffee.

"Yes."

"How did it go?"

"Fine. Good talk."

"He's an intelligent, perceptive young man," Douglas said, biting into his sandwich. "There's no need to worry about drugs or suicide. He's not the type. It's just not in the cards."

"Are you absolutely sure of that?" Monty asked.

"As sure as one can be about anything involving human behavior," Douglas said. "There are no absolutes. But, in my professional judgment, he's not suicidal. He's very well-motivated."

"Did my wife tell you about my mother?" Monty asked, voice low.

"No. Paul did, however."

"Paul? I didn't know he knew."

"Oh, yes. But don't be concerned about that. I don't believe in hereditary suicidal tendencies. That's an old-wives' tale. It's the *environment* that counts."

Monty stared at Douglas, with doubt in his eyes.

"Don't worry about it," Douglas said. "I'll go into it with you in more detail later . . . when we have more time."

"My wife said you condoned Paul's going to Canada."

"No, no. I don't *condone* it," Douglas protested. "Generally, I said, he's got to get out on his own."

"She was plenty upset."

"Not so much about Paul, I think," Douglas replied, again biting into the sandwich.

"Well, what did you say that got her so upset?"

"She had an absurd notion—a fantasy—about your retiring and starting life anew."

"Why is that absurd?"

"The way she was fantasizing it. Vine-covered cottage, all that."

"We all retire someday."

"Later it might be different. But not at age forty-six. Right in your prime. That, in my opinion, would be catastrophic for both of you. Tell me, why don't you sleep with your wife?"

"Who says I don't sleep with my wife?" Monty bridled.

"She does."

"Oh," Monty said, "I—"

"Are you concerned about your sexuality?"

"What do you mean?"

"Do you feel . . . impotent?"

"No, I'm just too goddamn tired when I come home."

"Do you have erections?"

"Of course."

"Do you masturbate?"

"Hell, no!" Monty shot back. "What do you mean?"

"Did you masturbate frequently at sea?"

"No," Monty said angrily. "Look, Dr. Douglas. I came down here at my wife's request to talk about Paul. I don't . . . "

"Paul is not the urgent problem. Now, if it is true you did not masturbate at sea, then I must pronounce you a medical oddity—the very first case I ever encountered. Have you considered there may be something physically wrong with your testicles?"

"Oh, hell," Monty conceded. "I guess maybe I did occasionally."

"That's better."

"But what the hell's that got to do with—"

"I'm trying to fathom why you haven't slept with your wife for thirteen months."

"I don't know why."

"You don't have a girl friend?"

"Certainly not."

"I see. Well, you should understand that your wife is having a sexual renaissance. Perfectly natural post-menopausal reaction. Release from fear of pregnancy and all that. I gave her a paper to read. You might read it yourself."

"All right."

"Her sex drive probably conditions most of her behavior, right now. It was eating away at her, bringing on the fantasy of the new life. The way to handle this, I believe, is for you to show her more . . . more attention."

"I don't understand why you say it's a fantasy . . . that retirement is absurd."

Douglas glanced at his watch, then drained his coffee cup, tossed it into the wastebasket.

"Captain," he said adopting a professorial tone. "I've spent a good bit of my life studying what I call the maritime family—the sea-going man and his mate. You must grant, initially, that it is, sexually, an odd arrangement. Right? Two people mate, knowing full well that they will spend most of their lives apart?"

"I don't think many of us expected to spend so *much* time away from home," Monty countered.

Douglas raised a hand. "The nature of the life dictates long periods of separation, right?"

"Right," Monty conceded.

"Now, you must ask yourself, why? Why would two people deliberately enter into such an odd matrimonial arrangement? My theory, based on many years of close observation of the maritime family, is they do it instinctively and deliberately, albeit unconsciously, and that the complaining later is merely a surface defense mechanism to disguise the reality, which is that they prefer it—the female in particular."

"Prefer it?" Monty exclaimed.

"Hold on. Let me finish. Your wife is a typical Navy brat. When she was growing up, her father was, more often than not, away. Gone to sea. She grew up with a feeling of rejection. She, unconsciously, longed for his love. Perfectly natural. She married you, a stand-in, so to speak, for her father. But deep down, in the unconscious, she confused the two —her father and you. So that now—"

"Dr. Douglas," Monty broke in. "Don't give me a lot of Freudian crap."

"You asked my views," Douglas said coldly. "Now let me finish."

"But I—"

"I remind you, Captain. Your wife came to me. I didn't seek you out. I don't need patients. I'm eating my lunch at my desk in order to talk to you."

"All right," Monty said impatiently. "Go on."

"She wants you, of course. But at arm's length. Otherwise, she's involved in what I call psychic incest."

"Oh, for Christ's sake, Douglas," Monty said. "What a lot of bilge."

"And you, of course, play the opposing role."

"I don't have time for this," Monty said, standing to leave. "I've got work to do."

"The fact remains," Douglas said, "whether you accept it or not, you two cannot go live in a vine-covered cottage and blissfully watch sunsets."

"Are you saying people can't change?"

"Yes. Not basically. Not the deeper instincts."

"Then what are you guys in business for?" Monty retorted, sarcastically. "I thought your job was to change people."

"Not at all. Our job is to open people's eyes to their true nature. That achieved, the people make their own adjustment to reality. But they don't change fundamentally."

"Well, you know what I think?" Monty sneered. "I think . . . I know damn well . . . I'm getting sick and tired of people telling me what I can and cannot do around here. I think you're dead wrong. People can change. You'll see."

The telephone jangled. Douglas answered. He passed the phone to Monty.

"It's for you. Your wife."

"Nancy? How in the world—"

"Monty!" Nancy said, in an urgent voice. "I'm so glad I caught you. Look, there's a problem. We drove Linda here to join her protest group. Paul got out with her and went to the camp. I tried to stop him. He wouldn't listen. Monty, I believe he's high . . . coming up on the drugs again. All morning he was acting very strange. Standing on his head, humming inanely, like Monday night. Monty, I'm afraid something dreadful is going to happen to him. You've got to help me get him out of there."

"Where are you, honey?"

"In the Pentagon. Down here where all the shops are."

"The Concourse?"

"Yes."

"What shop are you near?"

"Wait a minute. I'm . . . I'm just opposite Brentano's book store."

"Well, stay put. I'll be right there."

"All right. I won't move."

Monty hung up and turned to Douglas.

"Paul ran off with the girl to the protest camp," he said. "Nancy believes he's high. She's worried as hell! Wants me to go get him."

"Oh, for God's sake!" Douglas sighed. "Can't you two let that boy alone for five minutes?"

"If he's high, he shouldn't be running around loose. Especially not to that camp. You don't approve of that, do you?"

"What makes her think he's high?"

"He's been standing on his head all morning."

"Come on then," Douglas said, with exasperation. "I'll go with you. I want to talk to her again."

They went into the corridor.

★ 8 ★

They moved into the dense flow of lunch-time traffic, Monty leading. Suddenly Monty heard shouting and running footsteps. He glanced around. Coming toward him at high speed were Captain Davis and a dozen of his Special Police. The group halted not more than six paces away.

"Martin," Monty heard Captain Davis say agitatedly to one of his men, "take your squad to the Secretary of Defense area. On the double. Remember your orders. No shooting!"

One of the policemen, apparently Martin, ran up the pedestrian ramp. Four of the policemen followed him. What the hell was this, Monty wondered. A bomb threat drill? He moved in closer. Davis was giving orders to the other men. His face was grave. Five more police came rushing up from the direction of the cafeterias. One wore a white shirt, with a single gold lieutenant's stripe on the epaulet.

"What's up?" he asked Davis.

"The hippies have broken in," Davis exclaimed, in a loud voice. "All over the damn building."

"Jesus!" the lieutenant responded.

"Deploy your men for Plan Baker," Davis said.

The lieutenant and the men with him rushed down the corridor toward the police station.

"Did you hear that?" Monty said to Douglas. "The hippies are in the building! Maybe Paul and Linda."

Monty turned his attention back to Davis. The CID man, Lambert, had run up with two other men.

"Do you want the troops?" Lambert asked Davis.

"Not yet," Davis said. "I've got twenty-five men deployed, or being deployed. Damn them for picking lunch time. My men were scattered all over."

"I figured they'd pick lunch hour if they ever broke in," Lambert said. "I've alerted Fort Myer. The troops are on stand-by, if we need them. Buses ready. The bomb-disposal teams are standing by. The fire station is on full alert. Have you notified SecDef?"

"Yes."

"The door guards?"

"First thing. They got in, but they won't get out."

"Good," Lambert said, licking his lips.

Davis turned back to the knot of policemen, giving orders. They trotted off. At that moment, Monty heard a piercing shout. He turned. A band of hippies came racing down the pedestrian ramp. There were six or seven of them, young people with long flowing hair and a weird assortment of clothing. One was carring a Soviet flag.

"Here they come!" Davis shouted, staring wide-eyed.

"Bastards," Lambert spit. "Get 'em."

Monty turned to Douglas. "Go get my wife. She's opposite Brentano's at a phone booth. I'll see if I can find Paul and Linda and meet you back at your office."

"Right," Douglas said, hurrying off toward the Concourse.

Monty watched as Davis and Lambert ran up the ramp to intercept the hippies, who divided into two groups, running faster. Davis dived toward one group, making a flying tackle. He caught one hippie by a leg, bringing him down with a thud. The boy struggled free and ran. Lambert set a course to intercept the second group, one of whom carried the flag. The second group eluded Lambert completely, coming down the ramp directly toward Monty.

The hippies ran by Monty. One of them, a girl, wearing a floppy felt Australian hat, looked just like Linda. Monty caught his breath, then ran after the group. It dispersed into the crowds thronging toward the cafeteria doors. He lost sight of the girl for a moment. Then he saw the hat. He shoved toward it, pushing people aside. He caught the girl by the arm, spun her around. Yes! It was Linda. She looked around, wild-eyed, panting. Then she tore away. Monty ran after her, catching up, again grabbing her sleeve.

"Linda!" he shouted.

She turned, stared into his eyes, giving no sign she had ever seen him before.

"Where's Paul?" Monty demanded.

Linda shrugged her shoulders. Then she spit in Monty's face and hissed, "Fascist pig! Let go!"

Monty drew back, stunned. He wiped his face with his hand. Linda broke and ran. From the opposite direction, another group of hippies raced into A ring, shouting. The lunch crowds fell back, clearing a path, looking on in amazement. The new hippie group passed Monty. In their midst he saw a young boy with long, dark, matted hair, wearing an Air Force sergeant's jacket. He was either Paul or his double.

"Paul!" Monty shouted. "Paul, wait!"

Monty ran after the group. But they, too, were soon gone, tearing off down a corridor. Monty stopped to catch his breath, leaning against the wall, feeling suddenly a sharp pain in his back.

Now, from the direction of the fire station, Monty heard a siren. Then he saw the little red Cushman fire truck with its red light, coming down the corridor. There were four firemen wearing helmets, hanging on. It swung up the pedestrian ramp toward the second floor. Captain Davis and

Lambert followed it up the ramp. One of the firemen yelled at Davis: "They set fire to the Hall of Heroes!"

Oh God, Monty thought. No! Linda? Paul? Feeling dread, a premonition, he ran after the Cushman, oblivious of the pain in his back. The little truck did not have much power. It strained up the ramp. Monty caught up, running just behind Davis and Lambert, who were too preoccupied to notice him.

At the second floor, the truck turned into A ring. Immediately, Monty could smell smoke. Then a woman came running toward them, shouting hysterically: "He set himself on fire! He set himself on fire!"

She reeled and collapsed on the floor beside the truck. Davis stopped, bent over her.

"Call the infirmary," he said, standing up, speaking to an Air Force major who knelt beside the woman. Then Davis hurried off behind the truck.

Monty ran alongside the truck toward the Hall of Heroes, seeing the smoke, dense and black, pouring from the entrance. By now, a large crowd had gathered—backed up into the Mall Corridor, facing the Hall. They were civilians, Army and Air Force officers in uniform. They seemed to be frozen in shock. Two of the firemen, wearing oxygen masks and carrying axes, jumped off the truck and ran into the flaming Hall. Monty took a deep breath and followed them into the smoke.

Then he stopped, staring in horror. There, on the bright blue carpet, before the glass-domed display of medals, was a body. The long matted hair, the clothes—an Air Force sergeant's jacket—were a mass of flames. Monty could smell the terrible odor of burning flesh. The flaming body emitted a piercing shriek and flapped its arms in one last, futile effort to put out the flames.

The two firemen stood mutely looking on. Choking, coughing, fighting down nausea, Monty screamed: "Paul!"

He lunged blindly, ripping down one of the long purple

drapes behind the display of medals. But one of the firemen grabbed him roughly by the arm and pulled him back, shouting: "Get out! It's too late!"

Coughing, flailing, eyes and lungs searing, Monty struggled with the firemen. Then he felt himself going weak, consciousness ebbing. Then a blackness. He fell to the floor.

When he opened his eyes, he saw the ceiling passing rapidly. He was lying flat on his back. There was a mouthpiece over his lips. He inhaled pure, cool oxygen. He saw a man on his left in a white medic's jacket, another near his feet. He remembered, sat up suddenly, tearing away the mouthpiece.

"Lie down," the medic on his left said. "Take it easy."

Monty felt a firm hand on his chest, pushing him down. He lay back, eyes open, watching the ceiling. Then the mouthpiece covered his lips again. He inhaled and felt a searing pain in his chest.

Paul! he thought. Oh my God! My God!

The blackness returned.

★ **9** ★

Nancy waited by the telephone booth, watching the lunch-hour shoppers in the Concourse. Now that Monty was on the way to take charge, she had doubts about what she was doing. Had she overreacted again? If Paul was truly all right, what would he say if Monty appeared in the compound to take him home?

Perhaps she and Monty could find a place for a quiet lunch and a good talk. She would apologize first for what she had said last night. She would tell him she had been wrong about retirement. Then she would tell him about selling the stock at a great loss. He would know what best to do about Paul.

In the crowd she saw a familiar face coming toward her. Dr. Douglas! But where was Monty?

"Your husband asked me to pick you up," Douglas said, walking up. "The kids from the compound broke into the building to demonstrate. He thought possibly Linda and Paul might be among them, so he's off chasing them. You come to my office. He's planning to meet you there after the dust settles. O.K?"

"Of course," Nancy said, sharply sucking in her breath. That was why Linda insisted on being at the Pentagon to-day by noon! And why Paul insisted on going with her to the compound. If he took part in a break-in, surely he was high!

"Do they break in often?" she asked, walking by his side.

"No, this is the first time."

"Why are they doing it now?"

"I'm not sure. They may want to get caught, for the publicity, to keep the protest alive."

"What do you think the punishment will be?"

"Not much, probably. It's only a violation of a GSA building regulation against unauthorized demonstrators. They'll book them and fine them, probably. Nothing to worry about."

Nancy nodded.

"It's going to be a nuisance for me," Douglas said. "As the resident Department of Defense psychiatrist, I'm required by regulation to interview and write a report on every so-called undesirable and misfit the police pick up in the halls —the drunks, psychos, and so on. The hippies fall into this category. It'll take me a week of paper work. That's one reason, Mrs. King, I can assure you that Paul is well-moti-vated, and no cause for real concern. Certainly not, by comparison to the freaks that inhabit that compound."

They pushed through the lunch-time throngs to the Civilian Dispensary, a serene oasis with carpets, bright blue walls and pastoral paintings. There was a nurse in uniform at a reception desk, talking on the telephone. When she saw Dr. Douglas, she said into the phone: "Here he is now." Then she hung up.

"Doctor," she said excitedly. "That was the Army Dispensary. One of the hippies set himself on fire in the Hall of Heroes! That Captain King you had in your office just now tried to save him. He told the medics over there the kid was his son. They want you right away."

"Paul!" Nancy cried, feeling the breath knocked from her.

"Was the boy seriously burned?" Douglas said quickly.

"DOA," the nurse replied. "Charcoal."

"Oh God, no!" Nancy shouted hysterically. She felt one enormous blinding shock—then consciousness slipping . . .

When she awoke, she was sitting on the floor, head between her knees, shoes off. A hand was waving a bottle beneath her nose that gave off a powerful odor.

"She's coming around," Nancy heard the nurse say.

"Are you all right?" Douglas asked.

Nancy tried to say yes. She was numb. No words would come. She nodded her head affirmatively.

"I'm so sorry, Mrs. King," the nurse was saying. "I didn't know. I'm so sorry."

"Was Paul wearing an Air Force sergeant's jacket?" Douglas asked her.

Nancy shook her head negatively.

"Then it wasn't Paul," Douglas said. "The kid had on an Air Force jacket."

"Are you sure?" Nancy whispered. "He could have picked it up in the compound."

"I doubt it. Those kids don't have extra jackets lying around. Do you feel strong enough to stand?"

"I think so," she managed.

Douglas helped her to her feet. She slipped on her shoes.

"What kind of mood was Paul in when you dropped him?"

"Fey," she said. "He may have been high on drugs. A recurrence."

"Not paranoid?"

"No. Flip."

"It wasn't Paul," Douglas said again. "Your husband must be mistaken. He may be in shock."

"Was he burned?"

"He got some smoke inhalation, that's all. Do you think you could manage a short walk to the Army Dispensary?"

"Yes."

Douglas took her by the elbow and led her back into the corridor, past the cafeteria crowds to the Concourse, up the wheelchair ramp to the Army Dispensary. Inside, the reception room was jammed with reporters and radio and television men with portable tape recorders and cameras. They were shouting and pushing. One young long-haired reporter saw Douglas and came to him immediately.

"Doctor," he said. "Can you tell us what's going on? Have you identified the kid? Who's the Navy captain they've got back there? There's a rumor going around the kid was his son. Is this true?"

Nancy felt faint again, her knees going rubbery. She held fast to Douglas, heart thudding.

"I don't know a thing," Douglas said coldly to the reporter. "As you can see, I just got here."

"Who is this?" the reporter said, staring brazenly at Nancy.

"We'll give you what information we're authorized to give later," Douglas said, pushing on.

They went past the reception counter into a hallway. A bald man in white medical jacket and Army trousers came out of a swinging door.

"God, Brainard!" he said with a look of exasperation. "What a mess!"

"Somebody ought to get those damn newspaper people out of there," Douglas said, nodding toward the reception room.

"I've notified the Office of the Secretary. They're sending some Public Information types over right away."

"This is Mrs. King," Douglas said. "Captain King's wife. Nancy, this is Dr. Hull."

"I'm so sorry, Mrs. King," Dr. Hull said, voice low. "Your husband's in here."

Nancy nodded numbly.

"Come this way," Hull said, glancing darkly at Douglas.

He led the way back through a swinging door into an emergency room. Nancy saw Monty, lying on a wheeled stretcher, around which four white-jacketed medics hovered.

"He'll be all right," Hull said reassuringly. "Apart from the shock, there's just a little smoke inhalation, plus he aggravated a back condition."

Nancy pushed through the medics to the stretcher. "Monty!" she cried.

Monty looked up at his wife. His face was ashen, eyes racked with grief and pain.

"Honey," he said, raising himself on his elbows.

"Don't," she said, putting her hand on his chest.

She took his hand, looking down into his face, communicating the question with her eyes. She was determined to hold on, not to collapse again, no matter what.

"Yes," he said, with agony. "I got a good look."

"Oh, God!" Nancy moaned, clutching his hand, shuddering, feeling faint in spite of her resolve.

"Captain King," Douglas said, bending over. "You told the medics the boy was wearing an Air Force jacket?"

"Yes," Monty nodded.

"Paul was *not* wearing an Air Force jacket, according to your wife."

"I can't help that," Monty sighed. "I *saw* him. First in the corridor, then in the Hall. It was Paul."

"It couldn't have been," Douglas said firmly. He turned to Hull. "Is Captain Davis here?"

"He's on his way," Hull replied.

"My God! My God!" Monty cried out, in a voice full of

terror. Nancy held his hand tightly and soothed his brow.

Captain Davis and Mr. Lambert came into the room. Two of the medics left to make room. Davis and Lambert conferred with Douglas in low tones, Douglas all the while shaking his head negatively. Then Davis and Lambert came to the stretcher.

"Captain King, do you feel up to answering some questions?" Davis asked.

"Yes."

"You say you got a good look at the boy?"

Monty nodded.

"And it was your son, Paul?"

Monty nodded again and said, "Yes. My son."

"Are you certain? You made a positive identification?"

Monty nodded.

"What was he doing here?" Davis asked.

"He was with a girl, Linda—Linda Adams."

Lambert consulted a piece of paper. He leaned over and said: "We've got a Linda Adams on the arrest sheet, but—"

"That's her," Monty said. "I saw her. Wearing an Australian Army hat."

"Captain," Lambert said, leaning in close again, this time with a skeptical look. "We've kept a pretty close watch on those kids over there. Confidentially, one of our men had penetrated the group. I am not aware that either your son, Paul King, or the girl, Linda Adams, was associated with the people in the compound. Can you explain this?"

"They only got there this morning," Nancy put in. "Linda belonged to some group in Wisconsin. Paul was just . . . just visiting . . . helping Linda get squared away, I think."

"I see," Lambert said, nodding. But his eyes still expressed skepticism.

"They met in college," Nancy went on. "He brought her home. I brought them here this morning."

"I see. What *time* was that?"

"About eleven-thirty," Nancy said.

"Captain King," Lambert said, sighing heavily. "A thing like this can't be spontaneous. It takes some preplanning. He had to think it out . . . know where he wanted to do it. He had to get gasoline. Paul couldn't have arranged all that in less than forty-five minutes."

"Besides which," Douglas put in, "that wasn't his bag. I told you, Captain King, it's *not* in the cards."

Lambert turned to Davis. "Will you ask one of your people to bring the Adams girl over here?"

"Right away," Davis said, leaving the room.

"If you had a man in the group," Monty said, looking up at Lambert, "wouldn't he have known if they'd been planning the . . . the . . ."

"Not necessarily. I think it was an individual act by one of the speed freaks—not a group action. I don't think they'd have allowed it, if they had known. But, in all honesty, our man was not on his toes. He didn't know they were even planning the break-in today."

Nancy clutched Monty's hand tightly.

"There simply wasn't enough time, Captain," Lambert repeated. "And the jacket—" He broke off, shaking his head.

"He really believed," Monty said to Nancy, looking up sadly. "He told me last night, he'd die for what he believed in."

"He didn't mean it this way," Douglas said.

Captain Davis reentered the room. He said to Lambert, "Can I see you a minute?"

The two men went into the hall. In a moment they returned, leading a long-haired boy between them.

"Paul!" Nancy shrieked, running to her son, throwing her arms around his neck. Monty raised on one elbow, craning to look. With a look of disbelief, he slumped back on the stretcher.

Captain Davis came to the stretcher. He said to Monty, "Paul was waiting outside for the girl, Linda. When she didn't come, he tried to get in to find her. One of the door guards picked him up and brought him to the station."

Paul walked to the stretcher, looked down, and said: "Dad . . . I'm sorry. Sorry as hell."

He stood looking down at his father, tears streaming down his cheeks. Then he laid his head on Monty's chest. Monty put his arms around his son, holding tight. Nancy looked on through her own tears, silently thanking God.

★ **10** ★

Nancy came into the bedroom bearing a bed tray with a bowl of hot soup and a roast beef sandwich. She woke Monty, gently pushing his shoulder, saying: "It's six o'clock."

He opened his eyes, blinking.

"How do you feel?" she asked.

"I don't know yet," he said. He dragged himself erect slowly, gingerly, adding, "That smells good. I'm starved."

"I thought you would be. Dr. Hull said it was a really powerful pill. I was afraid you'd be knocked out before we got home."

She set the tray on the bed, then arranged the pillows behind him, bracing his back.

He spooned the soup, saying, "Delicious."

Nancy sat on the chair, watching him eat.

"What a horrible thing it was," Monty said, shuddering.

"Yes," she said.

"It *could* have been Paul," he said, looking at her.

"But it wasn't. Thank God for that."

"It was *some*body's Paul."

"I know."

"Imagine, believing that strongly . . ."

"Monty, he was probably very sick."

"Or dedicated."

She said nothing.

"What happened to Linda?" he asked, finishing the soup, turning to the sandwich, taking a bite.

"Paul arranged the bail. She's here . . . much subdued, I might add. They came home in the VW."

"Good."

"The phone's been ringing off the hook," she said, taking a piece of paper from her pocket. "Admiral Starr and Buzz Creighton and a man named Anthony de Lucca with the House Armed Services Committee, all called to ask how you were and to find out if you'd be able to make some hearing tomorrow morning."

"Please call them back and say yes. I'll be there."

"All right. Also Chief Zempfke called and Lieutenant Trimble. They asked how you were. Zempfke said not to worry, he was back in harness and had the office under control."

"Good," Monty said, eating the sandwich.

"I take it he got off?" she asked.

"Yes."

"I'm so glad," Nancy said. "Now, finally, a reporter called. He wanted to interview you, get your reactions. Some quotes and background. I told him you were asleep. He said never mind, he'd make do. He also said something cryptic . . . about not writing the other story because he couldn't have two Captain King stories the same day. Does that make sense to you?"

"It must have been the reporter in the courtroom when Zempfke appeared."

"I don't understand."

"I made a little speech in Zempfke's behalf. I guess he thought he could find a way to ridicule the military from that."

"He's going to make you a hero, I think. He was there when the medics lifted you out of the Hall."

"Oh, hell. We don't want that. Did he mention Paul?"

"No."

"Then he doesn't know the full story. Thank heavens. What else?"

"That's all the calls. But . . . Monty, I didn't have a chance to tell you. I sold the stock this morning."

"Good for you," he smiled.

"We took a terrible bath. We lost at least twelve thousand dollars."

"Oh, hell," he said lightly. "Easy come, easy go."

"I'm sorry. If I had asked your advice years ago, we'd probably have a small fortune in real estate or something."

"We don't need a small fortune."

"Monty, also, I want to apologize for last night. I must have been out of my mind. Of course, I don't really mean for you to choose between me and the Navy. My retirement idea was—"

They heard a sudden lusty shout in the hallway.

"Mike!" Nancy said, getting up excitedly.

The bedroom door opened. Midshipman William Montgomery King III, wearing his gray, high-collared uniform, walked militarily into the room. His blond hair was cropped short. His blue eyes were wide-set, inquiring, concerned. He kissed Nancy on the cheek, then came to the bed.

"I heard about it on the radio," he said, shaking hands with his father, then stepping back stiffly. "Are you all right?"

"Aggravated my back. Otherwise, I'm fine."

"It was a damn brave thing to do—risking your life to save one of those creeps!"

"No, it wasn't, Mike," Monty said somberly. "For a while I was certain it was your brother."

"Paul?" Mike said, in an incredulous tone. "But how—"

"Sit down and I'll explain," Monty said calmly.

Mike sat down on the chair, ramrod straight. Nancy

closed the door and sat on the edge of the bed, looking at her son.

"Paul dropped out of school last week or sometime and came home Monday night," Monty said. "He brought a girl named Linda—Linda Adams. Paul was in a bad way, Mike. On acid. He is quite a different Paul now. Radicalized. Very long hair. The girl, Linda, came to join the protest group at the Pentagon—the kids who broke into the building. Paul took her down there today just before the break-in, and for a while I thought he might be in the building. As it turned out, he wasn't. And that, son, is the main reason I tried to save that kid."

Mike stared at the carpet a moment, then said in a low voice: "How long has Paul been taking acid?"

"We're not sure," Monty said.

"My brother, a head!" Mike said sadly.

"I don't think so," Nancy put in. "We took him to a psychiatrist. He assured us Paul was not a serious drug problem."

"Psychiatrist!" Mike exclaimed, turning to his mother.

"We all went," Monty said.

"But, Dad," Mike exclaimed, staring at his father, "you always said they were quacks!"

"It seemed the necessary thing to do."

"God," Mike said. "I hope this doesn't get around. What if your Selection Board hears about it?"

"I'm disappointed to hear you say a thing like that," Monty replied. "I thought you were bigger. My chances of making Flag Rank are very slim, Mike. Just like everybody else's."

"That's not true! Everybody says you're the man to beat."

"Everybody?"

"Captain Singleton. Our Deputy Superintendent. He told me that yesterday."

"Well, anyway," Monty said. "Let's get back to your

brother. Paul and I had a long talk last night. I respect what he believes. He is a sensitive boy, moody at times, even quixotic. But he's extremely intelligent, and perceptive. I want you to try to respect him too."

"Dad," Mike returned gravely, "brother or no brother, I cannot respect an acid-head or a radical. Those people stand for the overthrow of our government. If they aren't all rounded up and thrown in jail, we run a very serious risk of losing our country. Have you read that essay in *Proceedings* by Captain—"

"I didn't give him your letter, Mike," Nancy broke in.

"Paul and the girl are here, Mike," Monty went on. "In the other room. I want you to sit down and talk to them calmly. Try to understand their point of—"

"The girl is *here*?" Mike cut in, again incredulous. "In *our* house?"

"Yes," Nancy said. "She needs help, Mike. She's all alone—"

"God!" Mike snorted. "I can't believe this."

"You should also know," Monty said, "that Paul has said he intends to go to Canada to evade the draft."

"He can't do that!" Mike cried, jumping up, glaring at his father. "You're not going to let him—"

"It's his decision, not mine," Monty said calmly.

"*Order* him not to," Mike said. "If it were I who—"

"I can't order him," Monty said.

"He's still a minor—just twenty!" Mike shouted.

"A minor in fact, not spirit," Monty said.

"If this gets out, I'll be *ruined*," Mike moaned, holding a hand on his head. "My brother, a *felon*. Why did this have to happen to me? Dad, what's gotten into you people?"

"I'm not sure I can give you an answer to that."

"Well," Mike said sullenly, "all this sure proves one thing to me. Paul *must* have been brain-damaged."

"Mike," Monty said sharply, returning his son's glare. "That's not true."

"I heard you say it," Mike said defiantly. "It's true too, isn't it? He's crazy, like Grandmother King. That's the truth, isn't it?"

"Mike!" Nancy cried. "Don't—"

"I have another shock for you, Mike," Monty went on. "Perhaps the biggest of all. But what I have to say, I want to say to all of you. Nancy, honey, would you mind getting Paul and Linda?"

She rose silently and went to get Paul and Linda. They entered a few minutes later. Mike stood in the corner, staring at his brother and the girl as though they were plague-ridden.

"Mike," Nancy said, "this is Linda Adams. Linda, this is Mike."

Linda walked to Mike and stuck out her hand. Mike ignored it, staring beyond her at Paul. Paul walked up to Mike, extended a hand, smiling, saying, "Stay loose, Mike."

"Shake hands with your brother, Mike," Monty said from the bed.

"No," Mike said. "Look at him! *Look* at that hair! When was the last time he bathed?"

"Shake hands," Monty repeated. "That's an order, Midshipman."

Mike shook hands.

"All right," Monty said. "I have something to say that will affect all of you. Especially you, Mike. Within the last twenty-four hours, I have been offered Flag Rank by two groups of people—opposing power blocs in the military establishment. In each case, there were strings attached, compromise of principle involved, which I found unacceptable."

He paused a moment to collect his thoughts. The others stared fixedly at him, waiting.

"I just wanted you to know before I get to my main point," he continued, "that your old man *could* have worn two stars."

"Dad," Mike broke in apprehensively, "What are you saying?"

"Wait a minute, Mike. Let me go on. Tomorrow morning, there's going to be a hearing on the Hill that is vital to the work I have been doing for the last twenty-one months. I am going to the hearing. But I'm not going to say what a lot of people think I'm going to say. My bosses want me to make a strong pitch for ULMS. I am not going to do that, I am going to suggest, rather, that we reexamine our plans, the Soviet threat, and raise the possibility that ULMS could, conceivably, touch off another, perhaps fatal, round in the arms race."

"Dad!" Mike shouted. "Have you lost your mind? They'll—"

Nancy looked at her husband in wonderment. Linda was wide-eyed. Paul smiled thinly.

"Let me finish," Monty said to Mike. "Now, the papers will blow this up. They're looking for dissent in the military. But, in my opinion, what I have to say will do no good in the long run. The military-industrial-scientific-congressional-labor-finance complex is so huge, so powerful, so irrevocably the core of our entire economy, that there is no way we can wind it down or dismantle it without bringing on economic chaos. It will go on and on, in spite of well-intended efforts on the part of many people to stop it. There is no way to stop it."

"This is crazy talk . . ." Mike stammered. "Crazy . . ."

"Now," Monty went on, ignoring Mike, "my Navy bosses won't like what I'm going to say. The Congress won't like it. They will do everything in their power to discredit me. They will, without a doubt, organize to destroy me. Perhaps they will try to claim I am crazy, as Mike is suggesting. And, believe me, they can destroy a man. I know. I've seen the whole, monstrous system from the inside. I know exactly how it works how it responds to threat, however insignificant."

He stopped.

"Dad," Mike said. "You're just upset . . . shocked . . . by that thing today."

"No," Monty said. "I made up my mind before that. I'm sorry for you, Mike. It's going to go especially hard for you. You see, you'll be remembered as the son of that traitor, Captain King. You won't even make lieutenant commander. They'll pass you over, no matter how brilliant your fitness reports. My advice to you is to do the Navy time you are obligated to serve in return for your education and then make plans to get out. Meanwhile, prepare yourself, spiritually, for civilian life."

Tears came into Mike's eyes. He bit his lip, clenched and unclenched his fist. Nancy looked on silently.

Monty turned to Nancy.

"Tomorrow afternoon," he said, "I'm going to resign my commission."

"Monty!" Nancy said. "No! Don't—"

"Yes, I shall," he said. "For two reasons: One—After the hearing tomorrow I obviously would never be selected by the Navy for Flag Rank. Two—I don't want to be accused of being a patsy for the new administration, possibly for my own gain."

"But—" Nancy said.

"Wait. Let me finish. Now, as for you, Paul and Linda, I want to say this. This country was born out of a kind of impatient idealism. Youth has always been impatiently idealistic. There's no crime in that. If it didn't exist, there would be no change. Without change, we would atrophy and die. But you can't express your impatience in violence, demanding change by Friday afternoon, or by running away in a pique. You can't tear down in a negative way all we've built—no matter how inadequate it may be—before you're prepared to put something in its place. You don't have a rational program. You don't know how to organize yourselves to effect change within the system. As I told you the other night, Paul, you have to bring change *within* the system. Otherwise, you'll provoke massive repression, and any hope for change. If that happens, you've really done the country fatal harm. Evolve a program. Get yourself elected. Pass new laws. But do what you must do responsibly. And, Paul, responsibility does not include running away to Canada. That's a cop-out."

He pointed to the space between Paul and Linda and Mike.

"Somewhere, right in there, equidistant between you, is where you should bring this country. That means you must get together at a table and talk. Stop shouting and reason it out. All of you will have to yield."

Paul, Linda, Mike, stared at the imaginary table between them.

"That's all I have to say to you kids," Monty concluded "Now I want to talk privately with your mother."

Mike and Paul and Linda left the room. Nancy turned to her husband and said: "Monty, I'm afraid."

"So am I. But this is what I have to do. It's what you really want, isn't it?"

"I want what's best for you, Monty. I don't want to think I pushed you into something against your will."

"You were only one part of my decision, honey. There were many other people and things."

"Dr. Douglas says it's the wrong thing—"

"I've heard his theory. But he's not God."

"He was right about Paul."

"Nancy, I don't have any illusions. Life is life. Impos sible . . unfathomable. But I see myself differently, perhaps more objectively. We'll work hard to make it work. Learn about ourselves. We have to now. I can't go back to the other life. I don't want any part of it. Fuck war! Let's make love.

ABOUT THE AUTHOR

CLAY BLAIR, JR., is the author of two earlier novels, THE BOARD ROOM and THE ARCHBISHOP, and of four nonfiction books: THE ATOMIC SUBMARINE AND ADMIRAL RICKOVER, BEYOND COURAGE, DIVING FOR PLEASURE AND TREASURE, and THE STRANGE CASE OF JAMES EARL RAY. Mr. Blair has collaborated on three other nonfiction books: THE HYDROGEN BOMB, with James R. Shepley, NAUTILUS 90 NORTH, with Commander William R. Anderson, U.S.N., and ALWAYS ANOTHER DAWN, with A. Scott Crossfield. The author spent five years in the Pentagon press room as a *Time-Life* reporter. and another five years in and out of the place as a magazine writer. For some years he was Editor in Chief of *The Saturday Evening Post*. Mr. Blair presently lives on Key Biscayne, Florida.